By Julia Quinn

Anthologies

Further Observations of Lady Whistledown
Lady Whistledown Strikes Back

The Bridgerton Prequels

Because of Miss Bridgerton
The Girl with the Make-Believe Husband
The Other Miss Bridgerton • First Comes Scandal

The Bridgerton Series

The Duke and I • The Viscount Who Loved Me
An Offer from a Gentleman
Romancing Mister Bridgerton
To Sir Phillip, With Love • When He Was Wicked
It's in His Kiss • On the Way to the Wedding
The Bridgertons: Happily Ever After

The Smythe-Smith Quartet

Just Like Heaven • A Night Like This
The Sum of All Kisses
The Secrets of Sir Richard Kenworthy

The Bevelstoke Series

The Secret Diaries of Miss Miranda Cheever
What Happens in London • Ten Things I Love About You

The Two Dukes of Wyndham

The Lost Duke of Wyndham • Mr. Cavendish, I Presume

Agents of the Crown

To Catch an Heiress • How to Marry a Marquis

The Lyndon Sisters

Everything and the Moon • Brighter Than the Sun

The Splendid Trilogy

Splendid • Dancing at Midnight • Minx

THE FURTHER OBSERVATIONS OF LADY WHISTLEDOWN

THE FURTHER OBSERVATIONS OF LADY WHISTLEDOWN

JULIA QUINN
SUZANNE ENOCH
KAREN HAWKINS
MIA RYAN

AVONBOOKS
An Imprint of HarperCollins*Publishers*

This is a collection of fiction. Names, characters, places, and incidents are products of the author's imagination or are used fictitiously and are not to be construed as real. Any resemblance to actual events, locales, organizations, or persons, living or dead, is entirely coincidental.

First Avon Books mass market printing: February 2003
First Avon Books hardcover printing: October 2022

Print Edition ISBN: 978-0-06-327326-9
Digital Edition ISBN: 978-0-06-174430-3

22 23 24 25 26 LSC 10 9 8 7 6 5 4 3 2 1

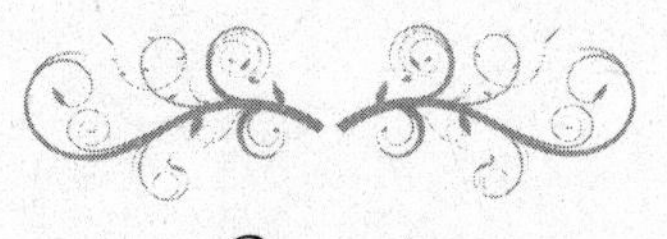

Contents

All Lady Whistledown columns written by Julia Quinn

THE FURTHER OBSERVATIONS OF LADY WHISTLEDOWN

One True Love

Suzanne Enoch

To the memory of my great-grandparents,
Vivian H. and Zelma Whitlock.
A West Texas cowboy and a sheep rancher's daughter,
their unlikely romance lasted for more than half a century.

Chapter 1

Lady Anne Bishop is back in town, along with the rest of society, eager to enjoy the frigid weather and overcast skies. London is suffering through a spate of cold unmatched in recorded history, and indeed, even the mighty Thames has frozen over. This Author cannot help but wonder whether this means that husbands all over town must now perform all the tasks they had put off by claiming, "I shall throw away my hideous mounted boar's head (or admit I have gout, or listen to the intelligently spoken words of my wife—you, Dear Reader, may insert whichever you like) when the Thames freezes over."

But despite the cold's tendency to turn one's nose a rather unattractive shade of red, the ton *seems to be enjoying the weather, if only for the novelty of it all. Lady Anne Bishop, as noted above, was spied making angels in the snow in the company of Sir Royce Pemberley, who, it must be noted, is not her intended husband.*

One can only wonder if this incident will compel the Marquis of Halfurst, who has been betrothed to Lady Anne since the occasion of her birth, to leave his home in Yorkshire and travel to London to finally make the acquaintance of the woman he will marry.

Or perhaps he is content with the situation at hand? Not every gentleman desires a wife, after all.

LADY WHISTLEDOWN'S SOCIETY PAPERS,
24 January 1814

Lady Anne Bishop laid the letters on the card table. "Now," she said, smiling, "we've each read all three. Your opinions, ladies?"

"Mr. Spengle's invitation seems to be the most fervent," Theresa DePris commented, chuckling as she brushed her fingers across the missive. "He used the word 'heart' four times."

"And 'ardent' twice." Anne laughed. "He also has the best penmanship. Pauline, what do you think?"

"As if you care about penmanship, Annie," Miss Pauline Hamilton said, giving a delicate snort. "All of us know you're going to go to the theater with Lord Howard, so please stop flaunting your love letters before us poor unfortunate souls."

"They aren't love letters, for heaven's sake." Less amused, Anne turned Lord Howard's letter to face her. Desmond Howard was the wittiest of her circle of male acquaintances, to be certain, but love? That was just nonsense.

"What do you call their correspondence, then? I-like-you-very-much letters?"

With a slight scowl, Anne returned the missive to its former position. "It's all in fun. No one takes it seriously."

"Why, because you've been betrothed since you were three days old?" Pauline pursued, grimacing. "I think you take that agreement even less seriously than your suitors do."

"Pauline, you are becoming quite the moralist, suddenly," Anne said, shuffling the letters into a brisk pile. "I do not have suitors, and it's not as though I've done anything wrong."

"Besides," Theresa added, rejoining the debate, "when was the last time Annie received a letter from Lord Halfurst?"

"Never!" her two friends finished in unison, laughing.

Annie laughed as well, though she didn't consider it all that funny. In romantic tales, one's betrothed fought witches and slew dragons for one. A letter should have been easy to manufacture, even in godforsaken Yorkshire.

"Exactly," she said, anyway. "Never a word, much less a sentence, in nineteen years. So I don't want to hear any more nonsense about my sheep-farming betrothed." She leaned forward. "He knows precisely where I spend my days. If he chooses to spend his own as far from London as possible, that's no concern of mine."

Theresa sighed. "So you'll never marry?"

Anne patted her friend's hand. "I have a monthly stipend, I get to spend most of the year in London because of Father's cabinet position, I have the most wonderful friends I could ever hope for, and I receive at least three invitations to every event, even in the middle of winter. If that's not perfection, I don't know what is."

Pauline shook her head. "What about your sheep-farming marquis, though? Do you think he'll stay in Yorkshire until he withers and dies? If he decides to marry, won't it have to be you?"

Anne shuddered. Miss Hamilton had always delighted in finding the pitfalls on other's paths. "I really don't care what he does."

"Perhaps he'll perish in a sheep-shearing accident," Theresa suggested.

"Oh, I don't want anything ill to happen to Lord Halfurst," Anne countered quickly. Heavens, if he expired, she would lose the only barrier between herself and her mother beginning an eternity of nagging that she needed to find a husband. This way, she could blame any lack of a mate on the absent marquis. And it would just be wrong if she married someone else without his consent. "I like him quite well exactly where he is—far away from here."

"Hm," Theresa mused. "You say that now, but—"

The drawing room door rattled and opened. "Anne, come at once!" her mother hissed.

Lady Daven's face was white, and for a moment all Anne could think was that something had happened to her father. "Mama, what's wrong?" she asked, shooting to her feet.

"It's him!" the countess continued, not even sparing the other two ladies in the room a glance. "Oh, why are you wearing that? Whatever happened to your new blue gown?"

"Mama, what in the world are you talking about?" Anne pressed, sending her friends an apologetic glance and hurrying forward. "Who is here? Papa?"

"No, *him*. Halfurst."

Anne's breath caught in her throat, her silent gasp echoed aloud by Theresa and Pauline. *"What?"*

"Stop dawdling," her mother snapped, grabbing her by the arm and pulling her into the hallway.

"But—what is he doing here?" A thousand questions jostled for position in her mind, and only that one managed to squeak out with any coherence.

Her mother sent her an annoyed look. "We can only assume. He asked for you. Poor Lambert didn't know what to do with him, but thank goodness the idiot had enough sense to put him in the morning room."

Her betrothed was in the morning room. The sheep farmer. The Marquis of Halfurst. The fat, bald, slovenly, short, smelly sheep farmer to whom her parents had given their word she would marry, and whom she'd never met in all her nineteen years of life. "I think I'm going to faint," she muttered.

"You are not going to faint. This is your fault, anyway, carrying on as you have been. He's probably here to insist that you cry off marrying him entirely."

Anne brightened a little. "Do you think so?" Now that the stupid marquis had invaded London, the prospect of her mother's nagging her about marrying someone else didn't seem so terrible.

They stopped before the closed morning room door. "I wouldn't doubt it," her mother whispered fiercely. "Now behave yourself." She pushed open the door and shoved Anne forward.

"Be—" Before she could finish, the door slammed closed behind her.

He stood before the fireplace, warming his hands. For a bare moment, Anne just stared at his profile. Not bald, nor short, and certainly not fat in the dark, closely-fitting jacket he wore. Aristocratic, she thought abruptly, in the old, elegant sense of the word. "You're Halfurst?" she blurted, then flushed.

With a slight stirring of air, he faced her. Dark gray eyes, one obscured by a stray lock of damp, coal black hair, studied her with a thoroughness that stopped her breath. "I am." His low tone was clipped at the end, though she wasn't certain whether it was from amusement or annoyance. "Lady Anne, I presume."

Not ugly, either, she noted with a slow breath, then shook herself and sketched a belated curtsy. "What . . . what brings you to London, my lord?"

"Snow angels," he answered, in the same level voice.

"Snow—beg pardon?"

The marquis reached into his pocket, producing a much-folded piece of paper. With his piercing gray eyes holding hers, he strolled toward her, hand outstretched. "Snow angels."

Anne took the paper, careful not to touch his hand. It was silly, but touching him would make his presence unmistakably . . . real. The large ruby signet ring on his right index finger flashed in the firelight, further lending the scene a dark, surreal quality. Glancing up at his lean, stony face, she unfolded the worn parchment. And blanched. "Oh. I . . . ah . . . Lady Whistledown exaggerates terribly, you know."

"I see," he murmured. The tone, soft as it was, vibrated down her spine. "So you weren't wallowing in the snow with Sir Royce Pemberley?"

Her astonishment at his appearance began to dim a little. Admittedly he had a tall, well-muscled form, and a lean, handsome face that would make a poet weep, but she had concerns other than his looks. He was rude, for one thing. She blinked, forcing her gaze away from his Greek-god countenance.

His wardrobe certainly didn't meet any proper London standards she'd ever heard of. His coat was well made, but easily a half dozen years behind the style. Dark buckskin breeches looked as though they'd seen much better days, while the quality of his boots was indistinguishable beneath the mud and snow covering them.

"I was not wallowing, Lord Halfurst. Sir Royce tripped into the snow, and as I attempted to help him to his feet, I lost my balance as well."

He lifted an eyebrow. "And the snow angels?"

Anne resisted the urge to clear her throat. Good heavens, her own mother hadn't asked so many questions, and certainly not in such a tone. "It seemed the thing to do, my lord."

His lips twitched. "I trust it doesn't happen often?"

Anne frowned. *Was he laughing at her now?* "You might at least have wished me good morning before you began railing at me, Lord Halfurst."

"Considering that I've spent the last three days riding through snow and ice and mud to discover why the devil my betrothed has been consorting with"—he took the clipping out of her hand—"with someone 'not her intended husband,' I think I've been quite civil."

Maximilian Trent, the Marquis of Halfurst, narrowed his eyes. He'd expected her to be surprised by his arrival, but not that she would give him an out-and-out argument about it. The slender young woman standing before him, her hands clenched into fists and her thick brunette hair coiled at the top of her head, didn't seem to care what he might have expected. And he found that interesting.

Little as he liked leaving Yorkshire, he had to admit that it was past time. Lady Whistledown's paper had made two things damned clear: first, he was going to have to go to London to fetch his bride, since she obviously wasn't going to come to him; and second, if his peers, in anonymous gossip or not, had begun questioning his manhood, then he'd been gone from London for too long, anyway. And when he'd set eyes on the woman to whom he'd been promised for nineteen of his twenty-six years, his first thought was that he should have come sooner.

"I was not 'consorting' with Sir Royce. He is a friend."

"Former friend," Maximilian corrected. Considering this was the first time they'd spoken—ever—the conviction he felt at that statement surprised him.

She was glaring at him, none of the earlier curiosity remaining in her moss green eyes. "I don't think you have any right to—"

"Be that as it may," he interrupted, "here I am." He took a slow step closer. "Where's your father?"

Her brow furrowed. "With the Regent. Why?"

"The sooner we get the details settled, the better. Then we can be off before you have any further snow angel adventures."

She took an equally slow step backward. "Off? Off where?"

"To Halfurst. At this time of year I can't afford to be away long."

Lady Anne halted her retreat, hands smoothing her heavy lavender gown. "Just like that? After nineteen years you appear, and—snap—we're to be married and flee off to the wilderness?"

"Yorkshire is hardly wilderness," he returned, pulling out his pocket watch. If they left before noon, they could be back at Halfurst by the end of the week, even with the slower pace that the weather and having a new bride with him would dictate. He pursed his lips, taking her in again. With the lady standing before him as his bride, several stops along the way might prove necessary—and pleasurable.

"No," she said distinctly.

Maximilian looked up from his timepiece. "What?"

He thought she hesitated, though her shoulders remained square and her chin up. "I said no."

With a snap he closed the watch. "I heard that. Just what do you mean by it, pray tell?"

"I thought it clear, Lord Halfurst. I mean that I will not leave London to accompany you to Yorkshire, and that—"

"You wish to be married here? I can probably obtain a special license without much difficulty, then." It made sense. She'd grown up in London, and he had no objection to marrying her in London.

"Allow me to finish," she continued, a tremor in her fine voice. "I am not going to Yorkshire at all, and I would rather drop dead than marry you."

Maximilian clamped his jaw closed in disbelief. "You can't just say no. That decision is not yours, Lady Anne," he protested, anger tugging at him. "Your parents—"

"I'm certain my parents must merely have neglected to inform you that they would not wish to see me married unhappily, to a man I've never met and who, I might add, has never even bothered to send me a letter or a note or a torn scrap of paper in nineteen years."

He lifted an eyebrow, wondering whether she was trying to convince him or herself. "You—"

"I know nothing of your character, my lord," she stated, "and I won't be dragged out of London by a stranger under any circumstances."

"Perhaps you might have thought to notify me about this previously." This female, seven years his junior, was not going to dictate the terms of their marriage. This very attractive female was not getting away simply because he'd neglected to write to her.

"Perhaps if you'd bothered to introduce yourself before now, I wouldn't be refusing your suit."

She had little ground to stand on; her parents would face ridicule and embarrassment if they allowed her to dissolve an agreement with a family as old as his, besides the fact that he *had* corresponded with her father, and knew perfectly well that both Lord and Lady Daven supported the match. Maximilian opened his mouth, then closed it again. He had already won, though she hadn't yet realized that fact. Whatever he might wish to say next, he was tired and cold and wet enough that it wouldn't be pleasant or helpful. And it would be pointless to make the circumstance of their anticipated union even more difficult.

For a moment he gazed at her. The high color in her cheeks, the quick rise and fall of her bosom, the way her fingers clenched the heavy material of her lavender gown—he wasn't going to make any progress by yelling at her. He did, however, intend to make progress. Winning by default was no fun at all.

With a last, regretful thought about what the continuing foul weather was likely doing to the North Road, he nodded. "Perhaps you're right."

"Per—yes, well, I *am* right," she returned, obvious relief softening her features.

Good God, she was lovely. He hadn't expected that. He hadn't expected *her,* at all. "Then I must make amends."

Her brow furrowed and then smoothed again. "That's not necessary."

"So you think I should return to Yorkshire posthaste?" he asked, amusement touching him again. However unexpected she was for him, Lady Anne was even more flummoxed by *his* sudden arrival.

"You did indicate that you didn't wish to be away for an extended period."

"So I did. First, however, I would be honored if you would accompany me to"—he flipped over the worn gossip sheet—"to the Theatre Royal, Drury Lane, tonight, to see *The Merchant of Venice.*" He looked up at her again. "I believe Edmund Kean is playing Shylock."

"Yes, he is," she said, a smile lighting her eyes to emeralds. "He's supposed to be quite remarkable. In fact—" She stopped, blushing.

"In fact, what?" he queried.

"Nothing."

"Good. Then I'll collect you at seven this evening." Feeling the need to touch her, Maximilian took one more slow step forward. Running his hand down her wrist, he uncurled her fingers from the material of her gown.

She made a small sound like a gasp as he brought her hand up, brushing his lips across her knuckles. Slow heat ran through his veins as she raised her face to his, gazing at him beneath dark, curling lashes.

"I'll see you tonight," he murmured, releasing her as his mind conjured all sorts of things he'd rather be doing with her than letting her go.

Without waiting for a response he strode out to the hall and the foyer beyond, collecting his hat and caped greatcoat. He had some things to take care of before this evening. And he didn't need to see the butler's expression at his old, out-of-fashion wardrobe to know what the most pressing of them was.

When he'd arrived in town a few hours ago he'd had little thought but to collect Lady Anne and return to Yorkshire without delay. After seeing her, however, the idea of doing a little courting didn't seem so repugnant, after all.

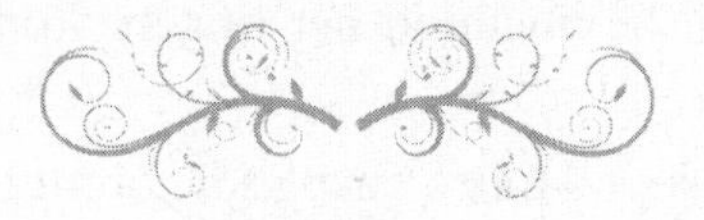

Chapter 2

This Author is not one to overstate one's own importance, but it is being said that This Author's own column, dated one week prior, is directly responsible for the recent town arrival of none other than Maximilian Trent, Marquis of Halfurst. It seems the good marquis took exception to his betrothed's snow angel escapades with Sir Royce Pemberley.

And if that weren't excitement enough, it was whispered that he is positively stalking Lady Anne. Consider, if you will, Dear Reader, what transpired Saturday evening at Drury Lane . . .

LADY WHISTLEDOWN'S SOCIETY PAPERS,
31 January 1814

"You refused him."

Anne continued pacing, ignoring her maid's piteous sighs as Daisy tried to put the finishing touches to her hair. "You should have heard him, Mama. 'Cease having any fun and accompany me to the middle of nowhere at once.' "

"He did not say that."

"He might as well have."

Lady Daven, seated on the bed and watching Anne's progress as she stalked back and forth, shook her head. "It doesn't matter. You can't refuse him. Your father and the old Marquis of Halfurst made—"

"Then let Papa marry him! I never asked to be exiled to Yorkshire!"

"Yesterday you were happy to be betrothed to Halfurst."

Yesterday she'd never thought he might actually appear. With a scowl Anne relented and sat, allowing Daisy to fasten the last few hairclips in place. "I don't like him. Isn't that enough?"

"You only just met him. And surely you can have no complaints about his looks."

That had been the most disquieting part of the meeting. He was handsome—far more so than she'd ever imagined. "Yes, his face was pleasant enough, I suppose," she hedged. "But did you see his wardrobe? Good heavens, it was positively ancient! And he was mean. How did he expect me to respond?"

Her mother sighed. "Perhaps he was nervous at meeting you."

"I don't think he was nervous about anything," Anne muttered.

"Whatever your initial misgivings, you will meet with him again, Anne. Short of our discovering some sort of mental imbalance on his part, the agreement stands. Your father's honor rests on it."

"He offered to escort me to the theater tonight." She frowned. "Actually, he practically ordered me to accompany him."

"Good. Your father and I shall await your account of the evening." With a rustle of material, Lady Daven stood and swept out of the room.

"It is *not* good," Anne said to the closed door. "I don't like being ordered about; and certainly not by an antique-wearing sheep farmer." *But such eyes.* She shook herself. "And I really don't wish to be seen in his company. Everyone will make fun."

"My lady?"

"Daisy, please go and inform Lambert that he is to let me—and only me—know when Lord Howard arrives."

"But—"

"No arguments, please. I am not going to spend my life imprisoned in Yorkshire."

As her maid hurried downstairs, Anne sat back to fiddle with her earrings. Her mother would've been livid if she'd known Lord Howard still expected to escort her daughter to the theater tonight. Anne wasn't entirely certain why she'd decided to be so defiant—except that the Marquis of Halfurst had arrived knowing he'd already won, and he hadn't bothered to be gracious about it, or to consider her feelings and her situation at all.

Someone scratched frantically at her door. "Come in," she said, jumping.

Daisy slipped inside. "My lady, Lord Howard is here, and I heard the countess your mother in the drawing room!"

Anne stifled a nervous breath. "Very well. Get your shawl, and let's be off."

A miserable expression on her face, the maid nodded. "As you wish, my lady."

"Don't worry, Daisy. I'll make certain any wrath falls on my shoulders."

"Oh, I hope so."

"So he just barged in on an ox cart and expected you to trundle back to Yorkshire with him?" Desmond Howard nodded at the footmen as they passed through the main doors of the Theatre Royal, Drury Lane, and up the stairs, where only those privileged enough to have box seats were permitted to tread.

Now that they'd reached the theater without being discovered or stopped by Lord Halfurst or any of her family members, Anne relaxed a little. "Yes, without even a by your leave or a good morning."

"Typical."

Anne looked sharply at the viscount's square-jawed countenance. "Do you know Lord Halfurst?"

With her hand wrapped over his arm, she felt him shrug. "In passing. We attended Oxford at the same time. I haven't seen him since he was last in London."

She hadn't realized he'd ever been to London before today. "When was that?"

"Seven or eight years ago, I'd wager."

"Hm. And he didn't bother to call on me then, either." Of course, she would have been only twelve or thirteen, but they were still betrothed.

"He left after a very short time—when the old marquis died, I believe." The viscount chuckled. "I imagine he was none too eager to stay once his solicitors let slip that he was nearly bankrupt."

Wonderful. Halfurst was arrogant *and* poor. Her parents certainly hadn't told her that, and they were insane if they thought she would willingly go off to live in some shack with him, handsome face or not. "How delightful," she muttered. If the marquis needed her money, escaping him would be even more difficult.

Lord Howard chuckled again. "Don't trouble yourself, Anne," he returned. "Tonight, you're with me. And rest assured that in his place I would never remove such a lovely blossom as yourself from the fertile environs of London."

"Thank you," she said feelingly, smiling as he held aside the curtain to his private box.

"My pleasure, believe me," he murmured, seating himself beside her.

As the patrons filled the theater, oblivious to the silly pre-Shakespearean farce being enacted on stage, a commotion in the pit caught her attention. Down below, among a crowd of amused-looking commoners, stood a very handsome, well-dressed gentleman in the company of an equally well-dressed and mortified-looking Miss Amelia Rellton.

"Who's that with Miss Rellton?" she asked, trying not to stare, though from the direction of the opera glasses in the other boxes, no one else had reservations about doing so.

"Hm. The Marquis of Darington, I believe," Howard said, sitting back again. "Obviously gone insane, to bring a lady into the pit with him." He shifted closer, then glanced back at Daisy, seated quietly in the corner. "All of the lost cubs are coming into Town for the winter—and for the women—apparently."

Abruptly Anne was grateful for her maid's presence. "Perhaps it's the cold," she answered.

"No doubt." He leaned even closer. "Tell me then, my dear, have you asked your parents to formally dissolve the agreement with Halfurst?"

The light in his blue eyes seemed too interested for such an innocent question, and Anne was reminded of Pauline's warning that she had suitors, whether she acknowledged them as such or not. "I've expressed some concern," she said carefully, at the same time wondering why she was being so cautious. Once she did convince her parents to deny Halfurst's claim, her mother would see to it that she married someone else.

" 'Some concern' isn't what it sounded like earlier," he returned, nodding at an acquaintance in a neighboring box.

The curtains went up on stage. "Shh. It's beginning," she whispered, sitting forward and never more grateful to see Edmund Kean perform than she was tonight.

She sat quietly, mesmerized, until intermission. She'd never seen Shylock played that way, nor so well; no wonder Mr. Kean's performance had been causing such a stir in London.

As the curtain closed, Anne joined in the applause. "My goodness," she exclaimed, smiling, "Mr. Kean is—"

"—completely engrossing," a quiet male voice interrupted from the doorway. "A remarkable performance, thus far."

Anne and Lord Howard turned at the same moment, and then Lord Howard lurched to his feet. "Halfurst."

The marquis didn't move, but remained in his relaxed lean against the rear wall, on the opposite side of the curtains from Daisy. From the maid's startled expression, she hadn't been aware of his entrance, either. His tall form was shadowed, but Anne sensed that his gaze was on her.

"Lord Howard," Halfurst continued in the same soft voice. "I recall that you had a fondness for wagering—and for other men's wives, apparently."

"I am not your wife," Anne whispered.

He pushed upright. "You *were,* however, to be my companion this evening, were you not?"

"I—"

"Lady Anne made the wise decision to join me, instead," Lord Howard broke in. "And I'll thank you not to insult my character, Halfurst."

The marquis took a step forward, into the dim light of the chandeliers. Anne's breath caught. The old, behind-hand garb he'd worn earlier was gone, replaced by a dark gray jacket and trousers that looked so precisely molded to his muscular frame that they couldn't have been borrowed. Her mind, though, refused to dwell on where they might have come from. Instead, her gaze traveled up the length of him, past his pitch black waistcoat and white linen shirt and starched white cravat to his gray, glittering gaze. "You've . . . changed," she managed, blushing.

"Only my clothes," he returned, his eyes still holding hers. "You didn't seem to approve of my garb this morning."

"I think you should leave," Desmond broke in.

Anne started. She'd nearly forgotten his presence. Lord Howard wore the self-assured look she'd often seen on his square, handsome face, the look that said he knew he had the advantage, and that he intended to use it. No doubt he would next hand Halfurst one of his scathing set-downs. It was almost a pity. She wouldn't have minded spending the evening looking at the marquis in that splendid attire.

"I have no intention of staying," Lord Halfurst returned with a slight, humorless smile. "The view from your box is horrendous. I'm only here to escort my fiancée to a better vantage point—namely, *my* box."

"She's with me. You'd best get that through your thick, Yorkshire skull."

"Lord Howard," Anne protested.

The viscount ignored her, even taking a step closer to the tall marquis. "Have you been gone from London so long that you've forgotten your manners completely? Go away."

Halfurst only shrugged. "If I'd forgotten my manners, I would presently be dragging you down the stairs and out to the alley, where I would then beat you within an inch of your life for presuming to step between myself and Lady Anne. As it is, I'm only asking my betrothed to join me in my box. I think that's quite polite of me." His gaze returned to Anne. "Don't you think so?"

Desmond's face reddened. "You . . . I . . . How dare—"

"Don't stammer, Howard," the marquis continued. "If you have something to say, say it. Otherwise, you merely sound blustery." He held out his hand. "My lady? I can promise you an unobstructed view of the remainder of the performance."

Anne felt dazed. No one bested Lord Howard in a battle of wits and words, and certainly not in only one volley. And the way the marquis looked at her, as though she were the only other person in the entire theater . . . "What if I don't go with you?" she asked anyway, forcing her brain to work again. She was not some bartered bride, for heaven's sake. Or was she?

"Then I will thrash Lord Howard," the marquis said, in such a matter-of-fact tone that she had no doubt he meant it.

She stood. "Then I'd best go with you, I suppose," she returned in her most composed voice.

"Anne," Lord Howard protested, moving to intercept her.

Halfurst's hand shot out and shoved the viscount back into his seat. "Good evening, Howard," he said, and stepped back to part the curtains.

Maximilian took Anne's gloved hand and drew it over his arm. He kept his face turned from hers as they proceeded around the curve of curtained boxes, her maid following behind them. Whatever reservations she had about marrying him were obviously more grave than he'd realized. At the same time, seeing her in that low-cut gown of faintest violet, the curve of her bosom drawing his attention, and with a string of pale pearls caressing her throat, he wasn't about to allow any other man near her.

He'd expected to find her pretty, but he hadn't expected the heat that coursed through him as he gazed at her, even warmer and deeper now than this morning. He would figure her out, and he would make her desire him as he desired her—because he wasn't leaving London without her.

"All of Edmund Kean's performances are sold out. How did you manage this?"

Maximilian pulled aside the curtain and ushered her inside. "I asked."

As he took his seat, he spared a glance at her. From her expression, she wasn't thrilled with this pseudo-kidnapping. He wasn't, either. Her parents obviously had no control over her, but even they'd been surprised to find her missing when he'd come to collect her for a night at the theater.

"I didn't join you because you have a better view, you know."

"Of course not. You were trying to preserve Lord Howard's health. Noble, I suppose, but I would have preferred that you join me because you said you would do so."

"No, *you* said I would do so."

"And you didn't contradict me. Keeping your word isn't so difficult, is it?"

Anne narrowed her eyes. "Be angry if you wish, but no one consulted me about any of this. Don't expect me to simply . . . surrender."

Apparently he'd underestimated both Lady Anne Bishop's sense of duty and the effort he would have to expend if he wanted her as his bride—and in his bed. "I do expect you to surrender," he said quietly, reaching over to take her hand.

Her fingers were clenched into a fist, and though he thought for a moment that she might attempt to punch him, he leaned over to brush his lips across her knuckles. Her hand, her glove, smelled of soap. The scent, so ordinary until tonight, intoxicated him.

She watched him as he straightened again. "If you expect me to surrsender," she said, a quaver in her voice, "then I will expect you to convince me to do so."

Maximilian smiled. "Let the battle begin."

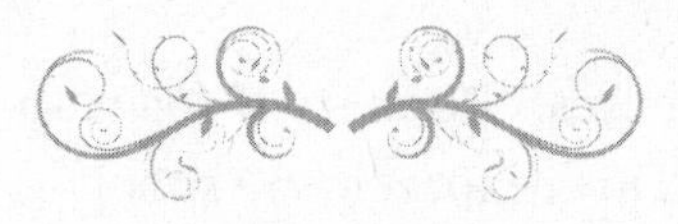

Chapter 3

Interestingly enough, Lord Howard was spotted leaving Drury Lane prior to the end of the performance. His mood was of a foul nature, and he was drinking quite liberally from a flask.

No bruises were spied upon his person, however, laying waste to all of the rumors that he and Lord Halfurst had come to blows over the lovely Lady Anne. Heated words were definitely overheard, however, leading This Author to wonder just how the altercation was avoided.

This Author is certainly not the bloodthirsty sort, but truly, Dear Reader, would not a purplish mark or two add a touch of character to Lord Howard's rather blandly handsome visage?

LADY WHISTLEDOWN'S SOCIETY PAPERS,
31 January 1814

Maximilian rose early. Sleeping had been a waste, anyway, considering he'd tossed and turned all night, visions of the woman who was supposed to be his bride, and who was sleeping in another house entirely, tangled in his dreams.

Half of Trent House remained covered in sheets and shut away to keep the cold from seeping into the main rooms. Even after his six-year absence from the premises, however, the servants had thankfully responded with alacrity.

His bride-to-be, though, didn't seem to be coming around at all. She expected to be wooed, when he'd expected to have her delivered to him at Halfurst as promised.

"Tea, my lord?" the butler asked as he reached the dining room.

"Coffee. Strong." Maximilian selected a hefty helping of ham and eggs from the sideboard and dug in. It was a moment before he noticed the short stack of letters at his elbow, atop the day's edition of the *London Times*. "What are these?"

"I believe they are invitations, my lord," Simms supplied, pouring him a large cup of coffee.

"Invitations? To what?"

"I couldn't say, my lord—though Mayfair does seem unusually . . . active for this time of year."

Maximilian grunted. "The rivers in Yorkshire freeze every winter. I don't see why half the populace of southern England has to come view it happening in London."

"It is something of a novelty here . . . as are you, if you don't mind me saying so, my lord."

As he leafed through the invitations, Maximilian nodded. "So it would seem. But these are mostly from families with single daughters, if I recall my Lady Whistledown columns correctly. Don't they realize I'm off the market?"

"I—"

"That was a rhetorical question, Simms. Please have Thomason saddle my horse."

"Your horse," the butler repeated dubiously.

"Yes, my horse."

"May I point out that it is snowing, my lord?"

"This is practically springtime in Yorkshire. I believe Kraken and I will manage."

"Yes, my lord."

As Maximilian ate, he opened the various missives. Apparently even with the rumors of his empty coffer which had been circling London for years, mamas wanted to offer him their daughters. In a sense, it was amusing. Women galore seemed available to relieve him of his bachelorhood—all but the one he'd been promised. And especially after last night, none of them would do but Lady Anne Bishop.

And while his earlier neglect of his betrothed might have been through complacency, and a choice to concentrate on the tangle of matters and confusion of properties his father had left him, he wouldn't make that mistake again. Anne had issued him a challenge, one he probably deserved, and he would answer it.

"Simms, would you happen to know an establishment where I might purchase some flowers? Roses, preferably."

"Ah. I believe Martensen's has access to a hothouse. Shall I send someone to—"

Max pushed away from the table. "No. I'll take care of it."

Most of the London nobility seemed still abed as Maximilian found Martensen's and then rode on to Bishop House. Considering that everyone claimed to be in London to enjoy the weather, the closed coaches and thick, cumbersome wraps of those who had ventured out of doors in the chilly morning seemed more than a little hypocritical. He was used to that from his peers, however.

The butler seemed surprised to see him. "I don't believe Lady Anne has risen yet, my lord," he said, smoothing a frown.

"I'll wait."

As the butler showed him into the cold, closed morning room, he glanced at the foyer table. A salver with calling cards from three other gentleman lay on it. So Lord Howard and Anne's snow angel companion Sir Royce Pemberley weren't his only competition.

"Did they deliver those in person?" he asked, slowing.

"It is snowing, my lord," the butler said, apparently considering that answer enough. "I'll send someone to light the fire."

"Don't bother. I'll manage it."

"Y . . . yes, my lord. I shall inform Lady Anne of your presence."

"He can't be here," Anne muttered, throwing off her dressing gown and rubbing color into her cheeks at the same time. Not that she needed to go to the effort. In Lord Halfurst's presence her cheeks seemed perpetually warm. "It's only nine o'clock in the morning, for heaven's sake."

"Do you wish the blue merino, or the plum velvet gown?" Daisy asked, half buried in the large wardrobe.

"The plum velvet, I think." Anne quickly brushed a restless night's tangles from her long dark hair. "But that's for outside. Isn't it snowing?"

"Yes, my lady."

"Perhaps the merino, then." But that would mean she would have to sit inside and chat with him. He'd seemed so . . . intriguing last night, and if there was one thing she didn't want, it was actually to like him. He only meant to drag her off to Yorkshire, and away from all her friends and family in London. "No, the plum velvet."

By the time she was dressed and descending the stairs, she was out of breath, and unsure whether her hands shook because of the cold, annoyance at his presumption, or anticipation of seeing him once more. Annoyance was the most likely. They'd parted only nine hours ago, after all.

"My . . . lord," she said, stopping in the morning room doorway.

The marquis crouched on the hearth, setting a match to the newly stoked coals. From the smudge of soot across the back of one hand, he'd done that, as well. He glanced over his shoulder at her. "Be with you in a moment."

"But—"

"Your servants were busy," he said, shrugging as he stood. Warmth touched the edges of the room as the fireplace roared into flame. "I offered."

So her sheep farmer knew how to make a fire—and a fine one, from the look and feel of it. Anne shook herself. He wasn't *her* anything. "What brings you to Bishop House so early?"

He approached, wiping the soot off his hand with a handkerchief. "I neglected something last night."

"I don't think you did," she answered truthfully. "I had a lovely evening." Except for the near brawl he'd gotten into with Lord Howard, but even the way he'd dismissed the viscount had been . . . interesting.

A soft smile touched his mouth. "Good. But that's not what I meant."

"What, then?"

Lord Halfurst stopped in front of her, taking a moment to run his eyes the length of her plum velvet gown and back up to her face again. Very slowly he reached out and tilted up her chin. "I forgot to kiss you good night," he murmured, his gaze focusing on her lips.

"You . . ." Anne trailed off again as he leaned down and brushed his lips against hers. Her eyes closed, almost against her will. Brief and gentle and soft, and yet full of promises, or something that made her want to throw her arms around his neck and demand more. With a sharp breath she snapped open her eyes again. "You take liberties," she managed.

He shook his head. "We are betrothed, after all." Halfurst drew her closer, and kissed her again.

When he released her the second time, she was actually leaning toward him. With a silent curse she straightened. "What . . . You already kissed me good night."

"That was good morning."

"Oh."

Returning for a moment to the fireplace, the marquis retrieved a splendid bouquet of flowers from the mantel. "Winter roses," he said, handing them to her.

Their bright scarlet color itself seemed enough to warm the room. In her heavy velvet gown, Anne was beginning to feel rather heated herself. "Thank you," she said, breathing in their spicy scent. "They're lovely. But not necessary."

"Evidently, they are necessary," he countered. "I have some things to make up for. This is merely the beginning."

"The beginning?" she repeated, watching the slow curve of his mouth. Somber, he was aristocratic and handsome, far enough from her imaginings that she could almost believe he was an imposter. When he smiled, though, the expression lighted his eyes, and in response her heart did silly little flip-flops.

"Of my courtship."

The pronouncement, so calm and matter-of-fact, stunned her, and it was a moment before she could get her jaw to work again. "I thought you intended to drag me off to Yorkshire."

Halfurst tilted his head as though trying to read her thoughts. "I could do that," he admitted in a low voice, "but I couldn't make you want to be there, and I certainly couldn't make you want to be there with me."

Anne narrowed her eyes. "Forgive my cynicism, but what happened to make you suddenly so willing to be reasonable?"

"You did. But it's not reason; it's patience. You were meant to be mine. I intend to have you."

My goodness, he seemed sure of himself. "Why, because I'm pretty and my family has money?"

The smile touched his mouth again. "Because you told me you'd rather drop dead than marry me."

"Because . . . That's absurd."

"And because you interest me, and intrigue me, and because after nineteen years without a word from me and as popular as you are, you only said no, and not that you'd chosen someone else."

Anne felt dizzy. It wasn't just his absurd turn of logic, but the way he held her gaze as he spoke, and the way he seemed to know what she wanted to hear. "So you intend to woo me?"

"I do."

"And what if I still resist?"

"You won't."

He did have a male's typical arrogance. "But if I do?"

For a moment he didn't speak. "Then I'll return to Yorkshire."

"Alone," she prompted.

"Without you," he answered, his eyes glittering, as if he knew she wouldn't like that response.

Heavens, he didn't think he could make her jealous, did he? She'd known *of* him all her life, but she'd only known him for a day, after all. He still gazed at her, so she grimaced at him, wrinkling her nose. "Good."

"Good," he repeated softly. "And now, would you care to go walking with me this morning?"

"But it's snowing!"

"Barely. We're both dressed for it." The marquis pursed his lips, looking her up and down again. Something akin to humor, but darker and warmer, touched his gray gaze. "Unless you'd care to sit here with me."

Anne cleared her throat. "I'll fetch my cloak."

"I thought you might."

"It doesn't mean I'm afraid of you, Lord Halfurst," she said as she made her escape.

"Maximilian," he corrected.

"No."

The marquis turned, keeping her in view. "Why not?"

Oh dear, she should just have given in. She was much more suave and confident with her other male friends. They, however, didn't question every word she said. They probably only listened to half of them.

"Calling a gentleman by his Christian name implies a certain . . . familiarity," she said, scowling as she realized how much she sounded like her mother.

With two quick strides he was between her and the doorway. "I heard you call Sir Royce and Lord Howard by their Christian names," he said in a low voice, meeting her gaze levelly. "What sort of 'familiarity' do you enjoy with them?"

Anne forced a short laugh. "Are you jealous, my lord?"

"Yes. And I become more so with each moment I spend in your company."

The proclamation stopped the coy, practiced retort she'd been about to make. Men pretended jealousy to garner further favor, and she usually found it tiresome. Men didn't admit to actual jealousy—not any men with whom she'd been heretofore acquainted. "I'm . . . I haven't been attempting to make you jealous," she offered, the heat in his gaze leaving her equal parts nervous and excited.

"I know that. It's another reason you intrigue me, Anne." He brought his hand up, tucking a strand of her hair back into the clip from which it had escaped. "Call me Maximilian."

A sheep farmer. He's a sheep farmer, she reminded herself fiercely. One who lived in Yorkshire, of all places. "Very well, Maximilian," she said. Her determination to remain unmoved didn't stop the slow swirl of lightning from coiling up her spine.

The light in his gray eyes deepened and darkened. All he said, though, was "Fetch your wrap, Anne."

He followed her into the foyer, noting that she didn't even glance at the silver tray holding the calling cards of her beaux. That was one point scored for early risers.

Lady Anne Bishop, he was coming to realize to his growing delight, was far more complex than he'd anticipated. Each moment the plans he'd worked out to win her needed to be modified and adapted as he learned something new about her.

The butler lifted a heavy gray cloak lined with ermine from the coat rack, and Max stepped in to intercept it. "Allow me," he said, taking it from his surprised fingers.

Approaching her again, he slipped the cloak over her shoulders, breathing deeply of the lavender scent of her hair as he did so. Moving around in front of her, he fastened the silver clasp beneath her chin. Her scent, touching her bare skin, intoxicated him. He'd thought to find a female to bear him an heir, and little else. The thought that he would actually desire her had never crossed his mind.

"Anne!" a voice called from the balcony. "Where do you think you're going?"

Lady Daven hurried down the stairs, a footman and two maids in tow. As she approached, ranting about her daughter's intentions much as she had last night when they'd discovered her missing, Maximilian stepped forward.

"Lady Daven, good morning," he said, sketching a bow.

She skidded to a halt, her fair skin reddening. "My goodness. Lord Halfurst. I . . . Forgive my intrusion. I hadn't realized you were here."

"No apology necessary. I merely thought to get a jump on my competition this morning. I've asked Lady Anne to accompany me on a walk."

"Your compet—" Anne began, frowning.

"I assure you, my lord, you have no competition. Lord Daven and I have always made Anne's duty perfectly clear to her."

"Mother, please don't—"

"Even so," he answered, "I have lately come to think that winning by default isn't precisely winning."

Anne threw open the front door and stalked outside. Stifling a frown of his own, Maximilian nodded to her mother and followed her. Whether

her parents had made her duty clear to her or not, convincing her to abide by their wishes was obviously something else entirely.

"Anne," he said, taking her hand and wrapping it over his arm, "I hadn't realized you were so anxious to take the morning air."

She shrugged free, increasing her pace. "If you're only being nice to 'win' some sort of competition for my favor, I can assure you that you have no chance, and you might as well return to Yorkshire right now."

His earlier good humor began to fade. "Don't be absurd."

"Abs—"

"Of course I'm here to win your favor," he cut in, grabbing her arm again. "I wouldn't be here otherwise." He leaned over, brushing her ear with his lips. "But just remember that I was not the one making snow angels. If you'd behaved, you might have avoided meeting me altogether." That wasn't quite true; he'd intended to come to London in the spring to bring her to Yorkshire, anyway. He would have been a fool, however, not to take advantage of the leverage her indiscretion gained him.

She looked sideways at him. "So if I hadn't appeared in Lady Whistledown's column, you never would have bothered to exert yourself to leave Halfurst? Now who's being absurd?"

His first instinct was to send her a retort about her own lack of respect for their parents' agreement. They'd already covered that territory, however, and he intended on moving forward—not revisiting the past. "Perhaps we should just agree that we haven't regarded our duties to one another as we should."

"That's my point," she insisted. "I don't have a duty to you."

"Then why are we walking together in the snow, my dear? You did seem to think it would be a horrific experience." He brushed a snowflake from her nose. "And yet it becomes you."

Anne glanced over her shoulder at her maid, but not before he glimpsed her sudden smile. "Humph. I'm most likely on this crusade because I've been rendered senseless by weariness and hunger."

He laughed. And he'd thought he would find her a malleable, if spoiled, chit. "I'll remember that you prefer to stay in bed late, then," he murmured, noting the flush of her cheeks. He didn't think her color was because of the cold, and that pleased him. "For this morning, though, I thought you might enjoy some fresh bread and butter from Hamond's bakery."

She evidently was hungry, because she didn't object when he led her to the bakery and ordered breakfast. "How did you know about this place?" she asked, between dainty mouthfuls of buttered bread.

"I'm not a stranger to London," Maximilian answered, resting his chin on his hand to watch her eat.

She looked up at him from beneath her thick, curling lashes. "Then why not visit more often?"

"I don't like it here."

"But why not? Friends, soirées, the theater, shops, the wonderful food—what's not to like?"

She'd left out the most alluring feature of London—herself. Generally at this time of morning he would be out in the far pasture, checking on his livestock. On occasion London did have its merits. For a moment he didn't want to answer, but he seemed to be developing a curious weakness for honest inquiry and moss green eyes. "Your experience differs somewhat from mine. I . . . found I was being judged by rumor rather than by my character."

"Perhaps that's because we had nothing else to go by." Her gaze darkened. "That's why I presume you're here as much for my purse as for me."

He smiled. "We were betrothed when I was seven, Anne. My only concerns at the time were horses and tin soldiers. I'm sorry to say, you were neither. Very disappointing, really."

She scowled, bread halfway to her alluring lips. "Do you mean to say we've met before?"

Nodding, Max ran a finger down the back of her hand. "I held you, when you were three months old."

"You did?"

"Yes. You sneezed on me, and poked me in the eye."

She laughed, a delightful, musical sound that made his pulse speed. "And you've no doubt carried a grudge against me for nineteen years because of that."

"Hardly." Max twisted his lips. Finding the words to say had never been difficult before. Before, though, he hadn't cared about the impression he made. Perhaps that was another reason he hadn't fared well in London. Directness didn't seem to impress many people here. But Anne seemed to appreciate it. "At fourteen, it seemed ridiculous to write letters to a seven-year-old. At twenty, you were still a babe of thirteen. And then my father died, and . . . other concerns took precedence."

"So you forgot about me."

He shook his head. "I just . . . assumed, I suppose, that that aspect of my life was taken care of." Maximilian met her gaze again. "It was wrong of me to do so. I'm now attempting to make amends for it."

"And you think I'm spoiled and self-centered to make you jump through hoops to prove something to me? I can assure you, Maximilian, that I am not—"

"Yes, I did think you were spoiled—until ten minutes into our acquaintance. Or reacquaintance, rather." Grinning, he wiped a smudge of butter from her lower lip with his thumb, because he couldn't seem to get past the desire, the need, to touch her.

"And what stupendous thing did I say to alter your opinion of me?"

"You saw my attire, heard my declarations, and then refused me because you didn't know my character."

To his surprise, she set aside the remainder of her meal and stood. "So I passed your test," she said, wiping her hands and pulling on her mittens again, "but you haven't passed mine. And unfortunately, you can't. Not while Halfurst remains in Yorkshire."

Back to that again, were they? Maximilian took a deep breath as he rose. "Keep reminding yourself of that, Anne Elizabeth," he murmured, tucking her against him as they left the bakery. Whether because of the cold or because she liked being touched by him, she didn't object. "Make it your battle cry. Whenever you see me, when you taste my mouth on yours, when you feel my hands on your bare skin, Anne, remind yourself that Halfurst remains in Yorkshire, and that so do I."

"I will," she said in an unsteady voice. "And it is argument enough."

They reached the front steps of Bishop House, and Lambert opened the door. Anne would have freed her arm from his, but Maximilian caught her, drawing her up against his chest. "I don't intend to give up the advantage that being engaged to you gives me, Anne," he said softly, and lowered his mouth to hers.

As he lifted his head from her, Anne's eyes were closed, her soft lips parted in warmth and invitation. Good God, what was he getting himself into? An arranged marriage wasn't supposed to feel so . . . arousing.

"We'll go for a carriage ride tomorrow," he forced himself to say, readjusting her cloak and barely able to keep himself from pulling her back into his arms.

"I . . . I have plans already."

"Cancel them. And tomorrow I will kiss you good morning again."

The deepening color in her fine cheeks aroused him even further. Thank Lucifer for heavy, caped coats. He pulled his closer around his front.

"You're very sure of yourself, Maximilian."

"No, my lady, I'm very sure of you."

Chapter 4

On Sunday, Lord Halfurst was spied paying a call upon Lady Anne Bishop.

On Monday, Lord Halfurst was spied paying a call upon Lady Anne Bishop.

On Tuesday, Lord Halfurst was spied paying a call upon Lady Anne Bishop.

This Author must deliver this column to the printer prior to Wednesday morning, but truly, does anyone think This Author would be lacking in journalistic integrity if the following were written Tuesday eve:

On Wednesday, Lord Halfurst was spied paying a call upon Lady Anne Bishop.

No? This Author thought not.

LADY WHISTLEDOWN'S SOCIETY PAPERS,
2 February 1814

"There is no imminent marriage."

Lord Daven opened and closed his mouth. "I beg your pardon?"

"I told him that you would not force me to marry him." Anne took a deep breath, gazing at her father's stony expression. *Best just to get it over with.* "I told you I didn't want to go to Yorkshire."

"Slow down a moment, Annie. If you . . . refused him—which I can't believe you did without consulting me—then why has Halfurst continued to call on you?"

She looked at her toes. "He's wooing me," she mumbled.

"I'm not as young as I used to be, daughter, so for God's sake speak up!"

"He's wooing me," she repeated in a louder voice, lifting her head again. "That's what he says, anyway."

The earl's lips twitched.

"Are you laughing at me, Papa?"

"At the moment, yes, I am." He sat back in his chair, a rare smile softening his features. "Just be aware that Maximilian Trent is not his father."

That stopped her, and she returned to her own seat. "What do you mean by that?"

"Oh no, you don't. You've kept me out of this, and so you can just continue to do so. As far as I'm concerned about it, all I meant was that you shouldn't think he does anything frivolously, my dear. He hasn't come to be where he is by accident."

Scowling, Anne leaned forward. "Papa, where is he, and how do you know? You haven't even mentioned his name in a year."

The earl chuckled. "Let's just say that I've followed his career more closely than you have, Annie. I've written *him* letters, and he's written back." He opened the accounts book on his desk. "Now if you don't mind, I have some work to do."

"You aren't being very helpful."

"Hm. Neither have you been. You might have asked my advice before you told him what I would or wouldn't do."

Still frowning, Anne left the office for the more congenial domain of the morning room. She'd expected her father to be livid when he'd finally summoned her to discuss Lord Halfurst. Maximilian. The sheep farmer, who apparently had some secrets.

She'd barely picked up her embroidery when Lambert scratched at the door. "Come in," she called, smoothing her skirt and trying to pretend that her heart wasn't racing. He'd come calling every day, and Lord and Lady Moreland's skating party on the Thames was that afternoon.

The butler entered. "My lady, Lord Howard is here to inquire whether you are at home."

"Lord Howard? Yes, of course." She'd barely thought of Desmond in almost a week, except to cancel the museum visit he'd suggested.

The viscount entered, still shaking snow from his tawny hair. "Anne," he said with a smile, coming forward to take her hand, "I'm pleased to find you home."

"Yes, I'm afraid I've been rather occupied the past few days."

"Monopolized is more like it," Desmond returned. "May I sit?"

"Of course."

He took a seat in one of the overstuffed chairs, while she sat opposite him on the couch. She'd known him since her debut in London, and as she thought about it, he'd always been available to dance with, to escort her to various soirées and fireworks displays, and most of the other amusements the town had to offer.

"Do you attend the Moreland skating party?" he asked.

"I'm invited. I haven't yet decided whether I—"

"You mean Halfurst hasn't asked to escort you yet."

"Desmond, I am obligated to spend a certain amount of time with him."

The viscount lurched to his feet, striding to the window and back. "I don't see why you should feel obligated to him at all. You've told me again and again how he's ignored you for your entire life." Abruptly he sat beside her, taking her hand in his. "Which makes me wonder—why is he here now, in London?"

A little uneasy at Lord Howard's outburst, she frowned. "He read about me making snow angels with Sir Royce Pemberly."

His grip on her hand tightened. "That explains it. He perceived that another man had an interest in you, and hurried to London to make certain he still had a claim on you—and your money."

Whatever his monetary situation, Maximilian obviously had enough blunt to purchase an all-new wardrobe and to open his house on High Street again. On the other hand, she knew of some families completely without funds who had still managed to dissemble for years before the truth came out.

"In all honesty, my lord, you're the only one who's mentioned Lord Halfurst's money problems."

"Ha. You don't expect him to tell you, do you? And if it's not money he's after, why hasn't he acceded to your wishes, dissolved your parents' agreement, and married one of the other chits who've been throwing themselves at him since he returned to London?"

Other women had been pursuing Maximilian? She'd had no idea. When they were together, all his attention seemed so . . . focused on her. "What do you suggest I do, then, Desmond?"

He leaned closer, near enough that his cheek touched her hair. "Whatever Halfurst's motives, Anne, we both know you don't belong in Yorkshire. And he isn't the only man who would welcome your affections."

With that, he brushed his lips against her cheek. When Anne looked at him, startled, he repeated the motion, this time against her lips.

Other than stunned surprise, the first thought to cross her mind was that with Lord Howard she didn't have to stop herself from flinging her arms around his neck. She didn't crave a deepening of the embrace, or even a repeat of it. "Please stop that," she said, pulling her hand free and standing.

He stood at the same time. "I beg your pardon, Anne. I . . . allowed my feelings to dictate my actions." The viscount seized her hand again. "Please forgive me."

"Of course," she returned, relieved that this oddness was over. "We are friends."

He smiled again, relief in his sky blue eyes. "Yes, we are friends. And as your friend, please allow me to escort you to the Moreland party. Whatever you decide about Halfurst, there's no reason you can't spend one afternoon simply enjoying yourself."

Well, he was right about that. Intriguing and tantalizing as she was coming to find Maximilian's company, she couldn't forget that he meant to take her off to Yorkshire. And if he followed his previous pattern, it would be at least six years before she saw London again. How could she bear that?

"Yes," she stated. "I would be happy to attend the Moreland skating party with you."

"Thank you, Anne. I'll come by for you at noon."

As he left, Anne turned to look at Daisy, seated in one corner and ostensibly sewing a stocking. "Do more gentlemen seem to be kissing me, lately?"

"Yes, my lady. None so well as Lord Halfurst, though."

"What?"

"You said yourself, my lady, that he kisses quite well."

She sighed. "Yes, I did, didn't I?"

Not ten minutes later, Lambert scratched at the open door again. "Lord Halfurst is here to see you, my lady."

Warmth swept beneath her skin. "Please show him in, Lambert."

Maximilian paused in the morning room doorway as the butler stepped back to allow him through. Soon he wouldn't have to ask anyone's damned permission to enter a room and see her. Soon he wouldn't have to stop at a kiss, and he wouldn't have to imagine what lay beneath the tantalizing curves of her gown.

"Good morning," he said, crossing the room as she stood.

"Good morning."

Already her gaze was focused on his mouth. Maximilian wrapped an iron fist around the abrupt desire to lay her down on the couch and make her his in more than just an old agreement on paper. Stroking her cheek with the back of one finger, he leaned down and touched his mouth to hers. Keenly aware of the maid seated in the corner, he held back, ending the kiss far sooner than he wanted to.

Her fingers had wrapped into his lapel, and she'd pulled herself close against his chest, so that he could feel the swell of her breasts as she took a deep breath. Sweet Lucifer, he should have come to London the moment she'd turned eighteen, whatever his personal feelings about the place and the people. He shouldn't have stayed away, no matter how much he disliked it, because by doing so he'd missed nearly two years of knowing Anne Bishop.

The maid cleared her throat. With a start, Anne released him and took a step backward. "Good morning."

He smiled. "You said that already."

"Did I? I forgot."

"Then perhaps you forgot our kiss as well, and I should remind you."

She closed her eyes for a brief moment. "I don't think that would be wise," she whispered, gazing up at him again.

"Amen," the maid muttered.

Maximilian glanced over at her. Daisy was right, as was Anne. He needed to show restraint; he'd already realized that pushing his betrothed only made her push back. And he had no intention of letting her get away now.

"Very well," he said, reluctance making him sigh. "Then might I instead ask you to join me this afternoon? I've been invited to an ice skating party on the Thames."

Her fine cheeks paled. "Oh."

Suspicion tightened the muscles across his shoulders. "What is it?"

"I've . . . Lord Howard was here earlier. I agreed to attend with him."

Damn that buffoon. "You kiss me, and you make plans with him?"

"She kissed him, too," the maid blurted, and ducked her head.

"Daisy!"

"What?"

Anne took several more steps backward. "I didn't kiss him. He kissed me."

Maximilian clenched his fists. "Has he kissed you before?"

"No! Of course not."

He believed her, but anger continued to charge through his muscles and his nerves. Desmond Howard had touched her, and she'd agreed to go skating with the bastard. "I'm not playing a game with you, Anne," he said stiffly. "And I would appreciate if you would do me the courtesy of not playing one with me."

"I wasn't—"

"Enjoy your skating." Too annoyed and too bloody frustrated to continue conversing in anything resembling polite tones, Maximilian turned on his heel to stalk back down the hallway, grab his coat and hat from the surprised butler, and stride back out to the street.

Cursing, he swung up on Kraken and trotted back toward Trent House. One damned thing was certain; he was going ice skating on the Thames that afternoon. Lord Howard might have the edge for the moment, but Anne Bishop belonged to him.

Anne sat between Theresa and Pauline on the bench provided for the ladies. The Morelands had invited nearly a hundred guests from the looks of it, and she fervently hoped the ice of the new-frozen Thames would hold all the resulting weight.

"I've been doing a gender count," Pauline whispered, as her maid helped her fasten the ice skates over her boots.

"What did you expect?" Anne returned in the same low voice, for Lord and Lady Moreland were only a short distance away at the end of Swan Lane Pier. The orchestra they'd hired for the outing seemed absurd in the extreme, but at least they were on the pier and not adding to the strain on the ice.

"What do you mean?" Theresa asked, tentatively standing in the last inches of snow before the river ice began.

"One hundred guests, and nearly seventy-five of them are female," Pauline said dryly. "What do you think it means?"

"Oh. Donald again."

For the past four years Viscount and Lady Moreland had been holding off-Season soirées, presumably because most of the other young bucks would be elsewhere, in hopes of convincing some young lady that their son, Donald Spence, was a fine catch. Everyone knew the ruse, and obviously no one was fishing. Each year the ratio of female to male guests grew greater, but still no one had fallen for Donald's lackluster charms. Anne had already spent ten minutes conversing with him, having been cornered nearly the moment she descended from Desmond's carriage. It seemed to be the price of admission to the soirée, but if anything he'd grown duller since last she'd seen him.

"Here comes Lord Howard," Pauline muttered. "I'm off. Wish me luck."

"Don't break anything," Anne called after her. The warning was unnecessary; Pauline swished across the ice as though she'd been doing it daily for years.

Lord Howard trudged over from the men's bench as Anne climbed to her feet. She hadn't skated in ages and barely then, but from the look of some of the other guests, Pauline excluded, she wasn't the only unsteady one.

"Shall we?" Desmond asked, offering his hand.

Her ermine muff hanging from the ribbon about her neck, and her right hand tightly gripping his arm, Anne nodded. They stepped onto the ice together, and thankfully she didn't collapse as they glided forward in a fairly competent fashion.

"Oh, this is fun," she exclaimed, relief making her chuckle.

"And even better, all chaperones must remain on the bank." Desmond slipped his arm free of her grip and skated a slow circle around her. "Green velvet becomes you," he said, continuing his circles. "And the cold brings roses to your cheeks. You are breathtaking, Anne."

That odd feeling started in her gut again. This was not how friends spoke to each other. "You look very fine yourself, Lord Howard," she returned, keeping the smile on her lips. "And I think you've been practicing your skating. You far outshine me."

"Nothing could."

Trying to gather her thoughts, Anne looked across the ice. Fifty or so guests had joined them already on the cold surface. As she watched, Moreland servants in socks emerged onto the Thames, pushing carts of sandwiches and Madeira before them while the orchestra launched into a country dance.

"You haven't answered me," the viscount said from behind her.

She shook herself. "Beg pardon. Answered you about what?"

His sky blue eyes narrowed for a brief moment as he passed in front of her, then cleared again. "I have to rescind my earlier apology, Anne. I *did* mean to kiss you."

Oh no. "Please stop circling," she snapped. "You're making me dizzy."

Immediately he returned to her side, taking her hand again as they neared the far bank and the higher piles of snow there. "Perhaps it's your feelings making you dizzy. I know this must be unexpected, but we have been friends for some time now. Surely you've realized my admiration and regard for you."

Anne swallowed. His recent declarations that he would never remove her from London and that he feared for her happiness in Maximilian's company abruptly made sense. It wasn't friendship he was after. "Desmond—"

"Damn him," the viscount cut in. "How did he manage to get invited? Obviously the Morelands had no idea what they were doing."

She turned. A clinging, slipping female on either arm, Lord Halfurst glided up and back along the ice. Something one of the ladies said made him laugh, the sound ringing merrily across the width of the river. Her heart jolted. He was supposed to be sulking somewhere, or thinking up their next outing. He *wasn't* supposed to be enjoying himself at the party to which she'd declined to accompany him.

"I suppose any chit with an income *will* do for him," Desmond murmured in her ear. "At this rate he'll be a married man by St. Valentine's Day, and you'll never have to worry about being dragged off to Yorkshire."

"But he seemed so . . ."

"Sincere?" the viscount finished. "Yes, he looks it."

Anne wanted a few moments to think in peace, without Desmond Howard echoing her own worst doubts aloud. As she continued to watch, unable to turn away, Halfurst returned to the snowy bank, released the ladies in his company, and amid much laughter collected two more. From the silly tittering and giggling, all the gathered females were supremely grateful both for his attention and for his clear skill on the ice.

"Come, my dear," Desmond continued. "You're upset. It's quite natural; you had no idea he was courting other females."

"Wouldn't you consider," she forced out, trying to shake free of Desmond's whisperings, "that he's merely being nice? This party does lack for male escorts."

"Ah, dear Anne. Always determined to think the best of everyone, aren't you?"

"Not real—"

"I have an idea to take your mind off this odiousness. At Queenhithe the commoners have set up food and gaming booths all across the Thames. They're calling it Freezeland Street or some such thing. It's just around the bend. Why don't—"

"Please fetch me a Madeira, Desmond," she interrupted, unable to listen to another sentence from him without shrieking, whoever's best intentions he might have in mind.

"Of course. Don't try to get about on your own. I'll be right back."

Maximilian was on his third or fourth pair of ladies, escorting them easily about the ice despite their obvious lack of skill and balance. This whole thing was a mistake, Anne decided; she should never have come, and certainly not with Desmond. Lord Howard's kiss should have been warning enough, both about his intentions and about her own feelings toward him. Perhaps without meaning to she *was* playing a game of some sort with Halfurst.

With a scowl and an awkward kick, she skated back in the direction of the pier, and Maximilian. Even when she ultimately refused his suit, she didn't mean to be spiteful about it. She certainly hadn't meant to behave like a coquette that morning.

He looked over to see her approaching, and for a brief moment their eyes met. And then he turned his back, he and his charges skating toward the shore.

"Anne, what's going on?" Pauline asked, sliding to a halt and nearly dumping the two of them onto the ice.

"Nothing's going on. I just need a moment to think." A tear ran down her cheek, and Anne brushed it away before anyone could see.

"This is a bad spot for thinking," her friend returned. "Let me help you to shore before you end up on your backside."

Just then Lord Halfurst, having relieved himself of his clinging chits, faced her again, arms crossed over his chest. *Ha.* So he thought to make her come to him, to apologize for daring to attend a party in someone else's company. And then he would expect her to dance off to Yorkshire and never see her dear friends like Pauline again.

"Go away, Pauline," she stated, turning her back on him. Let him see how he liked it.

"But Annie—"

"I'm fine. I don't need your help."

Pauline was *not* going to deliver her into the arms of her tormentor, no matter how handsome and kind and warm he seemed to be. She hadn't been wooed, and she hadn't been won—not by a few amusing outings and some arousing kisses. Misery lay just beyond them, and she knew it.

With a deep breath she pushed off in the opposite direction, ignoring Pauline's fading advice to keep her speed down. Sir Royce Pemberly appeared in front of her, his expression startled.

"Lady Anne—"

With a gasp she dodged, trying to avoid slamming into him. Flailing her arms, she went into a spin that she hoped looked daring and not desperate. Her left blade cut into the ice, and abruptly she was skating forward again at high speed.

In a blur a pretty blue wrap flashed in front of her, and she careened into someone. As she passed she heard a thud.

"Oh no, oh no," she quavered, looking over her shoulder. Susannah Ballister—whom Anne knew quite well from the previous Season—lay sprawled in a snowbank, her gown and wrap askew and her hair across her face. As she watched, still fleeing and unable to stop, Susannah sat up and shook snow from her front.

"Anne!"

She cringed at Maximilian's bellow, and faced forward again. Her face felt crimson, and she was absolutely not going to stop and be yelled at, much less by him and in front of everyone else. In a moment she'd rounded the bend, out of sight of the Morelands' idiotic skating party.

Finally she took in a breath, managing to slow down enough to guide herself onto the bank without falling. No one was in sight, but just up ahead she could hear the sounds of the frost fair Desmond had mentioned.

"Thank goodness," she gasped, wiping tears from her face again. She wanted a place to think, and a fair where no one knew her seemed perfect. Crossing her fingers for luck, she pushed back out onto the ice and skated at a much more cautious pace toward the sounds of music and laughter.

Chapter 5

Lady Anne Bishop proved herself to be quite the worst skater on the ice, with the possible exception of Lord Middlethorpe, who, it must be noted, is nearly four times her age.

Lady Whistledown's Society Papers,
4 February 1814

She'd been skating over to join him. It'd all been going quite well, Maximilian thought. Despite the torture of seeing Howard practically attached to her, he'd felt hope. Whatever the viscount said, she hadn't liked it, and when she'd started back to the shore, he'd returned as well, to relinquish his charges to the safer bank.

And then all hell had broken loose. Worse than Anne knocking chits into snowbanks, she'd vanished around the curve of the river—alone.

"Damnation," he muttered, skating through the remainder of the guests and after her. "Anne!"

She'd vanished. His chest tightening, Maximilian scanned the snowbanks on either side of the Thames as he sped along. He rounded another curve, and stopped short.

London was a very odd place. Spanning the river from shore to shore, a small village of wooden shanties had risen on the ice. Hundreds of citizens slid and walked and skated among the makeshift buildings while fiddle music and the shouts of vendors filled the air.

He'd been somewhat relieved to realize that Anne skated terribly. She wasn't perfect. On the other hand, a young lady alone in a crowd could find herself worse than embarrassed. With another low curse he skated onto the ice street between the rows of booths and carts.

He could scarcely advance a foot without being jostled by someone hawking gingerbread or meat pies. Drunken gamblers slipped and slid on the ice. A growing anxiety clutched at him. Chagrined or angry or whatever Anne had felt to cause her to leave the party, this was a dangerous place for her to be alone. Damn Howard for leaving her side.

"Stop! Thief!"

At the sound of the female voice, Maximilian whipped around. Anne clutched the arm of a large, hard-faced man, her green reticule gripped in one of his hands.

"Anne!"

The man shoved, and she went down onto her backside next to one of the shanties. With a leer the thief began a sliding run up the street.

Maximilian skidded to a halt beside Anne. "Did he hurt you?" he asked, crouching to brush hair from her face. "Are you all right?"

"I'm fine," she panted, her hands shaking in his as he pulled her to her feet. "But my brooch was in my bag. I feel so st—"

"Wait here," he commanded, thrusting her toward an approaching constable, and was off like a shot.

Some brute had dared push his Anne to the ground. For once he didn't have to be subtle or civilized or wait for another game piece to advance. As Maximilian caught sight of the fellow flashing through the crowd, he gave a grim smile. *No one* was allowed to harm his Anne.

Anne watched Maximilian vanish in pursuit of the purse snatcher. "There, there, miss," the constable said, gripping her arm. "No harm done."

She wasn't so certain of that. Her whole body shook, and not from the cold. She'd thought herself completely alone, and then Maximilian had appeared out of nowhere. And he'd vanished again—after what could be a very dangerous man, all because she'd been stupid and mentioned her silly brooch. "Please let me go," she said shakily.

"The gentleman said you should wait here."

"Lord Halfurst," she said distinctly, "might be in danger."

"Lord . . . Oh bloody hell," the constable muttered. "Right. You stay here, miss."

He skated off, his desire to be of assistance to a nobleman obviously outweighing his concern for a female who was in all probability a mere miss. Anne had no intention of correcting his misapprehension, if it would convince him to go help Maximilian.

Another constable appeared, demanding to know what all the excitement was about. Before someone could point her out to him, Anne pushed off in the direction Maximilian had vanished. He'd come after her when no one else had, and she would not let him be hurt on her account.

Maximilian caught up to the thief just before the shanty street ended. With a growl he launched himself at the man. Vendor carts and beer mugs and brandy balls went flying as they both went down in a flailing heap of fists and feet and skates.

They careened into the corner of one of the booths, bringing the flimsy thing down on top of both of them. Maximilian grunted as a boot slammed across his thigh. Thank God the fool hadn't been wearing ice skates, or his plans to produce an heir with Anne Bishop might have been extinguished. With a better purchase on the ice because of his own skates, he scrambled to his feet first.

"Bloody—" the thief began, and stopped when Maximilian's fist met his jaw.

Leaning across him, Maximilian yanked Anne's reticule from beneath a pile of beer mugs and oysters. "Thank you very much," he panted, stuffing it into his coat pocket.

"Lord Halfurst! M'lord, are you unhurt?"

Maximilian turned to see the constable skating through the mayhem and wreckage toward him. "Weren't you supposed to be watching after someone?" he snapped, trying to regain his breath. Damn it all, now Anne was alone again.

"She . . . she sent me to help you, m'lord," the constable protested. "I—"

"Maximilian!"

Max spun back around just in time to wrap his arms around Anne as she thudded hard into him. With another curse he landed in the beer and wood splinters and oysters again, Anne crumpled across him.

"Are you all right?" she asked, raising her head from his chest to look down at him.

"I'm a bit winded," he forced out. *Mostly from people and buildings falling on me*. "And you?"

"I feel horrid, knocking Susannah down, and then running off like an idiot, and sending you after a thief. Heavens, he might have had a knife!"

"But you're not hurt," he repeated, wishing she would stop wriggling on him. It was damned distracting, and they'd gathered quite a few onlookers with all the commotion.

"No, I'm not hurt."

"Good. Would you mind removing your skate from my knee, then? Slowly, if you please."

"Oh good heavens," she gasped, slipping with ungainly and exaggerated care off him and onto the ice. "I've hurt you!"

He sat up. "Only a scratch. My trousers have seen the end of their run, though, I'm afraid."

"I'm so sorry."

Now she looked ready to cry. "Don't be," he said in a quieter voice, smiling. "I've had much worse than this."

The constable had been joined by another, and together they hauled the reeling thief to his feet. "What do you wish done with him, my lord?"

Max pulled Anne's reticule from his pocket and handed it back to her. "Nothing. No harm done. Just see him away from here."

"Ah, yes, my lord."

Muttering to one another about all nobles being madmen, they dragged the thief off, presumably to give him a stern talking to. As long as Anne was all right, Maximilian didn't much care what happened to the man. Stifling a groan, he climbed once again to his feet, and pulled Anne up after him.

"I suggest we return to the party," he said, wrapping her gloved hand securely around his arm so she wouldn't be able to cause any further havoc.

"No, I can't," Anne blurted, her face going scarlet. "I behaved like such a hoyden." She looked up at him. "And besides, you're hurt, and wet, and you smell like fish and beer."

"Isn't that what you'd expect from a sheep farmer?" he returned evenly. "Or perhaps mutton and wet wool would be more in line with your thinking."

"You're just angry because I went skating with Lord Howard. And you *are* a sheep farmer."

His jaw tightening, Maximilian gave a slight nod. "Yes, I am. Why did you flee the party?"

"Because I wanted to."

She'd already convinced him that she wasn't the spoiled, flighty chit he'd expected at first sight of her. "With no thought to the danger you might be putting yourself in? Some of this ice is too thin to hold a rat. Not to mention your barging into the middle of a street fair. You're lucky our friend only wanted your reticule."

"I was managing quite well without you."

That was enough of that. He let her go. With a squeak Anne lost her balance. Before she could fall, Max slipped his hands beneath her arms and pulled her upright against him.

"Care to revise that statement?" he suggested to the back of her head. At her continued silence, he relented a little, pushing off in the direction of Queenhithe Dock. "All right. Then tell me why you decided to attend with Lord Howard."

"He asked me."

"You knew I would ask you."

"He asked first."

"I asked you to marry me first."

She looked up over her shoulder at him, and he was surprised to see tears in her green eyes. "You never asked me. No one ever asked me."

Anne expected him to say something cynical, like reminding her that no one had asked him, either, but he didn't. In fact, as she thought about it, he'd never said anything to bemoan his own part in this.

They reached the dock at Queenhithe, and with no visible effort Lord Halfurst lifted her onto the edge of the pier. While Anne watched, fascinated, he untied her skates from her half boots. His hands brushing the hem of her skirt and gripping her ankles left her feeling oddly . . . hot inside, despite the cold against her skin. She would never have thought a sheep farmer would know how to skate so well, and yet he obviously did.

He seemed to know how to do quite a few things well—things that made him fit into London better than she ever would have suspected. And yet in some ways, he didn't fit in at all. "I should have told Desmond no," she said slowly.

Max looked up at her as he tied her skates together and slung them over his shoulder. "Why?"

He wanted a truthful answer; she could see that in his warm gray eyes. "Because I knew you would ask me."

With a hop he sat beside her and leaned down to remove his own skates from his fine Hessian boots. "He doesn't own your heart, does he, Anne?"

She studied his profile. "No one owns my heart."

He straightened. "I've already accepted that challenge."

"I'm not sure why. I've told you a hundred times that I won't marry you."

"Ah." A slight smile touched his sensuous mouth, and then he leaned down again, his too-long black hair half obscuring his lean face. "Do you like to argue, or just with me?"

"I think it's my turn to ask you a question," she countered, abruptly wondering whether he had any lovers waiting for him back in Yorkshire. Sheep farmers were no doubt very popular there, and he was by far the most handsome farmer she'd ever set eyes on.

"Then ask."

"Do you *need* to be in Yorkshire all year long? Or is it just that you like to be there all the time?"

His skates off, he slung them over his other shoulder and stood. "I'm a landlord, the local magistrate, the farmer's almanac, and whatever else Halfurst needs. It's a responsibility, not a choice." Bending down, he helped her to her feet.

For a moment, Anne hoped he would take her arm around his again, as he had when they'd been on skates. Instead, though, he helped her stuff her hands into her warm ermine muff. "Am I a responsibility, Maximilian, or a choice?"

"What you are, Anne, is a conundrum. Shall I hire us a hack, or do you want to walk?"

"Walk? It's miles!"

"A hack it is."

He guided her back to the street. She liked that he'd called her a conundrum; it sounded so much more interesting than simply saying she was contrary or flighty. In truth, mostly what she felt lately was confusion—interrupted by moments of unexpected lust toward the man she'd sworn she would never marry. And even covered with beer and oysters, he enticed her.

"You must be freezing," she said abruptly, freeing one hand from her muff to take his arm as a hack stopped before them.

He handed her up, giving directions to Bishop House before he joined her inside and pulled the door closed. Even in the closed carriage she could see her breath. For heaven's sake, if Halfurst froze to death she wouldn't be able to argue with him any longer, and he wouldn't kiss her good morning.

"How wet are you?" she demanded, pulling him around to face her, and unfastening the top buttons of his greatcoat.

Maximilian lifted an eyebrow. "Beg pardon?"

"You're soaked all the way through," she said, stuffing her hand inside his coat, against his jacket. "Why didn't you say something earlier?" When she shoved the dark material of his jacket aside, even the fine lawn shirt covering his chest was cold and wet to the touch.

"Anne, I suggest you remove yourself to the opposite seat immediately," he said in a low voice.

"But—"

"Now."

She looked up. Maximilian's gaze was fixed on her hands, both of which had found their way inside both his greatcoat and his jacket. Jaw clenched, he gripped the door handle in one fist, and the back of the worn seat in the other.

Blushing scarlet, she yanked her hands back to her lap. "I . . . I was only worried that you might catch a chill," she managed. Good heavens, not even courtesans simply stuck their hands down men's fronts.

"I am quite warm, thank you," he grunted, his gaze still on her hands and his breathing harsh.

"Are you—"

"Anne?"

"Yes?"

"Shut up."

"Oh."

He muttered something she couldn't interpret, but it seemed unwise to ask him to repeat himself. Instead she watched as he closed his eyes tightly, his jaw clenched so hard she could practically hear his teeth grinding.

"Are you all right?" she whispered.

Maximilian shot to his feet, opening the flimsy door in the same motion. "I'm walking."

Anne grabbed his arm. "You can't!"

He swung his head around to face her again. "You're asking me to remain?"

"You're being ridiculous," she answered in her most matter-of-fact tone. She was being ridiculous, too, to insist that he remain with her, unchaperoned, in a closed carriage. "You will catch your death of cold if you go back outside." Releasing his arm, she moved to the opposite seat and folded her hands over her lap. "I promise not to assault your virtue."

He narrowed his eyes. "It's not *my* virtue I'm worried about."

"Just sit down."

With another deep breath he did so. "You do realize that if I did catch my death, you would never have to worry about being dragged off to Yorkshire."

At least he seemed able to converse again. "I won't be dragged anywhere, regardless."

"I'm beginning to realize that."

Did that mean he was giving up? The look in his eyes remained distinctly lustful, however, so she didn't think so. And whatever base thoughts he might be having, by the time the hack stopped, Halfurst was shivering, and making a valiant effort to pretend that he was not.

Maximilian stepped to the ground to hand her down. "In order to keep my virtue intact," he chattered, casting a glance up at the driver, "I'll forgo a goodbye kiss, just for today."

He was going to climb back into the hack and leave. And his home on High Street was another twenty minutes away. With a deep scowl Anne grabbed his arm again. "No, you don't."

"I'm beginning to think you like me," he murmured.

Not quite certain whether her concern was over his health or the proximity of his lips to hers, she decided to pretend it was the former. "That is not what I mean," she said flatly, tugging him in the direction of the front door. She could as easily have moved a mountain, but he went with her, anyway. "My father will have dry clothes you can wear. I won't have you dying and everyone blaming me."

"Fine." His shivering wasn't so bad that he couldn't dig a sovereign out of his coat pocket and pitch it to the hack driver, but neither was he faking a chill.

Lambert didn't appear at the door as they reached it, and Anne belatedly remembered that it was Thursday, the staff's weekly afternoon off. "Drat," she muttered, fishing in her reticule for a key and doubly grateful that Halfurst had recovered the bag for her.

"What is it?"

"Nothing. No one's home."

"Ah."

A low shiver went down her spine, one that had nothing to do with the cold. She'd never spent this much time alone with a man, and to have this large, muscular one in the house was foolhardy, to say the least. The hack was gone, though, and as she'd said, she couldn't allow him to walk home through the snow. "Whatever the circumstances," she said, as much for her own benefit as for his, "you are cold and wet, and you became that way because of me."

"I'm not protesting," he said in his low drawl, following her into the foyer. "I just want to be certain that one of us isn't delirious."

That would explain her actions, anyway. "My father's rooms are this way," she said, heading for the stairs.

His hand slipped down her arm to grip her fingers. "No one's home?" he asked, pulling her back toward him. "You're certain?"

Slowly he drew her closer. Leaning up on her toes, she met his mouth in a hot, hard kiss. Compared to this, his kisses of greeting had been chaste. Anne wound her hands into his lapels, and reality in the form of cold, wet beer crashed down on her.

"Ew."

Maximilian looked down at her, his expression amused and his eyes warm. "I usually don't get that reaction."

"You still need to change clothes. I don't know how you can stand being so cold and wet."

"I barely noticed."

He would have caught her in his arms again, but she dodged backward. "The spare bedchamber's right there. I'll fetch something for you to wear."

For a moment she was concerned that the fireplace in the spare room wouldn't be lit. Her sheep farmer, however, knew how to amend that.

Anne paused in her rummaging for a clean shirt. *Her* sheep farmer? Where had that come from?

"Well, someone has to watch over him here in London," she muttered, not believing it even as she said it. Maximilian Trent, despite—or perhaps because of—his preference for Yorkshire, was quite probably the most capable man she'd ever met.

She grabbed a shirt, trousers, a waistcoat, jacket, and cravat, none of them her father's best. This was, after all, an emergency. She hoped Maximilian wouldn't require anything further.

"Here you go," she said in a loud voice, pushing open the half-closed door. She didn't expect to find him naked, of course, but one never knew.

To her vast disappointment he was still fully clothed, even still wrapped in his caped greatcoat, as he squatted before the fireplace with outstretched hands.

"Get out of that coat, for heaven's sake!" she ordered, dumping the clothes on a chair.

He straightened again, grasping the mantel to pull himself up. "I tried," he said, his expression almost sheepish. "My hands were shaking too much."

It seemed an obvious ploy, but as he rubbed his hands together his whole body gave a shudder. "You truly are cold, aren't you?"

"I'm bloody freezing," he answered, shivering again. "I didn't realize it until I nearly burned myself with the tinder and didn't even notice." He gazed at her for several seconds, then cleared his throat. "I did get the fire started. Give me a few moments, and I'll be fine."

"I'll help," she decided, coming forward. He needed assistance, and besides, she really wanted to touch him. Not just his jacket or his shirt, but the smooth skin beneath.

"That's not necess—"

"Stand still," she ordered, spreading his arms and stepping between them to finish the job she'd begun of unfastening his coat.

Her hands were none too steady, either, as she stood well within the reach of his embrace. Still, she managed to get his coat open and push it down his shoulders.

His jacket followed. Anne could feel his gaze on her face, but she didn't dare look up at him. If she did, she wouldn't be able to pretend any longer that this was strictly for his own good.

As she started on the tight buttons of his waistcoat, one of his hands came around, and with a flick of his fingers, her heavy cloak pooled to the floor. She froze.

"I thought you might be warm," he murmured.

Though it occurred to her to point out that the dexterity of his fingers seemed to have returned, she didn't say anything of the sort. She opened his waistcoat, and from there it seemed necessary for her to run her hands along his cold, damp shirt. Hard muscles jumped beneath her fingers, and low heat traveled up the backs of her legs.

Anne leaned up against him, pushing the waistcoat down his arms and to the floor. Beer and oysters had never smelled so arousing. With her body pressed against his, she became aware of the hardness pushing at her through his trousers. She glanced down. "Oh my."

Finally she lifted her face to meet his gaze. With an exhalation of breath, as though the statue he'd become had awakened, he lowered his mouth to hers in a hot, openmouthed kiss. "Anne," he said, folding his arms around her waist, pulling her harder against him.

She closed her eyes, letting the feel of him soak into her. She kissed him back, the caress of his mouth leading her on. To where, she didn't know, but she desperately wanted to be there—with him.

The fastenings at the back of her gown loosened beneath his fingers. Heat burned through her, quelling the tiny voice of logic that remained and told her to run as fast as her legs could carry her.

Her legs wouldn't have gotten her very far, anyway, for she was beginning to feel very unsteady on them. The taste of him left her hot and oddly light.

Maximilian tore off his cravat one-handed, a low growl sounding in his chest. He yanked her against him, and abruptly they were on the carpeted floor, amid the growing piles of their clothes.

His hands caressed her everywhere, stealing her breath and leaving her moaning for more. He pulled his shirt off over his head and then slid the length of his lean, muscular body down her legs. Mouth and lips caressing every inch of her skin he exposed, slowly he drew her shift up.

Anne lifted her hips to help him, and his hand slid between her thighs. "Maximilian," she groaned, the pleading in her voice surprising her. This was close to what she wanted, what she needed, and any more of this tantalizing delay was going to drive her mad.

The shift passed her waist and then her breasts, and his warm lips followed. His tongue teased at her nipples, one and then the other and back again. And she couldn't even speak. Instead, she twined her shaking fingers into his dark hair and pulled him closer against her.

Still teasing and suckling her breasts, Maximilian twisted sideways, yanking off his boots and tossing them aside. His trousers followed.

As he moved up her body again to capture her mouth in a hot, plundering kiss, Anne was keenly aware of the heat and the hard shaft pressing against her thigh. A keen thrill of excited terror ran through her. Stopping him now, though, was out of the question. If Maximilian didn't finish what he'd begun, she was going to die. She felt it, the craving need to be part of him, stronger than any desire she'd ever felt in her life.

Sliding his hand down her breast, past her stomach to her thigh, Maximilian tugged her legs apart. He fit himself to her body, skin to skin, hip to hip.

"Anne," he whispered, lifting his head to look her in the eye. And then his hips shifted again and slowly pushed closer, and he entered her with a slow, deepening joining she could never have imagined.

A sudden pain made her gasp. Maximilian stopped instantly, balancing his weight on one elbow and teasing at her left nipple with his free hand.

"Relax," he said huskily, kissing her throat and the base of her ear. "It will pass. The pain only means that I'm your first. It won't happen again. Just feel me, Anne."

"It's better," she managed. Never had she been so aware of her body; never had she felt such anticipation and . . . satisfaction all in the same moment. "Don't stop."

He met her eyes again, nodding. "I don't think I could stop if I wanted to." With a slow, deepening thrust, he buried himself inside her.

Anne clutched at his shoulders as he began a deep, rhythmic plundering. Her breathing, the beating of her heart, seemed to match his thrusts. This was what she wanted. Nothing could be better, or feel better, than this. Ever.

Then his pace began to increase, and a deep tension swept through her. There couldn't be more. This was too much, already.

"Maximilian?" she gasped.

"The best is yet to come," he returned breathlessly, obviously sensing her question.

"How?"

"Just be, Anne. Don't think."

As if her mind could function, anyway, with his lean body pressing hers to the carpet and his arms cradling her, and his inexorable thrusting in and out between her legs. "Oh God," she whimpered, clinging to him.

She shattered, breaking into a thousand pieces of breathless pleasure. A moment later he shuddered inside her, and she knew that he joined her in this indescribable heaven.

They lay in a heavy breathing tangle of arms and legs for a moment.

Just as he began to feel heavy on her, Maximilian slipped his hand beneath her and rolled them over, so she lay atop him.

"How do you feel?" he murmured, brushing her long, brunette hair out of his face. He'd been as gentle as he could, but considering how badly he'd wanted her, he wasn't sure he'd been gentle enough.

"Disheveled," she answered, running a hand along his chest. "And very . . ."

"Relaxed?" he suggested, allowing himself a small smile.

"Yes. Very."

"I seem to be warm now myself." He sighed. Once they were at Halfurst, he would see that he made love to her before the fireplace as often as possible. The scent of beer and oysters came to him again as he inhaled, and Maximilian frowned. Even Anne smelled of their misadventure now, and it certainly wouldn't be very seemly for them to be discovered naked together and smelling of a low-class inn.

"You smell like beer," she said, her cheek resting on his chest. Her warm hands slid around his waist.

"And so do you, now," he returned. "I don't suppose there's a washbasin in here? We should probably at least smell sober when we see your father."

She sat up, her crumpled shift sliding down her breasts to her waist. "What?"

"I'll already be wearing his clothes," Maximilian said, sitting up as well, and tugging her against his chest. Even now he craved her again. "We should at least not reek of beer and oysters when we meet to arrange terms." Though any terms would do; he wanted Anne, and anything else was superfluous.

Now she was scowling. "What terms?"

"For our marriage."

Anne shoved at him, stumbling to her feet. "You tricked me."

"I did not trick you," he said flatly. "You wanted this as much as I did."

"Yes, *this,*" she said, gesturing between them, her gaze pausing for a moment below his waist. "But that doesn't mean I've . . . agreed to anything."

He stood as well, frustrated anger and lust burrowing through him.

"You are mine," he said flatly. "You may even be carrying my child. Aside from that, I already told you that this isn't a game, Anne. I came to London for you. And now—"

A door downstairs opened and slammed shut. "Lady Anne? Oh dear! Are you here, my lady?"

Anne blanched. "It's Daisy." She whirled to the chair and grabbed her father's spare clothes. "Get dressed," she snapped, throwing them at his chest.

"No."

For a heartbeat she hesitated. "Fine. Stay here naked," she returned, snatching up her own clothes. "I'll be elsewhere."

Maximilian strode to intercept her at the door, but she slipped out before he reached it. Damn her. He hadn't planned a seduction for today, and he'd dealt poorly with his desire to make her his. *Idiot.*

With a curse he dropped the clothes back on the chair and grabbed the trousers. Certainly he could use this to make her his wife, and no one in London would blame him for it—except for Anne. And above all else, he wanted what they'd had together today—desire, and even friendship. To drag her off to Yorkshire now would earn him nothing but her disappointment and their mutual misery.

He fastened the trousers. They were too damned short. Thank God for his boots, or he would end up looking like the sheep farmer she'd ridiculed. And obviously the less he resembled that, the better his chances.

Chapter 6

All London is abuzz with news of Lady Shelbourne's Valentine's Day ball. Invitations, This Author is told, are due to arrive today.

This Author is not certain, however, whether guests will be required to wear the Valentine-ish colors of red, pink, and white.

Red, pink, and white. This Author shudders to think.

LADY WHISTLEDOWN'S SOCIETY PAPERS,
7 February 1814

The best chance he'd yet discovered arrived four days later via the mail. A St. Valentine's Day ball, hosted by Margaret, Lady Shelbourne.

Maximilian turned the invitation over in his hands. If he'd received one, then Anne surely would have, as well. And considering her latest tactics, the ball might be his last chance to win her.

He'd called on her yesterday and the day before, and on both occasions she'd been out with Lord Howard. He could assume they hadn't gone ice skating again, but that hardly left him with enough information to hunt them down.

She'd enjoyed their lovemaking; he could sense that, in the language of her body beneath his and in the beat of her heart. He had been her first, and even more than before, he wanted to make damned certain he was her only.

Whatever she might say, they belonged together, and not simply because it said so on some old piece of paper. The idea that she was seeing Howard to avoid him annoyed Maximilian; the thought that she might accept a proposal from the damned viscount to avoid being dragged out of London infuriated him.

"So you have no idea where she's gone," he asked the Bishops' butler.

"None, my lord. I only know that Lady Anne said she would return in time for dinner."

The butler was probably lying, but that was part of the man's job. Well, the main target had vanished, but there were still other pieces he could fit into the puzzle. "Would Lord or Lady Daven be in, then?"

Lambert blinked. "Ah, if you would care to wait in the morning room, I shall inquire."

That meant someone was home. The question was whether they would want to speak with him or not. Anne's explanation for his presence the other day had sounded innocent enough to him, but he wasn't her parent, thank Lucifer.

"Lord Halfurst," a quiet male voice said from the doorway. "This is a surprise, though not an unexpected one."

Maximilian nodded. "Lord Daven. Thank you for seeing me. I know how busy you are."

"No need for that. Am I to assume that Anne has come to her senses? I wasn't certain I'd be seeing you again after she escaped to the theater without you."

"I'm persistent."

"So I've discovered."

At the earl's gesture Maximilian seated himself in one of the room's comfortable chairs. "I wanted to ask you a question."

The earl cleared his throat as a footman brought in a tea tray. "I'll avoid all assumptions."

"It's not about her dowry." Max leaned forward, rubbing his hands together. This was what he hated most about London—the artifice, the pretending, the veneer of politeness that meant no one would say what they really thought of you, except to your back. He preferred being direct, and it seemed important that Anne's family know that. "Do you wish your daughter to marry me?"

A scowl lowered Daven's brow. "Well, of course I do. An agreement between two families is—"

"No. Do *you* wish Anne to marry me?"

"Ah." The earl took a sip of tea. "You mean with the widespread rumors that your father left you bankrupt."

Apparently some residents of London could be direct. It was refreshing, in a way. "Yes."

"Well, to be honest—and I assume you want honesty—if that was all I knew about you, then no, I wouldn't want you marrying my daughter. Halfurst is an old and respectable title, but frankly that is no assurance of happiness."

For a moment Max remained silent. "But you know the truth behind the rumors. When I wrote, I made the facts as clear as . . . my being a gentleman would allow."

"Yes, I know that." The earl set aside his tea. "Which leads *me* to a question: do you wish to marry my daughter?"

"I wish to, and I intend to do so, my lord. At the moment, however, I still seem to be making up for nineteen years of not corresponding with her."

Daven chuckled. "Anne's hardly spent time anywhere but in London. She's convinced this is where the world begins and ends."

"Yes, I'd gathered that," Maximilian said dryly. "It's not actually my letter writing she disapproves of; it's my place of residence."

"There are solutions to that, my boy."

With a nod, Maximilian stood. "So there are."

First, though, he wanted to know something. Stupid and meaningless though it might be, he wanted to know that she chose him above all the other sugar-tongued nobles pursuing her.

With Lord Howard in the middle, that was going to be supremely difficult, unless he wished to play by the same rules as the viscount. And he really preferred to avoid that, if at all possible. Where Anne was concerned, however, he was willing to do just about anything. If she would take one step toward him, he would walk a hundred miles for her.

"Why do you keep looking over your shoulder?" Desmond asked, his own gaze on the snow-covered street. "Do you expect Halfurst to pursue us to Covent Garden?"

"He might," Anne answered, pushing her hands deeper into her muff.

Not even to herself would she admit that she missed Maximilian, that her body felt impatient for his kisses and craved his touch. She'd thought about asking Lord Howard to kiss her again, to prove to herself that this stupid feeling she had was just a general yearning for something her body had very much enjoyed. She knew, though, that it wasn't true; she enjoyed Halfurst, and only Halfurst. Having someone else kiss her would only prove a point she didn't wish to make.

"I should hand him a beating for making off with you at the skating party," the viscount went on, obviously annoyed. "And for frightening you into colliding with Miss Ballister."

"He didn't frighten me into anything," Anne retorted, flushing. "Please stop discussing it."

"I don't see why you should object. It's only another sign of his quaint Yorkshire manners." Desmond snorted. "No doubt his floors are covered with straw to accommodate the pigs with whom he shares his home."

"Oh, Desmond, stop it. You know that's not true."

"Well, yes, but only because Halfurst is in sheep country." This time he laughed. "Sheep are probably where he learned his lovemaking skills. You know—"

"*Lord Howard!* Stop this carriage at once! I will not be party to such crude—"

He pulled the team to a halt. "Anne, please calm down. I apologize for my very rude behavior. I got carried away."

"Obviously." Trying to hide the double attack of guilt and mortification that had hit her, Anne stuffed her hands deeper into her muff and glared straight ahead. If she looked at Desmond, she felt certain he would guess what she'd done—and how thoroughly she'd enjoyed Maximilian's skills. *Sheep, ha.*

"Come, Anne, looking for a way to spare his feelings is admirable, but it's been well over a week. You'll be risking the accusation that you're leading him on if you don't have your parents announce the break with Halfurst soon."

Taking a steadying breath, Anne faced him again. "We are friends, are we not?"

He clasped her elbow. "Of course we are. And we verge on becoming more to one another, I hope."

Not that again. Still, she had no more wish to hurt his feelings than Maximilian's. "All rumor, speculation, and innuendo aside, what do you know of Lord Halfurst?"

With a flick of his wrists, Desmond set the carriage moving again. "Not much, really. His father spent the entire year before young Viscount Trent arrived in town bragging to anyone who would listen about what a success he would be. It actually looked that way for a time, until old Halfurst expired at his own soirée and his widow went screaming through the ballroom proclaiming that they were all ruined."

"Lud. My parents never mentioned that."

"Well, they wouldn't, considering you were betrothed to him. After that, tales of the family's bankruptcy were everywhere. They even denied him membership at White's, as I recall. And then, practically without a word, he bundled up his mother and what remained of the family's belongings and fled to Yorkshire."

Intent as Maximilian seemed to be about straightforward truth, she could see why he hadn't made up some lie about his circumstances. She couldn't imagine him running from anything, either, but he'd been only eighteen. A year younger than she was now.

"So, as I said before, you know why he's here," Desmond continued. "He feared you and your money would escape him, and he's run to town to gather you both up and flee back to Yorkshire."

Yorkshire. She'd never been there, and it was without a doubt the most hated word in her entire vocabulary. "I suppose so."

The viscount glanced at her. "You 'suppose so'? Don't tell me he's charmed you with that quaint directness of his."

"It's not that," she hedged. "If he's so desperate for money, and if everyone knows it, how is he able to supply himself with a new wardrobe, and rent a box for a sold-out performance at Drury Lane?"

"I would assume he's lived like a pauper for the last seven years so he can make a good showing now. After all, if your parents reject him, he has no one else."

"He hasn't even met with my parents," she muttered, quietly enough that Desmond wouldn't hear. Obviously the viscount had forgotten his claim that any female would do for Maximilian. But she didn't agree. She'd always had the distinct feeling that the Marquis of Halfurst could have any female he wanted, and that he preferred her. His passion had certainly been very effective, and very unmistakable.

"I've made you blush. Let's speak of something else."

"Yes, please," she returned vehemently. Above all else she didn't want Desmond to know it hadn't been he making her blush; even thinking of Maximilian was enough to speed her pulse and leave her flushed with warmth and wanting.

"Annie!"

Starting, Anne looked up the street. Theresa and Pauline stood beside Pauline's family coach, waving at her. *Oh, thank goodness. Friendly faces.* "Let's stop, my lord," she said, waving back and grinning with relief. Conversing with men had never been as troublesome and problematic before Halfurst's arrival in London.

"But I wanted to spend some time alone with you," the viscount protested.

"You've spent the entire drive here talking about Halfurst," she retorted. "I really don't wish to hear any more."

"Then stop asking questions about him, my dear. One would almost think you've become infatuated with the sheep farmer."

How else was she supposed to get information, if not by asking questions? "Stop the carriage, Desmond. Daisy and I shall walk."

"Anne, don't be angry with me for enjoying your company," he said in a placating voice. "We'll discuss whatever you like."

Despite his peace offering, now that she'd decided it, she wanted nothing more than to escape his company. In all fairness, though, she had agreed to join him for a shopping excursion to Covent Garden. "Perhaps you'd escort all of us," she suggested. "I haven't seen Theresa or Pauline for days."

With a faint scowl he guided the phaeton to one side of the busy street. "As you wish, my dear."

So now he thought she was being difficult, and he had to humor her. Everything had been so much easier when her male friends had accepted that she was betrothed, and the only thing she had to offer was her friendship. Lately, though, all Desmond seemed interested in was trying to kiss her, and telling her how poor Maximilian's character was.

And that was the oddest part. She should have been happy to hear that rejecting the marquis would be the wise thing to do. Instead, though, for every blight the viscount offered, she seemed determined to come up with a reason to dismiss it. Why was she being so foolish? And why had she welcomed Halfurst's embrace, and his touch, and his body?

"Anne," Pauline said, grabbing her ankle as the carriage rolled to a stop in the snowy street, "I'm glad we found you."

"I'm happy to see you again, as well," she said, a bit surprised at the vehemence in her friend's voice.

"No. We've been looking for you," Theresa took up. "We went to your house this morning to see if you wanted to go shopping, and who do you think we saw there?"

She could guess. "Halfurst?"

"Yes! Did you know?"

"How could I? I accepted an invitation to go shopping with Lord Howard this morning." For the viscount's sake, she favored him with a smile as he came around and lifted her down to the street.

"Well, he's in your morning room. Apparently he's been there for over an hour. And your mother told us that she thinks he means to wait for you until you return!"

Anne closed her eyes for a moment, the familiar rush at the idea of his presence mingling with a distinct uneasiness. If he was at Bishop House and she wasn't, then no doubt he'd finally spoken to her father. And with the earl's cryptic comments about keeping an eye on Halfurst's career, her father seemed to favor the match. Good heavens, she might as well be married!

Desmond beside her was doing a poor job of hiding his displeasure at this latest pronouncement; no doubt he realized what she would ask of him next. "Desmond, please—"

"Take you home?" he interrupted. "Give me one good reason why I should."

She took an annoyed breath. "Lord Howard, if you would just remain pleasant for another few minutes, then we might remain friends, as well."

"And what does that get me?" he retorted. "A letter from Yorkshire every six months, describing how miserable you are and how much you wish you'd listened to your 'friend'?"

"This doesn't sound like friendship," she said crisply, taking Theresa's hand and hoping if her friend felt her fingers shaking she would think it was from the cold. "It sounds like jealousy. I have never made it anything but clear that I am betrothed, and whether I plan on marrying Lord Halfurst or not, that fact does not change."

"Only when it's convenient for you, that is," he sneered.

"Annie, Pauline and I will see you home," Theresa said in a tense voice, tugging her in the direction of Pauline's carriage.

"Yes, you do that," Howard snapped. "I'll be available when you return to your senses and decide you've had enough of your sheep farmer."

Before she could conjure a suitable retort, he climbed into his phaeton and lurched back into traffic.

"My goodness," Pauline whispered, taking Anne's other hand. "I've never seen him like that."

"Neither have I," she returned, her voice shaking to match her hands. "Will you please take me home?"

"Of course, Annie. Come on."

As she took her seat in Pauline's carriage, she was surprised to realize that she wasn't thinking so much of Desmond's jealous fit as she was of seeing her sheep farmer again. Four days seemed a lifetime, when all she could think of was how very good it had felt to be with him.

Thank God, Anne's mother had finally believed him when Maximilian had told her that she didn't need to keep him company, and that he would be quite content to read a book and wait for his betrothed. Her apologetic hovering set his teeth on edge, and Lady Daven's depictions of her daughter were woefully inaccurate and inadequate. Anne Bishop defied description, by anyone's definition.

For one thing, she was practically the only Londoner he'd encountered who didn't bother with affectations; she was who she was, and seemed quite content with that. And far from being shy and retiring, as her mother insisted she was, Anne was curious and forthright and utterly imperfect.

He'd meant to give her a sampling of what married life with him would offer her, and he'd meant to use his skills at lovemaking to convince her to give up her arguments about staying in London. While he thought he might have succeeded at the former, her continued insistence on parading about town with Lord Howard was proof enough that she hadn't succumbed to the latter. Nor was she likely to, if she was able to keep avoiding him.

She had to return home eventually, and then this nonsense would stop. He would convince her to marry him, and only when he'd run out of resolve and time would he surrender to London. After being inside her, his resolve had become boundless. And for the first time since he'd inherited Halfurst, he didn't care if it fell into ruin while he waited for her. He wasn't leaving London without Anne Bishop.

That didn't mean, however, that he intended to play by her rules. She was used to men throwing themselves at her feet, after her beauty or her money or her favor. He heard her enter the house, sooner than he expected, but he remained seated, reading the book he'd selected from the Bishop House library, when she stepped into the morning room.

"Lord Halfurst?"

He looked up. "Anne." Heat coiled through him at the sight of her, and he had to fight to keep seated, and to keep other parts of his body from becoming immediately erect, as well.

"What are you doing here? Didn't Lambert tell you I'd gone out?"

Her voice sounded unsteady, and the thought that his presence might be the reason for that made his relaxed slouch even more difficult to maintain. "He did. I decided to wait."

Slowly she came further into the room, and it took all his self-control to refrain from leaping to his feet and smothering her body with kisses. Her maid started to enter the room behind her, but at a feminine command outside, Daisy vanished behind the closing door. Lady Daven had some sense, anyway.

She tilted her head, glancing at the book in his hands. "*A Midsummer Night's Dream?* I didn't know you read Shakespeare."

Anne was nervous, and that was good. "You didn't? What did you think I read? Or you didn't think I could read at all, perhaps."

"Don't be ridiculous. I just couldn't . . . imagine you taking the time to read Shakespeare, is all. You seem so consumed by Yorkshire."

Did he? More likely, she was obsessed with it. His obsessions had lately taken a more feminine shape, with long, curling brunette hair. "I could quote something for you, if you like," he said, setting the book aside and standing, "but that wouldn't prove anything but my ability to borrow someone else's pretty words."

Anne took a small step backward as he rose. "You . . . didn't answer my question. What are you doing here?"

"You've been avoiding me."

"No, I haven't," she shot back, giving a nervous laugh. "I hope you don't think I just sit at home waiting for you to come calling. I have friends, and activities. This is my home, you know."

"I know." His gaze on her soft mouth, he slowly stepped toward her. "Nevertheless, I owe you a good morning kiss. Four of them, actually."

"I—"

If he let her argue, he'd never be able to touch her today. Maximilian closed the distance between them with one quick stride. Taking her shoulders in his hands, he leaned down and covered her mouth with his. She responded instantly, leaning up against his chest and curling her hands into the front of his jacket. He went hard, and felt her heat as she pressed herself closer against him.

As he drew his arms down the length of her and around her waist, she gave a stifled groan and pushed away. "Stop it!"

"Why?" he murmured, against her lips. "You want me again, and you know that I want you, don't you?"

Her hips moved against him, and he clenched his jaw, fighting for control. "Yes."

"Then don't ask me to stop."

He kissed her again, and he felt her give in—for a moment. "No!" she said again, shoving harder.

She couldn't have moved him if she wanted to, but he released her anyway. Persuasion only, he reminded himself, trying not to let his discomfort show on his face. Forcing her would win him nothing. "If you would agree to marry me, I would make you feel like this every day."

"That is not fair!" she shouted, as if volume equaled conviction. If her gaze hadn't trailed below his waist and back again, her parted lips still beckoning him, he might have believed her.

"Why isn't it fair? It's the truth. This is marriage, Anne. Being with me, skin-to-skin. I know you enjoyed it. I felt you, remember?"

"Fine. Remind me of my weakness," she retorted, a tear running down her cheek. "You're no better than Lord Howard."

The single tear bothered him, and suddenly it seemed more important to make her stop crying than to wear her down into a marriage agreement. "It wasn't weakness, Anne," he murmured, brushing the moisture from her cheek with his thumb. "It was desire. There is nothing wrong with desire. Not between us."

That earned him a glare, which he could only consider an improvement over her weeping. With a discontented sigh he seated himself again. If he made her flee, he might as well have stayed at home. He knew precisely what her objection to him was; what he needed to do was figure out how to convince her of the merits of Yorkshire. In the dead of winter, that wasn't such an easy task.

"Anne," he said, "sit down."

"Only if you'll tell me why you're here."

"I'm here to see you. Isn't that simple enough?"

"You're here to try to seduce me into marrying you," she said, her tone accusing. Even so, she sat—in the chair at the far end of the room.

Maximilian chuckled. "I've already seduced you, and we're still not married. I don't intend to apologize for continuing to find you desirable."

"If you know that seduction won't work, how do you intend to convince me of anything?"

For a moment, she almost sounded as if she wanted to be convinced. His heart leaped. "Have you ever heard of Farndale?"

She scowled. "Farndale? No."

"It's about three miles west of Halfurst. A small valley in the foothills of the Pennine Mountains. In the early spring the entire floor of the dale is carpeted with wild daffodils."

"It's lovely, I would imagine."

"You don't have to imagine it. I would show it to you." He gazed at her stony expression. "Anne, you've never been to Yorkshire. How do you know you would hate it so much?"

"Why do you hate London so much?"

"I . . . it was a difference of opinion, I suppose."

"You mean everyone treated you badly when they found out you had no money."

He narrowed his eyes, unable to stop the abrupt anger that drowned his damned lust for this outspoken beauty. "Lord Howard, I suppose?"

"Yes, he told me everything, but only because I asked him to. Don't blame him."

"I doubt he told you everything, Anne." *Damn Howard.* He hated this, the gossip and innuendo and one-upmanship. For Anne, though, he would tell the truth. All of it. "Why don't you ask *me*?"

She folded her hands in her lap. "Why should I? It doesn't matter, because in the end you'll still want to drag me off to Yorkshire. Daffodils or not, I will not spend the rest of my life in exile."

He cursed. "Would you spend it with Desmond Howard, then? Why don't you ask him about *his* finances? How long do you think he'd be able to keep you in your precious London after he finished going through your dowry?"

"You lie."

Maximilian lurched to his feet. "I do not lie," he snarled, striding over to her. Clamping his hands on either arm of the chair, he leaned down, forcing her to look him in the eye. "Ask him, Anne. And if you want to know anything—*anything*—about me, all you need do is ask."

Straightening, he stalked to the door and yanked it open. He hadn't meant to leave without securing her hand in marriage. He hadn't meant to leave without making love to her again. He hadn't meant to start bellowing about other people. He didn't do that. It wasn't right, and he knew firsthand how much it hurt.

"Are you bankrupt?" her shaking voice came. "Are you here for my money?"

Maximilian stopped. "No. I'm not. To both questions. I won't let it be that easy for you, Anne. And I'm not finished with you, yet." Taking a deep breath, he faced her. "I think I know you. I believe you to be honest, and honorable. And I am betting that you won't be able to leave it at this, without finding out everything. You know where I'll be."

"So you're going back to Trent House to sulk? I don't—"

"What I meant was, I intend to call on you every day between now and February fourteenth. And then I'll be at the Shelbourne St. Valentine's Day ball. On the fifteenth, though, I will be leaving London."

"Then you'll be leaving alone."

"We'll see. As I said, I think I know you, Anne." He lowered his voice to be certain none of the lurking servants would be able to hear. "And I know that you crave being with me again. Think about that."

Chapter 7

Ah, Valentine's Day. This Author personally detests the holiday. A girl must take the measure of her worth by the number of cards and bouquets she receives, and a young man is forced to spew poetry as if anyone actually spoke in rhyme.

It's a wonder the holiday hasn't been banned from the capital. Or the nation, for that matter.

But This Author supposes that there are those with more sentimental hearts, because Lady Shelbourne's first (annual? This Author prays not) Valentine's Day ball is sure to be a massive crush, if the number of affirmative replies is any indication.

And since this is Valentine's Day, This Author would be remiss if the question were not posed— Will any young couples make a match of it? Surely Lady Shelbourne cannot consider her party a success if the words "Will you marry me?" are not uttered even once.

Or perhaps that will not be enough. After all, what is a proposal without the proper reply of "I will"?

LADY WHISTLEDOWN'S SOCIETY PAPERS,
14 February 1814

Anne slammed the *Atlas of Britain* closed as her father entered the library. "Good morning, Papa," she said, trying to sound casual, and dismayed at the distinct squeak in her voice.

The earl lifted an eyebrow. "Good morning. What are you doing in here?"

"Reading." She forced a careless laugh. "What else would I be doing in the library?"

"Daughter, has anyone ever told you that you're an abysmal liar?"

One man had—not that that had endeared him to her. "Don't you have a meeting today?"

He crossed the room, sinking onto the couch beside her. "An atlas," her father said, tilting his head to view the book's cover. "Of Britain. Are you interested in any particular area?"

Anne grimaced. "You know what I was looking at. I was merely a little curious, for heaven's sake."

Maximilian had been telling her about western Yorkshire for a week, just little bits, obviously for the sake of whetting her interest. He also hadn't kissed her in a week. Given that strategy, she remained uncertain whether the craving that resulted was for him or for his blasted shire. Lord Halfurst could be very devious for an honest, forthright, virile male. An exceedingly virile male.

"There's nothing wrong with a little curiosity," her father commented, thankfully unable to read her thoughts. He paused. "Halfurst tells me he's leaving tomorrow."

Her pulse skittered. "Yes, he'd mentioned that."

"I suppose you'll be happy to see him gone?"

"What do you want me to say, Papa?" she asked, briskly, standing to replace the atlas on its shelf. "I . . . like him, but he still lives in Yorkshire."

"Believe it or not, Annie, I am trying to stay out of this. I could force you to marry him, but I have no wish to see you miserable."

"Then why did you make this silly agreement in the first place?" she burst out, surprised to find that she felt more exasperated than angry.

The earl shrugged. "Robert Trent was my dearest friend. When he had a son and then I had a daughter, it seemed the natural thing to do. And I did—and do—like young Maximilian."

His voice warmed as he spoke, the humor his political career often didn't allow touching his eyes. Anne felt wretched, squirming in her seat. The earl so obviously wanted this match, and she so badly wanted to be in Maximilian's arms again that she could barely think straight. "He's so stubborn," she said into the air.

"And so are you, my dear." He stood. "If you don't wish this match, then let him go. I'm sure your mother will be happy to find someone more to your taste."

She scowled. "More to *her* taste, you mean."

"Yes, well, with an estate closer to London, anyway. That seems to satisfy your requirements."

"Papa."

"Happy St. Valentine's Day," he said with a small smile, and left the room.

As soon as he was gone, Anne took down the atlas again. Thanks to Maximilian's vivid depiction, she knew precisely where Halfurst lay. From the way he described it, full of daffodils and green rolling hills and picturesque streams and waterfalls, he considered it another Eden. Even the grazing herds of sheep took on a pastoral beauty, nestled as they were among the hills and Roman and Viking ruins.

Part of her wanted to see it for herself, to have Maximilian show her the places he so obviously loved. The other part of her was terrified that if she loosened her grip on London, she would never see it again.

And the worst part of all was that she couldn't see any way around it. Yorkshire or London, Maximilian or . . . someone who wasn't him. "Maximilian," she murmured, her heart beating faster at the mere sound of his name. Butterflies came to life low in her belly.

Someone scratched at the library door. Anne yelped and shoved the book back into place.

"Yes?"

Lambert entered the room, a large bouquet of yellow daffodils in his hands. "These just arrived for you, Lady Anne. Shall I put them in the morning room with the rest?"

Daffodils. "Thank you, no. Leave them on the table, please." She spied the letter nestled among the blossoms, and clasped her hands to keep from springing forward and snatching it up.

"Very good, my lady." The butler set down the flowers, and left.

Since her debut, St. Valentine's Day had meant flowers; last year her mother had counted thirty-seven separate bouquets, most of them accompanied by candies and poems, and in one memorable case, a haunch of venison. Francis Henning had evidently thought her too skinny. The scent of roses filled every room of Bishop House today, as well. No one, though, had ever sent her daffodils.

Her hands abruptly clammy, Anne rubbed them on her skirt before she lifted the folded missive from the bright yellow blooms. She opened the heavy paper, and a smaller, weightier card fell to the floor.

On the back, in a dark, even hand it said, "As I remember it." When she picked the thing up, on the front was a six-inch-square colored sketch of a green pasture bordered by oak trees and boulders, and carpeted from one end to the other with yellow flowers. In the corner the initials "MRT" held her gaze for as long as the lovely rendering. "An artist as well," she said, running a finger carefully across the surface.

She took a seat and placed the sketch on the table. Then she turned her attention to the letter. All the other notes and cards she had or would receive today featured hearts and cherubs and declarations of heartfelt admiration.

This one, of course, was different. " 'Anne,' " she read to herself. " 'Nineteen daffodils for the nineteen years we've been promised to one another. I would wish one day to show you where they grow wild.' "

"A scholar, an artist, and a romantic," she whispered, her fingers shaking. "I would never have guessed."

With a hard blink, she went on. " 'I am thinking of you, as I hope you are thinking of me, with desire and anticipation. I shall see you tonight. Maximilian.' "

Tonight. The Shelbourne St. Valentine's Day ball. If she had any sense of courage or conviction, Anne decided, she would decline to attend. Then he would be gone, and she would probably never see him again.

With a sigh she stood to go examine her wardrobe. She already knew she would wear yellow.

Maximilian stood beside Lady Shelbourne's dessert table, doing his damnedest not to pace. She'd been invited, he knew, because he'd asked her father. She would come tonight, because he needed her to.

"Damnation," he muttered.

Others seemed to be waiting for her there as well, which only served to further blacken his mood. Lord Howard, of course, circled the room like a vulture, sampling the various available feminine sweets while he waited for the main dish. Sir Royce Pemberley was also there, though his attention seemed to be on a unique female in an equally unique pink gown that appeared in perfect harmony with the swathes of pink, red, and white silk that hung from the ballroom ceiling.

Well, turnabout was fair play. With another glance at his competition, he strolled toward Margaret, Lady Shelbourne, and the pink chit chatting with her.

"Might I have the pleasure of an introduction?" he asked, stopping before the ladies.

"Of course, my lord," Lady Shelbourne answered, swift dismay touching her face and then vanishing again. "Liza, Lord Halfurst. My lord—"

The pink chit grinned and stuck out her hand. "Miss Elizabeth Pritchard. Liza. Pleased to meet you."

He shook her hand. "A pleasure to meet you." Her light brown hair seemed to be coming out from its elaborate coif, the ends sticking out at odd angles, but she had an intelligence in her eyes that Maximilian couldn't help but notice. And for once a matron seemed reluctant to see him near a single female, which in itself made Miss Liza Pritchard the most interesting part of his evening thus far.

"Might I have this waltz, Miss Liza?" he drawled. "If it's not already spoken for, of course."

Unless he was mistaken, she sent a glance in Pemberley's direction. *Good.* "I'm afraid I'm all yours, my lord."

She was taller by several inches than Anne, and as they swirled onto the dance floor, he noted that her shoes were red. And then one of them trod on his left foot.

"I'm so sorry," she gulped, flushing.

"No need to apologize," he returned, smiling and hoping his eyes wouldn't water. She didn't appear that sturdy, but—

Miss Liza stepped on him again. "Oh no!"

"No worries, Miss Liza," he grunted. Good God, unique as she was in appearance, she danced with the grace of an elephant.

"I should have warned you," she mumbled, "dancing is not my forte. Perhaps if we counted the steps aloud?"

His left foot was going numb, but he couldn't help being amused. "The danger makes the adventure more worthwhile," he returned.

To his surprise, she laughed, and then, less amusing for him but to the obvious enjoyment of the nearest couples, she began counting. "One, two, three. One, two, three—oh drat."

He managed to avoid stumbling over her as she tripped on her own gown, then caught Sir Royce Pemberley staring at the two of them. A moment later he came forward, blocking their path.

"Might I cut in?" he asked tightly.

Maximilian met his gaze. He'd thought to find anger, or the snide disdain he was used to from Londoners, but instead he found himself nodding and stepping back, allowing Sir Royce to take his place. They said nothing else, but as Miss Elizabeth took Sir Royce's hand and met her partner's gaze, Maximilian abruptly realized that Anne had told the truth about the snow angels incident being nothing more than a moment of amusement. Royce Pemberley was not at the Shelbourne ball for Lady Anne Bishop. He'd already found his love.

Limping slightly, Max returned to the dessert table. The more circling Lord Howard did, the more nasty looks turned in Max's direction. He wondered whether Desmond Howard had ever bothered to tell Anne about the young maid he'd ruined when they'd both been at Oxford, and how much the viscount had resented Maximilian's intervention in seeing the girl safely to a position with his mother.

The air stirred. Without turning, he knew that she'd entered the room. Anne. His Anne. Straightforward as he'd been in stating he would leave with or without her, he wasn't quite certain he could manage to go a day, much less a lifetime, without her by his side.

He managed to intercept her before Howard. "You wore yellow," he murmured, taking her hand and brushing his lips across her knuckles.

Green eyes glowed in the chandelier light, and not just from the excitement of the dance, he thought. Could she be as drawn to him as he was to her? Dear God, he hoped so.

"Something put me in mind of daffodils, today," she returned, the soft timbre of her voice not quite steady.

"You outshine them all. Will you dance with me?"

"Maximilian—"

"Just dance with me," he insisted, drawing her toward the dance floor. Any protest that began with his name couldn't be good, and if he didn't take her into his arms at once, he had the distinct feeling he would expire.

She must have felt the same, because with an exhaled breath she relaxed and nodded. "One dance, and then we need to talk."

"Two dances," he countered. "After all, this piece is already begun."

"I can't dance twice in a row with you."

"Who'll notice? Besides, we're betrothed."

This was perfection. Holding her as close as she and etiquette would allow, he didn't even mind the additional maneuvering required to avoid crashing into Miss Elizabeth and Sir Royce. Unlike her ice skating, Anne's dancing was incomparable. With her swaying in his arms, he could forget he was in London, forget that a hundred other guests milled and chatted and gossiped around them, forget that Lord Howard waited in the wings for him to return to Yorkshire.

"Are you truly leaving tomorrow?" Anne asked, long lashes hiding her eyes from him.

"I can't stay forever," he returned, hoping that was regret he heard in her voice.

"Why not?" She looked up, meeting his gaze. "Why can't you just stay here in London?"

For a heartbeat he was tempted. "Halfurst is my home and my responsibility. I can't just abandon it, even for you."

"So you would have everything your way. That's not fair, Maximilian."

It *wasn't* fair, and he took a moment to consider before he responded.

"I hoped you would have more desire for me than for London, Anne. It's only buildings and some rather unpleasant people."

"They aren't unpleasant to me. If you had stayed, instead of running off, you would have seen that."

She'd been talking to Howard again. "I did not 'run off.' Halfurst needed—"

"You let everyone say whatever they wanted about you, and you didn't do anything about it."

"What they said didn't matter."

"Ha!"

Max lifted an eyebrow. " 'Ha'?" he repeated.

"Yes, ha. All of their silly gossiping *did* matter, and it still does. That's why you dislike London."

"I—"

"And it's your own fault," she continued.

In her enthusiasm for the argument, she didn't even notice that he pulled her closer in his arms. Six inches of space between them be damned. Anne Bishop intoxicated him as no woman ever had, or ever would again. "And how is it my fault, pray tell?"

"All you had to do was say something, you big oaf. Bankrupt or not, you might have defended your father's reputation—and your own, Maximilian."

"Did you just call me an oaf?"

She cuffed him on the shoulder. "Pay attention. This is important."

It seemed more important that she was fighting to keep him in London, but he didn't want to mention that yet. "If I were paying any more attention to you, you'd be naked," he murmured.

"Stop that. And don't just pay attention—do something!"

"So I should stand on a chair and bellow at all and sundry that I was grieving horribly for my father, and that I didn't give a hang what anyone said about either of us? Or should I simply declare that Halfurst was never bankrupt, and that my yearly income is somewhere in the neighborhood of forty thousand pounds?"

She blinked her moss green eyes at him. "Forty thousand pounds?"

"Approximately."

"Then just tell everyone—someone—that all the rumors were groundless, and they'll—"

"They'll like me again?" he finished. "I've told the one person whose opinion I care for."

"And who . . ." Anne blushed prettily. "Oh."

The waltz ended, and he reluctantly slid his hand from around her waist.

"Ah, splendid," a familiar male voice murmured from behind him. "It's my turn now, I believe."

Anne tightened her grip on his arm. "Desmond, I promised Lord Halfurst the quadrille, as well. I would be happy to—"

"Do you think the sheep farmer can dance a quadrille?" the viscount asked, sneering as Max faced him. "I'm surprised he managed the waltz. What did you trade for lessons, Halfurst, mutton?"

Maximilian gazed at Howard levelly. The guests had grown silent, the better to overhear someone else's business. Of more concern to him was Anne, practically quivering with anger and indignation beside him.

At that moment he realized he wouldn't—couldn't—lose her, no matter what it took. She'd made several good points in her argument. Whether he cared about his reputation or not, she did, and if they were to be married, their names would become joined.

"I have respected my fiancée's friendship with you, Howard," he said in a low, level voice. "But now you are embarrassing her. Leave."

" 'Leave'? I have no intention of going anywhere. You're the outsider here, marquis."

"Lord Howard, please stop," Anne hissed. "You've done enough damage."

"Oh, I've barely begun. Please, let's hear more of your witty repartee, sheep farmer."

That was enough of that. Anne had urged him to take action. "How's this?" Max returned.

He shot out with his right fist, catching Howard square in the jaw. With a grunt the viscount dropped to the polished floor.

"Much better." Maximilian faced Anne, ignoring the explosion of gasps and tittering from all around them. "Come with me."

"Good heavens," she whispered, staring at Howard's crumpled form. "One punch."

Max was unable to help a grim smile at her astounded expression. "You should have told me earlier that you preferred a man of action."

Anne felt too dazed to speak as the marquis led her out the nearest exit and down a narrow set of stairs. She'd only meant that he should defend his reputation verbally—knocking Desmond unconscious had not been part of the scenario, satisfying as the sight had been. "He's going to be very angry."

"Hence my escorting you from the scene," Maximilian returned, stopping at the bottom of the stairs. "Where in damnation are we?"

"These are the servants' stairs, I think."

As she spoke, a footman laden with a tray of sweetmeats exited through a swinging door, nearly colliding with Halfurst. "Beg pardon, my lord," he stammered, attempting to bow and balance at the same time.

"What's through there?" Maximilian asked, indicating the door.

"The kitchen, my lord."

"Is there an exit on the other side?"

"Yes, my lord. To the gardens."

"Good." The servant continued to gawk at the two of them, until the marquis nudged him toward the stairs. "Go."

As soon as the footman vanished up the stairs, Maximilian yanked Anne up against him and lowered his head to kiss her with a ferociousness that left her breathless and taut with desire.

"Someone will see us," she managed, tangling her fingers in his black hair.

"I don't care."

"I do."

He lifted his head again, gazing down at her with glittering gray eyes. "Because you don't want to be forced into marriage?" he breathed.

"Max—"

Grabbing her hand, he pushed through the kitchen door. A dozen servants froze in various stages of meal preparation. "Ignore us," he commanded. Heads lowered at once.

"Maximilian," she repeated, half wishing she'd kept quiet so he might have continued kissing her in the hallway, "what happens now?"

"Wait here a moment."

To her surprise he left her and went scouring about the kitchen, apparently looking for a snack. At the far end of the room he seemed to find what he was after, because with a murmured word to one of the cooks, he wrapped something large in a napkin and returned to Anne.

"You know your Greek mythology, I presume?" he asked, holding out his hand.

"Yes," she answered, dividing her attention between his intent face and the item resting on his palm, "though I don't see the relevance between golden—halved—apples and this situation."

A slow smile touched his mouth. "Wrong myth. Open it."

Her heart unexpectedly thudding, Anne pulled back the napkin. "A pomegranate," she said. *A pomegranate.*

Maximilian cleared his throat. "As you may recall, the lovely Persephone found herself torn between her lover, Hades, in the world below, and her mother, Demeter, in the world above, until they devised a way for her to have both."

Abruptly Anne couldn't breathe. "You would leave Yorkshire?" she asked, her voice breaking.

"That, my love, is up to you."

A tear ran down her cheek. "You called me your love," she managed.

"That is because I love you."

"Oh my, oh my," she whispered. She could have everything, now. She could have Maximilian Robert Trent. He would be hers, forever. Fingers shaking, she removed six pomegranate seeds, one after the other. "Six months in Yorkshire, and six months in London," she said.

"And you with me, Anne. Say you'll marry me."

She took the red fruit from his hand and set it aside, then flung her arms around his shoulders. "I will. Yes, I will marry you," she said, laughing and crying at the same time. "I love you so much."

He kissed her, lifting her in his arms and swinging her around and around. "Thank God," he murmured, over and over again.

Anne couldn't stop kissing him. Three weeks ago she would never have thought that she would agree to marry a sheep farmer, much less that she would want to do so. He would have to stay in town a few more days now, because she didn't think she could stand letting him leave without her. And if he obtained a special license quickly, they could be in Yorkshire by spring, and she would be able to see the daffodils bloom.

"Happy St. Valentine's Day," she whispered, hugging him tightly.

She felt him smile. "Happy St. Valentine's Day."

Suzanne Enoch

SUZANNE ENOCH grew up in Southern California, where she still balances her love for Regency romances and classic romantic comedies with her obsession for anything *Star Wars*. She has written more than thirty-five *New York Times* and *USA Today* bestselling romances. When she isn't writing, she is trying to learn to cook, and wishing she had an English accent.

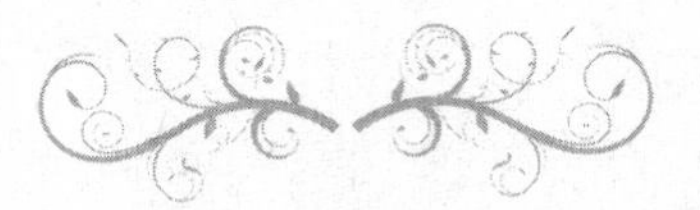

Two Hearts

Karen Hawkins

For my cat, Scat,
who graciously allows me
to sit in her favorite chair
while I'm working on the computer

Chapter 1

As if the frigid weather weren't providing the ton *with enough to talk about (and indeed, for a population so enamored of discussing the weather, this year's improbably cold winter is proving to be a boon for those who do not excel at the art of polite conversation) there is always Miss Elizabeth Pritchard, who seems to have set her cap rather astonishingly for Lord Durham.*

This Author does not believe this to be an impossible match—after all, Miss Pritchard is reputed to be quite plump in the pocket, and there is none who would find her personality unappealing (despite her obvious eccentricities). But it cannot be denied that she is rather a bit older than the average debutante, and indeed, older in fact than Lord Durham.

Will Miss Pritchard trade in her name for that of Lady Durham? Perhaps when the Thames freezes over . . . Ah, wait, the Thames HAS frozen over.

Nothing, apparently, is impossible these days.

LADY WHISTLEDOWN'S SOCIETY PAPERS,
26 January 1814

Lady Margaret Shelbourne marched to the ornate fireplace that graced one wall of the breakfast room. "There!" she announced grandly, tossing the paper into the crackling flames. "*That* is what I think of Lady Whistledown and her scandal rag!"

Her husband, Lord James Shelbourne, didn't even look up from his place at the head of the table where he sat perusing the latest edition of the *Morning Post*. After ten years of wedded bliss, he was far too used to his petite wife's theatrics to pay much heed. Thus it was left to Meg's brother, Sir Royce Pemberley, to respond.

He lifted his quizzing glass and eyed the curling ashes that had once been Lady Whistledown's latest efforts to beguile the *ton*. "I thought you rather liked Lady W. You certainly seemed anxious enough to read the thing; you snatched it off Burton's tray before he could announce it and almost vaulted over my chair in your eagerness."

"I did not. I merely leaned in front of you to—" Her gaze narrowed when Royce's grin slipped out. "Oh!" she said, stomping a dainty foot. "You're teasing me. That is the problem with you; you are *never* serious."

"Never," he agreed. "What did Lady Whistledown say that has irked you so?"

"It wasn't about me; it was about Liza."

Liza, known to the *ton* as Miss Elizabeth Pritchard, had been his sister's best friend since childhood. They were virtually inseparable, though one would be hard pressed to find two more different females. Meg was tiny, blond, perfectly coiffed at all times and a complete flutter brain, while Liza was tall, with light brown hair, mischievous cat green eyes, and a horrid sense of fashion. She was also one of the most logical women Royce knew. "What did Lady W say about Liza?"

"That she has formed an attachment, though how Lady W knew— Royce, that's the reason I asked you to come by this morning." His sister paused for a dramatic moment. "I fear Liza has decided to marry."

The words hung in the room, like the smoky haze of a newly lit candle. Though he knew he shouldn't feel anything but irritation at Meg's melodrama, the pronouncement was a shock. Liza? To wed? "Surely you are mistaken."

No one who knew Liza and understood the depths of her pragmatic nature would believe such nonsense. Liza's parents had died when she was only three and her maternal aunt had passed away the year of Liza's debut. She had been left alone at an early age with no one but a musty old solicitor who had believed his duties as guardian stopped at his office door.

A lesser female might have been distraught, but Liza had calmly gone on her way, purchasing a house, inviting an elderly, poverty-stricken cousin to live with her, and learning what she could from her guardian. On her twenty-fifth birthday, by then a confirmed spinster in the eyes of the *ton,* she'd surprised no one by pensioning off her hired companion and taking complete control of her fortune.

"I'm not mistaken about a thing," Meg said, clearly offended that Royce hadn't believed her. "The man's name is Durham."

"Never heard of him."

"He's new to town. He's a distant relative of Lady Sefton's, I believe."

Every two years or so, some ill wind would shake a handful of fortune hunters into the ballrooms of London and one or another would settle on Liza as his victim. With Meg's help, Royce had vanquished each and every potential threat.

Liza, of course, never noticed. She was supremely unaware of her own positive traits and the lure of her substantial income, which grew every year under her careful supervision. She also seemed completely content to remain as she was—single and unfettered by the demands of a spouse, much like Royce. Or so he had assumed. "I cannot believe Liza would do anything so scatterbrained."

"I didn't give the relationship any credence, either, but . . ." Meg hesitated. "She's been a bit blue-deviled since her birthday last month, you know. I'm afraid she's a little vulnerable."

Royce frowned at that. He'd seen Liza not two days ago. She *had* seemed a bit distracted, but nothing more. She certainly didn't display any symptoms of having developed a lifelong passion for a mysterious fribble. "Liza is not the type of woman to run into something as serious as marriage without thinking it through."

"She *has* thought it through. Why, she even gave me a list of all the reasons she thought Lord Durham and she would suit."

"Liza and her infernal lists! What does she think she's doing? Buying a horse?"

"She is thirty-one. Most women are married and have children by now."

"Liza isn't most women. I vow, Meg, have you been ragging her about marrying again? For if you have, I'll—"

"Of course I haven't," Meg said, her cheeks flushed. "I didn't say a word to her."

From the breakfast table, James rattled his paper in a telling way.

Meg's face pinkened even more and she hurried to say, "It's only natural Liza should meet someone and fall in love. I just wish she'd chosen someone we knew."

Liza in love? Why had Meg said *that*? It was one thing to decide to marry; it was another to actually be in love. The thought settled between his shoulders and produced a distinct restless feeling. Royce stood. The breakfast room seemed dark and oppressive while the bright light beaming through the windows from the snow-covered street offered escape. Escape from what, he didn't know, but he felt the very real need to breathe some of the icy cold air that hung outside the frosted window. "Meg, I really must go. Thank you for breakfast."

He turned toward the door, then stopped, a sudden thought gluing his feet to the carpet. "Meg? Do you . . . do you think she's really in love with this Durham fellow?" The question surprised Royce. He hadn't meant to ask it . . . not aloud anyway.

Meg's smooth brow puckered in thought. "No," she said slowly. "Not yet. But she feels that she's missing something. And you know Liza. If she wants something to happen, it happens." Genuine concern touched her voice. "Royce, what do we do? What if this Durham is not a nice man?"

Royce considered this for a long moment, a strange weight pressing on his chest. Finally, he said in a heavy voice, "I'm not sure we can do anything."

"What? You'd allow Liza to make the mistake of her life without a word?"

"She's a grown woman. If she really cares for this man—" He broke off, the words thickening in his throat. Bloody hell, what was wrong with him? This was Liza, for heaven's sake! The one woman he could trust to act sanely and logically. The one woman he respected above all others. Didn't he *want* her to be happy? Of course he did. She was like a—

He glanced at Meg and frowned. Well, not a sister. He certainly didn't take Meg into his confidence the way he did Liza. Nor did he have long, serious talks with Meg about . . . well, anything really. After all, she didn't understand him. Not really. And when he was feeling particularly blue, he certainly didn't seek out his sister, knowing she could make him feel better. Only Liza.

In fact, now that he thought about it, it had always been Liza. Over the years, she'd become his confidante just as much as she was Meg's. And now all that was threatened by some poppycock who was probably after poor Liza's fortune and would end up breaking her very tender heart. The thought angered him, which was a very unusual feeling for Royce. In fact, he was inundated with unusual feelings, none of which he recognized.

"Royce, I am disappointed that you are not offering to help." Meg crossed her arms, her gaze daggerlike. "I daresay you're too busy flirting with some new inamorata to bother with poor Liza."

"I never flirt."

"What a whopper! What about last week, when you were making snow angels in Hyde Park with Lady Anne Bishop? Lady W put it in her column and everyone was talking about it. I was never so humiliated in my life."

"Humiliated? By a snow angel?"

Meg squared her shoulders. "Royce, *someone* must discover Lord Durham's intentions. This man could be a fortune hunter or *worse*."

Shelbourne peered over his newspaper at Royce and mouthed the word "run" before retiring once more behind his paper shield.

Had Royce's head not been pounding, he might have smiled. "What else could Durham want from Liza other than her fortune?"

"Her virtue."

Blood roared behind Royce's eyes. Damn it, there was no way he'd let any man take such advantage of Liza! As much as he hated to admit it, Meg had a point. *Someone* needed to see about this Lord Durham.

And that someone would be Royce. If he didn't look into this Durham wastrel, Meg would, and God only knew what a mull she'd make of it. "Very well. I'll see what I can discover." And he would, too. He'd find out every blasted ugly thing that tainted the man's mysterious past and show it all to Liza.

Yes, that should do the trick. To his relief, Royce found that he could almost smile again. "Never fear, Meggie. I'll roust that rooster, one way or another."

She beamed. "Excellent! While you don't think Liza is attractive, other men—"

"Of course I think Liza is attractive."

Meg looked at him curiously. "No one would ever know it to see the two of you together. In fact, I've frequently thought you act as if she were more your sister than I. You treat her abominably."

Royce had been accused of many things in his life, but never of treating a member of the opposite sex like a sister. "Liza is my friend, so I daresay I do speak more freely to her than to other females. But that is all."

"Yes, well, it doesn't really matter. It's not as if she finds you attractive, either. She has grown rather immune to you over the years."

That stung his pride, so he straightened his shoulders and said in a lofty tone, "I should hope my relationship with Liza transcends such foolishness." There. That sounded impressive, even to him. But he was still unaccountably irked. "How the hell did Liza meet this man, anyway?"

"Lady Birlington introduced them."

"I should have known," Royce said. Lady Birlington was Liza's godmother. The old woman was brash, unconventional, and rude—the *ton* loved her.

No one could fault Lady Birlington's sense of duty. From the first moment Liza had set foot in London, her godmother had garnered Liza invitations to all the Season's most exclusive events, even gaining her a much-coveted voucher for Almack's. And when it became evident that Liza did not fit the standard of beauty established by society, Lady Birlington had taken her goddaughter even further under her wing and informed her that if she could not be stunning, she should at least be interesting. Liza took that bit of advice to heart.

Her tendency to dress against fashion increased, she'd become known for her shockingly frank speech, and she'd purchased a scandalously high perch phaeton and drove it wherever she went. Tongues had wagged, of course, but she blithely ignored them, and soon the *ton* came to expect the unexpected of Miss Liza Pritchard.

Not only that, but some of her quirks had become the rage. Last summer, Liza had appeared with a tiny monkey on a leash. Everyone, including the Prince, had been entranced with the animal's docile abilities. Within a week, every monkey in London was snapped up by women frantic to stay abreast with fashion, though they soon discovered that owning a monkey and keeping a monkey were not the same thing.

Mayhem ensued. Lady Rushmount's ill-behaved creature bit Lord Casterland's thumb. Casterland immediately took to bed for a week. Miss Sanderson-Little's monkey continually slipped its leash and scrambled beneath the skirts of every nervous female in sight. And Viscountess Rundell's pet showed a disagreeable tendency to swallow shiny objects, causing Lady Bristol to demand the return of a missing heirloom ring. After an elaborate search during which the ring was nowhere to be found, it was determined that the missing item must be resting in the bowels of the viscountess's monkey. Some awkward moments ensued, causing the viscountess to decide that perhaps she wasn't quite up to caring for a live monkey.

Royce sighed. "I hope this Durham fellow isn't a fortune hunter. I'd hate to have to—"

A discreet knock sounded on the door. Burton entered and announced in a grand tone, "Miss Elizabeth Pritchard."

A vision in crimson and green entered the room. *No, not a vision,* Royce amended silently. *More of a sight.* Liza had no clothing sense. Morning, noon, or night, she was always arrayed in the most outlandish colors. This morning, her crimson gown and matching pelisse were the height of simplicity, but the yellow half boots and the green turban were a shocking testament to the fact that she needed the advice of a good dresser.

Royce regarded her carefully, trying to see her as if he wasn't already perfectly familiar with her every expression and feature. And what he saw surprised him; Liza was a very striking woman. She possessed fine green eyes and a swath of curly, light brown hair that seemed to have a life of its own. While she was taller than most females, she carried it well, her height complementing her exceptional figure. She was long limbed, with a slender waist and a curvaceous form. At some time or another over the years of their acquaintance, all her features had softened, and the mature humor that lurked in her green eyes combined with her own natural vivacity to make her an eminently attractive female.

Or she would have been attractive, had she been better dressed.

"Liza!" Meg exclaimed. "What is on your head?"

Liza put a hand to the turban, a huge white feather sticking straight from the top and adding a good foot to her height. "Blast it, is it crooked again?" She pushed it to one side, the feather now pointing directly to the rear.

"Where did you get that atrocity?" Royce demanded, amused in spite of himself.

She patted the side of her turban now, moving it even more askew. "I got it from Madame Bouviette's on Bond Street. Do you like it?"

"It's the most ridiculous hat I've ever seen," Meg replied. "Only dowagers wear turbans."

"No! What a pity, as I believe I'm rather fond of it." She toyed with the feather, accidentally bending it almost in two. "I got it for an astonishingly good price; only ten shillings. I can't imagine what Madame Bouviette was thinking."

"I can," Royce said without pause. "She was thinking, 'I wager there isn't a person in London silly enough to buy such an atrocious turban even for ten shillings; I shall have to give the stupid thing away.' That, my dear Liza, is exactly what your precious Madame Bouviette was thinking."

Liza tried not to smile, but failed. How could she not grin when Royce teased her? She loved the ridiculous just as much as he. "That's quite enough merriment, thank you. It's too early and I haven't had my morning chocolate. Besides, I came to see Meg, not you." She glanced at Meg. "Do you needed some help with the invitations for your Valentine's ball? I have an entire afternoon free."

James sighed loudly, his breath rattling the paper.

"Ah, yes," Royce said. "Meg's Valentine's ball. I had forgotten about that."

"How could you?" Meg asked, plainly horrified. "I've been planning it since Lady Prudhomme tried to steal the Season with her wretched little soirée!"

Lady Prudhomme was Meg's archrival. The two had met in school and developed an aversion for each other that had been compounded over the years by the fact that they had married men of a similar station, had the exact same number of children, and were both held to be extremely attractive. Had one managed to overcome the other in some way, the rivalry might have abated. As it was, it had increased over the years until the two could barely maintain a polite face in society.

"Never fear," Liza said briskly, "once the world beholds the wonders of the Shelbourne Valentine's ball, no one will even remember the Prudhommes' paltry affair."

Meg smiled, a beatific expression on her face. "Liza, it will be spectacular! I've ordered over two thousand red candles. And Monsieur DeTourney has agreed to make six of his famed ice sculptures for the entryway. Royce, you are coming, aren't you?"

"Of course," he said promptly. "And I will dance with every antidote in the room, even the squinty-eyed ones."

Liza doubted that. Royce danced only with the most beautiful women. It was a depressing habit of his, and she wished he'd attempt to broaden his horizons a bit.

Meg shot a triumphant glance at the back of her husband's newspaper. "I'm glad I can count on my brother, at least."

"You can count on all of us," Liza said, aware of a wistful pang as she watched Lord Shelbourne peer over the edge of the paper at his wife, amusement warming his gaze. Though he wasn't one to show his feelings, Shelbourne could no more say no to his vivacious wife than he could fly. Meg and her husband were deeply and irrevocably in love. *It would be nice to feel like that, that I belonged to someone and he belonged to me.*

Of their own accord, her eyes were drawn to Royce. To her surprise, she found him regarding her intently, a question in his dark blue eyes. An instant prickle of awareness inched up her spine, a feeling she ruthlessly repressed. Heavens, that was no way to react to a mere look, especially not one from Sir Royce Pemberley, who gave intimate, intense looks to no fewer than forty females a day. Liza should know; she'd watched him do it for years.

Oh yes, Miss Liza Pritchard knew all about Sir Royce Pemberley. Far more than she should and certainly enough to keep her heart from leaping every time he cast a well-practiced glance her way. He was an atrocious flirt; notoriously unstable, his infatuations rarely lasting longer than a month; and circumspect only in public, where he was cautious never to cross the bounds of propriety in such a way as to cause him to lose his highly prized freedom.

That was why Liza thought she and Royce were such good friends—she knew him and accepted him without reservation. And she rather thought he did the same for her.

Of course, that didn't mean she wasn't aware of his charms. He was devilishly handsome, with dark brown hair that fell across his brow and contrasted sharply with his blue eyes. Eyes that laughed at one through thick, curling lashes in a way that could, if one was not careful, leave one quite breathless.

Worse, he was tall, broad-shouldered, and had a marvelous cleft in his chin that fascinated Liza in spite of her determination not to be fascinated. She rather wished he'd been born with a plain chin, and eyes a little less blue. And it would be nice if he had, over the years, managed to lose at least a little of his hair. Not all of it, mind you, but just enough to make it so that he wasn't so damnably handsome.

Unfortunately, God did not have a sense of justice, and Royce remained as handsome at thirty-nine as he had been at eighteen, only perhaps a trifle more so. Liza decided it was a testament to her astounding strength of character that she remained friends with the *ton*'s most successful heartbreaker, and had done so in a way that protected both her own dignity and his sense of worth.

Just to reinforce her thoughts, Liza gave him a firm, friendly smile and then turned back to Meg. "How many invitations do you need me to do?"

"Hundreds. Thousands, even. I'm inviting absolutely everyone." Meg bustled to the small escritoire that occupied one corner of the breakfast room. She collected a loose pile of heavy vellum invitations and then tore off the bottom of a long list. "Liza, thank you so much! You have saved me an entire day's work."

Liza took the invitations, straightened them into a neat pile, and tucked them under her arm. "We can send them out tomorrow." She slipped the scrap of paper into her reticule and pulled it closed. "Well, I'm off. I've errands to run."

"I'll see you to your carriage," Royce said with comforting promptness. He opened the door and stood to one side.

Liza pulled on her gloves, peering at him from beneath her lashes. Something was bothering Royce—she could see it in the way his gaze never left her, as if he were searching for something. Had Meg upset him? Whatever it was, Liza was determined to wrest it from him. After all, they were friends, and what else were friends for if not to worm every secret from each other?

"Of course you may escort me to my carriage. That would be very pleasant." She wiggled her fingers in goodbye to Meg. "I'll bring the invitations back in the morning." With that, she swept out and into the cooler air of the foyer, then waited for Royce to follow.

Outside the house, the air sparkled with cold, frosting Liza's breath to a puff of white lace. She glanced at Royce's heavy greatcoat a little enviously. She had on her best pelisse, and while it was nicely lined and trimmed with swansdown, it didn't ward off the chill nearly as well as thick layers of worsted wool. "I wish I could wear a multicaped greatcoat."

Royce glanced down at her as her carriage pulled to a stop before the stoop, a faint smile touching his mouth. "Shall I give you my coat? It would swallow you whole, but you'd be warmer."

"And what would you wear? My pelisse? I don't think so. Not even your good name could carry off that bit of foolishness."

"Trust me, if you can get away with wearing that atrocious turban, then I can get away with wearing a pelisse."

Liza grinned. "I'm beginning to get the idea that you don't like my hat."

"I hate it," he said promptly. "Not that you care."

"Of course I care," she said lightly as the footman pulled down the steps to her carriage. "Are you going somewhere? May I offer you a ride?"

"I couldn't trouble you."

"Pshaw! It will be fun to have a companion. Besides, the streets are nigh deserted, and we'll make excellent time." As a further incentive, she added in a confidential tone, "Sometimes the carriage slides a bit on the corners, which is perfectly delightful."

His teeth flashed as he grinned. "You are a complete hoyden. I suppose I should go just to keep you out of trouble." He glanced at the carriage, then lifted his brows. "I don't believe I've seen this carriage before."

"It's new and rides so smoothly that you won't even know you are traveling."

"How can I refuse such a tempting offer?" He sent her footman to dismiss his own carriage and then caught her elbow and helped her to get in, bending just enough so that his eyes were at a level with hers. "Come. You'll catch your death standing in this weather."

It was a simple gesture, one Liza was certain Royce had performed for countless other women without thought to the fact that he was making them feel special. Protected. Cherished, even. Fortunately, though Royce might not realize the effects his practiced gesture had on women who were not used to such, Liza did. She gently pulled her elbow free as soon as she was in the coach and busied herself with spreading a heavy wool blanket over her knees.

Royce seated himself opposite her as the footman shut the door. Within moments, the carriage sprang to life and they were soon on their way, comfortably ensconced, gently jolting over the icy paved streets.

"Very luxurious," Royce said as he examined the interior of the coach, touching the velvet seats and leather and brass trim. "I approve."

"I made a tidy profit on the market with my last venture, and I thought I was entitled to something nice."

He shot her a curious look. "The Duke of Wexford was complimenting you just the other day. Said he didn't know any other woman with a head so attuned to business."

"He just said that because I steered him in the way of a very profitable mining venture. He has a passion for gems."

"Nevertheless, he was very complimentary. He is not a man to give praise lightly."

"Nor am I a woman to take such nonsense seriously." She settled her feet on a small metal box that rested on the floor. "Here. Put your feet on this. It's delightfully warm."

Royce did as she instructed, his large feet making hers seem small. "What an astonishing color," he said, appearing amazed by the yellow boots that peeked out from beneath the edge of her crimson gown. "What bright shoes. I don't believe I've seen them before."

"They're new. I paid a fortune for them." She regarded her boot fondly. "I so love shoes. I have far too many, but somehow, it's still not enough."

He flashed a wide grin that made Liza's heart tumble in place. "If you have too many shoes, then I have too many waistcoats, and I refuse to admit to such folly."

She found herself grinning in return. One reason Royce had conquered so many female hearts was that he didn't dither over the things most men dithered over. He accepted that women loved clothing, and fashion, and talking, and tea. He accepted their fascination with gossip and the fact that many considered giggling a form of communication. Royce did not judge—he understood, encouraged, and listened. All simple enough things, yet combined, they left a woman feeling comfortable and loved.

Liza cleared her throat. "Do you like the hot bricks?"

He looked down at where their feet rested side by side on the box. "Very much." He hesitated for a moment. "Liza, I need to ask you something—" He broke off, looking so uncertain that she began to feel alarmed.

Something was bothering him. She could tell. "What is it?"

He flashed a rueful smile. "You know me too well. Liza . . . you know I have always valued your opinion."

Her heart sank. "Which woman is it this time?"

"Woman?" His smile faded. "Why would you think it's about a woman?"

"Because that's the topic upon which you usually request my opinions."

He blinked, as if shocked. "I do not."

"Didn't you ask me about the Pellham chit, the one with the blond hair and the large—" She gestured with her hands at bosom height.

His ears glowed. "I didn't think I'd—"

"Well, you did." And it was not a pleasant memory at all, now that she thought about it. The girl had been a nightmare; all false smiles and painted cheeks, and Royce had been too besotted to see. Of course, Liza had known his passion wouldn't last past the second week, it rarely did. Still, it had caused her some alarm, since the whole world knew the Pellhams were desperately looking for a wealthy husband for their only daughter and they possessed rather low connections. It was entirely possible the horrid girl had been pressured into setting a trap for Royce.

Fortunately, Royce's attention had waned before that could come to pass. "So, what female is it this time? Not Lady Anne Bishop, is it?"

"No, it's not Lady Anne Bishop."

"There's no need to get in a snit."

"I'm not in a snit," he replied stiffly. "I—I didn't realize I spoke to you about such inappropriate subjects."

"Lord yes. You even asked me if you should purchase a ruby necklace or ear bobs for an actress you were pursuing. You had enough sense to point her out to me when we were at the theater one evening, which was a very good thing, for I'd been thinking garnets would be just the thing, and it turned out she was quite an insipid blond."

Royce opened his mouth, then closed it as if unable to decide how he should reply.

Liza thought that perhaps he didn't remember the woman. After all, it *had* been four months ago. "Surely you remember her. Blue eyes, blond hair, and a large posterior. Oh, and I think she had a bad habit of wearing a beauty patch, which is quite out of fashion nowadays."

Royce leaned back in his seat, too stunned to speak. Meg was right—he did treat Liza abominably. He looked at her now, noticing how the cold had pinkened her cheeks and nose. She pushed an errant curl from her cheek with a gloved hand, the tips of her fingers tracing the slope of her cheek. His gaze followed every move. "Liza, I'm sorry."

"Sorry? For what?"

"For subjecting you to such inappropriate confidences. You are just so easy to talk to."

Her smile dimmed for the briefest second, then returned. "So I've been told. But that's neither here nor there. You wished to ask my advice? What about?"

"Oh. That. It's not about a female. At least, not about another female other than—" The words simply would not come, and Royce cursed himself for prevaricating. He apparently could tell Liza about his infatuation with a completely unsuitable actress, but could not find the words to ask her about a man she was rumored to care for.

Royce rubbed his neck, wondering when it had gotten so difficult to talk to Liza. This was *Liza,* for God's sake. Liza, who knew him better than anyone else. Liza, who laughed at his faults and teased him when he was low and always, always understood him.

Yet here he was, stammering like a tongue-tied boy of six. He wracked his brains trying to think of a subtle way to lead the conversation toward the unknown Lord Durham.

It was becoming increasingly imperative to discover what attraction, if any, Liza felt for the mysterious man. Royce straightened in his seat. "Meg and I had an interesting conversation this morning."

"Did you?"

"Yes, and, ah, well . . . she mentioned you. You and someone else."

There was an instant reaction in Liza's green eyes. But she gave a quick shrug, as if to reject an unwanted thought. "Sounds as if Meg is matchmaking yet again," she said calmly. "I can't imagine why she persists in doing so."

Royce thought it was very promising that Liza didn't immediately claim or deny knowledge of Lord Durham. Perhaps it was all Meg's imagination after all. Yes, of course it was all Meg's doing—it always was. Relief poured through him, and he grinned. "You know my sister! She delights in setting everyone on edge."

"I've noticed. Her penchant for matchmaking makes her dangerous. Perhaps we should flee London to protect ourselves. That would be easier for me than you, I'm afraid. I can change my name and hire myself out as a governess, but what would you do? Hire yourself out as a tutor?"

"I don't suppose anyone who'd ever heard my Latin would believe that."

"Never. Plus you need a more adventuresome trade. Perhaps you can make your way to the Indies aboard a ship. I've heard they are in dire need of cabin boys."

"Cabin boy? What about captain?"

"I'm afraid you'd have to work your way up to that position. It should only take seven or eight years."

"You are most unkind."

"But sadly truthful. You've never been to sea a day in your life, and I daresay you wouldn't know starboard from port."

"I know my port very well, thank you. I drink a glass every evening before bed."

"I take it all back, then. Obviously you would make an excellent sea captain." Sarcasm dripped from her voice.

Royce grinned. "Always ready to put me in my place, aren't you?"

"Only when you need it," she said with a faint smile.

"If that is true, then we'll never have a civil conversation."

"I don't believe we've ever had a civil conversation, but then that's one of the things I like about our relationship." Liza's gaze dropped to the stack of invitations in her hands. "I know Meg means well, but it is a pity we will have to run away to sea to get away from her efforts. She really should leave us to settle our own lives as we see fit."

"She worries about you. You are like a sister to her."

Liza's smile seemed a little strained. "Meg is like a sister to me as well. I don't know what I would have done without her friendship. Or yours, for that matter."

"I cannot speak for Meg, but I am always here for you. I always have been."

Her gaze flew to his. The silence deepened, intensified. Liza bit her lip and then lifted a corner of the leather curtain to look out the window. The bent feather on her turban flopped onto her shoulder. "They say the Thames is a solid block of ice."

Royce hesitated a moment, then accepted the change of topic. The quicker things were back to normal in their relationship, the better he'd like it. Damn Meg for stirring things up to begin with. It was obvious that there was nothing to this Durham man or Liza would have already told Royce about it—they were friends, after all. She told him everything.

But Meg had been right about one thing, and that was that Liza seemed vulnerable somehow. Beneath Liza's usual blithe manner lay a pool of sadness. He could see it in her eyes, especially when she attempted to smile. He watched her for a moment, wishing he could think of something to say.

She dropped the curtain and turned to face him, settling back in her seat. He couldn't help but notice how innately elegant she'd become. Sometime between her seventeenth birthday and her twenty-fourth or -fifth, she'd found her own peculiar sort of beauty. One that had little to do with her features, and more to do with the way she held her head and gestured with her hands.

Royce wondered if other men noticed the same things about Liza that he did. The idea made him shift restlessly in his seat. Damn it, he hated to think of someone harming Liza. She was special, different from all other women, and far more delicate in her own way. He eyed her with determination. Perhaps it would be better if he just took the bull by the horns and asked the question that had been hovering on his lips for the past half hour. "Liza, tell me about this Durham fellow."

Hot color flooded her cheeks, and Royce's heart lurched. Bloody hell, but Meg *had* been right—something was going on. Whatever it was, Royce knew he was not going to like it.

"Damnation!" Liza said, smoothing a gloved hand over her forehead as if to rub away a frown. "I suppose you read Lady Whistledown this morning. I was never so mortified as when she mentioned that I was older than Lord Durham, as if that matters—"

"Older?"

She blinked. "Didn't you read the paper?"

"Meg burned it, so I didn't get the opportunity."

"Heavens! Even I wasn't that upset. Yes, I'm a little older than Lord Durham. Only four years, which isn't that much. I don't know why Lady Whistledown made such a fuss."

That made Lord Durham more than ten years younger than Royce. The alarms in Royce's head intensified. *That insolent pup.* "Who the hell is this man?"

She opened her mouth as if to reply and then just as quickly shut it. "Why do you want to know?"

"Why? What do you mean, why? Meg is like a sister to you. Therefore, I have every right to ask you such questions."

"Royce, in the fifteen or so years we've been friends—"

"Twenty-one."

She frowned. "It can't be!"

"Well, it is. We met in August at the Chathams' house party. You were ten and I was eighteen. Meg and I arrived just as you and your aunt pulled up in your carriage."

She seemed astonished. "You remember all that?"

"Don't you?"

"Frankly, no."

A low grumble of dissatisfaction threatened to overset Royce's hold on his temper. "It doesn't matter. Tell me about this Durham fellow." He hadn't meant to snap the words, but they came out clipped and forceful.

She stiffened, her friendly demeanor disappearing in an instant. "I'd rather not. Especially not if you're going to be disagreeable."

The carriage rumbled to a halt. They must have reached Royce's lodgings, but he was too irritated to pay much heed. It wasn't like Liza to be so reticent. "Why won't you tell me about Durham? What's wrong with him? What are you hiding?"

"Nothing's wrong with him. It's just none of your business."

"How can you say such a thing?" He reached over and captured her hands and held them tightly. "Liza, I've been your best friend for twenty-one years. Surely it is natural for me to ask you about your beaux."

She looked down at where he held her hands, a strange expression passing over her face. "Royce, I am not a child. I will come to no harm at Lord Durham's hands or anyone else's. Besides, Lady Birlington speaks very highly of him."

"Your godmother speaks very highly of Lord Dosslewhithe, too, and he talks with his mouth full and has had fourteen illegitimate children."

Liza's lips twitched. She gently freed her hands from his. "Lady Birlington says Durham is a prosy bore, which means he is of exemplary character."

The door opened, and icy wind swirled into the carriage box. The footman fought to hold the door open as he waited for Royce to alight.

Royce struggled to find something to say—something significant that might protect Liza from . . . from what? Perhaps Lady Birlington was right and Lord Durham was as pure as driven snow. But Royce knew without any proof whatsoever that Durham was not the man for Liza. "Just promise you won't rush into anything."

Something flickered behind the mossy green of her eyes, only to be quickly hidden behind a bright smile. "You had better rush inside before you freeze."

"We haven't finished our conversation."

"Yes," she said firmly. "I'm afraid we have. Besides, George is waiting, the poor monkey. He has a cold, you know, and won't allow anyone else to give him his medicine."

There was nothing more to be said. He was being dismissed in a cool, friendly fashion, and he hated every minute of it. But what could he do? He alighted, nodding once to the footman, who promptly closed the door.

The curtain was almost immediately lifted and Liza leaned out into the cold wind. An especially sharp breeze careened up the side of the carriage and blew tendrils of her hair from the edges of her green turban and tossed them about her flushed cheeks. She looked fresh and healthy, pleased with herself and the world. "Royce, if you'd like to meet Durham, then come to the theater with Meg and me tomorrow evening. There's a new actor playing—Kean. They say he's quite good."

"I'd love to," he answered promptly. Anything to gain access to this Durham character. "I like a good play."

Liza chuckled, her eyes crinkling. "Oh, I know how you love the theater. I watched you sleep though *A Midsummer Night's Dream* just last month. Then you snored ever so gently through *Lord Kipperton's Last Request,* and that was a murder mystery with a smashing good ending. Try to stay awake this time, will you?"

He managed a mechanical smile, which she returned with such a bright, laughing look that he took an involuntary step forward. But she waved her hand and then dropped the curtain back over the window. The carriage jerked to a roll and moved down the street before Royce could compose his mind enough to speak.

What was there to say, anyway? Until he met this Durham fellow himself, Royce had nothing more than an uneasy feeling to use as a warning for Liza. And she was far too pragmatic to pay attention to such flimsy reasoning.

He remained standing on the walk in front of his lodgings for a long while, mulling this over. The wind whistled against the shutters of the row of neat houses behind him, bending the branches of the trees that dotted the avenue and swirling a scattering of snow across the frozen stones. There were a lot of things that bothered him about this Durham fellow, not the least was the claim he'd hold over Liza if they married. Chances were high that he wouldn't welcome his wife's friendship with Royce.

Royce hunched his shoulders against the cold. Bloody hell, what would he do without Liza in his life? It seemed as if he'd always had her to talk to, to confide in, to tease and laugh with . . . once she married, that would all come to an end. So would the easy camaraderie they shared.

Oh, they might remain acquaintances, and perhaps could engage in a serious conversation now and again, but the freedom that surrounded their current friendship would be lost forever. It was strange, but his whole life already seemed duller, less satisfying.

How long he stood there, staring down the street at the place he'd last seen Liza's coach, he didn't know. But his feet and face were numb before he made his way indoors. His housekeeper clucked noisily at his frozen state and bustled him into the parlor where she ordered a pot of tea and called for a footman to remove Royce's new boots. In an amazingly short time, he found himself sitting before a brightly burning fire, his feet in a pair of slippers, a cup of steaming tea liberally laced with brandy in his hand.

His mind thawed along with his toes. He had to find Lady Birlington and see what she knew about this upstart who was threatening the calm order of Royce's life. And then, armed with what he discovered, he'd go to the Theatre Royal, Drury Lane, and confront Liza. Oh yes, a day of reckoning was about to arrive for the mysterious Lord Durham, and Royce would be there to witness the man's fall.

Chapter 2

Speaking of Miss Pritchard, This Author would be remiss if it were not mentioned that she wore the following colors last week, all in the same ensemble:

Red

Blue

Green

Yellow

Lavender

Pink (of a pale shade, it should be noted)

This Author searched for an accent of orange, but none was to found.

LADY WHISTLEDOWN'S SOCIETY PAPERS,
26 January 1814

Liza entered the sitting room and smiled at the small brown monkey. George hopped up and down on his perch, screeching a welcome.

"Happy to see me, are you?" Liza stripped off her gloves and tossed them on a side table. "How are you doing this morning? Still sneezing?"

Poor George had a wretched cold, the product, no doubt, of the chilly weather and a sad tendency to take off his hat at every opportunity. He chattered loudly, making such a comical face that Liza laughed. He was very small, barely the length of her hand in height. She suspected he was the runt of his family, for she'd never seen a smaller monkey, and in the days following George's appearance in the *ton,* quite a few replicas had turned up. "Though none was as smart or well behaved as you, were they?"

George hopped in agreement. Liza opened a small drawer in the table where his perch rested and pulled out a packet of dried figs. He took the fig she offered, then swung up to his perch and nibbled his treat, his eyes fixed on her questioningly.

"It's a wretched morning. Far too cold, and I scuffed my new boot on the stoop." She held out her boot so George could see. He stared at it with polite interest, busily chewing the whole while.

Liza chucked him under the chin and then pulled the pins from her turban and tossed it onto the arm of the settee. Sighing, she dropped into a large winged chair and snuggled against the cushioned back. It was her favorite chair, purchased at an estate auction on a whim. She bought most of her furniture that way—a piece here and a piece there—which was why so little of it matched. But each chair and settee was unique and overwhelmingly comfortable. And that was the only thing that mattered.

She raked a hand through her hair, certain the turban had sadly flattened her curls, and wondered what was bothering Royce. Probably a woman of some sort—it always was. The man was a positive menace with all those women languishing after him. It was a wonder someone hadn't just shot him and put him out of their misery.

Liza pushed off her shoes and rested her feet on a low yellow and orange footstool. Her house was snug and warm even in this horrendously chilly weather, the fire was snapping merrily, her seat was cozy and comfortable, and there was sweet little George, looking on with an expression of contentment. Liza looked around her and realized that though she had every reason to be happy, she wasn't. She'd been aware for several weeks now that something was missing in her life—something big.

George finished his fig and inched to the edge of his perch where he could see Liza. He tilted his head to one side and chattered a question.

"No, no. Just a case of the winter doldrums, but . . ." She sighed. "I don't know. I just feel . . . lost. And then today, talking to Royce . . . I don't know, but it made me lower than before." He *had* seemed genuinely concerned about Durham, and had even made her feel . . . cosseted. It hadn't lasted, of course. He'd said Meg saw her as a sister and for an instant, she'd been tempted to ask him if *he* thought of her as a sister. But she'd decided not to—she was already blue enough, thank you. There was no need for her to torture herself senseless.

The really sad thing was that as special as Royce had made her feel when he'd helped her into the carriage and questioned her about Durham, she was sure it was nothing compared to the attentions Royce showered on the women he was interested in. Of course, he was careful not to pay too much attention to any woman, at least not in public. But in private . . . She sighed restlessly, wiggling her toes in the warmth.

What did she expect, after all? She was too old to believe in fairy tales. "Love," she scoffed to George, who looked properly disgusted with the topic. Liza'd never been in love. In fact, she wasn't even sure she was capable of the emotion.

Her heart tightened, and tears sprang to her eyes. *That* was why she was depressed; she'd waited for years to experience "the grand passion," but it never happened. Which was a great pity, for Liza was certain that being in love was the most wonderful feeling on the face of the earth. She knew just how it would feel—the giddiness, the excitement, the overwhelming emotion. She knew because she'd seen Meg fall in love with Shelbourne. Fall in love, and *stay* in love, which was even better.

But somehow, though Liza waited year after year, that most elusive of all sentiments had evaded her. She hadn't really thought of it, for she'd been busy living her life. But then, on her last birthday, she'd suddenly realized that perhaps she was not meant to fall wildly and completely in love. Ever.

The sad truth was that she was far too pragmatic for such emotion. And so she'd revised her thinking. She'd find the perfect man, marry him, and *then* she'd fall in love. Oh, it might not be the kind of love she'd originally dreamed of—passionate and astounding. It would be the more stable sort of love—one that would last a lifetime.

So far, Lord Durham seemed the most likely candidate. He was the most solid, honest, capable, correct, and forthright man of Liza's acquaintance. He wasn't bad-looking, either, providing one didn't seat him too closely to Royce. No one, not even the darkly handsome St. John men or the fascinating Bridgerton brothers, could compare to Sir Royce Pemberley. At least, not in Liza's eyes.

But Lord Durham had one advantage that Royce would never have—Durham was genuinely interested in Liza. All she had to do was make certain that he fit in well with the Shelbournes, and the deal would be struck. After all, Meg and Royce were her family, and she valued their opinion over all others.

Which was why she'd asked Meg to invite Lord Durham to the theater tomorrow evening. Things were progressing nicely, Liza thought, trying to talk her reluctant heart into feeling at least a little more sprightly.

A discreet knock sounded, and Poole, her butler, appeared. "Lord Durham, miss."

Liza waited, but her heart gave no excited leap. Perhaps she just needed to give it some more time. She sat up and looked for her shoes. "Send him in."

"Yes, miss." The butler hesitated. A long silence ensued, and Liza finally realized he wasn't moving toward the door.

She stopped looking for her shoes. "Yes?"

"I beg your pardon, but, ah . . . you might want to look into the mirror, miss. Your hair . . ." He gave a discreet cough.

"Mussed it, did I? It's that damned turban."

"Shall I have Lord Durham wait a few moments before sending him in?"

"Lord, no. It's rude to leave him kicking his heels in the morning room. Just bring him here. I'll fix my hair in a trice."

"Very well, miss." Poole bowed and withdrew.

Liza fished her shoes out from beneath the footstool and put them back on her feet. That done, she smoothed her dress and then crossed to the mirror that graced the wall over the mantel. She chuckled when she saw herself. Little brown curl-horns stuck out all over her head. She looked like a cross between Medusa and a devil. No wonder Poole had stared.

Still chuckling, she raked her fingers through her hair, managing to dispel some of the horned curls into smoothish bumps instead. "There," she said, turning to George. "What do you think?"

George cocked his head to one side and screwed up his face.

"I know it doesn't look good. But at least admit it looks better than before."

Before George could answer, the door opened and Poole announced quietly, "Lord Durham." He bowed and retreated, shutting the door behind him.

George bared his teeth at the newcomer. Then jumped off his perch and sat beneath it, his rump prominently displayed.

Durham, who had been eagerly striding across the room, slowed to a halt and frowned. "That creature doesn't like me."

"He's just in a bit of a temper. How are you today, Lord Durham?"

He reluctantly turned his attention from the monkey, his round face folding into a smile. "I'm better now that I've seen you and—" His smile froze when his gaze fell on her hair. "I—I see you've been sleeping."

She put a self-conscious hand to her crumpled curls. "I'm sorry. I was wearing a turban earlier."

"A turban? You are far too young for such a thing," he said gravely. "And far too pretty, as well."

Liza decided she liked being complimented. It gave one a feeling of well-being not unlike a good hot cup of chocolate. "Thank you." She took her seat and gestured to the empty one opposite hers.

He took the chair with a pompous sort of dignity. "I'm glad I caught you at home this morning. I was afraid you might be out running errands."

"I just returned." Liza eyed him speculatively. Of average height and build, he was an attractive enough man. He had brown hair and dark brown eyes and walked with a certain air of authority that she rather admired. She liked a man who knew who he was and what he wanted. Unfortunately, Durham's confidence was accompanied by a slight sense of arrogance and a touch of stodgery; both characteristics Liza would make sure were dispelled once they were married.

If she decided to marry him, she told herself. And only *if*. She wasn't desperate by any means, and she did not want to make a mistake.

He offered her a ponderous smile. "My mother sends her compliments."

"How lovely of her. Please tell her that I hope to have the opportunity to meet her sometime soon." Liza knew a good deal about Durham's mother. He mentioned her frequently. "How *is* your mother? I daresay she misses you dreadfully."

"Oh yes. Since my father's death, she looks to me for everything. Not that I complain, quite the opposite. I think you will find my mother is everything amiable." Durham gave Liza a look full of meaning. "I told her it wouldn't be long before I returned. And that I might have a surprise for her."

For an instant, Liza couldn't move. It was as if her mind, on understanding the not-so-subtle intention of Lord Durham's words, had retreated into the very back of her head and refused to emerge.

But Durham didn't need any encouragement. He smiled and said archly, "I don't mean to be forward, Miss Pritchard, but I have been rather plain in my intentions. I hope you don't think I'm being overeager if I give my poor mother a hint as to why her only son remains in London after so many weeks. Would you mind?"

A hot blush crept up Liza's neck. Yes, she would mind. Though she shouldn't. After all, this was the man she might marry. *Might* marry, she reminded herself.

Good God, what was wrong with her? This was what she wanted, wasn't it? Durham was a solid, respectable, honorable man. He was far from destitute, owning several large holdings, most of which he cultivated. And he was pleasant, courteous, and polite. What more could she ask for?

Unbidden, an image of Royce slipped into her mind, looking at her with that unmistakable glimmer of laughter in his eyes that never failed to make her grin in return. Liza frowned. How often would she get to see him if she married? Heavens, would she see him at all?

Liza suddenly realized that Durham was waiting for her answer. Unable to think of one, she blurted out instead, "I'm looking forward to the play tomorrow. *The Merchant of Venice* is one of my favorites."

"It was very nice of Lady Shelbourne to make me a member of her party. Normally, I am not one to engage in such frivolous activities, but when in Rome . . ." He smiled. "Are you much addicted to the theater,

Miss Pritchard? I fear Somesby is not a very large town. Until recently, we did not have the opportunity to see many plays, but I hope that one day . . ." He rambled on, unaware that Liza was no longer listening.

She was far too busy trying to imagine herself living in a small town without the conveniences of London. It would be quite different. She looked about at her comfortable home, at her cherished belongings, at her new shoes, and wondered what she'd do with her time.

"Miss Pritchard, what do you think about cows?"

She blinked. Cows. What did she think about cows. "Well," she said cautiously. "I like horses."

"Yes, they are necessary creatures. But cows . . ." Lord Durham beamed. "I own over a thousand. And they're the best money can buy."

Good Lord, the man owned a thousand cows and he was *proud* of it. "Whatever do you do with them?"

"I breed them. Durham cows are renowned for their quality."

Yes, but what about the Durham bull? She suppressed a giggle. Had she been with Royce, she'd have blurted the thought without worrying about his reaction, for she knew he would have laughed. They shared the same irreverent sense of humor. But she didn't feel that easy with Lord Durham. Of course, she hadn't known him that long, either. With time, she was certain she'd be able to share her every thought.

"You will enjoy seeing my farms," Durham said. "They are without compare. Miss Pritchard . . . Liza . . . may I call you that?"

She took a deep breath. The relationship was progressing. Just as it was supposed to. But why did that make her feel so . . . restless? *Liza, you are just experiencing cold feet, a normal reaction for a young lady about to embark on a flirtation that could possibly lead to more.* She smoothed her skirt and said firmly, "Of course you may call me Liza."

"And you may call me Dunlop."

She choked. George must have thought she was choking to death, for he began to screech and jumped up and down at the bottom of his stand.

Durham sprang from his seat. "Mi—Liza! Are you ill?"

"Monkey hair," she managed to choke out, gesturing for him to sit back down. Good Lord, she didn't think she'd heard of such a silly name. She thought she'd just continue to call him Durham for her own peace of mind. She frowned at her shrieking monkey. "George, that is quite enough."

The tiny monkey gave a huge, toothy grin, then swung up on his perch and settled down as if to watch the festivities.

Durham eyed the monkey with some misgiving. "Does he understand everything you say?"

"Most of it. What he doesn't understand from the words, he can tell from tone of voice. But we weren't speaking about George. Your cows, do you pet them?"

He laughed, his face relaxing until he no longer looked quite so stern. In fact, when he laughed he looked . . . nice. She suddenly felt guilty for giggling at his name.

"I don't pet the cows, but you may if you wish."

"How lovely. Do you wish to live in the country all year round?"

"Oh no." His smile bordered on a superior smirk. "I'm a man who enjoys the finer things in life. I plan on coming to Town quite frequently. I daresay I will spend several weeks a year here."

"Weeks? Wouldn't you stay for the entire Season?"

"Not with cows to care for. You see, many people think you just have to assign their care to a herder. But I believe that with more attention, you can double, even triple their value. Imagine that, Liza." He shook his head in wonder.

"That's . . . quite impressive." And she was sure it was. To someone else. Someone more interested in cows than she.

He gave her a rueful smile. "I'm certain you've more important things to discuss than my cows. Tell me about Lady Shelbourne's ball. It should be quite an event."

She told him about Meg's plans, skirting the more mundane issues of decoration and refreshments. As soon as she finished, he leaned forward and took her hand in his. Only a half hour hence, Royce had held that same hand. He had, in fact, held *both* of her hands. And though she'd had her gloves on at the time, the casual touch had sent strange tingles up her arms. Lord Durham's grasp, while pleasant enough, did nothing more than warm her cold fingers. She stared down at his hand.

She wasn't ready for this. Not now. She needed at least another week before she made her decision. Yes, a week would do nicely. The ache in her knees grew.

"This has been a lovely visit," she suddenly said, standing. Durham stood as well, looking a bit startled. Liza didn't blame him. "But I just remembered a very important appointment to—" She wracked her brain, but that organ was no longer functioning. Good God, she was only thirty-one and there was no reason she'd succumb to senility so quickly. "I have an appointment to, ah . . ." Her gaze fell on the turban, now lying discarded on the arm of the settee, looking like a scrap of green felt. "Milliner's. Yes, I have an appointment at the milliner's and I'm already late."

"I wish I could escort you, but I am to accompany Lord Sefton to White's. He offered to sponsor me." Durham wagged a roguish brow. "I fear I'm becoming something of a wastrel. I hope I don't end up wagering away the family farm."

He was just so nice. Liza wondered if perhaps she was being hasty. She wasn't a young girl anymore, and she'd long ago given up her dreams of finding a prince. There were no princes.

Durham took her hand again, only this time he bowed low. "Good day, Liza. I shall return tomorrow to escort you to the theater. At seven?"

She nodded mutely, feeling more wretched by the moment.

"Seven it is." He gave her fingers a significant squeeze, then left.

As soon as the door closed, George swung from his perch and chattered a fierce warning, all brave and brash now that Durham was out of the room.

"Oh hush!" Liza said. It was all so confusing. Her head and heart were at odds, one demanding one thing, one demanding another. "Damn Lord Durham," she said loudly.

That made her feel better. A little. But it still wasn't enough. So she added in loud ringing tones, "And damn Sir Royce Pemberley and his damned clefted chin." Somehow, those words were infinitely more satisfying, but they still left her feeling very alone. Sighing, she collected Meg's invitations and went to work, hoping to keep her mind busy with more productive thoughts.

Chapter 3

This Author has a confession to make.

When This Author sees Lady Birlington walking her way, This Author runs (quickly) in the opposite direction.

LADY WHISTLEDOWN'S *SOCIETY PAPERS,*
28 January 1814

Early the next day, Royce set out in search of Lady Birlington. It took the better part of the day to find the old woman, but he finally managed to track her down. She and her grandnephew, Edmund Valmont, were just entering a lending library. Lady Birlington was dressed in an alarming puce pelisse, which clashed horribly with her ruby gown and hideously purple muff.

Royce hastily hopped down from his carriage and followed them into the library, head down against a smattering of snow. He brushed icy flakes from his coat as he closed the door. "Lady Birlington, may I have a word with you?"

Edmund turned, brightening when he saw Royce. "Sir Royce! I was just speaking to someone about you the other day. Well, not you precisely, but about your horse—the gray you sold at Tattersall's two years ago. Remember it? It had a mark on its shoulder that looked for all the world like Italy. Strangest thing I ever saw. Do you know if the horse had ever been to Italy? I thought perhaps it was born there or maybe had just traveled through the country and the experience was so vivid that it marked—"

"For the love of heaven!" Lady Birlington said, thumping her cane dangerously near her nephew's toe. "Stop blathering and help me out of this damp pelisse. I shall die of an inflammation before you reach a point, if you even have one." As soon as her nephew began to assist her out of her coat, she snapped a sharp glance at Royce. "Well? What do you want? Don't owe you money, do I?"

Royce lifted his brows. "Not that I'm aware of."

"Good. I was at the Markhams' rout last night and I distinctly remember losing a goodly sum, but I can't for the life of me remember to whom."

Edmund folded Lady Birlington's pelisse over his arm and said to Royce in a confidential tone, "Age, you know. My Uncle Tippensworth was like that. Couldn't remember his own name at times, but he had a devilish way of remembering things one would just as soon he'd forget. He must have told every person he knew about the time I was three and stripped naked right in front of the parson's wife—ow!"

"I wouldn't smack your shins," Lady Birlington said, "if you'd stop talking long enough for someone else to get in a word. I'm not losing my memory because of my age, you ninny. I had too much to drink." She sent a slightly self-conscious glance at Royce. "Champagne. Tasty stuff, but it muddles me every time."

"Of course. Lady Birlington, I wanted to ask your opinion of Lord Durham."

"Durham. Hm. Sounds familiar. Not one of those new Methodist speakers, is he? Went to hear one the other day. If you want my opinion, all that depressing talk about hell will just incite the population to fornicate all the more. I know it made *me* want to fornicate, anyway."

"Forni—Aunt Maddie!" Edmund blustered.

"Demme, Edmund! It's for-ni-*cate*. Try to listen, will you? And stop dawdling about and return my books. I don't have all day, you know."

Edmund sent Royce a harried look, but he obediently took the books to the nearest desk.

As soon as he was out of earshot, Lady Birlington's sharp gaze narrowed on Royce, a faint lift to the corner of her thin mouth. "As for you, I can't imagine you wish to speak to me about a Methodist. Must be some other Durham."

Royce had the distinct impression he was being teased. "I am speaking about the Lord Durham you recommended as a potential suitor to your goddaughter."

"Ah, *that* Durham. Why didn't you say so? I know him quite well. But you've got one thing wrong: I didn't recommend him as a suitor."

Royce almost grinned. He couldn't wait to tell Liza how sadly she was mistaken. He opened his mouth to thank Lady Birlington for her time when she added, "But I *did* recommended him as a potential *husband*."

Husband. The word cut as sharply as the icy air.

The old woman sniffed. "Don't look at me like that! There's no need for Liza to dither about like a schoolroom miss. She's a smart gel and not getting any younger. She has too much sense to throw away her chances because of a bunch of lame courtship nonsense. That's for dewy-eyed youngsters."

"Liza may not be in the first bloom of youth, but she is very attractive and incredibly wealthy."

Lady Birlington's blue eyes shimmered, as hard as agates. "I know that Liza has the capabilities of attracting a man in her own right, with or without a fortune, if that's what you're getting at."

Royce's ears burned. "I didn't mean to suggest that you didn't appreciate her merits," he said stiffly. "I just wanted to be certain that whatever man she settled on was worthy of her attentions."

"Lord Durham is levelheaded, respectable, and as boring as they come. Can't stand him, personally, but I thought he might be the thing for Liza. Between the two of you, you and your sister, Liza never gets to meet any interesting men."

"I beg your pardon."

"Don't play the innocent with me! I've seen you chase off any number of men over the years."

"Only ineligible ones."

"Ineligible for whom? You've been selfish with Liza long enough. It is time you let her live her own life."

"I am willing to let her live however she wishes, so long as she doesn't bring harm to herself."

"Humph! I know you mean well, but perhaps Liza *likes* fortune hunters. She seems to have a penchant for handsome rakehells."

Rakehells? How could Durham be respectable *and* a rakehell? Royce's jaw tightened, and he was aware of a slow, thick rumble of frustration weighting his chest. Liza was steadily slipping out of his life; he had no time for boring homilies. "I only want what's best for Liza."

Lady Birlington's gaze softened slightly. "Liza is bound to make mistakes. Plenty of 'em. We all do. But that doesn't give you the right to take choices away from her."

"And if she falls for the flattery of a scoundrel?"

"Liza's too smart for that, and you know it. Leave her be. She's more than capable of handling Durham. Now if you'll excuse me, I must find Edmund. The last time I left him alone in the library, he found a section of completely inappropriate books and they shocked him so much he was unable to sleep for a week. Good day."

Royce clamped his jaw into a forced smile and bowed. As soon as Lady Birlington moved away, he turned on his heel and walked back into the frigid wind. It blew hard, slamming the door closed behind him and seeping into the buttonholes of his coat and down his collar. It was colder than yesterday, but inside Royce simmered, anger bubbling a heated path all the way to the soles of his feet.

How dare Lady Birlington accuse him of standing in the way of Liza's happiness? The idea was ludicrous. Everything he'd ever done for Liza had been in her best interests. Fortunately, in a few hours Royce would have his answers about Durham. He'd meet this paragon and make up his own mind as to the proper course of action. For the first time in his life, Royce found himself actually looking forward to attending the theater.

"Waiting for your coach?" a warm, feminine voice asked.

He turned to find the object of his musings standing before him, resplendent in a red pelisse over a burnt orange gown. Liza's footman stood discreetly behind her, loaded with bandboxes.

Royce grinned at the sight of the purchases piled so precariously in the arms of her footman. *This* was the Liza he knew. "Been shopping, eh?"

"Of course. What else is one to do in such weather?" The wind blew wickedly, and Liza shivered, pulling the edges of her hood closer about her face. "Raspberries and cream!" she exclaimed. "It's cold enough to freeze a fire."

"Yes, is it. I was looking for my carriage, but it appears my coachman has taken the horses for a walk to keep them warm."

Liza peered down the street, loosened tendrils of hair dancing about her cheeks. "Why don't you come with me while you're waiting? I'm just going to that shop on the corner. Meg swears they have the best selection of ribbons in London, though I have my doubts."

"Lead the way. It will be warmer in a shop than out here on the street." He fell into step beside her, her footman still following. They entered the neat building, and he was glad to be out of the frigid wind.

Royce waited patiently while Liza peered at all the goods lying on the tables. She fingered a thick trove of ribbons. "George has chewed all my red ribbons to tatters. He loves that color."

Royce picked up a lavender ribbon. "What about this one? It would look good with your hair."

"Too tame." She took the ribbon and replaced it on the table. "I'm looking for something more vibrant." She picked up a cherry red ribbon and examined it in the light. "You are coming to the theater tonight, aren't you?"

"I wouldn't miss it for the world."

Her gaze settled on him for an instant, a flicker of impatience in their green depths. "Perhaps it is a good thing I ran into you. Royce, please do not quiz Durham too much. He's a bit of an innocent."

Royce frowned. "I mean him no harm. Surely you know that."

"I know. It's just that . . . Well, you and I both have a tendency to say what we think. It can be rather disrupting to those who are not used to it."

"I shall try to restrain myself." Royce found a sea green ribbon that matched her eyes. He laid it across her shoulder. It hung there, against the light brown tendril of hair that had escaped her hood. Meg had accused him of not really seeing Liza, but she was wrong. Royce did see

Liza. He knew the curve of her cheek, the exact color of her eyes, the way her bottom lip stretched just a bit wider than her top one when she smiled. A slow heat crept through his heart as he regarded that very mouth. Lush and inviting, it was perfectly shaped for ki—

"You look frozen to death. Even your nose is red." Liza pulled the ribbon free and dropped it back on the table. "Are you taking ill?"

Wonderful. He was thinking of her lovely mouth and she was wondering if his red nose meant he was catching the ague. Nettled, he shrugged. "I'm perfectly fine, thank you. I was just thinking about something Meg said."

"Oh? What did Meg say?"

There was something particularly beguiling about the way Liza spoke. Simple and direct. Most women tormented a man to death with scarcely thought out words and half-developed thoughts. But then this was Liza, and she was far superior to any woman he'd ever known.

Superior? Since when had he begun thinking of Liza as superior to all other women? He blinked. "Where are you going after you've procured enough ribbons to twine yourself into a tizzy?"

She chuckled. "Home, to dress for the theater. You know, I'm surprised to find you in this part of town. You don't usually shop. Did you have errands for Meg?"

"Lord, no. That's your department as her best friend. I am merely to show up at her balls and dance with all the plain women in sight."

"You never dance with any but women of the first water, diamonds every one."

"That's unfair. I danced with Sara Haughton-Smythe just last week."

"She does have a sad squint." Liza collected the handful of ribbons she'd selected and handed them to a waiting clerk, then pulled open her reticule and took out a coin. "But she is a lovely girl. I hope you dance with her again."

"I shall," Royce said promptly. He was rewarded with a grateful smile that made him feel as if he'd just saved a baby from certain death.

Liza handed her now neatly wrapped ribbons to her footman and waited while he set down her other purchases and then tucked them into a pocket. "There," she said brightly. "I'm all done. Now all we need to do is wait for the carriage. We should be able to see it from here."

Royce followed her to the window. The wind rattled the thin glass in the pane, and small puffs of cold air leaked into the shop.

Liza tightened the string on her reticule. "Where are you off to now?"

"Tattersall's. I wish to see Milford's breakdowns. He had to sell his horses due to gambling debts, and I heard they could be had for a song."

"And I heard they were short on the haunch and easily winded. I thought about bidding on them myself, but I've no wish to be rooked twice in one year."

"When did anyone ever cheat you?"

"When I purchased Halmontford's matched set of grays. Don't you remember?"

"Ah, yes. The front one had an odd kick to his gallop."

"And nearly overset me the first time I had him to harness."

Royce watched as she brushed a strand of hair from her face with her gloved hand. Her hair had always had a tendency to escape every attempt to secure it. He wondered what it would look like loose, flowing down her back. To his shock, his unruly imagination went a step further and stripped her of clothing. She was long-limbed and well proportioned, her skin smooth and creamy, her breasts high and—*no*. Those were thoughts better left unthought.

He shifted uneasily and tried to remember what they'd been talking about. "What did you do with that horse? Did you send him to the tannery?"

"He's in my barn, eating his head off and growing absurdly fat. I can't decide *what* to do with him. He's a beautiful animal, and though I have my groom take him out for a ride every day, it isn't enough exercise for a high-strung animal."

"Sell him."

"A horse with a lumpy gait? I'd rather cut off my arm. I'm not like you, able to ignore my conscience at a whim."

"When have I ignored my conscience?"

"Last summer, when you played the Contessa d'Aviant at cards. You counted the queens and knew she couldn't possibly draw the card she needed to win."

"Counting cards is not cheating."

"No, but you knew she could not cover her debts and yet you allowed her to wager an incredible sum and then you offered to allow her to work off her debt by—" A delicious color bloomed in Liza's cheeks. "I heard the rumors and I know what happened."

Bloody hell, who had told her about that? Royce found he could not quite meet her gaze. "You shouldn't listen to gossip," he said, and then winced because he sounded so damned *old*. And somehow, it seemed a happening worse than death for Liza to think him old.

"Royce, you know me." A half-shy, half-devilish grin touched her lips. "I love a good gossip. One hears the most deliciously naughty things."

Royce wondered why he'd never noticed how lovely she looked when she blushed. He resolved then and there to make her blush as often as he could. "Yes, well, whoever filled your head with such a ridiculous story should be shot."

"I notice you aren't denying it. You have to admit you were shameless with the poor contessa."

He had been shameless. But it wasn't as if Regina hadn't enjoyed the encounter. In fact, the wager had added a certain piquancy to their subsequent meetings. They even continued seeing each other long after the contessa had earned off her losses.

Liza peered out the window for her carriage. "That wasn't the only time you ignored your conscience. There was also the time you asked that actress to—"

"We weren't speaking of me," Royce said hastily, "but of your horse. The fat one eating his head off in your stables. Remember him?"

Her expression softened. "Prinny is a fine horse."

"Prinny? You named him after the Prince?"

"I had to call him something. Halmontford gave him a name that was entirely inappropriate."

"What?"

To Royce's delight, Liza's cheeks pinkened again, this time even more deeply. "I'm not telling," she said firmly. "Suffice it to say Prinny is a *much* better name." She met Royce's gaze and gave a wry grin. "At least it is until the Prince hears of it, which will not happen unless he strolls into my stable and asks."

Royce wondered what it was that made Liza unique. It wasn't just her clothing, though that was unusual in itself. It was something more. Perhaps it was the intelligence in her green eyes, or the way her face crinkled up when she laughed, but whatever it was, it roused in him the most peculiar desire to grin and never stop.

Yet Liza wasn't smiling now. Instead her brow was furrowed in thought. "I really should purchase an estate in the country somewhere. I could send Prinny out to pasture then. It would be much nicer than leaving him locked in my pitifully small stables."

"You can't purchase an entire estate just so you have a place for one fat horse."

"No?" she said, obviously unconvinced. "It's just . . . poor Prinny." Suddenly she brightened. "Perhaps I should ask my friend Lord Durham to take him for me. He has quite a large amount of farmland and he is certainly willing to—"

"I'll take him."

Royce blinked. Dear God, was that his voice? How in the world had he come to offer to care for a fat, slovenly, ill-gaited horse? Yet he had. Anything to keep Liza from indebting herself to Durham.

Liza should have looked happy—thankful, even. Instead, she regarded him with disbelief. "*You* would take my horse?"

"Of course. I have more than enough pastureland at Rotherwood. I daresay my head groom would welcome an addition to the stables. All I have are a few hunters."

She appeared astounded. "That's . . . that's quite the nicest thing you've ever done. Are you well?"

He made an exasperated noise. "Of course I'm well! How can you even wonder? As for that being the nicest thing I've ever done, what about the time I drove you to Brighton so you could visit that Terrance woman? You were dying to go as I recall, and no one would take you."

"Her name is Lillith Terrance; her husband is an admiral. And if I remember correctly, the only reason you offered to drive me was because you needed an excuse to go there anyway. Something about a woman named . . . oh, what was it? Olivia, perhaps?"

Royce opened his mouth to refute Liza's claims when a vague memory tickled his conscience. Oh yes. The fair Olivia. She'd been a week's worth of entertainment, now that he thought about it. But little else.

He suddenly saw himself through Liza's eyes. His entire life seemed filled with short-lived entertainments. Some brunette, some blond, some redheaded. All perfectly lush and willing to flirt, pass the time, or romp in bed, depending on their circumstances. They'd all been attractive, merry, and, for some reason or another, completely unsuitable.

Royce caught Liza's knowing gaze. But instead of condemnation, a laugh lurked in her eyes, her lips pressed together as if she was trying to keep from falling into a spate of mad giggles.

"Don't even say it," he said testily. "Your memory is too damned accurate for my peace of mind."

"Poor thing," she said, chuckling all the same.

The footman appeared. "The carriage has arrived."

"Thank goodness," she exclaimed. She went out into the cold, Royce close behind her.

He assisted her into her coach, waving off the footman who lingered to help.

Liza leaned down to smile at him, ignoring the cold wind that whipped across her and blew her hood from her head. "Thank you for accompanying me. I hate to shop alone."

"It was my pleasure, though I am beginning to believe I owe you an apology for embroiling you in my contretemps over the years."

"Whatever for? I enjoyed every last one." She sent him a frank look and hesitated. Finally she said, "We've always been close, haven't we?"

He took her hand in his and pulled off the glove, exposing her bared fingers. Long and elegant, they were unadorned, yet another characteristic that was all hers. He lifted her fingers and brushed his lips over her knuckles, savoring the warmth of her skin against his lips.

For an instant, desire pulsed through him, hot and ready. It took him completely by surprise. Startled, he looked up into her eyes and realized with a shock that she felt the same thing.

She yanked her fingers free. "I—I—that is not necessary." Where she'd blushed before, now she looked positively ablaze, her cheeks so red it appeared she had been slapped. "Thank you for your offer to take Prinny."

"I didn't just offer," he said with forced lightness, stepping back from the carriage. It seemed imperative that he put some space between them. "I'll send a groom this week to take him to Rotherwood."

"Thank you, Royce."

"And thank you for a lovely afternoon." Without giving her time to respond, he closed the carriage door and nodded to the coachman to go on.

Strange as it sounded, Royce was beginning to believe that some evil spirit was at work, making him think and feel things he shouldn't think and feel. And now he was the proud caretaker of a fat, odd-gaited horse. He supposed he was just lucky Liza didn't want to be rid of George or he'd have ended up with a very feisty monkey.

Shaking his head at his own folly, Royce pulled his collar up about his ears and walked down the street, trying hard not to watch Liza's carriage as it rumbled out of sight.

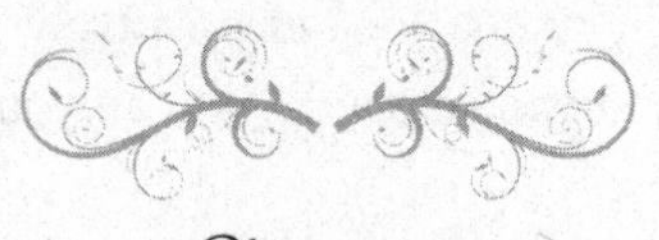

Chapter 4

Sir Royce Pemberley. Ah, now there is a man that This Author can write about for weeks without ever repeating a word.

No, no, that is not quite accurate. Rake, dashing, rogue, wicked, and devilish would surely worm their way into the columns over and over again.

But while the words might be repeated, the actual stories would not. Sir Royce's exploits are legendary, and yet he always manages to evade any actual censure due to his almost lethally charming personality.

Truly, the only woman who seems immune to his smile (aside, of course, from his sister) is Miss Liza Pritchard, about whom This Author could also write for weeks without ever repeating a word.

Quite the couple they make, and certainly an exemplary example to those who insist that the males and females of our species cannot be friends. Indeed they were spied together, shopping near Bond Street on Saturday afternoon.

And then again, that night at Drury Lane, although Miss Pritchard had been officially escorted by Lord Durham.

Lady Whistledown's Society Papers,
31 January 1814

The Theatre Royal was a-hum with excitement as appreciative theatergoers, seeking amusement for the long cold winter nights, filled the boxes and packed the pits. Everyone was dressed in his or her finest finery, and the house buzzed with excited voices, most of them talking right over the opening farce.

"I vow, but I cannot wait to see this Edmund Kean!" Meg said. "Lady Bancroft says he is a genius." She cast her eyes toward the box that bordered theirs, then said in a low, excited voice to Liza, who sat directly behind her, "Did you hear the Earl of Renminster speak to me a moment ago? He promised to attend my ball!"

Liza glanced to where Meg's cousin, Miss Susannah Ballister, spoke quietly to the earl. Though Liza had had the opportunity to see Miss Ballister on occasion and thought her quite a handsome girl, Susannah looked particularly pretty this evening. Liza grinned. "I daresay Renminster will be sure to come to your ball if you invite Miss Ballister."

Meg's eyes widened. "Do you think—oh no! He couldn't possibly—not after, well, you know what happened."

"Yes, but that was a while ago. And she is certainly a well-behaved young lady. And lovely to boot."

Meg's chin bobbed up and down in agreement. "Indeed, she is. She's such a wonderful—" Her attention suddenly riveted on a box across the theater. "Oh my! There's Lady Anne Bishop sitting with Lord Howard. Do you think they will make a match of it?"

Liza nodded absently and set her fan on the empty seat beside her. Usually she enjoyed a good gossip, but tonight she found her attention wandering. What she wanted was to ask Lord Durham if he enjoyed the theater and what were some of his favorite plays. Perhaps *that* was an area they might have in common. For some reason, it had become imperative that she find as many commonalities as she could.

But it was quite impossible to speak to Durham, for he was deep in conversation with Lord Shelbourne over the merits of a farm taxation bill due before the House of Lords. She cast a morose glance his way. Must every topic always focus on his blasted cows? She was going to have to learn to like bovines. It was a depressing thought.

Sighing, Liza looked down at where her new red slippers peeked from beneath the edge of her green silk gown. The slippers were embroidered with gold thread and sparkled as shamelessly as the rubies encircling her throat and dangling from her wrists. Most women wouldn't have worn green silk with rubies, but Liza liked the contrast. It reminded her of Christmas, and that could never be a bad thing.

"You look far too serious. Looking forward to Kean's performance?"

Liza looked up, startled to find Royce leaning so close. His eyes seemed a darker blue than usual, his gaze so direct that a skittering of heat flashed through her. She sent a self-conscious glance past him to Durham, but now Meg was monopolizing the young lord's attention. Reluctantly, Liza pulled her attention back to Royce. "I wasn't thinking of the play; I was admiring my bracelet." She held it up. "It glimmers quite loudly in this light."

His gaze slowly slid from her eyes, down to her chin, lingering a halting moment on her mouth. "That's a lovely bracelet," he said, his voice unaccountably low and husky. The sound dripped over her and rippled across her, leaving a trail of delicious goose bumps.

As if aware of how he'd affected her, he smiled then—a tantalizingly lopsided smile, his white teeth briefly appearing between his firm lips. "You look lovely tonight, too. Every bit as lovely as your bracelet."

Liza could only stare at him. Good God, was *this* how he spoke to the women he pursued? No wonder so many of them fell beneath his spell. The thought sharpened the edges of her already frayed nerves. "Stop that."

He lifted his brows. "Stop what?"

"You know what—trying to make me feel—" *Pretty*. She couldn't say that. Anything but that. "You're trying to discomfort me."

"No, I wasn't. I was, however, going to tell you that I've made arrangements for Prinny. I will send a groom to your house tomorrow to fetch him out to my estate."

Liza knew she should feel grateful, and indeed she was. Very grateful, in fact. But mixed in with the grateful feeling was something else. Something larger and infinitely more confusing.

She tried not to look down at her shoulder where it grazed Royce's. Heat slithered up her arm and down her collarbone, sparking an excited thump from her heart. She realized with dismay that somehow in the last few weeks, she'd lost her immunity to Royce.

Not that she'd ever really been immune to him—who could be?

But she'd prided herself on not reacting to him at every turn. Now she couldn't even look at him without some sort of tremulous tingle disrupting her thoughts. She moved her shoulder impatiently. "Must you sit so close?"

His gaze darkened. "Liza, what's wrong?"

"You are crowding me and I don't like it. Please move away." She knew she was being unreasonable. The chairs were closely set and Royce couldn't have kept from brushing against her even if he tried. But somehow that didn't matter. She just wanted him gone. Now.

He leaned toward her just a tiny bit more. "Perhaps I *like* sitting this close."

Liza refused to budge. Life had shoved her about enough this week, and she wasn't about to let Royce do it, too. Instead of moving away, she leaned forward, exerting her own pressure against his shoulder. *"Move."*

A flicker of something lit his eyes, something more than anger. A strange mixture of humor and interest. "You're the most infuriating woman I've ever met."

Considering the thousands of women Royce knew, that was hardly a compliment. Thinking of those thousands of women set her teeth even more on edge, and she pressed harder.

He laughed and shifted in his chair, matching her efforts without hesitation. For several moments, neither spoke, both intent on their silent battle.

Liza suddenly realized that if Royce moved, she'd probably shoot right past him and land headfirst in Durham's lap. What would she do then? But she couldn't quit. For one brief shining moment, she just wanted to win. At something.

She balled her hands into fists and made sure her fake smile stayed on her lips in case anyone happened to glance their way. "I hope this isn't the way you treat your amoratas," she said through her clenched teeth.

He choked. "Amor—damn, Liza! What will you say next?" Slowly, he relaxed. "You have no idea how I treat anyone, much less my amoratas."

Liza realized that he was no longer pressing against her. She'd won, by God! Her spirits lifted momentarily.

But before she could crow her victory, Royce said in a low voice,

"*This* is how I treat a woman I want." He reached in front of her, his arm brushing against the lace front of her gown as he picked up her discarded fan from where it sat on the seat beside her. He moved slowly, his arm rubbing intimately against her, making her breasts peak beneath her silk gown, her skin burn as if the sun kissed it.

Liza gripped the arms of her chair, her breath suspended as Royce leaned back in his seat. It seemed a slow, delicious, and thoroughly agonizing hour passed before he finally removed his arm. In reality, it had been but a moment. Still, her body clung to the feeling, lingered over it, savoring every second.

Royce held the fan before her startled gaze and swung it back and forth, then dropped it into her lap.

She looked down at the fan and tried to find her breath. Her entire body quivered with a strange heat. "Why—who—I—" Her cheeks were so hot that she was certain she'd explode into flames at any moment. "You are impossible!" she managed to hiss. "What if someone saw?"

"No one did," he said, his voice a bit rough. There was a look in his eyes she'd never seen before. Something dangerous and thrilling at the same time.

Liza cast about for something to say. Something that would show the braggart that she was completely unaffected by his touch. But nothing came. All she could do was look into those damnably gorgeous blue eyes and wish she'd never pushed Royce so far.

Royce, meanwhile, was trying to figure out how a simple touch had muddled him so badly he couldn't utter a coherent sentence. He'd been with swarms of women, engaged in flirtations too numerous to count, and generally had whomever he wanted, whenever he wanted. He'd let Liza's infernal teasing force him into treating her in a way he never had before. And in that moment, something changed. She'd gone from being a protected, beloved friend to a maddeningly challenging woman. One, he found to his deep dismay, that he wanted badly. So badly he ached with need.

Bloody hell, I want Liza. A thick fog of desire swirled through him and he had to force himself to breathe. He wanted Liza, his best friend, the one woman who really knew who and what he was. The idea was astounding. Disturbing. And utterly impossible. What the devil was he supposed to do now?

"Sir Royce, did you enjoy the farce?" Durham beamed down at them. "I thought it was particularly well executed."

Royce had to clear his throat before he could speak. "Ah, yes. Yes, the farce was very well done."

The bumpkin wasn't paying Royce the least heed, but was staring at Liza like a lovesick puppy. "And you, Liza? Did you enjoy it?"

Royce glowered. Since when had Liza allowed Durham use of her Christian name? Royce cut a hard glance at her.

She lifted her chin in response. "Lord Durham asked if he might address me by my given name and I assured him he could."

Royce had quite a bit to say about that, but Meg interrupted. "Liza, come look!" She was sitting on the edge of her chair, trying to look down into the pits without appearing to do so, which would be unaccountably vulgar. "Lord Darington is in the pits. At least, I *think* it is Lord Darington."

Liza jumped up with an alacrity that Royce was certain had more to do with getting away from him than anything else. She made her way to Meg's side and peered down, leaning way over the balcony. "It can't be Darington. He hasn't been to Town in ages."

"I know, but I'm almost sure I saw him before he disappeared into the pit." Meg stretched up, trying to see over the railing without leaving her seat. "Of course, if it is Darington, he wouldn't be seated down there, would he?"

"Pardon me," Lord Durham said, his heavy brows drawn low. "Liza, my dear, perhaps you shouldn't lean over the balcony quite so far."

A normal woman would have been pleased at such solicitous concern, but this wasn't a normal woman. Royce had to hide a grin when Liza sent Durham an exasperated glance.

"I'm fine," she said in a flat tone. "I have my foot hooked in a chair." She turned away then and leaned even further over the railing. "Lud, yes, that's Darington! I'd recognize him anywhere. I should wave hello."

"Liza!" Meg gasped. "Don't wave. It's vulgar. People will talk."

"I don't care." Liza tilted her head to one side. "He looks a bit thinner. I'd heard he'd been ill."

Meg stretched up in her seat as far as she could, trying desperately to *see* over the railing without actually *looking* over the railing. "Is he still as handsome as ever?"

"Lord, yes," Liza returned. "And more so." She waved to Darington. It wasn't a petite, delicate wave, but a huge whoosh of her arm. Her bracelet flashed in the lamplight and glittered gaily. Several older women in one of the neighboring boxes appeared scandalized, but Liza ignored them all, turning to Meg to say with a grin, "Look! He bowed in return. I wonder what's kept him out of Town?"

Royce's spirits were buoyed when he noticed Durham still frowning, only more so now. Well! At least Durham would see what he was in for; Liza never followed the dictates of politeness. She made her own rules, and so far, society had allowed her full rein.

"She's a bit impulsive," Royce said, trying not to grin.

Durham shot him a considering look. "Miss Pritchard needs a man's influence in her life. Once that has occurred, I'm certain her natural feminine delicacy will return."

"I'm not certain Liza has ever possessed 'natural feminine delicacy.' " Royce met Durham's disapproving gaze with a shrug. "She has led a very free, unfettered existence. It's possible she enjoys her freedom and has no wish to exchange it for any other state."

"No woman likes being completely independent, no matter what she says," Durham replied with a self-satisfied smile that made Royce's humor evaporate. "Sir Royce, shall we fetch some lemonade for the ladies? There is just enough time before the play begins."

Perhaps it would be wise to move this conversation out of the box, Royce decided. There were things he'd like to say, none of which could be freely aired with Liza sitting only a few feet away. "Of course. Let us go."

No one seemed to notice them leaving. Meg was chattering loudly to Liza, while Shelbourne settled into his seat as if planning a nice snooze.

Susannah, meanwhile, was engaged in speaking to Renminster over the partition.

Royce held the curtain and allowed Durham to pass through.

Liza's beau was dressed like a country squire. From his plain, functional boots to the faint sheen of perspiration on his upper lip, he looked uncomfortable and out of place. Quite the opposite of Liza, who, in her unmatched clothing and sparkling jewelry, always seemed to fit, no matter where she was or what she wore.

What *was* Liza thinking? The man was little better than a farmer. He would drag her to the country and bury her there, a fate worse than death for someone like Liza, who thrived in the excitement and elegance of London.

As they made their way to the routunda, Durham cleared his throat. "Sir Royce, I wanted to speak to you about a matter of great importance."

Royce found a table filled with champagne glasses. He offered one to Durham who refused with a brief shake of his head. Royce chose one for himself and took a sip. "I'm not sure why you'd have anything of importance to say to me, but by all means, speak away."

Durham pulled out a handkerchief and mopped his brow. "I must apologize for seeming a little nervous, but I . . . Sir Royce, I wanted to talk to you about Miss Pritchard. She sees you as part of her family. Almost as a father—"

Royce choked, champagne going down his throat and up his nose at the same time.

Durham gave a muffled curse, then pounded Royce on the back, causing more damage than the champagne.

Royce held up a hand in an effort to stop the onslaught. "I think I can breathe now. I was just—Liza does *not* see me as a father."

"An older brother, then," Durham said easily. "Ever since I first met Liza . . . well, you know what she is. She's unique. Strong willed. And has a delightful turn for business, which could be handy if I wish to expand my farm. She's exactly what I've been looking for in a wife."

Royce's chest began to burn with something other than champagne gone wrong. The man was looking for a wife. And he'd settled on Liza.

Damn the man for his impertinence. Royce barely managed to keep his tone civil. "Durham, have you said anything to Liza about this?"

"Not yet. The time hasn't been right." A smug smile curved the farmer's mouth. "I believe I am fairly safe in saying that Liza does not view my suit with indifference. Sir Royce, you see Liza every day, so you are immune to her, but for me . . . she's everything I've ever wanted. She's wonderful."

The man appeared completely besotted. Royce finished his champagne in one swallow and set the glass on the table, then grabbed another. He tossed it back without tasting a drop.

Durham watched, shifting from one foot to the other. "Sir Royce, are you well?"

The champagne was working its magic, and slowly, Royce's chest and throat loosened. "I'm fine. Just answer one question, Durham."

"Anything. I'm at your disposal."

"What do you have in common with Liza?"

"In common? Well, we—" The man clasped his hands behind his back and stared at the ornate ceiling, his thick brows lowered. "She, ah . . . hm. In common. I hadn't really—in common, eh?"

Royce waited for the man to realize the dismal truth; the only thing he and Liza had in common was . . . nothing. Not a damned thing.

Durham's gaze suddenly focused. "Liza loves animals and I have a farm with over a thousand cows."

Cows? Royce shook his head. "Liza loves horses and monkeys. Actually, to be more precise, she likes horses and one *particular* monkey."

"I have horses, too," Durham said hurriedly. "Several, in fact."

Plow horses, every one. Royce would wager money on it.

"But my cows . . . Sir Royce, do you know much about cattle?" Durham's eyes positively glowed. "My cows are specially bred. My father began to develop a slightly larger breed before I was born and I have carried on his work." A faint color touched Durham's face. "This may sound silly, but my cows are heirlooms in a way. They are my most prized possessions."

Good Lord, the man was serious. Royce tried to imagine Liza in the country, surrounded by cows and perhaps a dozen or so thick-waisted children, all carrying butter churns or some such nonsense. The thought was so nauseating that he had to press a hand to his stomach.

Bloody hell, it was madness. And he'd be damned if he'd just stand aside while Durham ruined Liza's life. Liza *and* Royce's lives, for she was *his* best friend and he couldn't live without her.

Thus it was that he heard himself saying in a firm voice, "Lord Durham, I fear only one thing."

"What's that?"

"It's—" Royce bit his lip as if uncertain to continue. He watched Durham out of the corner of his eye, waiting.

The man's expression darkened with concern. "Come, Sir Royce, we are to be family, for I know Liza thinks of you and Meg as such. You can tell me anything."

"Oh. Well! If we're to be family, I suppose I should at least mention . . . I was just wondering how your cows will take to Liza's monkey? George can be quite fierce when he chooses. He bites, you know."

Durham blanched. "Bites?"

"Indeed. Of course, he only does so when frightened. But a small monkey like that is bound to be frightened of a cow. Especially a very large cow."

"Oh dear. I've heard it said that a monkey's bite can be very painful."

"In some instances, I believe they cause death. And if he began to prey on your cows . . ." Royce supposed he should feel bad laying so much on George's tiny shoulders, but he felt he had to do something. Something dire. Something to save Liza. He turned away and replaced his empty glass on the table behind him, wondering if he'd yet said enough.

Durham was silent a moment, mulling this over. After a bit, he said, "That creature has always made me a bit nervous. Perhaps Miss Pritchard can be persuaded to leave him in London."

"Never. She's mad about that silly animal."

"Oh dear. I was hoping . . ." Durham collected himself with a visible effort. "Well! That certainly makes one think. But no matter. I'm certain we'll be able to work something out. Sir Royce, I know you and Lady Shelbourne are quite close to Liza and I find myself . . . that is, I want you to know that my intentions are entirely honorable."

Royce fisted his hands and shoved them into his coat pockets.

Unaware of how close he was to being beaten into dust, the farmer continued, "Furthermore, I am well able to take care of Liza. She will want for nothing," he said proudly. "Sir Royce, is there anything you wish to know about my circumstances?"

Lord, yes. Royce wanted to know how Durham would deal with Liza's penchant for doing as she pleased. And her sad addiction to shopping. What would she shop for out in the country? Certainly they wouldn't have the quality of clothing she was used to. And where would she get her shoes? Certainly they'd have to come to London once a week, perhaps more.

But most importantly, Royce wanted to know how the hell was he going to live without Liza. She was such an intrinsic part of his life—always there for him, no matter what ailed him. He looked down at the champagne glasses on the table, watching the bubbles dance to the surface, bright dots of light that disappeared the instant they hit the surface. "How often will you come to Town once you are married?"

"Several times a year, and I daresay we'll stay for a week or so each time."

Only a week? Royce didn't think he'd ever heard a more horrible statement. He racked his brain to think of something else he could say about Liza to show Durham how they didn't suit. Something to make the besotted fool realize that marrying Liza was the last thing he should do. "Have you mentioned this to Liza? She may have a differing opinion, and she's not a woman to take suggestions well. She's as stubborn as they come."

"So is my mother. I'm quite adept at dealing with strong females."

"Liza is strong for a reason—she's had to deal with life's difficulties in a way few understand."

"Which is why one should never give a female too many decisions to make. It goes to their head."

Royce lifted his brows. "Liza *likes* making decisions."

"Only because harsh circumstances have prevented her from developing in the delicate way nature intended. Fortunately I'm blessed with an affectionate mother who will be more than happy to show my wife all the courtesies necessary to correct such unfortunate tendencies."

"Liza will be glad to discover that," Royce said, gritting his teeth.

"Sir Royce, you need not fear. Miss Pritchard and I will suit very well. In fact"—the man preened a bit—"I've decided to give Liza a very special wedding gift. Her very own bull."

Royce picked up another glass of champagne and took a hurried drink. "A—a bull. How unique."

"I haven't told Liza yet. I thought it might make a good surprise."

"Oh yes, I think that would be an excellent surprise. I'm surprised right now, in fact. What, ah, is she to do with this bull?"

"Raise it. If she tends it closely, it could easily grow to be worth two or three hundred pounds."

Which was about how much Liza spent on shoes in a week. Royce had to swallow a reluctant sigh. God, but he'd give his best pair of grays to see Liza's face when she found out she was to receive her very own bull. But of course, the only way that would happen was if she lost her mind completely and agreed to marry Durham.

And that, Royce decided, would never happen. Not while he was breathing. "Durham, are you aware of Liza's worth?"

The younger man shrugged. "If you are speaking about her person, then I can honestly say I find her priceless."

"I was talking about her fortune. She's a very wealthy woman."

To Royce's surprise, an actual shadow passed over Durham's face. "I know. But I will not let it be a detriment. Once we are married, we will live on my income alone."

"You would? But . . . why?"

"Sir Royce, I am not a man who could accept money from my wife. If Liza loves me, she will accept that. Besides"—Durham pinkened—"I hoped she might put her funds in trust for whatever children we have."

Royce turned away under the pretext of setting down his now empty glass. His mind whirled. Liza married. Liza buried in the country. Liza with Durham's thick-necked children. Good God, this was worse than he'd thought. After a moment, he managed to say, "It sounds as if the play is about to begin. I'm sure everyone is wondering what has kept us."

They procured lemonade for the ladies and then made their way back to the box, Durham talking animatedly about how fond he was of

London. The pompous ass looked pleased with himself—and he should be, Royce decided sourly. If things worked out for the young peer, he would have secured a wife of infinite intelligence, one guaranteed never to bore him, or wear him down with endless conversations about dressmakers and which pelisses were in style.

She might, of course, argue with him about politics, or the best way to feather a tight corner in her high perch phaeton. And she'd been known to stomp about when she was angered. But she was never out of temper long, and she always came back with a smile.

A pang of something uncomfortably like envy went through Royce. Good God, was he actually *jealous* of a cow farmer? It wasn't possible. Yet it was with a very heavy heart that he took his seat in the box and watched Durham monopolize Liza to such an extent that even Meg and Miss Ballister looked impressed.

Royce raked a hand through his hair and wished he was anywhere else but there. God, he'd never hated the theater so much. Still, he felt a sense of relief when the lights finally lowered and the play began, cutting off Lord Durham's effusive compliments.

Chapter 5

Preparations have already begun for the Shelbourne Valentine's Day ball, to be held (quite obviously) on Monday the fourteenth. This Author has heard rumors that Lady Shelbourne plans a fourteen-piece orchestra, five hundred pots of roses (of pink, white, and red), and ten separate refreshment tables.

Where she plans to fit all of that in her ballroom, This Author hasn't a clue, but such accoutrements will certainly guarantee Lady Shelbourne the crush that every hostess desires. Even if only half of her invitations are accepted, the ballroom will be packed.

Although one can hardly call a party a success when the flowerpots have stolen the dance floor from the guests.

LADY WHISTLEDOWN'S SOCIETY PAPERS,
31 January 1814

Tuesday morning, Meg sat at her escritoire trying desperately to figure out where to place a twelve-piece orchestra *and* three hundred pots of roses *and* eighteen refreshment tables so that her ballroom didn't look quite so cramped.

The door opened and Royce strolled in.

Meg hopped up from her desk, glad for any interruption she could find. "Royce! What brings you—"

He stalked right past her and took an impatient turn about the room. The early morning light revealed that his cravat was hastily knotted, his hair mussed as if he'd been raking his hands through it, and his eyes underlined with deep circles. "Dear God," she said, genuinely alarmed. "What has happened?"

"Liza has—" He clamped his mouth shut and took another swift turn, this time stopping in front of the window. He stood for a second, his gaze fixed unseeingly out at the snowy vista, before he turned back and stalked about the room again.

"Royce, have a seat and tell me—"

"Damn it, I cannot be still! Meg, if Liza—" He broke off, obviously in too much of a passion to speak.

Meg lifted her brows. She'd *never* seen Royce in such a state. Nothing ever seemed to bother him and, if she admitted the truth, life had been too easy on her handsome brother. He'd never had to worry about his income, and women practically threw themselves at him. But what made it worse was that Royce didn't find this plentitude the least disconcerting. He was perfectly satisfied to flirt away his life, having no goals, no desires, and leaving a trail of broken hearts so long that one could make a footpath out of them.

It was really most distressing, Meg decided, thinking of the large number of her friends who had sat in this very room and sobbed aloud, crying over her brother's indifference. But it was equally distressing to see him so uncharacteristically overwrought. "Let me ring for a hot cup of tea."

"To hell with the tea." Royce turned on his heel and paced to the window and back. "We have to do something about Liza. This . . . thing with Durham, it's far more serious than either you or I realized."

Meg's heart sank. She'd had hopes for Durham, especially after last night. "Oh dear. He is a fortune hunter just as we suspected."

"No," Royce said heavily. "No, he's not that."

"He's not a fortune hunter? Then what did you find out about that makes him an ineligible *parti*?"

Royce stopped a moment and opened his mouth as if to say something, but then closed it just as abruptly, and resumed his pacing. He seemed caught in some sort of internal turmoil, striding angrily up and down the room, raking a hand through his hair and making it stand even more on end. Finally, he stopped before Meg and said, "Durham doesn't intend on touching Liza's funds. He feels it would be dishonorable. He doesn't even want her to use them to support herself."

"That's . . . that's good news, isn't it?"

"No," Royce said in a vehement voice. "Meg, he is wrong for her. If they marry, he will expect her to live in his house in the country."

"And?"

Royce's brows snapped lower. "Isn't that enough? Can you imagine Liza living anywhere other than London? This is her home. It's all she's ever known."

Meg struggled to understand. "Yes, but I've known plenty of couples who—"

"Furthermore," Royce said without stopping. "Durham is not a man to appreciate independence. He will do what he can to depress her spirits. We cannot allow that to happen."

"Liza *is* a bit unruly at times," Meg conceded fairly. "She should never have waved to Darington last night."

"Why not? She didn't harm a soul. I daresay no one even noticed it."

Meg wasn't so sure about that. Still . . . She glanced at her brother, noticing the white lines about his mouth. This was a most unusual turn. Something else must have happened. She bit her lip and tossed about for an answer. "Royce, did you speak to Lady Birlington? She knows Durham's family. Maybe she—"

"Oh, I spoke to her," Royce said in a grim tone. "She believes him above reproach, though she doesn't think the same of you and me."

"What could she possibly think about us?"

"That we have kept Liza from marrying by chasing off every eligible male."

"We have not," Meg said hotly. "We've never kept a truly eligible man from Liza. All we did was remove the ineligible ones."

That *was* all they'd done, wasn't it? A tiny niggling of doubt tickled Meg. She frowned, trying to remember the reasons they'd dismissed various men who'd burst into Liza's life.

Royce waved a hand in the air. "Yes, you and I are painted black as sin, while Lady Birlington suggests that Liza might *like* fortune hunters."

"Liza has too much good sense to like fortune hunters," Meg said absently. "She doesn't like fribbles, either; she's never given you the time of day."

Royce's pacing came to an abrupt halt; his eyes blazed. Meg recoiled a little.

Never had she seen such a look on her brother's face. She gave an uncertain laugh. "I—I didn't mean that the way it sounded. I just meant—" She bit off the word, trying desperately to sort through her thoughts. After a moment, she said slowly, "Royce, do you think perhaps Lady Birlington is right? Have we chased off all the eligible men in our determination to protect Liza?"

"Of course we haven't."

"But . . . if Durham is not a fortune hunter and the worst you can discover about him is that he wishes his wife to live with him in the country, then . . ." Meg shrugged, though she kept her gaze on her brother's face. "I don't know how we can stop Liza."

"If this Durham fellow loved her, he would accept her for what she is—town life, fortune, even George."

"Her monkey? She loves that creature."

"Durham cares more for his precious cows." Royce raked a hand through his hair. The last two nights had been sheer hell, and this morning didn't seem to be any better. After leaving the theater, Royce had returned home only to find he couldn't sit still, couldn't eat, couldn't sleep. Over and over, he'd relived the moment when he'd brushed his arm against Liza's chest. His reaction had been purely physical. Hot and instant.

Could he feel that way about a mere friend? Bloody hell, what *did* he feel about Liza? The answer sent his mind spinning. There were a very few, precious things that were certainties in his life, and one of them was Liza. That she understood him, sometimes better than himself. That she would always be there. Always and forever.

But now, Durham was determined to rip Liza out of Royce's life. *That selfish bastard.* "Meg, what kind of marriage is based on changing the other person?"

To his surprise, she didn't immediately answer. She pursed her lips and tilted her head to one side. "In a way, *all* marriages are based on change. Just being in love changes you. At least, it makes you want to change, and usually for the better." She sent him a dire look. "That's something for *you* to think about, dearest brother, if you ever decide to wed."

"I don't want to marry and I don't want to change," he said firmly. The problem was, he didn't want Liza to marry or change, either. He wanted them to be the same as they always were. What could be wrong with that?

A flash of irritation marred Meg's expression. "Royce, if you don't wish to change, then don't. Die old and alone. Fortunately, Liza has decided that path is not for her. Furthermore—" Meg stopped, a dawning light in her eyes. "I'm going to do what I can to help her win Lord Durham!"

Good God, no! What was this? "Liza doesn't need your help."

"Nonsense. It's the least we can do, especially if Lady Birlington is right." Meg bit her lip. "What if we *have* kept all the eligible bachelors from Liza?"

"Would you have had her marry that Handley-Finch fellow? The one who owed so much money he was on the verge of being tossed in gaol?"

"Well, no."

"What about the man from Devon, the one who'd had two previous wives who had both died under mysterious circumstances?"

"There was never any proof."

Royce snorted, so Meg added, "What about the widower from America, Mr. Nash? He was very pleasant and was quite heartbroken when you hinted him off."

"He had four children. Liza would have gone mad. She can barely handle George. Look, Meg, we're Liza's family. It's our job to make certain she's happy."

"But whose job is it to decide *what* will make her happy? Royce, unless you have a serious, specific objection to Durham, then it is our duty to help her attach his interest so firmly that he will ask her to marry him without delay."

"How? By making her into something she's not?" Royce turned away from Meg and went to the window. He crossed his arms over his chest and leaned against the frame, wondering irritably why he'd come to Meg anyway. She was too bubbleheaded to understand the importance of what was happening. Outside, the wintry street sparkled under the blue sky, cold air seeping around the windowpane. "I refuse to help Liza ruin her life. If you cared about her, you'd do the same."

Meg sniffed. "You're just upset because you finally realized there is a woman immune to your charms and she was right under your nose the whole time."

"Nonsense!" he scoffed. "I'm not upset; I'm worried. That's an entirely different emotion. Furthermore, Liza is not immune to me whatsoever. And I'm not immune to her—"

"What?" Meg's mouth dropped open, her eyes wide. She leaped from the settee and was at Royce's side in a trice. "What happened? Tell me now!"

Royce cursed his rash tongue. "Nothing happened. I just leaned forward at the theater and my arm brushed—" He passed his hand over his eyes. "Forget it."

"Forget it? If Liza and you have a physical attraction after all, then that's all you needed since you already lo—"

"Meg, do *not* read more into this than is there." God, how he hated this! He should have known better than to tell his sister anything.

She pursed her lips, gazing at him with a damned knowing look that made him want to shout with vexation. "I see what it is," she said slowly. "You don't want Liza, but you don't want anyone else to have her, either."

"Bloody hell! I didn't say that."

"You didn't need to." Meg drew herself up to her full five-foot-one-inch height and assumed a lofty air. "Royce, you have made up my mind."

"What?"

"I am going to Liza's and I am going to offer to help her ensnare this Lord Durham. I am going to make her the best dressed, most beautiful, most sought after woman in all of London. I can see it now—she'll be the most talked about woman at my Valentine's ball. Men will line up for miles just for one dance with her."

"She doesn't dance," Royce said, wondering if he could convince

Shelbourne that Meg was having an acute attack of nerves and should be shipped off to the country at the first opportunity.

"She will when I'm finished with her. If you want to help, which you should, considering how boorish you've been, then I will let you. I daresay it would be quite impossible to obtain the services of a good dance instructor at this late date anyway."

"I don't want any part of this."

"Fine," Meg said airily, drifting toward the door. "I'll find someone else. Perhaps Lord Durham would be willing to assist us. That might make more sense anyway, for certainly there is nothing so intimate as dancing the waltz. Just picture it, Durham with his arms about Liz—"

"Don't start throwing them together! They see too much of each other as it is." He scowled at his sister's too wide grin. "You are leaving me no choice, are you?"

"Not one."

"Damn you," he said bitterly. When she didn't respond, he made an impatient noise. "Very well. I'll be your bloody dance instructor."

Meg gifted him with a pleasant smile. "How kind of you!" She opened the door to the foyer and gestured for him to leave. "Thank you for coming to visit. It has been very enlightening. However, I've too much to do to sit around and gossip. Be here tomorrow. I'll make sure Liza's here as well."

"Wonderful," he growled. This was just perfect—now he was going to help Liza become even more attractive so that dirt farmer would be even more smitten than he was. Was there no justice in this world?

Meg left the door to give an excited twirl about the room. "This is going to be such fun! Oh, but I have so much to do. We'll need to work on her clothing, her comportment—really, the dancing is the least of our worries."

"Liza'll never agree to any of this."

"Leave that to me," Meg said smugly. "I know just what to say."

Royce swallowed a very rude retort and rubbed his neck, suddenly too weary to argue. At least by helping Meg, he could keep his eye on Liza. And perhaps . . . His tired mind began to churn, an idea lurking.

Perhaps this was a good opportunity for him to show Liza the error of her thinking. She wouldn't be satisfied with such a dull, pompous boor. She needed someone with more sophistication and a deeper appreciation for who and what she was. Someone like . . . well, like him, for instance. Only not him, of course.

"Meg, you are absolutely right," Royce said slowly.

Her joyous expression darkened with suspicion. "What are you thinking now?"

"Only that I'm glad I'll be here to help Liza. You win, Meggie. I'll be your dance instructor and anything else you want. What time do we begin?"

"I don't want to learn how to dance."

"Liza, you must," Meg said earnestly. "It's *crucial*."

George made a loud, disgusted noise, then scratched his rump and yawned. Liza hid a grin. That was exactly the way she felt about dancing. "I tried to dance when I was younger and I was a complete and utter failure."

"No one is a failure," Meg said earnestly. "At least say you'll try."

Liza stifled a sigh. Meg had arrived just ten minutes ago, looking so petite and pretty in a pale blue pelisse with matching swansdown hood, that Liza'd begun to rethink wearing her walking dress of burnished orange, though it did contrast nicely with her new lavender boots. She peered over at Meg's half boots of blue kid. "Where did you get those? I love the heels."

"I found them on Bond Street in that new place near the—wait. We are not talking about shoes, we are talking about dancing."

"*You* may talk about dancing all you wish. *I*, meanwhile, will talk about shoes."

Meg looked hurt. "Liza, I only want to help."

"You can't help me with dancing. I've had private lessons. Monsieur DeGrasse completely gave up."

"That was years ago. Besides," Meg said with a mischievous look, "I have a better instructor than Monsieur DeGrasse. Royce is going to teach you."

Liza's heart gave a queer leap so sudden that she pressed her hand to her chest. Raspberries and cream, was that an honest-to-God heart palpitation?

"Liza? What's wrong? You look very strange."

"I'm fine," Liza said. She was dying of some strange heart disorder, of course, but other than that, things couldn't be better.

"Liza, listen to me. I'll admit I wasn't too thrilled with Durham when I first met him, but he seems very worthy."

Worthy. If he was so worthy, then why did the thought of spending the rest of her life with him make her stomach ache? "He's a very nice person."

"Yes, and he would make a lovely match for you. You're both very distinct and your coloring is quite similar—"

"Similar coloring? You make us sound like matching mittens."

"That's not a bad way to think of it. Come, Liza. Let me help you. With just the right tweak here and there, Durham will be on bended knee before you know it."

"I don't want him on bended knee. I want—" What? To die in peace? She already had that. To be left alone? She had that, too, if she desired. "I don't know what I want, but I *do* know that I don't want to learn how to dance. If Lord Durham cannot accept me the way I am, then I'm not the wife for him."

Meg gave a disgusted sigh. "Now you sound just like Royce! Everyone changes when they get married."

"You didn't."

"No, but Shelbourne did. He was so reticent when I first met him. Never a word. You remember, don't you?"

Liza thought about Shelbourne, who was usually asleep or hiding behind a newspaper. "He's quite the talkative sort now, isn't he?"

Meg gave her a reproachful look. "Not in public perhaps. But in private he rattles my ear off."

Liza found that hard to believe, but she kept her tongue still. She wasn't in the mood for an argument, not that she and Meg ever argued. They usually just agreed not to agree. Unlike Royce, who would match her snip for snip whenever they brangled over something.

Liza liked that about Royce. He never spoke down to her, or treated her as if he was afraid she might break in two if she heard a bit of racy language. Instead, he treated her as an equal. Her mind drifted to the play. She hadn't slept a wink after arriving home. She'd lived over and over the way Royce had brushed against her, awakening feelings she was quite certain she'd never have for . . . well, for anyone. Or would ever have again, for that matter.

Meg clapped her hands excitedly. "Royce is willing to start tomorrow. You can practice in my sitting room and then surprise Durham at my ball." A beatific expression crossed her face. "Perhaps we will even announce the engagement there. I vow, but my ball will be a night no one will forget!"

"I don't know," Liza said, trying to feel some enthusiasm, when all she felt like doing was crawling back into her bed and pulling the covers over her head. Perhaps she could fake an illness. Like dropsy. She frowned. No, that had a distinctly unpleasant sound to it. If she was going fake an illness, it would be something more exotic. Like the Westchester ague. Now *that* was a distinctive sounding illness.

"Oh, at least try it," Meg urged. "It will be fun. Royce is going to help and—"

"What *does* Royce think about all this?"

"Oh. Well, it was practically his suggestion. I'm certain he feels the same way I do—if you've set your heart on Lord Durham, then you shall have him."

Liza found that she couldn't smile. She couldn't even move her lips for fear of loosening a sudden sadness that pressed against her throat. Royce knew of Meg's plan to help her win Lord Durham. And he approved. He'd even offered to assist in remaking her so that she was more palatable to eligible males. It was the most lowering thought Liza had ever had.

"I suppose it won't hurt," she heard herself say in a toneless voice. "I'll do whatever you suggest." And she would. If Durham was the only man she could have, then she'd take what she could get and make the best of it.

The logic of the thought should have buoyed her spirits—logic usually did. But this time it only made her sadder. And the sadder she felt, the madder she got.

Damn it, she was only thirty-one years old, not a hundred! She was trim, attractive, and didn't squint a bit, except in very strong light. Meg was right—Liza deserved more. Why shouldn't she try to attach Durham? Or any other eligible soul, for that matter? What could be the harm in improving oneself? None. None at all. And if, in the meantime, she managed to attract the attention of a certain hard-hearted rake who needed to be taken down a peg or two, well, that would just be so much the better.

"Meg, you're right. What do you want me to do?" Thus it was that Liza entered into Meg's scheme the same way she did everything else in her life—heart and soul.

Chapter 6

As for Lord Durham, This Author confesses that very little is known of the gentleman, as he prefers country living and does not spend much time in town. What is known:

He is a dutiful son.

He owns many cows.

Whether those are marks of an ideal husband, This Author leaves up to you, Gentle Reader.

LADY WHISTLEDOWN'S SOCIETY PAPERS,
2 February 1814

Royce arrived at the Shelbourne town house at three the next day, exactly as Meg had requested. The butler took Royce's coat and hat and escorted him to the sitting room.

Upon entering the room, Royce came to an abrupt halt.

Liza sat alone on a settee, arms crossed over her chest, looking somewhat forlorn. As soon as she saw him, she hopped nervously to her feet. "Royce! I—I daresay you are looking for Meg. She is with Mr. Creighton, who is responsible for procuring flowers for her Valentine's ball. Apparently there is some problem with getting pink roses at this time of the year."

"I see." Royce could use this time alone with Liza to his advantage. He didn't dare say too much about Durham in front of Meg, since that traitor had decided to support that insufferable boor's suit. But here he was, alone with Liza . . . He smiled. "How are you this morning?"

"Miserable. Meg wants me to wear this to her ball." Liza dropped her arms to her sides. "What do you think?"

"Good God," he said, as the full impact of her gown hit him. The woman was wearing yards and yards of pink sarcenet. And not a soft, feminine pink, either. More of a rabid pink. Like one associated with a cow's udder. "Where did she find that?"

Liza smoothed her hands down the bow-laden skirt, an uncertain expression flittering over her face. "Meg thought the pink would go marvelously with the draperies."

"Draperies or no,'" he said, lifting his quizzing glass and regarding her from head to foot, "it's ridiculous."

"But very feminine." Liza grabbed the pink ruffled skirt and held it out to both sides. She craned her neck so that she could see as much of the gown as possible, presenting him with the top of her head, where an improbable mass of curls was rather ruthlessly tacked. After a moment, she dropped her hands to her sides and sighed. "It *is* rather hideous, isn't it? I was afraid it was just me. The modiste said it was all the crack."

"I daresay your precious modiste saw an opportunity to get rid of a gown that had no doubt been haunting the place for four or five years. One ordered by some pathetic country miss and then returned once they realized their error."

"Oh dear. Am I out of fashion?" She plucked at a loose string that hung from the neckline. "What if we add more ruffles? Perhaps that would make it appear to advantage."

"Add a ribbon and you can wear it as a hat."

Her face crinkled in merriment as she chuckled. It was an unladylike sound, rich and low, and extremely hoydenish. But it suited her, and he found himself responding in return. God, how he was going to miss her.

But no, he wasn't going to miss her, because he was going to see to it that she never left. "I am here to instruct you in the fine art of dance."

"It's very kind of you to help."

"Oh, I like helping. In fact, I plan on helping until it hurts."

She lifted her brows. "That doesn't sound very pleasant."

"Trust me, it will be very pleasant indeed." He looked her up and down. "I suppose that, besides allowing you to trod upon my toes while instructing you to dance, I shall have to go shopping with you, too."

"I thought you detested shopping."

"I do. But I will make an exception for you."

"You really *are* determined to be helpful, aren't you."

Was that a note of discontent he sensed? "I want what's best for you. I'm not certain it's Durham, but . . . We shall see, won't we? Meanwhile, that dress is not adequate. And your hair . . ." He frowned. "Did you have it cut?"

"Oh, that. The iron was too hot." She fingered the hair over her left ear where some of her short-lived curls had broken off. "I don't know how women put up with such silliness. It's enough to put one in a temper."

"Most women stay in a temper. Perhaps you've hit upon the very reason that is so. Still . . ." He regarded her narrowly. "You don't look that bad."

She crossed her arms and fixed a steady gaze on him.

He tried to keep from grinning, but couldn't. "You never were one for dissembling, were you?"

She plopped back on the settee and stretched her feet before her so her blue shoes were evident. "Dissembling wastes time. And time is what I do not have."

He joined her on the settee, turning so he could see her face. "Liza, just what is your hurry? Why the rush to find the right man?"

She hesitated a moment, then sighed. "I just turned thirty-one, Royce. And it dawned on me that I'm not getting any younger."

He shrugged, genuinely perplexed. "So? I'm thirty-nine and could easily say the same. You don't see *me* rushing to the altar, do you?"

"No, but you are a man. Men can wait until they're sixty and still . . ." A faint heat touched her cheeks and she said primly, "Women aren't so fortunate."

"You want . . ." He straightened. "Good God, Liza. You want to get married because . . . because you want a child?"

That's not quite what she'd meant. She'd meant that men didn't lose their looks at such an early age, which only proved that the Creator was a male, or he'd have seen the injustice in it. Still, now that Royce mentioned it, Liza thought she might indeed like a child. A boy. With black curls and blue eyes.

The heat in her cheeks exploded into a conflagration. "Oh, I don't know what I want," she said irritably. "Women tend to desire things like children and . . ." What? A house? She already had a house. A fine one, at that. And she had a lovely life, very fulfilling, with friends like Meg and Royce. But somehow, that wasn't enough. Not anymore.

Not that she enjoyed *this,* either—the flounces and the ribbons and bows. And she could definitely do without the silly courtship games and mindless flirtations, thank you very much. She wanted someone to hold, someone who was all hers.

"Liza, I'm not one to give advice on such things, but don't you think you should discuss this with someone before you . . ." He gestured vaguely at the pink dress.

"Before I what?"

"Before you do something silly."

"All I want is to find a pleasant husband. A companion. That's not silly." She sent him an exasperated look. "Don't *you* ever think about getting married and having children?"

He sighed, then crossed his arms. "There are times when I've wondered—" He frowned. "But it was nothing that a good glass of port couldn't fix. I suggest you try the same."

"Port makes me gaseous."'

His lips twitched, his blue eyes twinkling. "We really are going to have to do something about your tendency to blurt out whatever it is you're thinking. If you cannot have port, then have some sherry. I vow that this urge to procreate will pass."

"I don't want it to pass. But I do want a drink. Sherry is too sweet, so perhaps I'll just have some brandy." She stood. "Would you like some?"

"Now?"

"It may be only three in the afternoon, but I rose at ten, took a very hot bath, burned off all the hair over my left ear, and dressed in a pink gown completely covered with flounces. *You* may not need a drink, but *I* do."

"You're never going to get a man talking like that."'

"Well, I'm not talking to a man," she returned lightly, "I'm talking to you."

His amused expression vanished so quickly that she was somewhat taken aback. But before she could say anything, he offered her a bland shrug. "I suppose one drink won't hurt anything. Maybe it will get you to relax a little when we dance."

Liza wasn't so sure she wanted to dance with Royce. Her skin tightened at the thought, and she resolutely made her way to the silver salver that sat on a table at the end of the room.

"I know," Royce announced, as if the sight of her pouring a drink had spurred him to some decision. "While you sip that, we're going to make one of those lists you are so fond of."

"A list?"

"Of things you need to work on to become more accomplished."

"I don't need a list—"

"Do you or do you not want my help?"

"I don't." She splashed an extra measure of brandy into the snifter.

He rose and picked up a pen from the escritoire that graced the space between two windows, then found a bit of foolscap. "What should we work on first?"

She took her glass and plopped into a chair.

He took the chair opposite hers. "Ah, yes. Seating . . ." The pen scratched across the paper.

"Blast it, Royce, I know how to sit."

Royce continued writing. ". . . proper language . . ."

"Proper . . . You can't mean to teach me to—"

"Perhaps I should just shorten the list to include overall comportment. It will save ink."

"Bah!" She clunked the glass onto a side table and crossed her arms.

He regarded her thoughtfully, his brows lowered.

After a long moment, she said rather testily, "What?"

"Nothing."

"It has to be something; you're staring at me as if you'd never seen me."

"Was I staring? Sorry. I was just thinking . . ."

She leaned forward, her elbows on her knees, her gaze locked on his. "Yes?"

A wicked gleam heated his blue gaze. "You know, it might behoove you to wear a wig. That hair . . . it will not do."

She jumped to her feet. It was difficult enough having to change her every way of thinking and doing things, but this—sitting here while Royce criticized every aspect of her person—it was just too much. "I have changed my mind about having you assist me!"

"Ah, you are contrary. At least that's one feminine trait you seem to have mastered." He read through the list. "There it is." With a flourish of the quill, he crossed it off.

"Oh, just stop it!" she snapped, crossing the room and making a mad grab for the paper.

Royce jerked it to one side, and Liza, solely focused on getting that ridiculous list, leaped for it. She landed across his lap, her hands wrapped about the paper. "Aha!" she said, waving her prize.

Strangely, Royce said nothing. Liza tried to twist about to see his face, but she was caught, the weight of his arm pinning her legs to the chair, his hand resting squarely on her bottom. Liza could feel the weight of that hand, the warmth of it seeping through her skirts and making her restless in the oddest way. She wanted to protest, but no words would come.

"Hoyden," he said, his voice low and husky.

"Let me up."

"Not yet." His arm moved slowly down the backs of her legs and then returned to her rump.

Liza closed her eyes against the maelstrom of feeling that touch ignited. "Royce . . ." But she didn't ask him to release her. She didn't want him to.

Royce held completely still, his hand still warm on the curve of her derriere, his other hand resting on the small of her back. But something was different. A slow tension began to build in her breasts. "Royce," she whispered.

He turned her so that she faced him, no longer sprawled across his lap, but held in his arms. "Liza?" His lips brushed her hair. "Can Durham make you feel like this?"

Raspberries and cream, he was going to kiss her. She closed her eyes and lifted her face to his. His lips descended over hers, at first softly, with a teasing, almost tentative touch. Heat sparked and flared, sending tremors to her stomach and lower. She leaned into him, tightening her arms, opening her mouth beneath his. Royce moaned and deepened the touch, his mouth hotly possessive.

Every thought in Liza's head melted into a swirl of passion. But before she could do more than grasp Royce's lapels and pull him closer, Meg's voice rose from the hallway.

Royce broke the kiss. "Damn," he swore, his gaze so dark as to appear almost black. "I could shoot my sister."

Liza suddenly realized how it would look if Meg walked into the room that very moment. "Oh my—Royce, let me up!"

For a second, she thought he'd refuse, but then he gave a short nod and released her.

The second he removed his arms, she stumbled upright, her face as flushed as the rest of her body. She was as disoriented as if she'd been spinning in a circle. She glanced down at the crumpled list she held in her hand. That's what she got for imbibing before dinner. No more brandy for her. Ever.

Royce stood as well, but he didn't move away from her. Instead, he smiled and brushed her cheek with a careless finger. "Liza, I hope you learned something. Passion is a necessary ingredient in a successful marriage. Do you have that with Durham?"

Liza stiffened. Royce had attempted to seduce her for no other reason than to win his point about Durham. Anger sifted through her. "Who are you to tell anyone about the factors that make up a successful marriage. You've never even been engaged before."

"I've never broken a leg, either, but I can tell you it would hurt," he retorted. "I was just trying to say that—"

"I will inform Meg that you had to leave."

The frosty timbre of Liza's voice made him pause. "Liza, I only want what's best for you. Durham is not it."

She met his gaze calmly enough, but he could see from the glitter in her eyes and the way her pulse beat so wildly at her throat that she was anything but calm. "You'd better leave."

"Very well. We'll talk about this tomorrow," Royce said, turning toward the door. He'd known she'd be furious—after all, he was interfering with her life. But still . . . he thought she'd gotten the message rather nicely. "I'll call on you at noon."

"I won't be home."

That was his Liza, always challenging and cheeky. He grinned at her over his shoulder. "If you aren't there, then I'll just have to hunt you down."

To infuriate her a bit more, he winked. Grinning to himself, he walked out into the corridor and waited. Within moments, something hard hit the door and shattered. Royce chuckled. A few more sessions like this one and Liza'd never look at another man.

Feeling supremely satisfied, Royce collected his coat and hat from the butler and went on his way, whistling a merry tune and imagining the fun he was going to have convincing Liza of all the reasons she shouldn't marry Durham.

The next day, Royce arrived at Liza's neat town house at noon. The day was sparkling bright, the air clear and invigorating, and for some reason, Royce felt invincible. His plan to show Liza the error she'd be making if she settled for a dirt farmer was going perfectly—the kiss had proven that. He absently hummed a tune as he raced lightly up the steps. It was amazing, the passion that had sizzled between them. And it required further investigation.

Royce paused on the landing to adjust his cravat, then reached for the ornate brass knocker. But before his fingers closed over the ring, the door opened and there stood Liza dressed in a red velvet pelisse with a matching hood. She looked damned attractive as the vibrant color brought out the delicate bloom of her skin and made her brown hair seem darker.

"Sir Royce!" Durham said, stepping out onto the landing beside Liza. "What a pleasant surprise. But I'm afraid we're on our way to the Moreland skating party."

Royce managed a smile even though he felt as if someone had punched him in the stomach. "Indeed?"

"Oh yes!" Liza stood aside so Durham could join them on the landing, then she tucked her hand into the crook of his waiting arm. "It's a lovely day to go skating." To further compound the injury, she smiled up into Durham's face as if he were the only man in the world.

Royce tamped down a very uncivilized desire to pound Durham into dust. "I daresay you don't have the opportunity to skate often in the country, what with all those cows to see to."

"Oh, we work hard, but I'm not adverse to some fun now and then. I'm quite proficient at skating." Durham placed a hand over Liza's and said in a voice deep with hidden meaning, "Liza will learn to skate in a trice. I'm certain she's a very apt pupil."

Royce thought he might be ill, though whether it came from Liza's simpering demeanor or Durham's heavy-handed attempts at flirting, he couldn't say. "I hope you have a lovely time, the both of you." Perhaps the ice would break and Durham would get a good dunking.

Durham smiled benignly. "I'm certain we'll have a very memorable afternoon. Where are you off to, Sir Royce? Perhaps we can give you a ride—"

"Sir Royce's carriage is right behind him," Liza said briskly. "So there's no need for us to bother."

Royce could think of no more unpleasant occurrence than sitting in a carriage while Durham and Liza flirted before him. "I believe I'll make my own way to Swan Pier."

Liza blinked. "*You* are going to the Moreland skating party?"

"I never miss a good skate," Royce answered promptly.

"I didn't know you *could* skate."

"Of course I can." At least he could when he was six.

"Excellent!" Durham winked at Royce. "We'll see you there, then!" He made a great show of assisting Liza down the steps to where his carriage waited. Royce watched, seething, as Durham waved off the footman so he could personally help Liza into his carriage and then had the audacity to tuck a rug over her lap.

What made it even worse was that, just as the carriage began to roll down the street, Liza looked out the window directly at him and waved. A happy, gay, aren't-you-sorry-you-aren't-with-me sort of wave that made him grind his teeth.

"Blasted woman! I should just leave her be. She'll marry that fool and the two of them will be miserable for the rest of their lives." Yes, that would do the trick.

Unfortunately, Royce was committed to halting such foolishness. After all, he'd given his word to Meg. So as soon as Durham's rather antiquated coach disappeared from sight, Royce spun on his heel and stalked to his own carriage. He tossed an order at his coachman as he leaped inside and slammed the door behind him.

What the hell did she think she was doing, playing with Lord Durham's affections in such a way? Royce almost felt sympathy for the poor man. The kiss Royce had shared with Liza proved that she couldn't feel anything for Durham.

Or at least that's what it had proven to Royce. Uncertainty gripped him. What if the kiss had proven something else to Liza? What if, instead of showing her that Durham was not the man for her, the passion of that kiss had frightened her in some way and made her all the more determined to seek out the safe, passionless presence of a frumpy farmer?

Royce pressed a hand to his forehead. Bloody hell, he'd as good as chased Liza into Durham's waiting arms. Royce leaned out the window and ordered his coachman to hurry, though it did no good. Within moments, they were caught behind a hideously slow dray, the creaky cart barely moving, the long lines of carts and carriages hemming them in.

It was twenty minutes before he finally arrived at the pier. The Morelands had obviously put a considerable amount of thought into their skating party. Decorations abounded, and servants swarmed the area, handing out skates and pushing carts of refreshments over the uneven ice.

Royce hurried through the crowd, looking for Liza's red pelisse.

"Royce? Is that you?"

He turned to find Meg standing at his elbow. "Have you seen Liza?"

"She and Lord Durham arrived several moments ago." Meg frowned. "I didn't think you were coming."

"I didn't know about it."

"Yes, you did. I told you not a week ago and you said you'd rather be strung up by your thumbs than attend." Her gaze narrowed. "What *are* you doing here?"

He was looking over her head, trying to find some sign of Liza. "Are they skating?"

"Who? Lord Durham and Liza? Not yet. Durham saw the ice carts the Morelands had provided and he decided Liza would enjoy a ride."

Royce looked out at the ice. A cacophony of colors crossed the white expanse of the Thames, frozen now in a solid sheet. Well, not so solid, if the thinning patches near the bank were any indication. Royce frowned. "What do these carts look like?"

"There's one over there." Meg pointed out on the ice.

A large cart, placed on sled runners and decorated with a fake sprig of flowers and ribbons, went sliding by. A young lady sat in the cart, gripping the sides and laughing as her beau pushed her along.

"Meg, I'm going to see if I can find Liza." Royce turned on his heel and made his way toward a servant who was handing out skates to guests who had not brought their own. He took the closest set and strapped them to the bottoms of his boots. All too soon, he found himself skating on the Thames.

Well, not skating precisely. More like walking with an occasional effort to glide, which usually ended up with a lurch. Skating had evidently changed since he'd last tried it, as it was much more difficult now. Worse, the ice was rough and filled with dips and ridges and an occasional slush patch.

It took him almost fifteen minutes to find Liza. She was sitting in an ice cart a good distance from the pier. Durham, who appeared to have told the truth about his skating abilities, was making quite a show of pushing her about. He slid the cart in a full circle, and Liza's delighted laugh rang across the ice.

Damn the man, Royce thought irritably. Someone could get hurt doing such a thing. What if they hit a weak spot? The cart would go under in a moment. His gaze fixed on Liza, he increased his efforts. He wasn't sure what he was going to say, but he had to make certain that Liza wasn't running from him—especially if it meant she would head straight into Durham's waiting arms.

He tried to move forward, but a ridge of ice stopped him. To his chagrin, at just that moment, Durham leaned forward, his dark head near Liza's cheek. Bloody hell, was the bastard kissing her cheek?

A dull roar exploded in Royce's head. The bounder! The cad! Royce had seduced enough women that he knew exactly what that slovenly bastard was about and the thought burned all the way to his stomach.

Royce's concentration was entirely on Liza, so it was a shock when—*whap!* Something—or more correctly, someone—ran into him. Royce recognized Lady Anne Bishop in the split second before he stumbled back, trying desperately to right himself. He had no time to do more than gasp her name before he was flailing wildly back toward the shore, off balance and out of control.

Lady Anne, meanwhile, was propelled forward at an astonishing rate. Royce winced as she went sailing against Shelbourne's cousin Susannah Ballister. Though an exceptionally good skater, the poor woman had no chance of saving herself, and she fell into a snowdrift.

Off balance himself, Royce staggered forward, trying desperately not to fall on or in front of anyone else. He managed to save himself at the last moment, grabbing a pole that supported the pier and clinging to it until he'd regained his balance. "Bloody hell," he muttered. He hated ice skating almost as much as he hated romantic little ice carts.

Royce looked about for some sign of Durham and Liza, but they had once again disappeared. He supposed he should go and assist Miss Ballister out of the drift, but he didn't dare leave Liza alone with a practiced rakehell like Durham. Royce squinted across the ice and absently noted that Renminster had just reached Susannah. There was no sign of Durham and Liza.

"Sir Royce!" Durham's deep voice boomed directly behind Royce.

Bloody hell. He carefully turned without letting go of the pole. "Durham."

"We saw your performance. It was magnificent."

Royce's jaw ached where his fake smile was plastered. He truly hated dirt farmers who stormed London in an effort to steal away all the best women.

"Royce," Liza said from the safety of her damned ice cart, her voice brimming with laughter, "I didn't know you knew how to spin in quite that manner."

She should have been sympathetic to his plight—she didn't skate at all. But no. She was laughing even harder than Durham, if that was possible.

"Good to see you again, Sir Royce!" Durham turned Liza's cart around. "We'll leave you to enjoy the festivities. Liza and I are going to find something warm to drink." They were gone before Royce could think of a brilliant comment to halt their smirks.

That did it. Something inside Royce had snapped the instant he'd seen Durham's lips so close to Liza's cheek. He was through being gentle. Liza didn't know the force of his personality if she thought to maneuver him away with such paltry efforts. If anything, she made him want her all the more.

Royce took a deep breath and released the pole, then made his way to the bank. He untied his skates and tossed the stupid things into the nearest snowbank and stalked to his waiting carriage. This was no longer about keeping a friend; it was war. And to the victor went the spoils, every delectable, irritating inch of her.

Chapter 7

Another standout in the I-Clearly-Have-Not-Skated-Since-Early-Childhood category was Sir Royce Pemberly, who was seen desperately clinging to one of the Swan Lane Pier poles while his feet made a mad scramble for purchase beneath him.

It is probably a good thing, don't you think, Gentle Reader, that Sir Royce was not aware that the ice was thinning near those poles? This Author should not like to have seen the number of people knocked to the ice if Sir Royce's feet had instead been making a mad scramble for safety.

LADY *WHISTLEDOWN'S* SOCIETY *PAPERS*,
4 February 1814

"Pardon me, miss. It's Sir Royce Pemberley."

"Sir Royce? Here?" Liza was somewhat surprised. When she'd seen him earlier that day at the Moreland skating party, she'd rather thought her calm, aloof air had warned him away.

Poole nodded gravely. "He says he has come for your dancing lesson. Shall I show him in?"

Liza bit her lip. Memories of their passionate kiss flooded through her, and it was in a slightly panic-stricken voice that she said, "No."

Poole bowed. "I will tell him you are not at home."

Then he would leave. For some reason, that wasn't an acceptable answer, either. "No."

The butler raised his brows. "Shall I tell him you *are* at home, but are not receiving?"

Liza bit her lip. If Poole told Royce that she was at home, but not receiving guests, he might think she was avoiding him. And she wasn't. Not really. She was just a bit befuddled, though not too befuddled to realize the dangers of being alone in her own house with a man who could send her common sense spiraling out the window with just one heated look.

What she needed was a valid reason for not seeing Royce. Something innocuous. But what? Perhaps she should just have Poole inform him that she was on her way to the modiste's—she *did* need a new gown for Meg's ball.

But no, he'd just offer to go with her.

Maybe she could claim an inflammation of some sort.

But then he might think she had a red nose or something equally repulsive.

Which left the truth. She didn't want to see him for fear of losing her virtue.

Actually, "fear" wasn't quite the right word. She didn't fear Royce *or* his touch. She craved them. If she married Durham, she knew she'd never experience the kind of spine-tingling excitement she'd felt in Royce's arms. Ever. That much had become clear the second Royce had kissed her, and then today's little visit to the Moreland skating party with Durham had confirmed it. Though she'd had a lovely time, it was painfully obvious she would never feel the way she should about him.

The question was, then, was calm companionship enough to sustain her throughout her life?

"Pardon me, miss." Poole's warbly voice intruded on her thoughts. "What should I tell the gentleman?"

If she had any sense at all, she'd avoid Royce Pemberley like the plague, even if all he wanted to do was teach her how to dance. That was exactly what she should do, and Liza almost always did what she should do.

Thus it was with a mild sense of astonishment that she heard herself say, "Show him in." As soon as Poole left the room, Liza jumped to her feet and raced to the mirror by the fireplace. For once, thank God, her hair was not trying to make its own way in the world. And her green-striped gown was quite presentable, too. She pressed a hand to her heart where it thudded like a badly played drum.

Not that she was nervous or anything. Of course not. Everyone had to learn how to dance, sooner or later. Liza was just an example of a "later."

"I'm always a bloody 'later,' " she mumbled to herself.

The door opened, and Royce entered, looking indecently handsome. Dressed in a dove gray coat over a deep wine-colored waistcoat, his black hair falling over his brow, he seemed to be examining her intently, as if searching for something. Poole closed the door quietly.

To Liza's chagrin, her heart gave that strange little beat. "Damn it," she muttered.

He lifted his brows. "Pardon?"

"Nothing. Just thinking aloud. Poole said you came for our dance lesson. I wasn't aware we had an appointment."

A wicked gleam lit his eyes, sending a shiver of expectation through Liza. "I love dancing." His deep voice lingered over the last word, giving it new, sensual meaning. "Don't you want to learn how to dance, Liza?"

Yes. The word rang clearly through her mind. It was exactly what she wanted. And now. "Of course."

Royce smiled then, his gaze never leaving her. "I promised to meet Wexford at White's at seven. That gives us only two hours."

Hours? Surely he didn't need a whole two hours to— Liza frowned. Perhaps he *was* talking about dancing. *Real* dancing.

To mask her disappointment, Liza fixed her gaze on her new lavender shoes. "Royce, I don't think I feel like dancing now—" She looked up and found herself face-to-face with a snowy white cravat. Blast the man, didn't he know what being near to him did to her poor, ragged nerves?

Liza smoothed her hands down her skirt. *This is just Royce*, she told herself. She'd spoken to him, sat beside him, whispered to him, laughed with him, more times than she could count. Dancing, even real dancing, would be nothing new.

Then why am I shaking like jellied calf's liver? "Royce, I can't—"

"If you can go skating with that clod digger Durham, then you can dance with me." His hand slid to her waist. "Come. What are you afraid of?"

Liza looked dumbly down at his hand. Large and warm, it rested lightly on the curve of her hip. "Durham? Who is that?"

He laughed softly, and her other hand was captured and held by his other hand, which proved to be just as large and just as warm.

"This . . . what dance is this?" She dared to lift her eyes and found Royce smiling down at her, a wicked glint in his gaze.

"The waltz," he said softly.

"Oh. The waltz," she repeated stupidly, too befuddled by the nearness of him to do more than repeat his words like a mindless parrot.

"You *have* heard of it?"

"Of course I have," she lied, hurriedly reviewing the dances she *did* know. Was it the quadrille that began with a curtsy? Or the boulanger? "Raspberries and cream, how does one keep up with all of this nonsense?"

"Perhaps you begin by realizing it's not nonsense at all."

"Humph." Liza realized now why she'd climbed the ranks of the eccentrics with such willingness—she didn't have an ounce of nonsense in her solid, plainspoken soul, and it hurt her shins to pretend otherwise.

Still, there was something to be said for an activity that allowed one to stand so close to—well, she might as well admit it—to such an attractive man. Royce was more than attractive; he was dashing and oh so dear. That was the problem; she knew him so well that such close contact was bound to cause some sort of a reaction.

Especially since he smelled so good. Spicy and masculine, the scent drugged her senses worse than any brandy she'd ever consumed. Liza took a step back. "Perhaps instead of dancing, we should practice playing piquet. I daresay Durham has a liking for the game, or could develop one, once someone taught it to him."

Royce pulled her back into place, the ruffles on her dress just brushing against his waistcoat. "You play piquet like an ivory turner. In fact, you play all card games well and you know it. I daresay I've lost over a hundred pounds to you in the last year."

That was true, but only because she could always tell when Royce was going to trump—he was so expressive. His eyes would light and he'd get this adorable little triumphant smile that quickly turned to frustration when she won. She peeped up at him now and noticed that he was wearing that exact same triumphant grin. "I—how is Prinny?"

"Your horse is fine. You must come and visit him sometime."

That would be lovely, she told herself, trying to think about something other than the way Royce's long fingers looked clasped about her hand. Yes, she would enjoy visiting Prinny in the countryside. Perhaps she and Royce could even go for a ride and—it wasn't working. Just as she fixed a safe picture in her mind of the very fat and unattractive Prinny the horse, she'd have another, less safe picture of her and Royce, in the country, frolicking in the hay, like two—"We can't dance," she said with a touch more urgency.

"Why not?"

"No music."

"I'll hum."

"That table is in the way."

"We'll dance around it."

"I don't like dancing."

"Neither do I, but if we wish to silence Meg's requests, we must. She has asked me no less than ten times if we're doing as she's asked."

"She's very bossy."

"Isn't she? Now, put your hand here." He placed her hand on his shoulder, and her fingers brushed across his wool coat. "I'll hold your other hand like so."

They were standing toe-to-toe, her hand resting lightly on his shoulder. He clasped her other hand loosely, her fingers curling over his. His skin warmed hers, a delightful contrast to the freezing cold outside.

She peeped up at him, feeling as awkward as a newborn foal. "Now what?"

"Now we move. Like this . . ." He hummed a soft tune; his deep voice reverberating through the breakfast room. He really had a lovely voice. She remembered hearing him sing just this past Christmas and commenting on it.

"Now," he murmured, "just follow me. One. Two. Three." He hummed again, tightening his hold on her hand, and began to move.

Liza gulped some air, then began to count in her head. *One. Two. Three. One. Two. Three.* This wasn't so bad after all. She took a step back, pulling him with her.

Royce stopped, amusement and exasperation in his voice. "You aren't letting me lead. Just relax."

How humiliating! She tugged, trying to free her hands. "I hate dancing. I always have."

He tightened his grip. "Then don't think of it as dancing."

She stopped struggling. "What should I think of it as?"

"Think of it as an emotion and not a thing."

"An emotion? Like fear?"

"I was thinking of a friendlier emotion. Like passion."

Good heavens, he wanted her to *pretend* to feel passion. Pretend when in reality, she was beginning to feel passion all too often. "No."

He frowned down at her. "I promised Meg I'd teach you how to waltz. Do you want me to go back on my word?"

Liza thought she detected a very real flash of disappointment in his eyes. He *wanted* to dance with her. She didn't know what to think about that. After a moment, she said in a very small voice, "Meg would be very sad if we didn't at least try, wouldn't she?"

"Very much so."

"And she *is* my best friend."

"She thinks the world of you."

Liza closed her eyes, aware that her heart was beating far faster than necessary. Why did she have to feel this way for Royce, of all men? The fates were as brutal as they were fickle.

He leaned forward so that his chin brushed her hair. "Close your eyes, Liza. Let me take care of you for just one moment." He began to hum again, and Liza tried to relax.

"One, two, three," she whispered. It wasn't easy and she twice trod on his feet, but Royce didn't seem to notice. He just kept humming, moving to the music, his warmth and the deep timbre of his voice pulling her on.

She relaxed just a touch . . . and danced. Perhaps it was because she hadn't had her luncheon yet. Or perhaps it was because she had her eyes closed. But whatever the reason, she could feel something . . . more.

Something almost magical. It was as if for an instant, she and Royce became one.

The thick rug scuffed beneath her feet, softening her step and impeding her ability to glide the way the music seemed to ask. But it didn't matter. Everyplace Royce touched her—his large, warm hand over hers, his palm resting on her hip, his broad chest brushing against her breasts—felt alive and warm, as if the music had invaded her body and moved it for her.

Royce's hum deepened. It rumbled through his chest and down his arms, through his fingers into hers. She could feel the sway of the music and she went with it, letting him lead. One. Two. Three. One. Two. Three. She stopped thinking and just felt. Felt warm and loved. Felt happy and cherished. They were swirling now, slowly still, as if Royce knew this state was fragile. But each swirl sent her a little further into Royce's arms. Her breasts no longer brushed his chest—now they were so close that it was rare that they parted. And Liza reveled in every second, forgetting everything except the feel of this one moment.

Suddenly, they were no longer dancing. His lips had found hers and he was kissing her, tasting her, his tongue gently teasing hers. Liza kept her eyes tightly closed, wanting the moment to last and last. It wasn't real, just a figment of imagination brought on by the heady dance and Royce's presence. She flowed with the kiss, melting into it, accepting it without thought or reason. And her soul flew, expanded like a winged hope, wider and wider.

"Royce, please . . ." she whispered.

The words sifted through Royce, feeding the heat that built within. Liza lifted her gaze to his, her eyes dark with some emotion. He saw in that instant that she wanted him as badly as he wanted her.

Silence filled the air, deepening the tension, teasing and tormenting. Royce found that he could not look away. It was as if she'd melded him to her and he was powerless to resist. He wanted to call her name, to tell her that he cared about her, that he didn't want her to marry Durham. But the words wouldn't come. Instead, other words formed and spilled out, words about the smoothness of her skin, the silk of her hair, the curve of her lips.

Royce heard himself speaking, some of the words old and familiar. Words he'd used to lure various females to his bed. But this time, they weren't just words. They were thoughts—thoughts entwined with feelings so powerful he thought he would explode from the pressure of it.

Liza drank in everything he said. She seemed to glow before his very eyes, her cheeks flushed, her eyes sparkling. He brushed his fingertips across her cheek, down her jaw to her neck. Her skin was soft, with just a hint of moisture. The tension grew and thickened, and Royce's body responded. He was mad for her, yearning with a passion he'd never felt. This was Liza, his friend, his conscience. And somehow this was right. They were meant to be together at this moment, in this way.

She twined her arms about his neck and pressed herself to him. "Royce. Please."

She was so exciting—her sparkling eyes, soft lips, the warmth of her skin begged for his touch. His body yearned for her, his manhood hardening in response. He forced himself to breathe slowly and evenly in an attempt to remain in control, though he knew it was tenuous at best. What was he doing? This was Liza, who trusted him and believed in him, even when he didn't deserve it.

Which was why he had to protect her from Durham, who would hide her magic and never let her be herself. If she ever tasted true passion, she'd never accept anything less.

She sighed softly, her breath brushing Royce's cheek. "Royce, please," she said again, only with more urgency.

He didn't give her time to rethink her decision. He bent to capture her lips with his, molding her body to him, his hand sliding down her back to cup her firm behind through her skirts. She was well made, strong and lithe, with a body capable of providing hours of enjoyment. And this would be her first time. The realization made him hesitate, but Liza wouldn't allow it. She slipped her arms around his waist and pressed against him, her hips raking his. Desire, hot and immediate, poured through him. Royce swooped her into his arms and carried her to the small settee that graced the corner of the room.

Moments flew, moments of teasing and tasting, of tormenting pleasure so perfect that it was painful. He loosened the ribbon at her neck and pushed the material aside, baring her breasts. They were perfectly formed, each firm mound topped by a tight berry-colored nipple. Royce groaned and lowered his mouth to them, tasting first one and then the other.

Liza gasped, threading her fingers through his hair and arching against his mouth. Royce delighted in her shivered response and he trailed his fingers up her leg, pushing aside the voluminous skirts as he stroked the insides of her thighs. She shifted, opening for him as if divining his intent. Every move was so easy, so right.

He kissed her, touched her, showed her that she was more beautiful than words could express. He trembled in his eagerness to touch her, to caress her creamy skin, to feel the pressure of her most intimate places against his fingertips. He worshipped her lips, her slender throat as he loosened his waistband. Soon he was where he'd dreamed of being—between her thighs, her bared skin against his.

All he cared for in this world was lying before him, innocent and warm. She was his, by God. And he would prove it.

Yet despite the blood pounding in his body, despite a hunger so intense that he almost didn't recognize himself, he came to her slowly, carefully.

She shuddered beneath him, lifting her hips instinctively. He poised on the brink, and he suddenly realized the implications of their actions. She was a virgin. If he took her now, honor decreed that he marry her. To his utter astonishment, the thought didn't dim his need one bit. "Liza, we—"

She thrust upward, enclosing him with her strong legs, pressing herself around him. Royce reacted impulsively, pushing forward, burying himself deep within her. She cried out, a flicker of pain in her wide green eyes.

Royce captured her cry with a kiss, his hands smoothing, soothing. "Easy," he murmured, stroking her softly. "Kiss me."

She did, as hot and passionate in her response as he had been. Gradually, the tension on her face eased, and a deep moan sounded in her throat as she moved against him. Royce gently kissed her even as he thrust once more. Heat built and increased, and soon Liza was meeting him thrust for thrust, her body perfectly in tune to his. But of course it was—this was Liza, his best friend, his companion, his soul mate. Each movement was exquisite, almost painfully perfect. She arched against him, and he groaned with pleasure.

"Liza," he gasped. "Stop moving. If you'll just wait . . ."

She held still, pressed firmly against him, her legs wrapped about his waist. He pressed further, grinding himself tightly against her, worshipping her delicate neck with his mouth as he waited.

She gave a sudden gasp. "Royce!" She arched against him as waves of pleasure gripped her. Her reaction fueled his and he was soon lost as well, falling mindlessly over the edge.

Slowly his breath returned to normal. They were no longer on the settee, but the floor. Royce held her clasped to him, her head tucked against his shoulder, her arms about him. He didn't move, suddenly afraid to destroy this perfect moment. For the first time in his entire life, he felt warm, safe, satiated, complete.

He tightened his arms about Liza, and she buried her face against his neck. He welcomed the warmth of her breath, holding her as her trembling subsided. Moments passed, the clock ticking away each second.

After a long moment, Liza sighed and pulled away. She peeped up at him with an uncertain smile that stole his heart all over again. "I believe I understand your fascination for this state," she said in a husky voice.

He lifted up on his arm and looked down at her, aware of a rush of unusual feelings that made him want to hold her tightly and never let go. "You have only begun to understand the wonderment."

A noise sounded in the hallway, and Liza sat upright. "Oh dear! That will be Poole."

Royce didn't question, but helped her to her feet. Once there, they stood awkwardly for a moment, then Liza managed a brittle smile as she began to adjust her clothing. Royce helped her silently, feeling the need to say something, but too full of feelings to give voice to his thoughts. Once she was back to normal, he began to adjust his own clothing. He was a little startled when she reached up and straightened his cravat.

In all the times he'd made love to women, none of them had ever helped him to dress. He looked down at her though all he could see was the top of her head as she smoothed his lapels in place.

"There!" she said brightly, stepping away. She didn't meet his gaze, but stood there, looking adorably embarrassed, her hair still falling about her shoulders.

He retrieved some of her missing hairpins from the rug and handed them to her. "I didn't know you could turn so many shades of red."

Her blush deepened, and he impulsively bent and kissed her lips. "Put your hair up. We've things to do."

"Oh. Yes. The dance lessons—"

"Why do you need to learn how to dance now? You should send a note to Durham as soon as possible."

She slid the last hairpin into place. "And tell him what?"

"That you aren't going to marry him."

Her luminous gaze darkened. "Then who *am* I going to marry?"

For a stunned second, he couldn't think. But then, from the very depths of his heart came the answer. *Me.* He wanted her to marry no one else. The words echoed in his head, growing louder by the second. But somehow, he couldn't say them. This was Liza, the one woman above all others that he cherished, cared for . . . *loved.*

Wait a minute, he told his stunned mind. He cared for Liza, of course he did. But love? Real love?

Good God, he *did* love her. The realization left him reeling, and he found the settee with a groping gesture. Something seemed to be wrong with his knees, for they no longer supported him. He loved Liza with all his heart. But love was one thing . . . marriage—that was something else altogether.

Wasn't it? He struggled to make his mouth work. "Liza, I—you . . . you can't marry Durham."

A glimmer of something flashed in her eyes. "Royce, I want to marry someone who is kind. And considerate. Someone with a steady character. Someone who will always be there for me, and with me. A partner. That's what I want."

Royce tried to digest this. He was many things . . . but kind? Considerate? When he thought of the way he'd used Liza in the past—confiding in her on so many unsavory topics—he could not find it in himself to call his behavior either kind or considerate. As for being steady in character . . . A sick feeling clenched his stomach, and he realized in that instant why he'd never attempted to secure Liza's interest in all the years he'd known her—he wasn't good enough.

He never had been.

She looked away, her lashes shadowing her eyes. "You . . . you aren't speaking."

He swallowed, drowning beneath so many unfamiliar feelings. "I—I can't . . ." He shook his head, his throat closed. She deserved so much more than he was capable of being.

After a strained silence, she gave a soft, painful laugh. "Silence is an answer of a sort, I suppose."

Royce raked a hand through his hair. He loved her, he really did. But . . . could he make her happy? What if he failed? Disappointed her in some way? He didn't think he could bear it.

"Royce, don't—" Her voice broke, and she bit her lip, closing her eyes tightly. She stepped away, swiping angrily at her eyes with the back of her hand. "You cannot come to see me anymore."

"Liza, I—"

"If Durham proposes, I am going to accept. I hope you will wish me well." She walked toward the door unsteadily. She placed her hand on the knob, then turned to look at him with tear-bright eyes. "Whatever happens . . . wherever you go, I wish *you* well."

She ducked her head, then left, shutting the door almost silently.

Royce stared blankly ahead. It was almost too much to grasp. How long had he loved Liza? Days? Months? Or had it been years? Had he not been silently comparing every woman he knew to her? It was as if she'd always been in his heart, tucked away in a safe corner, waiting for the right time to reveal her true beauty.

But now that she had, he was caught . . . *was* he the man for her? All the years of protecting her came to the fore, and he realized that he was exactly the type of man he'd always warned her about. The realization did little to ease the questions pounding through his mind. All he knew for certain was that he loved her and couldn't live without her.

He raked a hand through his hair and wondered dismally what the hell he was supposed to do next.

Chapter 8

There is so much to report from Lady Shelbourne's Valentine's Day ball that This Author scarcely knows where to begin. But do not worry if you were not present (or not invited). There is no need to feel that one is not au courant *when This Author takes such splendid notes.*

Ah, Gentle Reader, read on . . . .

LADY WHISTLEDOWN'S SOCIETY PAPERS,
16 February 1814

The Shelbourne Valentine's ball exceeded even Meg's wildest expectations. By ten o'clock, waiting carriages lined the avenue in front of the house for almost a mile. Liza stayed with Meg for a short time in the front hall, issuing orders to servants and doing what she could to help. Of course, Meg was beside herself with excitement, especially since Shelbourne's cousin Susannah had married the Earl of Renminster earlier that week in a surprising move that had shocked them all.

"Oh Liza," Meg said for the hundredth time, "the Shelbourne name is set! Not only will it be a horrid squeeze, but I will have the felicity of being the first hostess to introduce Renminster and his new bride!"

"How lovely," Liza said absently, thankful Royce hadn't yet appeared. By relying on Lord Durham's constant presence, she'd successfully avoided Royce since their last "lesson." Oh, he'd tried to see her, but Liza had thought it best if she maintained a safe distance. Her heart could not take another beating. Besides, she was sure that, in time, Royce would forget all about her. He forgot about all his other "loves."

The thought was so deflating that Liza had to blink back tears.

"Look, here's Lord Durham yet again," Meg said, glancing over her shoulder where the gentleman hovered. "He's anxious to have you to himself."

As soon as he caught Meg's gaze, Durham approached. Dressed with tiresome gallantry in a black coat and a sober brown waistcoat, he bowed over Meg's hand. "Lady Shelbourne, you look lovely this evening!"

Meg simpered. "So you've told me twice now. I begin to think you are flirting with me."

"I never flirt," he said somberly. "Especially not with a married woman."

Meg's smile disappeared. "Oh. Well. Lord Durham, why don't you take Liza into the ballroom and try some of the cake? I heard the cake at the Prudhomme ball was somewhat stale, and I was determined that would not be the case here."

Lord Durham looked inquiringly at Liza. All she wanted to do was go home and sip a cup of tea before her fireplace, confide all her woes to George, and perhaps indulge in a nice, refreshing spate of tears. But she could see that that was not to be.

"Along with you both!" Meg said, shooing them away.

Liza didn't want to sit, and she didn't want any cake. But apparently what she wanted was of no moment, for she soon found herself cozily installed in a chair near the refreshment table, a piece of cake before her.

Lord Durham sat beside her, talking of this and that, eventually trailing off into silence. He stared into the distance as if contemplating a weighty matter.

Liza watched him with some trepidation. He was going to ask to marry her, she just knew it. Dread weighted her shoulders, and she found she couldn't think of a thing to say to stall off the inevitable.

The silence increased until even Durham noticed it. He shifted uneasily, then said, "I, ah, I meant to say that you look ravishing tonight."

"Ravishing? In this gown?" She was wearing the pink atrocity that Meg had chosen simply because she'd been too disheartened to order another. The reason she was so distraught crept back into her thoughts and she had to blink back tears.

Durham pulled back a little. "It's a truly lovely gown," he said earnestly. "And you do look wonderful."

No, she didn't. Royce had been right; it was too frilly and the color was unattractive, at best. "What about my hair? Do you like it?" Meg's French maid had specially prepared her coiffure. It was twisted and pinned until she felt as if her eyes had been pulled back a full inch on each side.

"It is perfect," he said without really looking. "Liza, I wanted to talk to you—"

"Do you think we'll get more snow?" Liza said in a rushed voice. Anything to keep him from saying the words she dreaded. "Poor George has just recovered from one cold. If he gets sick again, I fear it could be fatal."

Lord Durham smoothed his hands on the knees of his breeches. "You are quite fond of George, are you not?"

"Some people treat their dogs and cats as children. I suppose, in a way, that is what George is to me: a very sweet, noisy child."

Lord Durham blinked. Once. Twice. He stood so suddenly Liza jumped. "It's quite hot in here. I'll fetch some orgeat."

He was gone before Liza could say anything, which might have been his intent.

Disconsolate, Liza placed her piece of cake on his empty chair and looked about the ballroom. Meg had outdone herself. The whole chamber was draped in swathes of red and pink silk. And she must have ordered two or three thousand red candles that burned brightly on a number of tables, all of which were covered in white lace. The effect was magical.

Everything was perfect. Except that Liza was quite certain her heart was completely broken. She tried to tell herself it was her own fault. After all, she'd known a dalliance with Royce would lead to nothing but heartache. It was just that he was so damnably delectable that it was quite easy to forget that fact once he was near.

Not that she had any regrets. She didn't. But having been in Royce's arms, she was finding it very difficult to fall into Lord Durham's. Worse, she found that she missed Royce's arms almost every moment of the day.

She supposed that at some time, she was going to have to face him. It would be difficult, but she'd do it. She'd force herself to act normal, as if nothing had happened. And it would cost her dearly.

Durham returned at that moment and sat down beside her, a faint sheen of perspiration on his upper lip. "Here you are!" he said, handing her a small glass.

She hated orgeat. And it was just like Durham to bring her a drink that she disliked. Still, she supposed she should thank him. "Lord Durham, I appreciate—" Her gaze fell on the edge of his chair, where a bit of napkin stuck out from beneath his bottom. An unexpected burble of laughter tickled the back of Liza's throat. Lord Durham had sat on her piece of cake.

Her strained nerves didn't help, and a horrified giggle caught in Liza's throat. It was probably squashed flatter than a piece of foolscap. She looked at Durham again and bit her lip. Strange that she hadn't realized it before, but he was just the tiniest bit pudgy, quite unlike Royce, who was ideally fit. "Lord Durham—I—you—"

"Liza, I must say something."

Good Lord, he was going to propose right now, this very second. Liza shook her head desperately. "Lord Durham, please. Before you say anything, you should know—"

"No. Let me speak first." He wiped his brow with an unsteady hand. "I've made it no secret that I came to London to find a bride. I flatter myself that I'm a bit more sophisticated than the average landowner, and it seemed only fitting that I attain a higher level of wife than most. After much consideration, I have realized—"

"Please, Lord Durham, do not say another—"

"—I cannot ask you to marry me."

She froze. "Can*not*?"

He nodded.

Relief flooded through her, and she pressed a hand to her heart. There was a God, after all.

"I can see you are upset," Durham said gravely. "I want you to know there is nothing in your person that I find repulsive. Indeed, I believe you are a very charming woman."

"Thank you," she managed, wondering if Meg would notice if she slipped out now. She could go home this moment, throw this horrid dress into the fireplace, and slip into bed. All she wanted was to pull the sheets over her head and forget she had ever met a man named Royce Pemberley. A man she couldn't have, but couldn't seem to live without, either.

Durham took her limp hand and held it between his. "I don't mean to offend you, Liza, but after spending time with you, it has become apparent that you are more of a . . . a monkey person."

She blinked, wondering if she'd heard correctly. "I beg your pardon. Did you . . . did you just say I was a 'monkey person'?"

His cheeks bloomed a rich red. "I've noticed how you dote on that animal, while I cannot abide the creature."

Liza tugged her hand free. Every bit of her discontent rushed to the fore, and, combined with her aching heart, led her to say with some asperity, "My monkey is very well behaved. Better, I daresay, than your cows!"

He stiffened, his neck turning a mottled red. "My cows do not bite! Furthermore, no matter how well behaved George is in the city, he would not be so agreeable in the country. That would be another matter all together."

"Why would George be different in the country?"

"Because monkeys dislike cows. And if he were to bite one of them—"

"George bite a cow? Who on earth told you such a shocking whopper?"

"Why . . . I believe Sir Royce mentioned it at the theater, though I've been asking various persons and it seems quite common knowledge that monkeys can be quite aggressive. Lord Casterland almost lost his thumb to one."

"Only because he poked it and scared the poor creature half to death."

"Yes, well, I cannot risk the health of my herd." He frowned. "Liza, it's more than the monkey. I've enjoyed your company, but I feel as if perhaps . . . perhaps your heart is not available."

None of her was available. Not to Durham, anyway. Liza's irritation faded, and instead, she felt nothing but relief.

Her reaction must have been obvious, for Durham managed a weak grin. She eyed him for a long moment where he sat beside her, sweating in his stiff evening clothes, an apologetic smile on his broad face, a piece of cake squashed on his rump. For some reason, all those horrid facts made him seem very dear. "Lord Durham, you are right. We wouldn't suit at all, but I do hope we can be friends."

"Of course. Liza, it has been a pleasure, but I believe my time in London is done. I'm returning home tomorrow."

"Your mother will be glad to see you."

A wide grin crossed his face. "Yes, she will." He patted Liza's hand one last time, then stood.

Liza's gaze was immediately drawn to the chair Durham had just vacated. There, sitting in solitary splendor, was her empty napkin. She leaned to one side and glanced at the floor behind him, looking for some sign that perhaps the cake was somewhere other than stuck to Durham's slightly too tight pants. The floor was completely clean. "Lord Durham, you should perhaps—"

"There you are!" Meg stood before them, beaming brightly. "I left Shelbourne to tend the receiving line. Can you believe how many people have already arrived? Everything is going so well! The Duke of Devonshire specifically complimented me on the orchestra, and Lady Birlington said the cake was the best she'd ever had."

"I personally can attest to the cake," Lord Durham said gravely. "It was very light and airy."

"I don't know about airy," Liza said with a dubious glance at the empty napkin. "Lord Durham, before you leave, I must tell you that you have ca—"

"Liza, please," he said, holding up a hand. "We've said all there is to say. Let's not make this any more difficult than it already is." He gave her a very meaningful glance, then turned to Meg. "Good evening, Lady Shelbourne. I am sorry to inform you that I must leave your delightful party and return home with all possible haste."

"Oh dear. Right this instant?"

"I'm afraid so."

Meg glanced at Liza, who managed an encouraging smile. "I see."

Durham bowed deeply, took Liza's hand, and gave it a significant squeeze, and then he left, making his way through the crowd.

Meg frowned after him. "What has happened? And what on earth is that on his breeches? It looks as if—oh! There's Royce!"

Liza leaped to her feet and saw Royce crossing the room, his dark blue gaze locked on her. He looked devastatingly handsome in his evening attire. Handsome and determined.

Liza's breath shortened. She didn't want to speak with him now. Not until she had time to shore up the weak banks of her own traitorous heart. It would take at least a bottle of brandy and perhaps an entire cake, maybe two.

"Liza, what's wrong?" Meg asked, alarm on her face. "You look as if—"

"Might I have the pleasure of an introduction?" came a smooth masculine voice.

For just a second, Liza thought it was Royce. But a quick glance told her that her ears had played a cruel trick on her heart.

"Of course, my lord," Meg said, quickly masking a frown. "Liza, Lord Halfurst. My lord—"

"Miss Elizabeth Pritchard," Liza said. She stuck out her hand. To hell with trying to be all pink and frilly. It was uncomfortable and damned itchy. "Liza. Pleased to meet you."

He shook her hand, a reluctant grin touching his mouth. He was actually quite a handsome man. Large and powerful, though he didn't have Royce's sense of style. She was beginning to realize that for her, no man could measure up to Royce.

Halfurst offered an easy grin. "A pleasure to meet you. Might I have this waltz, Miss Liza? If it's not already spoken for, of course."

Meg opened her mouth as if to protest on behalf of her brother, who was bearing down on them as they spoke, but Liza halted her with a sharp glance. If Liza danced off with Halfurst, Royce would be forced to wait for her to return from the dance floor. It would only stall the inevitable, but it would give her some time to calm her nerves and think up a good explanation for Durham's obvious absence. And if she knew Royce, that would be one of the first questions out of his mouth.

Liza smiled blindingly at Halfurst. "I'm afraid I'm all yours, my lord."

She only hoped she could remember how to waltz. The thought of the outcome of her one and only dance lesson made her stumble a little, and she trod heavily on poor Halfurst's foot. "I'm so sorry," she gulped, her cheeks heating.

"No need to apologize," he said smoothly, reassuring her with a friendly smile even though his eyes were obviously watering a bit.

Well! He was far more pleasant than Lord Durham. Liza tried to relax, to let the music move her, when she caught sight of Royce glowering from the edge of the dance floor not ten feet away.

She immediately stepped on Lord Halfurst's other foot. "Oh no!"

"No worries, Miss Liza," he managed to say through a somewhat less robust smile.

"I should have warned you, dancing is not my forte. Perhaps if we counted the steps aloud?"

His lips quivered a little before a grin broke through. "The danger makes the adventure more worthwhile."

Liza had to laugh at that, noting out of the corner of her eye that Royce was now making his way through the crowded dance floor toward them. She fixed her gaze upon her feet, determined to appear gay and carefree. "One, two, three. One, two, three—oh drat!" The flounce she'd just torn caught her heel and she hopped.

Halfurst narrowly missed stumbling over her and came to an abrupt halt.

But it wasn't because of her stumble. Halfurst had stopped because Royce stood before them, blocking their way. "Might I cut in?" he said in a clipped voice.

Halfurst lifted his brows, and for an instant, Liza wondered if the young lord would relinquish her. But something happened—a fleeting sign of recognition seemed to flash between Royce and the younger man. And then Halfurst nodded and stepped back and Liza found herself in Royce's embrace.

At once his arms, his scent, his heated gaze surrounded her. It was pure heaven and she found, to her shock, that she could actually dance without counting. Damn it, that was not fair. Dancing should *not* depend on the level of attraction one felt for one's partner.

As they turned, he pulled her closer, his breath fanning her ear. "Liza, I know you don't want to talk about this, but we must."

"Why?" she asked, trying desperately to put into words the avalanche of feelings she'd been fighting. "Why can't we just go back to the way we were? Royce, I want us to be friends again. Why can't we—"

"Because we can't. And you know that as well as I."

She did know it. And the thought made her feel so lonely that tears threatened to choke her. He'd always been her best friend, and once his passion faded, there would be nothing left. She'd seen it too many times to hope for more. *Why* had she allowed her passion to ruin everything?

His fingers tightened over hers. "Liza, I've been thinking about you. Every day. Every night."

"Have you?" she said, trying hard for some insouciance despite the fact her cheeks burned, her heart was beating painfully against her third rib, and her knees were threatening to buckle. "I haven't thought of you at all."

He drew back a little, a question in his dark eyes. "Not once?"

"Not one single time." Except when she ate, drank, slept, walked, talked, or breathed. He invaded every moment of her day and every long and lonely hour of her night. The bastard. "I daresay you haven't really been thinking of me, either. And why should you? Royce, let me make this easy for us both. We enjoyed a . . . what you would call a flirtation. And now it's over. And that's fine. I'm a mature woman who—" Her voice broke.

"Liza, don't. You just caught me off guard. I'm not the marrying kind of man."

"And I'm not the dallying kind of woman," she said with a shaky smile. "I suppose that leaves us back where we were before."

The music came to an end. Liza stepped away from Royce. "Thank you for the dance. If you'll excuse me, there is a cake awaiting my attention." With that, she collected her bruised and battered heart, and walked determinedly away.

Too wound up in his own emotions to speak, Royce watched her go. She was wearing that ridiculous pink gown, and her hair was already falling from its pins. She was Liza and she was his. Desire heated him through and through, and without a thought, he followed her. She was already standing with Meg at the refreshment table when he reached her, all his feelings suddenly crystal clear as they tumbled from his heart. "Liza, I have something to say to you, and by God, you are going to listen!"

"No, I'm not. I don't want to hear anything you have to say. Now leave me be!"

Meg looked from one to the other. "Well! Perhaps you two should retire to the library and—"

"No," Liza said, a breathless tone to her voice. "I'm staying right here. With the cake."

So Liza feared being alone with him again, did she? He looked at her closely, noting her high color, the sad twist to her lips. For the first time in a week, a faint spark of hope buoyed his spirits. "If you will not have private speech with me elsewhere, then we'll have our discussion right here, in public."

An elderly matron who was gathering a piece of cake looked up at that, a hopeful expression in her faded eyes.

Liza's color heightened, but she didn't budge. "We have nothing more to say to one another."

"Like hell." He glanced around the room. "Where is Durham?"

"I don't know. I'm not his keeper."

"He left," Meg offered. She leaned toward Royce and said, "He looked upset, too."

The spark of hope that flamed in Royce's heart warmed into something else, something more powerful. Royce took Liza's hand. "Why did Durham leave?"

She pulled her hand free and took a step back, coming up against the edge of the refreshment table. "It was nothing, really. Lord Durham and I discovered we did not suit. He is more attuned to cows while I'm more attuned to monkeys. *Not* that that's any of your concern."

"You're wrong. If it has anything to do with you, then it's my *first* concern."

The matron leaned over to Meg and said in a loud whisper, "Lady Shelbourne, this sounds quite promising!"

Meg nodded emphatically.

Liza made an exasperated noise and whirled to face the refreshment table, presenting Royce with her back. Her hair, which had been pinned in an array of sophisticated curls, was rapidly falling down. Two large brown curls stuck out at odd angles, while one thick curl clung to her ear. "Liza," he said softly, aware that if he but bent forward just a little, his lips could graze the soft skin of her neck. "Liza, I'm sorry. With all my heart, I beg your forgiveness."

Meg grabbed the matron's arm, her eyes wide. "He's *never* apologized in his life. *Never.*"

Liza covered her face with her hands, but didn't say a word.

Royce gripped her arms at the elbow. "The other day . . . I didn't answer you because I couldn't. I didn't realize how much I cared about you until that very moment. I kept telling myself we were just friends. That I wanted to save you from making a mistake. But I know the truth now. I didn't want to save you *from* Durham, but *for* myself. I love you."

"You . . . you say that quite frequently. To lots of women." Her voice was muffled by her hands.

"Liza, I've never said it this way, with such strong feelings in my heart." He leaned forward until his lips grazed her ear. "And I've never said this to anyone: Liza, I love you and I want to marry you. I want to be with you forever." There. The words were said. They seemed to fill the room around them, dancing on air like so many motes of golden dust. Royce held his breath and waited.

Meg and the matron both sighed loudly, holding on to each other as they watched, blinking back tears.

Trembling from head to toe, Liza dropped her hands from her face and looked down at her feet where her new shoes peeped out from beneath the horrid pink dress, the torn flounce lying limply on the floor beside her foot. Royce's hands held her firmly, his breath warm on her cheek.

He loved her. He loved her enough to say so in front of a stranger. Enough to say it in front of his sister. Enough to want to marry her. Forever.

Deep inside her heart, something broke open, and joy, pure and strong, poured through her. The emotion was so overwhelming that all she could do was stand there, staring down at her silly shoes, tears gathering.

"Liza? Please—" His voice deepened, his hands tightening on her arms. "Tell me that you love me. I can wait for everything else, if you'll only tell me that."

"Royce," Meg said impatiently, "*do* something! Can't you see she's too overcome to speak?"

To Liza's dismay, Royce gently turned her to face him. She kept her chin tucked, afraid that if she moved, the tears would fall. And they would not be gentle tears, but great guffaws of love and pain and joy.

Royce placed a finger beneath her chin and lifted her face to his. Then he bent and gently kissed her cheek, looking at her with a gentle, almost awed expression. "Liza Pritchard, will you marry me?"

The elderly matron gulped and dabbed at her eyes with a napkin. "Lord love you, Miss Pritchard. If you don't marry him, I will!"

Liza's laugh was strangled by a sob. She couldn't help it. Of all the women Royce had courted, flirted with, cajoled, and dallied, he'd never asked a single one of them to be his wife. Only her.

She looked up into his eyes, finally finding her voice. "Oh, Royce. How can I say no? I love you, too. So very, very much."

He roughly enveloped her in a warm hug, crushing her against him as he tilted back his head and laughed—long and loud, the sound drawing the attention of everyone within earshot. "God, I love you!"

And then Royce, Liza's dear best friend, the man who knew her every foible, her every flaw, her too-large feet, her inability to dance—and loved her anyway—picked her up and spun her around once, then kissed her full on the lips right in the middle of the Shelbourne ball.

Karen Hawkins

New York Times and *USA Today* bestselling author KAREN HAWKINS writes novels that have been praised as touching, witty, and heartwarming. Her historical romances have garnered praise and awards, and her contemporary women's fiction is a nod to the many books that opened doors to more adventures, places, and discoveries.

A Dozen Kisses

Mia Ryan

This one I could not have done
without Karen Hawkins.
Thanks for knowing exactly when
I needed you to call,
for knowing exactly what
to say, and for being my best friend
when I needed one desperately.

Chapter 1

New to town for our odd little "Winter Season" is the Marquis of Darington, who has not been spied in London for over five years, not since his soldiering days. Rumor has it that he was wounded in action and spent many months convalescing at Ivy Park, in Surrey, which he inherited (along with his title) at the death of his fourth cousin twice removed, the former Lord Darington, who leaves his wife, the dowager Lady Darington, and his daughter, Lady Caroline Starling.

The details of Lord Darington's injury and recuperation are unknown (indeed, the entire affair is a mystery, even to one as proficient at ferreting out secrets as This Author.) However, it IS known that upon his return from the continent, Lady Darington and her daughter were given very little time to vacate Ivy Park, which they had called home for several decades.

All in all, a most unpleasant affair, indeed.

LADY WHISTLEDOWN'S SOCIETY PAPERS,
28 January 1814

Ernest Wareing, Earl of Pellering. She was going to marry a man named Ernest Wareing, Earl of Pellering. For the love of all things holy, the man's name rhymed.

Lady Caroline Starling didn't know whether to laugh or cry.

Since she was in a public place, though hidden away in a corner, she really ought not to do either.

But since it seemed that in the last month she had pretty much lost any control she had ever had over her emotions, Lady Caroline Starling started sobbing right there in the rotunda of the Theatre Royal, Drury Lane.

It did not make sense that a lady should lose her decorum so, but it made even less sense for Lady Caroline Starling, who hardly ever cried.

Of course, that being said, she had cried more in the last week than she had in her entire twenty-five years upon the earth.

But most importantly, Lady Caroline should not cry, because in the last month, her life had finally, after years of upheaval, come very close to being perfect.

Shouldn't that mean she would be sitting cheerfully in the box seat next to Lord Pellering, excited to witness Edmund Kean's portrayal of Shylock?

Yes, of course it should. She ought to be thrilled. Ecstatic. With this thought, Linney started crying even harder.

"Are you all right?"

Linney jumped, her heart nearly stopping at the shock of another human's voice, especially a distinctly masculine one. She had carefully secreted herself behind some very heavy drapes and a potted plant before turning into a sniveling watering pot.

"Here."

She blinked at the snowy white linen handkerchief thrust unceremoniously beneath her nose. The handkerchief was held in equally snowy white gloves, which encased fingers that seemed to be of a nice proportion and size.

Linney stopped crying, her attention completely caught by the sight of some anonymous man's gloved hands.

And, since she could not see the details of the man's hands, it did strike Linney as strange that she would notice them at all. And, though Linney had never considered herself even close to normal, she felt a bit taken aback that unseen hands could trigger a heretofore unfelt flutter in her stomach.

It was the type of reaction one might have if startled, perhaps.

No, that was not truly the feeling.

Actually, it felt more like the time she had eaten some bad sausage.

With a shake of her head, Linney's gaze traveled up the dark blue arm of a well-tailored silk jacket, across impressive shoulders to a lovely strong neck, and then, there before her, Linney looked upon the most breathtaking man she had ever seen.

She hiccupped.

"Take it before you ruin your gown," the man said, shaking the bit of linen beneath her nose once more.

He was truly a gorgeous man, but he had the manners of a heathen. Not that Linney had ever met a heathen. Still, it was suddenly perfectly clear to her that there was no such beast in the world as a man who possessed good looks, good breeding, and sensitivity.

Oh Lord, she was going to cry again.

She grabbed the handkerchief and bunched it against her nose as tears resumed leaking from her eyes. Her knight in shining blue silk simply stood there staring as if she had just stripped naked on stage.

Linney blew her nose, loudly, and then folded the handkerchief so she could use a nice clean patch to wipe her face.

"Thank you," she said, glancing at the lovely man and holding out his soggy handkerchief to him.

He stared at it for a moment, and then Linney clutched it back to herself in horror.

Well, of course, she could not give it back to him. How incredibly disgusting. "I . . ." She waited for a moment, hoping he would be the gentleman and suggest she keep it, thus releasing her from this awful and embarrassing experience with some dignity intact.

And, of course, the man continued to stand there staring at her.

The beautiful dolt. He might have the manners to offer her a handkerchief, but, quite obviously, that is where his sense of etiquette ended and his rather pompous bearing took over.

"Well, here, then," she said, standing and shoving the soiled piece of linen right in his front pocket.

He glanced down at his chest pocket, and then looked back at her.

And Linney instantly wished herself to the nether reaches of China.

Why on earth did she let herself do such horrible things? It was the very reason she usually stood up against the wall trying to blend into her surroundings. Whenever she was singled out, she inevitably defied propriety.

Instead of glaring at her, though, as most were wont to do, Lord Gorgeous smiled. Actually, it was a full-blown grin.

And, though she bit at her lip, Linney could not help but grin right back at him.

"You have a dimple," she said then. Linney slapped her hand over her mouth. She really did need to stop speaking altogether.

Still, he did have a dimple, one, only one, denting his right cheek in a rakish way that made her knees weak.

"And you have passion," he said.

Linney blinked.

"You do not cry anymore," he said softly. "This is good. That is . . ." The man glanced away and then back at her. And he lifted her fingers away from her lips and gently pressed his mouth to them.

She was going to swoon, seriously.

But, thankfully, the man left before she could do anything so incredibly stupid. Although she had already cried her eyes out in front of him, blown her nose loudly into his handkerchief, then shoved the soggy thing back in his front pocket, so, really, she had done much more stupid things in the last five minutes than swoon.

Linney sighed. She really ought not to be allowed anywhere in public. Taking a deep breath, she smoothed back her hair and straightened her shoulders. She *was* in public, though, and she was at the theater with the man who would surely propose to her tonight.

Oh God, she wanted to cry again.

No! Linney closed her eyes. Marrying Ernest Wareing, Earl of Pellering, was a good thing. It was what she wanted desperately. She *hoped* he would ask her to marry him, and soon.

This was *exactly* what she wanted.

Linney forced herself not to think anything else as she left her hiding place and marched, rather determinedly, back to the grand seats Lord

Pellering had obtained for her and her mother and her mother's fiancé, Mr. Evanston.

Actually, the thought of Mr. Evanston was nearly as unpalatable as her strange moods of late. The man made her absolutely want to run screaming from humanity.

And she had another uncomfortable thought when she spied the back of Lord Pellering's head. That ring of brown hair around his slightly pointed domed pate was becoming quite familiar, but it wasn't tugging at her heartstrings or anything so sentimental as that.

Shouldn't it, though?

No, of course not. She wasn't some featherheaded ninny with thoughts of love and sweetness guiding her. As if the back of someone's head could make one's heart flutter.

Suddenly Linney saw the back of Lord Gorgeous's head in her mind, and though her heart did *not* exactly flutter, she had to admit to a slight shiver.

She was obviously tired, or hungry. Or something equally debilitating. With a slight shake of her head, Linney straightened her shoulders and excused herself into the seat just in front of Lord Pellering.

Her mother glanced over at her, a bit of reproach in her gaze. Linney did not see that look often, as she did try to skirt her mother's displeasure, usually by staying out of the woman's presence altogether. But when the urge to cry had come upon her so suddenly, Linney had known that she really must retreat to a more private sanctum than the box her family occupied at the moment.

She folded her hands properly upon her lap and stared out at the stage, which was just far enough away to make the faces of all the actors a blur. Add to that the fact that the column to her right obscured the entire right half of the stage, and she knew that even Edmund Kean could not salvage the night for her, if he ever took the stage. The farce seemed to be taking forever.

Her mind wandered, and suddenly she realized that she was once again thinking of Lord Gorgeous, who, admittedly, had a nice head of hair. Admitting that a man had nice, thick dark hair that curled just enough to be endearing was absolutely *not* admitting anything too horrible.

And letting herself ruminate on what some man's hands must look like without gloves was not completely ridiculous, either.

Not at all.

"Well, well," her mother said, and Linney realized that the players had retreated, finally. The first show was over. "I see Lord Darington has made an appearance."

Linney came completely into the present, all thoughts of beautiful men with large hands and soggy linen disappearing with the cold reality that name brought to mind.

Her mother was leaning toward the edge of the box, staring down at the pit, of all places. "I cannot believe that man. The audacity!"

Mr. Evanston stood behind her mother. "I've heard, of course, that the young bucks like to sit in the pit with the peasants. They say the view is better."

As she had just sat staring at a column with occasional glimpses of the stage beyond for the last hour, Linney had to believe the young bucks were onto something.

"But he has a woman with him! I think it is Miss Amelia Rellton, a woman of breeding. How dare he."

Linney couldn't have cared less who sat where or that some man had a woman of breeding—*why did people have to use such a term for a person?*—sitting down in the pit with him, but the fact that it was Lord Darington, there in the same building with her, made Linney suddenly feel extremely ill. He had never deigned to make her acquaintance, after all. In fact, he'd gone so far as to send a letter requesting that she and her mother leave their home, and giving them two days to accomplish the act.

Terrance Greyson, Lord Darington, was the last man Linney ever wanted to see, much less meet. She had hoped, actually, that Lord Darington had decided to spend the rest of his days locked away at Ivy Park.

Maybe even locked away with gout and chronic toothaches. And, if he ever married, she imagined him sequestered with a horrible harridan of a wife who would kick him in the shins with her pointed shoes.

Still, even though, of course, she never wanted to know the man, Linney found herself inching forward in her seat and peering over the short wall of their box.

"I swear, that man is horrible. Do you know that he basically gave me the cut direct two nights ago at the Worth ball?"

"He did not give you the cut direct, Georgie," Mr. Evanston soothed, patting her mother's shoulder.

Linney, who had not gone to the ball, just looked at her mother in shock. Though she realized her mother barely remembered that they breathed the same air, Linney believed she ought to have been told that Lord Darington was in London.

"Well, when we were introduced, the cad stared at me for a moment as if I were some sea creature from the depths, and then just turned away and left."

"I do think he excused himself," Mr. Evanston said.

"*Horrendously* abruptly!" Her mother glared at Mr. Evanston, and the man obviously realized that he really ought to shut up.

"I have heard," he said, "that Darington has become a complete bore and a pompous ass to boot. Thinks much too highly of himself, really, and doesn't even converse with those above him, socially speaking."

Good old Mr. Evanston. He surely knew exactly how to sweet-talk her mother. Not that it was all that hard. Just agree with her and give her center stage.

"You did hear what he said to Mrs. Kilten-White?"

"I did not," her mother whispered dramatically.

"Well." Mr. Evanston leaned forward and glanced around furtively. They were alone in the box, for heaven's sake.

"You do remember that Mrs. Kilten-White was dressed from head to toe in that hideous purple costume at the ball. She even had a purple feather in her purple turban." Mr. Evanston arched his powdered brows—he liked powder still, even though it had gone out of style, and it made Linney sneeze horribly. "Lord Darington said, right to her face, and with no introduction whatsoever, that he hated purple."

"No!"

"Yes!"

Linney couldn't say that she enjoyed the color all that much, either. And just the thought of Mrs. Kilten-White's rather large frame swathed in the hue as well as her enormous head wrapped in a turban with a feather, well, Linney was pretty sure that it had not been the loveliest sight to behold.

But, of course, she would not have said anything.

She would have thought it, but she surely would not have said it.

"Look at that!" her mother whispered harshly. "That girl just waved at him!" She pointed a few boxes down from them.

"That *girl* is Miss Elizabeth Pritchard, dear," Mr. Evanston said, smiling over at the lady as he did. Smiling, actually, was lending a rather nice description to a rather disgusting leer.

Linney couldn't help grimacing herself.

"Well, someone needs to tell Miss Elizabeth Pritchard that rubies do not go with that horrible green dress."

Distracted from her oily future stepfather, Linney glanced over at Miss Elizabeth Pritchard and sighed softly. She had always envied Liza Pritchard, who had the confidence to say and do and wear exactly what she wanted.

"I am sure I have never seen anything so outrageous," her mother continued, looking away from Liza Pritchard and back toward the milling crowd beneath them. "Lord Darington just bowed to that Pritchard character."

Dragging her gaze from Liza Pritchard's grinning face, Linney stood a bit and leaned forward so that she could truly see Lord Darington for the first time. She raked the crowd once, twice, and then stopped.

That could *not* be he.

It *was* he, she was sure. But if there was a God in heaven it absolutely should *not* be he.

"Is that Lord Darington?" she asked quietly.

Of course her mother did not hear her.

"Really! I never!" Georgiana Starling was still going on about Liza waving and Lord Darington bowing. "Just acts the rake to all the girls, but gives such as me the cut direct. Harrumph!"

The tall man in the dark blue jacket standing beside Miss Amelia Rellton was, indeed, smiling up at Liza. Even from so far away, Linney could see his dimple. Her heart pounded out a strange double beat that made her feel as if too much blood surged in her veins.

And then he glanced a bit to his right, and Lord Darington was looking straight up at Caroline.

And he winked.

Linney nearly stopped breathing.

"Oh my!" her mother said on a shocked intake of breath.

But Linney ignored her and just stared at Lord Darington. Did he know who she was? Had he known, even as he stood watching her cry her heart out behind a potted palm, that she was the very same woman he had kicked out of Ivy Park?

Had he been laughing at her as he offered his hanky with that little grin?

And then Lord Darington's smile deepened and she knew that he was laughing.

The wretch!

Linney swallowed hard and wished with all her might that the man would burst into flames and return to the devil, which is obviously where he had come from in the first place.

With a little tip of his head in Linney's direction, Lord Darington returned his attention to Miss Amelia Rellton.

"I feel ill," she said, turning quickly and stalking past Ernest Wareing, Earl of Pellering. "Take me home." Since she did not speak very often, and never did she demand, Linney was rather sure that every person in the box was taken aback by her tone. But she did not care.

She walked out into the hall and started for the rotunda. She would not stay in the same building as Lord Darington, and she would never allow the man to laugh at her again.

It was bad enough that he had taken away her home in such an abrupt manner. She would not allow herself to give that man even one second of mirth, especially at the expense of her dignity.

For once, her mother and Mr. Evanston were exactly correct. Lord

Darington was a horrible rogue, who thought himself too high in the instep to be civil to her mother, the wife of the man from whom he inherited his title. His fourth cousin twice removed.

Add that all to the fact that he laughed at her.

Actually, she now wished that she had blown her nose even harder into the man's handkerchief.

And she really ought to have kept it. And never returned it to him.

Better yet, she should have ripped the soggy bit of linen into tiny shreds and shoved it right up *his* nose.

Chapter 2

And while we are on the topic of Lord Darington, and his eviction of the dowager Lady Darington and her daughter from their lifelong home, perhaps it is past time to mention the aforementioned daughter, Lady Caroline Starling.

This Author confesses that Lady Caroline's name has not often graced these pages, but it must be noted now that this quiet miss seems to be headed toward the altar with none other than Ernest Wareing, Earl of Pellering.

(As an aside note, does anyone other than This Author feel the need to recite nursery rhymes upon the recitation of the earl's name?)

This Author hopes that Lady Caroline enjoys country pursuits, and most especially hounds and hunting, because it is well known that Lord Pellering loves nothing so much as his canines.

LADY WHISTLEDOWN'S SOCIETY PAPERS,
28 January 1814

It was truly an abomination of nature that one always found the most comfortable spot in the bed five minutes before one had to leave it.

Especially when one's bed was very warm, and one's room could have kept ice solid for a week.

From the fact that she could not feel her nose, Linney surmised that this last bit of conjecture was exactly true. The first part was true because everything was aligned just right, the pillows were perfect, her body completely cocooned in warmth and comfort. Ahhh.

And then someone rapped on her door. And it wasn't a nice soft knock, either, but a hard, staccato rap, rap, rap.

"Linney!" Her mother.

Bloody hell.

Without waiting for a summons, Georgiana bustled in, her hair in curling papers and her face free of the paint she liked to slather on.

Not a pretty way to be awakened.

Duchess seemed to agree, for Linney's constant companion, who had been curled at the end of the bed with her head toward the door, stood elegantly, turned her bottom toward Lady Darington, and lay back down.

"Really, dear, I do wish you would not allow that cat to sleep in your bed."

That cat twitched her tail in indignation.

Linney did not say anything. She rarely did, but her mother never seemed to notice.

"Well, you will not believe," Georgiana continued, cinching her wrapper tighter. "That man is in our drawing room as we speak!"

Since Linney had not uttered a word, it seemed rather presumptuous of her mother to use the pronoun "we."

"I mean, really!" Lady Darington paced. "It is not even noon. Nobody calls before noon, does he not know this?"

Obviously not, whoever the culprit was.

"And he is so . . ." Here her mother appeared unable to find the right words. Amazing, that. If there was something that Georgiana Starling, Lady Darington, was never at a loss for, it was words. "Well, if he thinks that he can give me the cut direct at the Worth ball and then show up in my drawing room nearly a whole two hours before noon and act as if we are bosom friends, he is most sadly mistaken."

Linney's heart fluttered, truly it fluttered. How horribly melodramatic of her stupid, awful, *tender* heart. Perhaps she needed to have Dr. Nielson around to have a look at her.

But, of course it only fluttered because Lord Darington was an awful cad. That was exactly why her heart fluttered and her head felt light.

"Lord Darington is here?" Linney heard herself ask. "Now?"

Her mother stared at her, blinking. Georgiana liked to talk; conversation, though, was rather beyond her.

"Go to him," her mother said with a flick of her wrist. "I shan't, that is certain. As *if* I would be ready to receive at this indecent hour. I haven't even had my tea."

Neither had Linney, but obviously that mattered not at all.

"And I will certainly not receive Lord Darington, ever." Georgiana turned on some imagined companion who, obviously, had the audacity to question her. "No, I will not! I do not approve of him at all. You saw him!" and suddenly Linney was the center of her mother's attention once more, imaginary companion be damned. "Saturday night, flaunting his horrible manners by taking that poor girl to the theater and then sitting among the rabble. Your father would be appalled that his title is being so abused." Lady Darington bit the back of her hand to stifle a sob. "Now I am overtaken." Georgiana swept from the room.

Linney sat for a moment contemplating the door her mother had just left through. She often wondered if her parents hadn't found her at the side of the road. Her mother was absolutely beautiful. Well, she had been when she was young. Now she had to work at it a bit.

Her father had been the same; a man so lovely to look upon he could see no reason to focus beyond his mirror.

And then there was Linney, pale, beige Linney. She was neither too tall nor too short, too thin nor too fat, too beautiful nor too ugly. "Too" was absolutely never used before her name.

In fact, she blended right into the woodwork. No one ever noticed her.

When her father had been alive, her parents had fought like a midnight storm, both of them constantly vying for attention, but never letting any of that attention spill over onto their progeny.

She rather thought they did not remember her, most of the time, even though she sat in the same room with them.

It had been like living with two three-year-olds as parents. At least now there was only one of them.

Duchess picked up her head and gave Linney a look.

"Oh, I know, I know," Linney said. She eyed the washbasin across the cold floor. The water would be absolutely freezing, and that was not an exaggeration. In the last week, Linney had actually had to crack the ice to get at her wash water.

Her mother, of course, got warm water and her fire stoked each morning by Annie. Since no one made a fuss that Annie didn't attend to Linney, the maid didn't bother.

Duchess swished her tail.

"Right, I'm off then." Linney threw off her covers, and with great courage braved her morning ablutions.

It was she.

Could his crying wood nymph be Lady Darington? But no, he had met Lady Darington at the Worth ball. This must be Lady Caroline Starling.

All his thought processes stuttered to a halt, and Terrance Greyson, fourth Marquis of Darington could only stare.

"Lord Darington," she said as she entered the small drawing room and bowed her head. Her eyes were duller without tears, not quite the bright emerald he remembered from the theater. And God knew he had remembered them, especially as he tossed and turned and tried to sleep.

No, he shouldn't say they were duller, just muted.

But her skin was still an ethereal pale pink.

The cat Terrance had been petting rubbed its head beneath his fingers, and he automatically continued scratching behind the kitty's ears. She, the woman, that was, stared at him as if he had just forgotten to stand in her presence.

Dear God, he *had* forgotten to stand.

Terrance stood quickly, dumping the poor cat unceremoniously at his feet. The feline made a horrible sound and shot from the room like a ball fired from a cannon.

This was not a good way to start. With all that he had to overcome when conversing with others, the very least he could ask for was a smooth entrance so that his tongue did not get tied up in knots.

It was not that his mind did not work, it was just that, ever since a bullet had lodged in his skull on a soggy battlefield in France, Terrance

Greyson had a hard time finding the words to show that his brain worked perfectly.

"I see you have met Miss Spit," the lady said succinctly. "She doesn't take to most people, usually. And I daresay she shall not be jumping up again on your lap anytime soon."

Lady Caroline Starling frowned, the delicate skin just above her dark brows furrowing. "That is to say . . ." she said quickly. And then she stopped and just looked as if she wished she might disappear.

Terrance knew that feeling intimately. "Lady Caroline," he said, trying desperately to fill the silence with words that were not easily recalled. "I . . ." Words, words would be very nice. Please? Words? English, French would suffice. *Ah, Lady Caroline, your neck was made for kissing.*

No, those were not good words to begin the conversation at all.

Lady Caroline took a deep breath and stood very straight, waiting.

"Damn," he said, realizing only after the word came out of his mouth that he had said it aloud.

Good work, Terrance.

"Excuse me?" Caroline Starling's eyes rounded.

It would have helped immensely if he had not been shocked to discover that the crying wood nymph of Saturday night was his fourth cousin thrice removed, Lady Caroline Starling, late of Ivy Park.

To be shocked speechless was rather a detriment when one had to work so hard at speech in the first place.

Terrance could not help but chuckle.

Lady Caroline stiffened and cleared her throat. "I'm sure I do not know why you are here, Lord Darington. Especially at so early an hour. But if you think to . . . to tease me about what happened at the theater . . ."

"I would never!"

"Good then."

And they stared at each other.

He had a whole speech prepared and memorized. He realized, of course, that he had incurred Lady Darington's wrath when he had been introduced to her at the ball. But, for the life of him, he had been unable to find the words when suddenly faced with the dowager of the late marquis.

And he knew that he must find the right words for such an important relationship. And so he had returned home, written a small speech for Lady Darington, and put it to memory.

Of course, now he was faced with her daughter, so nearly half the speech had to go, and the rest altered.

This was not good.

Especially seeing that the daughter was making it extremely difficult for him to concentrate on words. She had the most delicate skin he had ever seen. There was a spot, actually, right at the base of her throat, which certainly needed to be explored further. Preferably with his tongue.

Terrance closed his eyes for a moment, trying to dig through his paralyzed brain for a word. Lady Darington. That was it, Lady Darington. That was how the speech started.

"Lady Darington," he began then stopped at her perplexed look.

God no, 'twasn't Lady Darington standing before him, but Caroline. He had, of course, realized this right off. Terrance wished he could rip his tongue from his mouth and give it a good talking to. *Just say the words, damn it.*

Okay, Miss—no, Lady Caroline Starling. "Lady Caroline," he started again, and couldn't help a twitch of a smile. *Good, Terrance, you got the name right.* "I come with greetings from your former tenants." All right, that was fine. But then he had some sentences that would only sound right if said to Lady Darington.

Oh, but he did have some letters for Lady Caroline. She seemed to have been a favorite, actually, of the Ivy Park servants and many of the tenants. "I have letters addressed to you in my command."

Good, good. He was almost giddy with pride since he was getting through this all so well even though he was speaking to a person he had not prepared himself for, and, even more mind-warping, that Lady Caroline was quite a vision, poised as she was in a golden splash of sunlight angling in from one of the windows.

"Also," he continued. "I wished to tell you that Ivy Park does very well. Miss Elizabeth Bilneth married last month, a boy from farther south. The Lawry children are all in school now, and their mother is working for the cook at the Park, she wanted me to tell you. She also said that Lady Caroline . . . er." Whoops, he had gotten a bit too sure of himself and slipped up.

"That is . . . I mean, you would like to know that the roses are doing beautifully and Mr. Lynch has kept them up very well since your absence."

Silence again.

Caroline stared at him as if he were a three-headed snake in a freak show. Was that truly necessary? Yes, his words had come out a bit stilted; still, he had said everything he meant to say, and even though it had all started out rather oddly, it wasn't that bad at the end, was it?

And, though he had not anticipated his crying wood nymph—so named in his thoughts because he had first spied her through the leaves of a potted palm—to waltz into the drawing room just now, it was rather nice to have a name for the face that had stayed with him through two sleepless nights.

Not a remarkable face, really. Not at all like Miss Rellton, who was quite incredibly beautiful, though about as scintillating as dishwater. No, Lady Caroline had a face one might overlook unless one had first met it in the throes of a passionate cry, her teary eyes like a bottomless forest pond.

Wasn't he turning into the poet?

Actually, he had to admit that the reason he could not get her out of his mind was the spark in those eyes when she had stood and shoved his dirty hanky in his front pocket. She had made him laugh.

He smiled now at the memory.

"Oh!"

Terrance blinked at the anger in Lady Caroline's exclamation.

"You are horrible!"

It had been a rather long time since Terrance had ventured into society, but he was pretty sure he hadn't done anything that could be called horrible.

"You are laughing at me!"

No, he wasn't. "No, I'm not."

"How dare you, Lord Darington! I do not know what it is you think you are doing, or why you would even want to spend your precious time teasing someone as unnoteworthy as I, but I will tell you right now that I will not have it! You come in here with the obvious intent of making me squirm for the circumstances you found me in at the theater, say your little piece as if you are reading it off a note card, and then you laugh at me? Well, I never! And it means nothing at all to me that Miss Spit actually sat on your lap. Nothing at all!"

The girl stamped her foot. "And it means nothing at all that you have hair on the back of your head or that my heart flutters. I think it flutters because I hate you!" She turned on her heel, walked through the door of the drawing room, and stomped down the hall.

And then Terrance heard the distinct sound of a door slamming. He could have sworn, as well, that the door that had just slammed was the one he had come through to enter the house.

That would mean that Lady Caroline had just screamed at him and then slammed out of the house. Her house. He had just run the girl from her own home.

Though he had a problem with words, he knew that his mind worked just fine. But the last few minutes left him completely flummoxed.

What on earth did his hair have to do with anything?

Terrance glanced around the empty room, waited for a few minutes while silence pounded off the walls, and then went out into the hall.

"Hellooooo?" he called, and then waited a bit more.

No one came. He could spy no bellpulls, either. He *did* see his hat and coat on a rack at the end of a hall off the front door.

"Excuse me," he tried again. But the little maid who had let him in did not appear. Well, fine then. Terrance went and took his hat and coat.

He'd quite bungled that.

Still, he thought as he let himself out of the small town house, he had said what needed to be said. Probably he should stay well away from Lady Caroline Starling in the future.

She made his mind feel jumbled, and he really needed to keep confusion to a minimum.

Anyway, she did seem a bit touched.

Why, then, did he feel this strange need *not* to stay away from her?

Maybe *he* was touched.

There was nothing like making a fool of oneself first thing in the morning. Add to that, freezing to death on one's own stoop. In her humiliating rush out the front door, Linney had forgotten her hat and coat. She had forgotten, as well, that it was her own front door she was rushing out of. Stupid woman. She had just made a scene and stomped out of her own house.

And now she was going to freeze.

For she most certainly could not go back in until Lord Darington left.

Oh, the downfall of pride. And the downfall of allowing herself to speak at all. She did much better when she kept all her queer musings tucked up inside her own head, thank you very much.

Linney marched down the stairs to the deserted walk and spied Lord Rake sauntering up to her. He flicked her a superior glance, twitched his tail in disdain, and continued on his way. Obviously, he was just back from a night of debauchery.

Horrid male. All males were horrid, even feline ones.

Lord Rake went another couple of yards, and then turned about the railing and picked his way delicately down the stairs to a small alcove beneath the main entrance that hid the servants' door.

Well, at least she now realized how to reenter the house without being seen. Linney followed the cat and rapped on the kitchen door.

As they waited for Cook to let them in, she and Lord Rake stood in silence. He was nothing at all like his grandmother, her very best friend growing up at Ivy Park, Mr. Winky.

Mr. Winky had obviously turned into Mrs. Winky when Linney had discovered her ensconced on a bed made of her mother's best satin dress, a litter of six kittens about her.

One of those kittens had been Duchess, who, in turn, had given birth to Lord Rake and Miss Spit. And though Lord Rake rarely acknowledged her and Miss Spit was nearly always in a snit, Linney loved them all. They were, in fact, a major reason she wanted to marry Lord Pellering.

Her dearest barn cats desperately needed a barn.

Linney heard the front door above them open and pushed her back against the far wall. The last thing she wanted was for Lord Darington to find her shivering outside the kitchen. What a horrid way to ruin a most embarrassing, but truly dramatic exit.

It was that damnable pride. One would think she hadn't any pride, really, but had it she did, in spades.

The heels of Lord Darington's boots struck each stair sharply as he descended to the street. Linney held her breath, and then cringed when Cook finally decided to open the door.

"And what you be doin' out here, Lady Caroline?" she cried loudly. "You'll catch your death!"

Lord Rake slithered through Cook's feet and disappeared.

"Lady Caroline?" It was, of course, Lord Darington. It was much too much to ask that he had not heard Cook.

Linney wished she could slither and disappear as well. Wouldn't it be nice? But, instead, she glanced up at Lord Darington, who was now leaning over the railing, a questioning look on his incredibly beautiful face.

At the very least he should have looked like an ogre, being one as he was.

"I did not mean to offend," Lord Darington called down to her with what seemed sincere earnestness.

Cook stood looking perplexed. And Linney just wished she could go back to only a half hour before and inform her mother that she certainly could not and would not meet Lord Darington in the drawing room.

She never said or did the right thing, ever. So she did try to say and do nothing at all. This whole horrible scene was proof that she ought to get married as soon as possible and retire to the country, forever.

"I am sure you did not offend, Lord Darington," Linney said quickly. "But . . ."

Cook was obviously out of her comfort level as well, for the traitorous woman backed into the house and shut the door.

Lord save her. Linney shivered.

Lord Darington hurried down the stairs, doffing his coat as he did. "Here," he said, thrusting the piece of superfine cloth at her.

She did not want to take his coat, and they both stood staring at the article of clothing for a rather long and very cold moment.

He shook the coat out and then tried to help her on with it.

Oh for goodness' sake. Linney stuck her arm in one sleeve, then bent to put her other arm in, and stopped suddenly as she felt Lord Darington's breath upon her neck.

It was warm and brought out goose bumps all along her back and down her arms. Lovely.

"Are you all right?" he asked, bending closer.

Oh Lord, oh Lord, oh Lord, oh Lord. Linney shivered again, only this time it had nothing to do with the fact that she was a few short minutes away from freezing to death.

She shrugged into the coat and turned around quickly. Only they were now standing in a very small alcove and so there just wasn't enough physical space between them. Linney could see the dark hairs just under the skin of Lord Darington's jaw. She could feel his breath fan warmly against the top of her head, and she could now smell him all around her, a mingling of spice and cigar, coffee and man.

Oh Lord.

Lord Darington just stared at her, and then he frowned. He seemed awkward, and with all that Linney knew of him, she knew that he would never be awkward.

She sighed. "Really, Lord Darington, I do not understand . . ."

"Will you go with me to the Morelands' skating party?"

Now that was unexpected. Linney glanced around, wondering if maybe someone weren't listening to this. Perhaps this was all some sort of joke or a dare or some other stupid male prank.

"I'm engaged, Lord Darington," she said, even though she wasn't. "Well, at least, I will be soon." She hoped. At least she thought she hoped.

And then she again felt that horrible sensation burn the backs of her eyes, and her heart just felt like a stone anvil beating away at her chest.

Lord, she was going to cry.

She really must stop thinking about Lord Pellering and his impending request to marry her while in the presence of others, because without fail it made her wish to cry.

And, really, it was bad enough that she was such a horrible hanky drencher in the seclusion of her room. When she started displaying her newfound weakness to all and sundry, it just did not bode well.

Linney bit hard at her bottom lip and stuck her chin in the air. She would not cry in front of Lord Darington. Of course, she knew that her eyes were probably a bit shiny, because she could feel those tears burning and trying to be free.

It would be awfully nice when she just got the married part over and she could be sensible once more.

And it would have been really nice if her tears had at least waited until she was inside, and preferably alone.

And it would have been really, really nice if Lord Darington hadn't been standing in front of her, staring at her, watching her fall apart . . . again.

No, damn it, she would not fall apart.

Linney took a deep breath, clenching her fists at her sides and shivering again, just as Lord Darington said something.

She didn't really understand what he said, but then he shook his head sharply and put his arms around her and pulled her against his wide chest.

Linney spent a tiny second shocked, a part of her brain telling her to shove the man away for he was taking liberties. And he was most probably laughing at her or something more horrible.

But then her brain basically stopped functioning as it should entirely. Lord Darington was the only man in her whole life to hold her so, and, once her brain sort of melted into mush, she found that she most definitely liked it.

Who knew that one could feel so incredibly warm when the world about them was gripped in the tight fist of a winter freeze?

And was it not truly amazing to spend a few precious moments held in such wonderfully strong arms against such a nice muscular chest, listening, as she was, to the soft thump of another's heart beating?

She had forgotten entirely that she had been fighting to keep from crying. Why on earth had she teared up, anyway? And, oh bloody hell, what was she doing in Lord Darington's arms?

Linney pushed away.

"Are you all right?" Lord Darington asked, his voice low and really very nice sounding.

No, goodness no, she was most certainly not all right. "I must go. Immediately!" Linney turned and banged on the door with all her might.

It opened quickly as if Cook had been standing there the whole time. Wonderful. This incident would be old news among London servants within the hour. Linney made a small sound of distress and then did just as Lord Rake had before her; she slithered past Cook and disappeared.

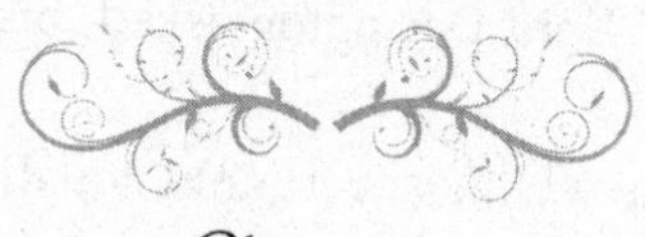

Chapter 3

Lord Darington appears to have dispensed with all semblance of normal behavior and etiquette. Upon meeting Mrs. Featherington in Piccadilly last week, he informed her that she appeared to have a dead bird on her head. (This Author shall—uncharacteristically—refrain from comment about Mrs. Featherington's unfortunate choice of headwear.) Not to mention that when he asked Miss Ballister to dance with him at the Worth ball last week, he did so by looking her in the face and quite bluntly stating, "I want to dance."

Such candor would be refreshing if it weren't so bizarre.

And if that weren't enough, Lord Darington was seen Sunday last, walking along the streets of Mayfair without a coat.

Good heavens, has no one told the poor man that the Thames has frozen over?

Lady Whistledown's Society Papers,
2 February 1814

"Well, first of all, Dare, you called upon them way too early yesterday."

Terrance sat back with a sigh. "Right, I forgot about that."

Ronald Stuart shook his head. "A week in London, and you are still on country time. I shall have to keep you out late tonight, perhaps then you might sleep at least until noon."

Terrance laughed and sipped his tonic.

"You know, you could have a brandy. It's only me you're with. No one you'll need to keep your wits up for."

Terrance glanced around White's. "Thanks, but I like my wits." It had been a very long time since he had last sat with Stu at White's like this, a lifetime, really.

"Secondly, Lady Caroline is not anyone you should waste another thought on. Though it's a bit of a slight to lose such a fine coat."

"She had it sent to my home. I did not lose it."

"Well, good then. Now." Stu pulled a bit of parchment from the pocket of his waistcoat. "Miss Rellton isn't going to do?" He dipped a quill in an inkpot on the table beside him and held it above the paper.

"No."

"Then we shall go on to the next." Stu scratched out Miss Rellton's name.

Terrance frowned. Stu had the subtlety of a rampaging bull and the tact as well. A fine man, and the most loyal friend Terrance had ever had. But suddenly the businesslike way they were going about finding Terrance a bride seemed rather crass.

And he did not think Lady Caroline should be dismissed out of hand quite so quickly. "I asked Lady Caroline to the skating party."

"Excuse me?"

"I asked—"

"Are you mad? She's exactly what you told me you did not want in a wife, Dare. And, if I remember correctly, you wanted to get this done in a timely matter." Stu stuck the quill back in the inkpot. " 'I need to get married, Stu, help me find a wife. But for God's sake don't make me stay through a Season.' Does that ring a bell, Dare? That was you giving me instructions on this whole thing, wasn't it?"

Yes, but how horrible his words now sounded coming from Stu's mouth.

"And, anyway, Lady Caroline does not meet your requirements in the least," Stu continued. "You asked me to find you someone who would be able to represent you well in society. Someone who—how did you put it?—glitters? Someone who can keep up a good conversation so as to divert the attention away from the fact that yours isn't as glib. Well, I'll tell you now, Dare, Lady Caroline is most definitely not the one to do that. She's positively"—Stu grimaced—"positively bland, Dare, is what she is."

Bland? Terrance thought of Caroline's dewy complexion and large eyes, then remembered her strange words and obviously passionate demeanor.

If there was one thing that Lady Caroline Starling was not, it was bland.

"She refused me," he said. And if he thought this information would calm his friend, Terrance was sadly mistaken.

"*She* refused *you? She* refused *you?*" Stu stood. "How dare she! As if she could do any better!"

"Stu," Terrance said quietly. "Sit."

Stu sat. "Well, really, she does think she's quite the thing, doesn't she?"

"No." Terrance stopped for a moment, trying to find his words. "Actually, she seems not to like me."

"She doesn't like you?"

"That's what I said."

"Of course, but you don't always say what you mean, now do you? Or at least you really never use enough words that I am sure I understand completely. And I really must understand this completely: Lady Caroline doesn't like you?" Stu held up his hands as if surrendering to someone. "What on earth does *liking* you have to do with anything? I mean, Lady Caroline is the quintessential ape leader. She really ought to be most grateful to anyone who offers her a way off the shelf. She has no room to be picky."

"I must disagree. Lady Caroline should be very picky. She is a beautiful woman."

Stu furrowed his brow. "Fine, she's beautiful. But no woman with any kind of intelligence would turn down an invitation from a well-heeled bachelor with a title in front of his name. Especially a woman who is well past her prime." Stu waved his hand in the air. "Beautiful or no. It has nothing to do with liking at all."

"Well, Lady Caroline doesn't like me."

Stu just shrugged. "Women, strange bunch, the lot of them. And it doesn't matter anyway, because she's not for you." With a shake of his blond head, Stu returned his attention to the list. "But Miss Shelton-Hart most definitely is." He looked up, his dark eyes alight with triumph.

A bit premature to think in terms of triumph, it seemed to Terrance. And anyway, he did not want to think of the next person on the list. He wanted to think of Caroline Starling.

So much for staying away from her.

"I shall call upon Miss Shelton-Hart this very moment and tell her that you shall be escorting her to the skating party," Stu announced.

Lovely, he could just see Stu pounding into Miss Shelton-Hart's drawing room and demanding that the woman go to the skating party with Lord Darington. "Shouldn't you *ask* her, Stu?"

Stu blinked. "Right, that's what I said, Dare." His friend leaned in toward him and whispered, "Really, do try not to say things that make you sound touched. *We* know you are fine, but if others know of your problem, they will give you horrible grief. And believe me, this list of probable brides will be whittled down to nearly nothing."

Terrance's lips twitched, but he carefully did not laugh at his friend. "Anyway, I don't want Miss Shelton-Hart."

"And how would you know? Have you met her? Have you seen her?" Stu did not wait for Terrance to answer. "No," he said succinctly as if to a child in the midst of a tantrum. "I'm off, then, to *ask* Miss Shelton-Hart to be ready at half past eleven, three days hence, for the incredible pleasure of being escorted to the Morelands' skating party by Lord Darington himself." Stu launched himself from his chair with great enthusiasm. "Will you be all right here alone?"

Dearest Stu. "Of course."

"Right, then, I'm off." Stu tipped his head at Terrance, shoved the list of names in his breast pocket, and took off with a light step toward the exit.

Terrance watched him go, and then he glanced around at the other gentlemen talking and smoking in White's drawing room. Ever since his injury, he spoke less and saw more. It was amazing, really, the things he now understood whereas he would have completely missed them before.

Terrance watched as some young man twitched and stammered his way through some request of the Earl of Stanwick. Though he was too far away to hear, Terrance knew it was a request, one the young man wanted desperately and was rather sure the old earl was not going to give him.

Poor sod.

Terrance stood. He remembered a time when he would come to White's and wile away hours doing nothing more than drinking and smoking and talking. And now that seemed infinitely boring to him.

He was actually more interested now in finding his way into Lady Caroline's good graces. It didn't matter what Stu said, or even what Terrance had said he wanted before. Now that he had met Lady Caroline, Terrance did not care about anything he might once have desired.

He wanted to get to know Caroline. And he most definitely wanted to explore the base of her neck with his tongue. Very important, that.

With a nod to the Earl of Stanwick, Terrance left his club in search of Lady Caroline Starling.

One of the things Linney was most definitely looking forward to, when married and living in the country, was the freedom to go anywhere she wanted without having to find a chaperone. It was just such a horrible bother, especially since most of their servants were usually on some errand for her mother.

Usually, she would have sent a note around to Emily Parsons, her one and only friend and always willing to go with Linney and bring along one of the fifty million footmen her father retained. But, unfortunately, Emily's family had decided that the frozen Thames was not sufficiently fascinating to warrant a winter trip to London, and so they had elected to remain in the country.

Thus, she had been forced to corner Teddy, their butler/footman/all-around errand boy. Her mother would probably burst a vein when she realized that Teddy would not be there to put on his butler hat for the callers who would be showing up at any moment, but Annie would be able to do it. And Linney needed to get out.

Anyway, sitting in the drawing room, as she was always asked to do for some unfathomable reason, and listening to her mother talk a mile a minute, as well as enduring her disgust of Mr. Evanston who leered at their female visitors, was beyond her at the moment.

No, now she would much rather be right where she was. Linney stood in a deserted marble hall of Montagu House, Bloomsbury, in which the British Museum was kept, staring at the Rosetta Stone. Teddy was gossiping with a guard in the other room, with Linney's blessing.

Linney touched the stone, letting her fingers play over the strange markings. She let herself wonder about what they said, about the world the stone had come from. The mysteries surrounding the stone intrigued her.

It made her sad, too. Somewhere there was a space this stone had once occupied that was now deserted. The Rosetta Stone had been taken from its resting place of thousands of years, stolen really, and taken miles and miles and worlds away.

And though she really could not put words to the idea, it didn't feel right, just another one of the strange thoughts that she would never say out loud.

"Interesting, isn't it?"

Pulled from her musings by a low voice just over her shoulder, Linney let out a shriek that echoed through the entire Museum and was probably heard on three different continents.

"Sorry," the voice said.

She turned to find none other than Lord Darington. For a man to whom she was related, albeit distantly, but had never seen in her life, it seemed a little strange that she had now encountered him three times in as many days.

A little strange, and very disconcerting.

"My lady?" Poor Teddy came at a dead run around the corner, his face the color of the ice that now covered the Thames.

"Sorry, Teddy, 'tis nothing." Linney frowned up at the "nothing." "I was just startled, is all."

Teddy gulped some air and nodded, but didn't leave, either. Good boy.

"I did not mean to startle."

No, he didn't mean to startle, or offend; what on earth *did* he mean, then?

They stared at each other for a moment. Which was a bit on the uncomfortable side, but really fine since he was the most beautiful man she had ever seen. And he smelled good, too. That was not usually a point in favor of most men, she had to admit.

Mr. Evanston, for example, always smelled like the inside of an old shoe.

When it was warm out, the man went absolutely sour.

"Do you enjoy Egyptology?" Lord Darington asked, tipping his thick head of hair toward the Rosetta Stone.

She faltered a moment, a rather strange and altogether disturbing image of her fingers running through his hair causing her to swallow a touch loudly before answering him.

"Errr, no, actually." She glanced at the stone. "Not particularly. I like the stone, though. I like to wonder about it, especially in the quiet of the museum." Linney frowned. That hadn't really made any sense, had it? "I mean . . ."

"Yes, I know."

She narrowed her eyes at him. If he truly understood, then she was a fairy princess.

He touched the stone, right at the exact spot she had put her own fingers. "I see some poor sod, hunched over this rock . . ." Lord Darington stopped for a moment and took a long breath. "Chipping away. Who was he? It makes you wonder, doesn't it?"

Yes.

Lord Darington glanced up at her with eyes the color of a summer sky. "It is sad," he said softly, "that this stone is so far from home."

Well, her fairy godmother would be dropping in at any moment, then. She blinked at Lord Darington.

He put out his arm. "Walk with me," he said.

It would have been *awfully* nice of him to put that in the form of a question rather than a demand, but for some reason, Linney just slipped her hand around his elbow.

Mmmm, Lord Darington was warm.

In fact, for a moment, Linney had the strangest urge to curl right into him and breathe in his lovely scent and just be warm. She had not been truly warm in a horribly long time.

"You aren't at all bland," he said.

Linney stopped walking and just stared. "Well, thank you so very much."

His face darkened as if he were blushing, which was exactly what he should be doing, but she doubted that was the cause. He was probably just getting prickly at her sarcastic tone.

Well, that was just too bad, because she was already prickly from being called not bland. "Are you trying to compliment me, Lord Darington? Or perhaps you are trying to put me in my place?"

He took a very deep breath. "It was a compliment."

"Really?"

"Actually . . ." Lord Darington stopped and glanced up at Teddy, who stood at a discreet distance behind them, pretending profound interest in some piece of cracked pottery.

"I'm not sure why," Lord Darington said, looking back at her. "But I really like you."

"Well, goodness, I may swoon."

Lord Darington frowned and a small muscle ticked along his jawline. For some reason, the sight of that muscle made Linney almost *really* swoon.

Lord Darington was a cad and a snob, and he said the most horrible things. And yet he was absolutely beautiful, and his very nearness made her feel all light in the head and . . . well . . . swoony.

And it was especially bad at this very moment, for Lord Darington was watching her lips with an intensity she had heretofore never seen in another person's eyes. Especially someone looking at her.

Linney ran her tongue along her front teeth, and then tried, surreptitiously, to lick her lips, an altogether impossible feat, seeing that Lord Darington watched her like a cat eyeing a mouse.

And then Lord Darington kissed her.

Holy mother of God. Lord Darington was kissing her!

Linney stood frozen in shock as Lord Darington pressed his warm, full lips against hers. She had never been kissed before, of course. Actually, she had wondered if the act weren't horribly disgusting.

It most definitely was not anything close to disgusting.

In fact, she quite liked being kissed.

Lord Darington pulled away slightly, but then returned, angling his head just a touch to the side and a bit higher so that her top lip was sweetly embraced by both of his.

Yum.

Yes, she definitely enjoyed this. If it was this much fun to kiss Lord Darington, the cad, maybe it would be very wonderful to kiss her soon-to-be fiancé, Ernest Wareing, Earl of Pellering?

He was not at all exciting, of course. But at least he wasn't a cad.

Lord Darington opened his mouth slightly and sucked her top lip into his mouth. Linney's hands lifted of their own accord, and she felt Lord Darington's upper arms against her fingers.

His arms were solid, strong. And she *suddenly* remembered when she had first seen his hands; those lovely hands were now gently holding either side of her rib cage.

Since it seemed that all rules had been thrown to the pigeons, Linney decided to indulge—well, indulge even more than she was at the moment—and she inched one of her hands up and curled her fingers in the hair at the back of Lord Darington's neck.

It was exactly as it looked, soft and thick. Oh, she did like Lord Darington's hair. And his smell, and his hands, and his strong arms, and . . .

No, kissing Ernest Wareing, Earl of Pellering, would not be this thrilling. She was pretty sure of that at the moment.

She was also sure that she would like to kiss Lord Darington more than just this one time.

It was much too nice to do only once. "I would like to kiss you at least a dozen times," she murmured.

Lord Darington leaned away from her and touched the side of her face with the tip of his finger. "A dozen?"

Caroline felt her face burn. Her legs were actually shaking, and she felt horribly light-headed.

Lord Darington's arms tightened around her as if he understood completely that she might turn into a puddle at his feet at any moment.

"At least a dozen," she heard herself whisper. Well, wasn't she just making a cake out of herself?

"I like you, Lady Caroline."

Hm, yes, swooning might definitely be in her future. "I will go with you," she said then, her mouth working with absolutely no input from her brain. "To the skating party."

He blinked, his hands leaving her sides.

Oh no, why on earth had she just said that?

"I think I'm going with Miss Shelton-Hart," he said slowly.

"You think?" she said stupidly. And then she pushed away from Lord Darington. Oh, what a horrible fool she was, Linney thought, as she whirled around and nearly ran from Lord Darington's presence.

Teddy looked away quickly, but she knew very well he had been staring intently.

Wonderful. She had completely forgotten that Teddy was standing there watching them. In fact, she had forgotten everything. Bloody hell, they were standing in the middle of the British Museum. Anyone could have seen them.

Seen her be an idiot.

She stopped and turned back to the man who had just kissed her. "I would very much appreciate it if you just left me alone. I'm not sure what it is you are about, but I *am* rather sure it is not anything a gentleman should be doing." And Linney swirled around on her heel and walked as regally as she could manage away from Lord Darington.

The cad.

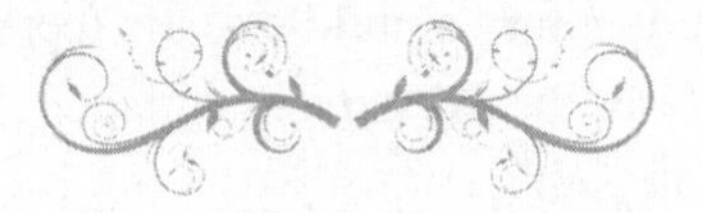

Chapter 4

This Author has it on the best authority that an elegantly dressed couple was seen kissing in the hallowed halls of the British Museum on Monday afternoon.

Unfortunately, This Author has not been able to definitively identify the persons making up this couple, and as all Gentle Readers know, while This Author may be a gossip, This Author is the best sort of gossip and only prints that which is one hundred percent, certifiably true.

Hence, no names will be named.

It must be noted, however, that it is difficult to imagine any two members of the ton *anywhere in the vicinity of the British Museum, an institution which does seem to imply a certain degree of intelligence among its patrons.*

The again, perhaps the amorous couple chose that lofty edifice for their tryst precisely because it is such an unlikely location for members of the ton.

LADY WHISTLEDOWN'S SOCIETY PAPERS,
2 February 1814

Lady Caroline Starling had been cornered by Donald Spence on the icy banks of the Thames. She had, in fact, been forced to deal with the idiot for nearly ten minutes now. And though Terrance realized completely that Lady Caroline absolutely hated him at the moment, he was rather sure that she would actually see him as a blessing in the face of Donald's rather buffoonlike attentions.

In fact, he was a bit upset with Lord Pellering, Caroline's escort to the Morelands' skating party, for not rescuing her. But Lord Pellering, it seemed, was deeply engrossed in a conversation with Lord Moreland, dull Donald's even duller father, about hunting dogs.

Anyone who could find the subject of hunting dogs more compelling than Caroline Starling was destined for Bedlam, surely.

"You are going to skate over there and be the gallant Sir Knight, aren't you, Dare?"

Terrance squinted at Stu, over the top of his glass of Madeira.

His best friend just rolled his eyes. "I must say, Dare, I miss the old days. You know, when the thought of marriage made you wince, and you did not know the definition of the word 'morals'?" Stu, rather unsteady on borrowed skates, stood beside Dare, as they watched everyone pretending to have a grand time at the worst skating party ever concocted, and grumbled.

"And you spoke more than three words a sentence," Stu continued.

Terrance arched one brow at his friend.

"Right, completely unfair of me, old boy, but God, Dare, you now remind me of an uptight snob who either thinks I'm an idiot or doesn't want to lower himself to my level to speak to me."

"Both being true, I think it fair to say."

Stu laughed without any humor and raising his hands as if praying mightily, said, "He speaks," in a horribly dramatic fashion that did not become him at all.

Terrance just chuckled. "I am about my knightly duties." He slapped his now-empty glass in Stu's outstretched hand and pushed off to rescue the fair Caroline.

Miss Shelton-Hart had abandoned him, demanding that he turn his carriage around and return her home before they had gotten even halfway to the Swan Lane Pier where the Morelands had decided to hold their skating party. She was cold and tired and about a dozen other horrible inconveniences that Terrance had quit listening to almost the minute they had left the Shelton-Hart town house.

And, though it was truly horrible of him, Terrance could not have been happier. The chit was altogether hellish, and the fact that she was second on Stu's list of marriageable females made Terrance even more certain that Stu's list was not worth a tuppence.

Terrance maneuvered himself around a servant struggling with a serving cart on the ice and glided nicely to Caroline's side.

"Caroline," he said, placing his hand around her trim waist. "Skate with me."

Donald scrunched up his rather prominent nose. "Lord Darington," he said with a bit of a sneer. The boy really ought not to sneer, it did not help his looks in the least. "I had heard that you decided to leave your country cave and rejoin society."

"And you heard right." Terrance pushed off, taking Caroline with him, and leaving Donald to his sneering.

They moved in silence, Caroline quite proficient on her skates. He noticed that they fit perfectly against each other's sides. Just as they had fit perfectly facing each other.

Conclusion: they definitely fit.

"Thank you," she said finally.

Terrance glanced down at her in surprise. She was beautiful. The hood of her fur-lined pelisse framed her face, soft against her glowing cheeks and shining eyes. "You look lovely," he said. "I like you in pink."

Caroline's cheeks reddened even further, and she looked away quickly, assuming great interest in the ten-piece orchestra set up on the pier. "I daresay you are an incredible liar, Lord Darington." She made a soft sound that was probably meant to be a laugh, but Terrance knew it wasn't. Not really. "I am sure no one would ever describe me as lovely."

"But I did."

She blinked up at him, and this time she really did laugh. "Yes, I guess you did."

Terrance tried to think of how to say what he wanted to ask her. "You cannot believe that you are ugly" was what came out. Not quite right, but good enough.

"Oh, of course not," she said quickly. "Well, that is to say . . . I am not saying that it is fact that I am not ugly, I mean . . ." She shook her head.

"Obviously, I have no idea what I'm saying, but, suffice it to say, Lord Darington, I know that I am not ugly, but I am not lovely, either. I am most definitely not an extreme, you see, just very much in the middle."

"You are perfect, then."

She stumbled over her skates and nearly fell, but Terrance held on to her tightly. Perfect, most assuredly so, he thought, his hand at her waist. Not too thin, but not too thick, absolutely perfect.

He remembered the feel of her soft lips beneath his own, her sweet breath mingled with his, and decided that Lady Caroline Starling was beyond perfect. And it really was not just because he wanted to throw her down right there on the ice and ravage her until her eyes shone green like emeralds.

Really, it was not because of that at all.

Well, maybe a little.

But mostly it was because her eyes turned green, a startling fernlike color, when she cried. And when she kissed him, or yelled at him. Lady Caroline Starling had a passion within her that would make some man very happy someday.

If that man even realized that it was there. Terrance shot a dark glance at Lord Pellering.

Lord Pellering would *never* realize that passion lurked within Caroline. The man probably had no idea that passion lurked in anyone that didn't bay at the moon and chase foxes up trees.

Actually, in the last few days, Terrance had begun to hope that maybe he might be the perfect man to uncover that passion and keep it burning at more regular intervals than it did at the moment.

In fact, he was rather sure that he was.

But to convince Lady Caroline was going to be rather difficult. Worth it, but difficult.

He had been holding her hand very lightly, but now Terrance threaded his fingers through hers.

She shivered, and he felt it against his chest.

"Are you cold?"

Rather than answer, Caroline just shook her head.

"Why did you cry at the theater?"

She stiffened, but then just as quickly she seemed to wilt against him. She shook her head, and this time she sighed as well. "I do not know," she said quietly.

"Ah."

She stiffened again, and this time she stayed that way. Terrance knew that somehow, somewhere he had once again flirted with her ire. He did seem to do that a lot.

Caroline moved as if she would try to push away from him, but though it nearly put them into a snowbank, Terrance held on to her.

"You know, Lord Darington, I think you are even more pompous than Lord Rake."

Lord Rake. Terrance wracked his brains. Did he know a Lord Rake?

Pompous? Terrance could not help but laugh. Him? Pompous? Being that he could barely speak his thoughts, that he had been declared brain damaged, actually, only two years before, he rather thought "pompous" an unfair description.

But suddenly he remembered that Stu had basically just called him the very same thing. Terrance's silence must make him seem that way.

Stu understood. Caroline did not.

In fact, the servants and people of Ivy Park had seemed to take a very long time to get used to him as well.

"I . . ." He tried to find the words to tell Caroline. But finally he just said, "I would never make you cry."

Now that was good: short, but sweet and rather romantic if he did say so. He congratulated himself even as he suddenly hurtled toward a snowbank.

It wasn't until he was firmly imbedded in the treacherous mound of cold snow that he truly realized that Lady Caroline Starling had just pushed him headfirst into the thing.

Hm. Perhaps he had not been as romantic and sweet as he thought? Right. He was starting to understand with new clarity how very much easier it had been to woo women as a scoundrel and a rake than as a man in love and with marriage on his mind.

Good God, he was most definitely in love. Terrance knew this completely, because when he shook the snow from his hair and levered himself onto his knees, he did not wish to throttle the glaring Lady Caroline.

Well, maybe he did, but just a little.

No, he actually felt more compelled to make her understand.

Interesting, that.

"You wouldn't make me cry, Lord Darington?" Caroline asked with definite tears glistening in her very green eyes.

"You are the only reason I have ever cried." And with that cryptic statement she shot off away from him, away from the entire party, in fact, moving quickly out of sight and around a bend in the river.

"I think, Dare, that you have lost your touch with the ladies."

Terrance looked over to see Stu reaching down to help him up.

"Yes." He took his friend's hand and steadied himself on the ice. "It is confounding. I finally try to understand one of them, and I am now more confused than ever."

Stu just shrugged. "Still, Dare, I must say that you might be right about that chit." His friend squinted at the spot they had last seen Lady Caroline. "She may not be all that bland. She looked quite fetching today, actually."

Terrance turned a glare on Stu. The man put his hands up as if to ward off an attack. "Not that I noticed."

They both looked again at the bend in the river.

"I am going to marry her," Terrance said.

"Right." Stu nodded. "I thought so. Could tell, actually, as you were skating."

"But she is very angry with me." Terrance looked back at his friend again, who stood tapping his right forefinger against his bottom lip. "I don't know why, exactly." Terrance cocked his head. "Do you think *you* might?"

Stu tapped some more. "I just might."

"Yes, I thought so. Could tell, actually, when you started tapping."

Stu curled his right hand into a fist and folded his arms in front of himself. "That gets me in trouble at the gaming tables as well."

"Yes, I know." Terrance nodded. "I used to beat you often."

"Right, right."

"So."

"It *is* cold today, isn't it? Coldest winter I've ever known, I think."

Terrance did not say a thing.

"I think I was rather abrupt with them . . . no, I know I was very abrupt with them, Lady Caroline and her mother, that is, when I was terribly worried that you would die."

Terrance arched one brow.

"I hate it when you do that."

Terrance did not move.

"Okay, then, I knew you were not going to die, of course. You came through well enough in the hospital in France. But you looked awful, really, your head all bandaged up. And the doctors all said that you would never speak again, and probably have a damaged intelligence even if you did."

Stu grinned at him, but Terrance did not even crack a smile.

"Yes, well, the intelligence is still there, isn't it?" Stu said morosely.

"I'd say."

"But, anyway, I had to bring you home, and I didn't want to take you to London. So I wrote a letter to Lady Darington and told her she had to leave Ivy Park."

Terrance spent a short moment trying to remember the exact word he needed to say. "Leave? How quickly?" Terrance asked finally, a very bad taste in his mouth.

Stu started to tap his lip again. "Goodness, it has been nearly, what, three years, Dare. I can't really remem . . ."

"Stu?"

"Two days, yes that was it. I gave them two days." Stu shuffled closer. "But, Dare, I was at my wits' end. I mean, I didn't want anyone to know about your injury. I wasn't sure what you would want. Or if you'd ever want anything again. I was just trying to do the best I could under the circumstances."

Terrance sighed heavily, and then he closed his eyes. "Shh," he said, finally.

Stu stuttered to a halt.

"You are a loyal friend, Stu."

Stu bowed his head, scuffing the ice with the toe of his skate. Which made him fall. But he scrambled up quickly.

"You did me a . . ." Terrance knew the word in his head, but he had to work to make his mouth say it. "Justice," Terrance finally got out. He glanced over the skating party and shook his head on a sigh. "They would have ripped me to shreds."

"Yes, now they all just think you're a pompous ass."

Terrance frowned fiercely.

"Which is good!"

Terrance realized that his friend was right, and his frown eased. And then he chuckled softly. "Yes. They don't think I am . . ." The word would not come.

"Damaged?" Stu supplied helpfully.

"Yes."

With a grin, Stu slapped Terrance on the back, and fell again.

Terrance helped Stu to his feet. "Still, I have to woo. But I never say what is right." Terrance pushed against his brow with his forefinger. "This courting business produces horrendous headaches."

"Ha! That has nothing to do with the bullet in your head, old boy. It has to do with women. They speak some other language none of us can comprehend. Communicating with females isn't easy for even the best of us."

Terrance glanced over at his friend. "You being 'the best of us'?"

Stu frowned. "Well . . . I, er . . ."

"Who can't speak?" Terrance teased.

"Right then, I'll race you to the pier, that'll put you in your place, all right."

"No, the ice is too thin at the pier."

Stu rounded his mouth as if dramatically surprised. "Long sentence there, man."

Oh yes, Stu was good at tit for tat. He was also wonderful to tease. Terrance loved that about his friend. He needed it desperately. "Around Lady Witherspoon and back. On your count."

"Go," Stu said without counting, and they were off.

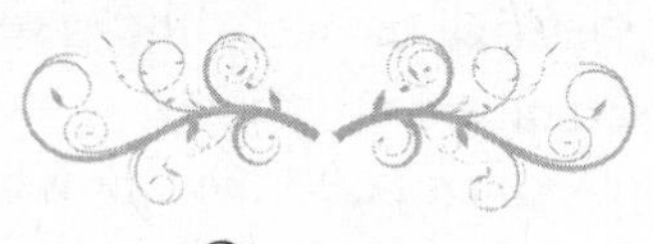

Chapter 5

It was clear to all onlookers that Lady Witherspoon was not at all amused when Mr. Ronald Stuart, while racing upon the ice against Lord Darington, crashed into her and knocked her into a most awkward prone position, causing her skirts to rise in a most indelicate manner.

Copious attempted apologies, tendered by both Mr. Stuart and Lord Darington, were, by all counts, rebuffed.

LADY WHISTLEDOWN'S SOCIETY PAPERS,
4 February 1814

"Oh Duchess," Linney moaned. "I think I am going to die."

Duchess just burrowed closer to her under the covers.

Linney was sick, very sick. She was hot and achy. Of course, it was entirely her fault. It was only a matter of time, after all, if one started running out her very own front door without her coat on and taking off from skating parties with nowhere to go, and no escort to take one home.

"Linney, dear!"

Linney squeezed her eyes shut against her mother's strident tone.

"Oh, leave me alone," she muttered into the down of her blanket.

The door opened. "Linney, Lord Pellering is here. You *must* get up."

"I don't feel well, Mother."

"Be that as it may, Lord Pellering is here!"

Save me from Lord Pellering. This thought popped into Linney's head, and she really did want to run away suddenly. She could not possibly marry someone who made her so completely miserable, could she?

And it was not fair at all to Lord Pellering that he made her miserable. He was quite an agreeable man, really. But, well, he had no hair.

And he liked his hounds altogether too much. That just could not be right.

Oh Lord, she was just as pompous and horrible as Lord Darington to think such awful thoughts.

Lord Darington. A jumble of emotions made it feel like her skin was hot and cold at the same time. No, her skin *was* hot and cold at the same time. She was sick, for the love of pete.

Now she really did want to run away.

Her mother barged into her room and stood over her bed. "He is going to ask for your hand, Linney. I'm just too thrilled. I rather thought you would *never* make a match."

"Thank you so much, mother."

"Well, you are to be six and twenty, after all, Linney. When I was your age, I was married already with a child."

With a long sigh, Linney peeked out from beneath her covers. "I am truly ill, Mother. Please tell Lord Pellering that I shall see him at another time."

"I shall do no such thing." Georgiana stripped Linney's beloved down-filled coverlet from the bed.

Oh, it was cold.

"Linney, Lord Pellering is more than you deserve. You will get out of bed this instant and go accept his suit."

"I can't."

"Fine, then, I shall do it for you."

"No!" Linney cried.

Georgiana, halfway to the door, turned around with a frown. "Whyever not? If you are so ill, than I shall at least accept on your behalf. Really, Linney, you must make this official now, or you may just lose Lord Pellering. And then what will you do?"

Linney moved slightly, and every bone in her body ached horribly. And she was so cold.

She remembered the warmth of Lord Darington's embrace and ached even more.

She knew her mother well. Georgiana Starling could care less if Linney ever married. Her mother just wanted Lord Pellering to provide a bit of pin money to his darling mother-in-law. At least until Mr. Evanston's uncle died. Mr. Evanston was, unfortunately, penniless. But he was heir to a rather large fortune, assuming his ailing uncle ever stuck his spoon in the wall.

The ailing uncle had been ailing for nearly ten years, it seemed.

"Why don't *you* marry Lord Pellering?" Linney said, only half jokingly.

"Oh really, Linney!" Her mother went to the clothespress and grabbed a gown. "I don't know what has gotten into you lately. You have been abominable."

"No, I am serious, Mother. Why are you marrying Mr. Evanston? You could have any man you choose. Why don't you just marry someone who can give you what you want right now?"

Georgiana looked entirely confused.

"Dearest Linney," her mother finally said. "Mr. Evanston does give me what I want. He gives me attention, and very soon, he will give me money. Lord Pellering, and really most of the men of society, give their attention to their paramours, their carriages or hunting dogs, but most of all to themselves." Here Georgiana stood a bit straighter.

That last comment, Linney was sure, was directed straight to her father, wherever his soul happened to be at the moment.

Duchess meowed and moved closer to Linney, lending her warmth. Using the last strength in her body, Linney leaned up on her elbow, found the corner of her blanket, and pulled it back over her. She closed her eyes and sank back against her pillows. "I think I want attention, too, Mother," she said. "I can't marry Lord Pellering."

Duchess made a sound, and Linney put her arm around her cat. Poor dear, she wasn't going to have a barn anytime soon, it seemed. And Linney was probably doomed to spend the rest of her life a spinster, living as if she did not exist in the home of her glittering mother and her decidedly oily stepfather.

And at the moment, she did not care, since she was probably going to expire from the ache in her head at any moment anyway.

"Linney."

"No more, Mother. I can barely think with the pounding in my head."

There was a long, lovely silence, and then Georgiana's silk skirt rustled. "I shall tell Lord Pellering that he should come back in a few days when you are feeling better."

Georgiana opened the door to leave. There was a God.

"Really, Linney, I don't know what's gotten into you at all. You have not been this obstinate since you were two."

Perhaps she had known more at two than she did now.

"Maybe this will teach you a lesson, though. You really should not have run away from the skating party yesterday. It is your fault entirely that you are sick."

Didn't some mothers kiss their children when they were sick?

"And you most definitely ought to stay away from Lord Darington. You are not pining after someone so incredibly beyond you, are you, Linney?"

Linney felt a strange anger burn in her heart. Beyond her? Ha! He was beyond the pale, was what he was!

Georgiana waited as if she expected Linney to say something. But Linney had neither the strength nor the inclination, and finally the door closed behind her mother.

Silence. Lovely, gorgeous, beautiful silence.

If she lived in the country with a husband who loved his hounds more than he would ever love her, she would be able to have silence often and most probably always.

And in that single moment, during that very thought, Linney finally understood why she had been crying the week before at the theater.

Perhaps even why she was so affected by someone of Lord Darington's ilk.

Because what her mother had said to her today, and nearly every day of her life, was just not true. Lord Pellering was not more than Linney deserved. No man was.

She deserved to be happy and content.

And Lord Pellering could not give her those two things, not really. Some woman would deserve him, and he her. But that woman would not be Linney.

Thank God, because she really had no inkling to kiss Lord Pellering as she had kissed Lord Darington.

Oh goodness, Linney thought, as she again felt rather swoony.

Though, in all seriousness, that could have had everything to do with the fact that she was probably delusional with fever, and nothing at all to do with thoughts of a tall, dark, and gorgeous man with curling thick hair and eyes the color of a lazy summer sky.

Nothing to do with him at all.

Linney smiled softly as her foggy brain took her off into a lovely dream. Interestingly enough, Lord Darington took center stage in that dream. And it was a really, *really* good dream.

Chapter 6

Good heavens, but Lady Caroline Starling has refused Lord Pellering's offer of marriage! Linney, my dear, you are well into your third decade! Whatever can you be thinking?

Maybe that she'd rather enter into marriage in which she was considered of greater importance than a pack of hunting dogs?

Yes, yes. That is exactly what This Author believes she is thinking.

LADY WHISTLEDOWN'S SOCIETY PAPERS,
9 February 1814

Linney had had one too many glasses of rum punch. But, really, it was horribly cold outside, and the rum punch did warm one to one's very toes. Add to that the fact that she stood at the Shelbournes' Valentine's ball, where every single person seemed to have some special person to swan over, except for Linney, who was most positively alone. And, most importantly, Linney was terribly nervous about seeing Lord Darington again, for the last time she had seen him, she had been so gauche as to shove him into a snowbank, and since that moment she had dreamed of him every time her eyelids dropped shut.

And the dreams were far from those an aging miss ought to have.

Yes, she did think she had reasons enough to imbibe rum punch. Still, since it was imperative that she guard her tongue at all times, Linney did try to stay away from anything that loosened it.

And at the moment, she felt decidedly loose.

Probably not a good thing.

She scanned the crowd nervously. At the very least, Linney knew she would not see Lord Pellering. When she had finally been well enough to see him, two days after the skating party, Linney had refused his suit.

The earl had grumbled mightily about wasted time and informed the entire household, Annie included, that he was off to Stratfordshire to wed the daughter of some squire who knew the worth of a good hound, and whom, Lord Pellering said as he thrust on his beaver hat, he should have married in the first place and never set foot in London.

So that was the last she had seen of Lord Pellering.

And she could not say that she was sorry. No, the urge to cry at every turn of the hour had disappeared completely, and Linney felt rather more like herself in the last few days.

Of course, there was still the problem of Lord Darington.

He had come while she was sick as well. Only her mother had absolutely refused to allow Annie to inform Linney of the fact. But the maid had managed to relay the message, and even give Linney the one pristine pink rose that Lord Darington had brought for her.

The message had been simple and short: "Sorry."

Linney was quite perplexed, of course. There were moments when Lord Darington seemed to be absolutely the opposite of what everyone knew him to be.

He seemed, really, like someone to whom she could actually tell all the strange thoughts in her head.

And he seemed as if he might understand them.

That, in and of itself, was a miracle.

The fact that the man also seemed taken with her, and that he was God's aesthetic gift to the universe, just made it all perfect, sort of.

Still, these things were all tempered by the fact that Lord Darington had the manners of a toad.

Anyway, Linney was quite decidedly confused by it all.

A now-familiar tall and broad figure hovered into her peripheral vision, and once again Linney felt the telltale flutter of her heart.

It made her feel positively light-headed, especially since she was about half a glass of rum punch away from singing a tune at the top of her lungs and doing a dance alone across the Shelbournes' ballroom floor.

Actually, she really ought to turn around and go home, and leave her intended mission of the evening undone until another time.

But obviously she was not really thinking right. Linney straightened her spine and keeping Lord Darington's wide back in her sights so as not to lose him, marched around some lace-covered tables, through a bunch of pink and red streamers that had come loose of their moorings and hung lamely from a crystal chandelier, and tapped Lord Darington on the shoulder.

He turned and glanced down at her, and she had to catch her breath. The man was so unearthly handsome, in a dark jacket and white waistcoat, that her fluttering heart nearly caused her apoplexy.

Well, that would never do. She had a mission, after all.

"Lord Darington," Linney said, and then realized that she had rather yelled his name a bit too loudly.

He frowned.

Oh Lord, he was being awful again. He had taken on his Lord of the World manners. Lovely.

"I am sorry," she said quickly, just wanting to get this whole thing over with. The thought that Lord Darington actually fancied her danced like a taunting bully in her head. How on earth could she have ever thought such a thing?

Be that as it may, though. She did need to apologize for pushing Lord Darington into a snowbank. Even if he were the most abominable man on earth, she ought not to lower her own manners so.

"I should not have pushed you at the skating party."

Lord Darington blinked, but said nothing at all.

"Right, then," Linney said. She absolutely refused to be rude to him again, but she did so want to throw the rest of her rum punch in his face.

Well, that was, if she had had any more in her glass. Which, funny enough, she did not. She glared for a moment at the empty glass in her hand as if she could will it to fill up on its own.

"Dance with me," Lord Darington said.

Did he never ask? Just order all the underlings around him to do his will?

He took the glass from her hand and gave it to a tall, thin, blond man who stood at his side. And then Lord Darington grabbed her arm and escorted her to the dance floor.

Linney hesitated. This was probably a very bad idea. She was most definitely dizzy, and trying to remember the steps and moves of a dance would not help that disability in the least.

"I really . . ."

Lord Darington turned toward her. "We shall dance," he said.

God, was there anyone else on the entire earth as pompous as Lord Darington? Linney could feel her ire churning in her stomach, along with the rum punch, unfortunately.

It was terribly difficult to keep her dignity around Lord Darington. The man did tend to make her want to thump him over the head. Of course, at the same time, he made her want to jump right into his arms and demand that the man who found a sad quality in the fact that the Rosetta Stone resided so far from its home come out and play.

"I'm not feeling well, Lord Darington," she said. "I do not want to dance."

Lord Darington stopped, his brow furrowed in consternation. "Let's dance."

Linney just shook her head. "No!" She pushed away from him, even as she realized that she was about to lose her decorum again. Lord Darington was such a horrible influence on her. "Really, Lord Darington, you are such an *ass*!"

A few couples around them stopped mid-dance step and stared, and Lord Veere, who had been standing behind them, began to chortle.

Linney just felt completely disgraced. How horrible of her, really. "I'm sorry," she said quickly.

"Here. Take this," Lord Darington said, shoving a piece of folded paper at her.

She frowned at it, feeling as if the whole room revolved slowly around her, making her wish to lose her dinner all over Lord Darington's highly polished boots.

"Take it, please."

Please, he had said please. She grabbed the paper, thrust it down her décolletage, and spinning about, ran for privacy.

She was most definitely going to see all the rum punch that now churned in her belly once more. And she rather thought it would be nice to do such a thing without the world watching her.

Let's not *dance.* He had meant to say, *Let's* not *dance.* Terrance watched Caroline wind her way quickly around chattering partygoers and disappear from the room. He had given much thought to his predicament, and realized that if he could not seem to woo Lady Caroline, then he really ought to go back to Ivy Park and practice his speech a bit more before going out into the world again.

But he did hope that Lady Caroline might want to go with him. He could no longer picture his world without her funny little ways in it. He loved to just look at her. It was as if he could read every thought in her head through her eyes.

He had seen her grapple with what must have sounded like total savagery on his part. And he had never wanted to speak so badly in his life.

No, he wanted to cry, *no, I don't mean to demand or make you upset. I want more than anything to make you happy. I want to dance with you. Or not dance. I want to walk with you, or stand, or sit. Anything, just let me stand near you, feel your soft skin beneath my fingers, taste your lips, and listen to your voice.*

And most definitely, let me take you out from the shadows and let the world realize what they have been missing.

He had hoped that he could make her understand this, but he had not completely trusted himself. In fact, he had not trusted his tongue at all. And he had spent the last few days trying to write on paper his feelings.

Now he could just stare at the path that Caroline had taken and hope that she could glean his real meaning from the words he had written.

Chapter 7

Could it be that Lady Caroline Starling refused the suit of the Earl of Pellering because she prefers the Marquis of Darington? Darington???? Isn't he the very same cretin who evicted her from her home three years ago, giving her only two days to pack her every belonging?

This Author does not presume to know Lady Caroline's heart, but the lady was heard (by a great many people, This Author might add), calling Lord Darington a very nasty word at the Shelbourne Valentine's Day ball.

And it is This Author's experience that only true love could ever compel a lady to lose such total command of her verbal faculties.

LADY WHISTLEDOWN'S SOCIETY PAPERS,
16 February 1814

Linney awoke to all three cats sitting at the bottom of her bed staring at her. This had not happened in all her lifetime, so she realized immediately that she must have been the topic of feline conversation the night before.

"Oh, leave me be."

Duchess meowed.

"Right, I know, I acted horribly last night. And I emptied my stomach upon Lord Rake's tail, but I have been sick, you must remember."

Lord Rake cocked his head to the side regally, and in that second he completely reminded her of Lord Darington. "Well, obviously I also had too much rum punch. But, be that as it may, you must all take into account the fact that I had the most horrible cold only a few days ago."

Miss Spit actually spit.

Linney just shook her head, and then groaned. She pushed back her coverlet and placed her feet on the floor. She still wore the silk petticoat she had put on under her pink dress for the Shelbournes' ball.

She had worn a pink dress because Lord Darington had told her she looked pretty in pink. Could she be any more pathetic?

The much-contemplated dress sat in a crumpled heap on the floor, completely ruined and reeking. She would burn it.

And she would absolutely never have rum punch again, ever.

Beside the dress lay a folded piece of paper. Linney squinted at it for a moment, trying to remember what it was.

Holding her head with one hand, Linney leaned over carefully and picked up the paper. She unfolded it, just as a memory flickered through her fogged brain of Lord Darington thrusting the thing at her and demanding she take it.

"He does like to thrust things at me, and demand, doesn't he?" she asked.

The cats didn't seem to care as they all waited for her to read the paper. "I'm reading, I'm reading," and she glanced down at the thing.

Dearest Caroline, it started out. That was nice.

I must explain myself in writing for my words do not come easily. I had thought, perhaps, that I could get past this problem and woo a wife, but obviously my speech is even worse than I believed.

Caroline frowned.

First, I must apologize for making you leave Ivy Park as I did. I will not make excuses, but I will say that I was not myself at the time and did not realize what was happening. In fact this brings me to my next confession. And I do hope you will choose to keep this to yourself, even if you do not see fit to accept my suit.

Accept his suit? Linney dropped the paper, but then scrambled to grab it again.

I was wounded in the war. And I have a problem making my mouth utter the words that my mind wants to say. I realize this sounds very odd. And I know that society would not understand such a thing. They would probably lock me in Bedlam, actually. But I believe in my heart that you will understand. My mind is sound, I promise. It seems to be a connection between my mind and my tongue that is damaged.

Oh yes, she understood that very well.

I will now just tell you that I love you. I love your eyes and your throat and your mouth and your lips. I love the words that come from those lips when you say the things you try so desperately not to say. I loved you the moment you put my soiled handkerchief back in my pocket. I feel something for you that I have never felt for another person in my life, and I know with all my heart that I want to feel it forever. Please, I know I am not worthy, but will you marry me? I shall spend the rest of my days loving you, and listening to everything you want to tell me. It will be a burden for you, I know, since you will have to smooth over my rather rough ways. But if there is anyone in the world who can do such a thing, I believe it is you. If you do not want me, I think I shall retreat to Ivy Park, as I do not believe I was quite ready for London. I shall leave in the morning, but keep a hope in my heart that you will impede my journey home.

"Oh my Lord!" Linney cried. She jumped from the bed, her headache completely forgotten. "What time is it?" The cats looked at her as if she were daft.

Grabbing a wrapper, Linney threw the thing about her and ran from her room. "What time is it?" she yelled as she pounded down the stairs.

Teddy stepped out of the drawing room, but with eyes the size of saucers, he beat a quick retreat.

"Teddy!" Linney followed the poor boy. "What time is it?"

Teddy turned away, shading his eyes. "Er, um, I think it is noon, Lady Caroline, or very close to it at least."

"Oh no! Lord Darington is an early riser."

"What?" Her mother glided in from the dining room and stopped short. "Linney! What on earth are you about? And how in the world do you know Lord Darington's sleeping habits? Lord, child, get some clothes on."

"Mother, I'm going to marry Lord Darington, but I must let him know that I don't find him altogether repugnant."

"Excuse me?"

Linney grabbed a bonnet from the stand and flung open the front door. "I'll explain later," she said and ran down the stairs and off in the direction of Lord Darington's town house.

As she ran, she tried to pull the bonnet on, but realized that she had grabbed her mother's by mistake. The frilly bit of haberdashery was much too big. It kept slipping over her eyes.

It was about two blocks away from her mother's town house and just a block away from Lord Darington's that Teddy caught up to her.

"Lady Caroline!" he sputtered, grabbing her arm. "What are you doing?"

The poor boy looked as if he could not breathe.

Linney, on the other hand, felt as if she were running on the wind, and she most definitely did not want to stop and speak to Teddy about it. "I can't stop, Teddy." She shook off the butler's hand and pounded down the walk.

Teddy kept up with her, barely. "La . . . dy . . . Car . . ." Teddy stopped and gulped some air. "You can't . . . you have no shoes!"

Linney spared a glance at her bare feet. Goodness, they were rather cold. But instead of stopping, she sped up, rounded a corner, and ran smack into a very large and imposing figure who was directing a footman with a trunk.

"Lord . . ." Linney's voice drained away, for it was not Lord Darington at all, but his friend. The man he had been speaking to at the skating party and the Shelbournes' ball.

The man blinked a few times, his mouth open in a large O. "Lady Caroline?" he said incredulously.

"Lady Caroline!" Teddy yelled with obvious confusion, skidding to a halt behind her.

"Halloo, Lady Caroline," Liza Pritchard called from her seat at the reins of a high perch phaeton, the handsome Sir Royce Pemberley at her side. Caroline waved automatically, and Liza grinned as if there was absolutely nothing out of the ordinary as she whisked by.

"Caroline," Lord Darington's low voice said with complete understanding.

Linney glanced up the stairs, and then she ran up them and threw herself into Lord Darington's arms, just as she had wished to do so many times in the last fortnight.

His strong arms closed around her, his beautiful hands lifting her against him.

And they did not have to say anything at all. She finally understood. And she knew with all her heart that he did, too. And she was home, at last.

"We have . . ." He stopped.

Linney glanced behind them. "An audience," she said.

"Yes."

The street was filled with people, servants, street vendors, carriages, couples walking, and at the bottom of Lord Darington's steps, three cats.

"You must marry me now," Linney said, "I am thoroughly compromised."

"If I must." Lord Darington turned and carried her up the stairs and into his home. Duchess, Lord Rake, and Miss Spit followed just behind, slithering in before the door closed, obviously realizing that they had a new home as well.

Darington did not stop, though, in the hall. And she was awfully glad of that, since she was most definitely aware now of her lack of dress, and gaping servants seemed to stand at every doorway.

He walked sedately down a long hall, and up a curving staircase.

Obviously, acting pompous did come in handy at moments like this.

And then they were in a dark room, Darington kicked the door shut behind him, and Linney heard an offended yowl. Miss Spit.

"I love you," Darington said, placing her on a bed. "And I will make love to you."

Linney frowned. "You know, you could *ask* once in a—" But he covered her mouth with his, and she forgot completely what she was going to say as he pushed her back against the coverlet.

"How's this, then? Shall we begin on those dozen kisses?" he inquired against her mouth.

"Much better—and most definitely," she answered.

He kissed her most thoroughly, and then moved back slightly, his voice ragged. "Could we up the count?"

"One hundred?" she said.

"Let's start with a few million."

Linney thought for a moment. "That is rather a lot . . ."

But with a dark chuckle, Terrance pulled her body against his and bit lightly at her neck.

Linney shivered; it was as if every nerve ending was right at the surface of her skin, waiting and shuddering.

"That's just for today. Tomorrow we start over."

"Oh, that's lovely," she said breathlessly as Lord Darington's large, strong hand moved up her side and cupped her breast.

She closed her eyes, and threading her fingers in her lover's beautiful hair, pulled his mouth back to hers. "I will kiss you a dozen times, a million times, I don't care. Just kiss me forever. It is the most wondrous thing in the world."

"I shall show you an even more wondrous thing," he said and moved his kiss down her jaw, against her collarbone and then lower, his tongue wetting the light fabric of her nightgown.

Linney gripped Terrance's shoulders as his mouth found her nipple. Her nerve endings rippled against her skin. She moved beneath him and moaned.

"That is wondrous," she managed to say.

And Lord Darington laughed. “That isn’t even what I was going to show you.”

“Show me. Now.”

“Don’t you ever ask?” he said, his hand moving down to cover her belly.

Linney opened her eyes. Terrance was watching her with an intensity she had never seen in another person. And she felt excited and safe and happy all at once.

“I love you,” she said.

“I love you, too,” he said.

And she could tell that was truth just by the look in his eyes.

“But, you know,” she said, “you hardly speak at all, and now, when that particular trait would be a good one, you are speaking full and long sentences. It is terribly annoying.”

He grinned, his lonely dimple deep in his cheek. And then he winked at her, the rat.

“Sorry,” he said, and kissed her.

“That’s four,” she said, and then completely lost count after that.

Mia Ryan

When not carpooling, scraping gum off seatbelts, doing laundry, and staring insanity in the face, MIA RYAN likes to escape into her writing. You can also read Mia Ryan's "The Last Temptation" in *Lady Whistledown Strikes Back*.

Thirty-Six Valentines

Julia Quinn

For Karen, Suzie, and Mia—
what chutzpah!

And also for Paul,
even though he almost threw
my laptop off the balcony.
(It wasn't the computer's fault, honey.)

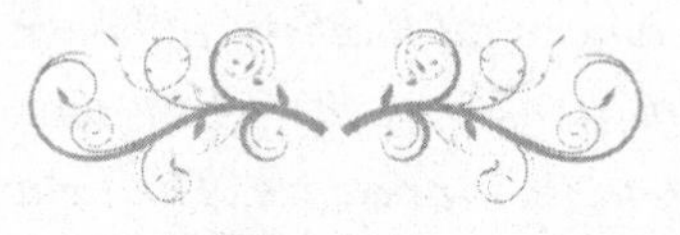

Prologue

In May, Susannah Ballister met the man of her dreams . . .

There is so much to report from Lady Trowbridge's ball in Hampstead that This Author scarcely knows how to contain it all in one column. Perhaps the most astonishing—and some would say romantic—moment of the evening, however, was when the Hon. Clive Mann-Formsby, brother to the ever-enigmatic Earl of Renminster, asked Miss Susannah Ballister to dance.

Miss Ballister, with her dark hair and eyes, is recognized as one of the more exotic beauties of the ton, *but still, she was never considered to be among the ranks of the Incomparables until Mr. Mann-Formsby partnered her in a waltz—and then didn't leave her side for the rest of the evening.*

While Miss Ballister has had her share of suitors, none was quite as handsome or eligible as Mr. Mann-Formsby, who routinely leaves a trail of sighs, swoons, and broken hearts in his wake.

LADY WHISTLEDOWN'S SOCIETY PAPERS,
17 May 1813

In June, her life was as perfect as can be.

Mr. Mann-Formsby and Miss Ballister continued their reign as society's golden couple at the Shelbourne ball late last week—or at least as golden as one can imagine, given that Miss Ballister's locks are a rather dark brown. Still, Mr. Mann-Formsby's golden hair more than compensates, and in all honesty, although This Author is not given to sentimental ramblings, it is true that the world seems a touch more exciting in their presence. The lights seem brighter, the music more lovely, and the air positively shimmers.

And with that, This Author must end this column. Such romanticism rouses the need to go outside and let the rain restore one's normally grumpy disposition.

LADY WHISTLEDOWN'S SOCIETY PAPERS,
16 June 1813

In July, Susannah was beginning to picture a ring on her finger . . .

Mr. Mann-Formsby was seen entering Mayfair's most exclusive jewelry establishment Thursday last. Can wedding bells be far behind, and can anyone truly say they don't know who the prospective bride will be?

LADY WHISTLEDOWN'S SOCIETY PAPERS,
26 July 1813

And then came August.

The foibles and affairs of society are usually mind-numbingly easy to predict, but every now and then something occurs that confounds and startles even one such as This Author.

Mr. Clive Mann-Formsby has proposed marriage.

But not to Miss Susannah Ballister.

After an entire season of rather public courting of Miss Ballister, Mr. Mann-Formsby has instead asked Miss Harriet Snowe to be his bride, and, judging by the recent announcement in the London Times, *she has accepted.*

Miss Ballister's reaction to this development is unknown.

LADY WHISTLEDOWN'S SOCIETY PAPERS,
18 August 1813

Which led, rather painfully, into September.

Word has reached This Author that Miss Susannah Ballister has quit town and retired for the remainder of the year to her family's country home in Sussex.

This Author can hardly blame her.

LADY WHISTLEDOWN'S SOCIETY PAPERS,
3 September 1813

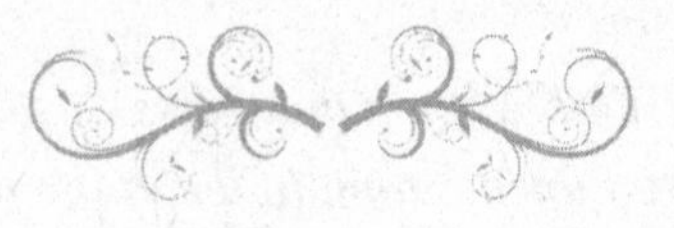

Chapter 1

It has come to This Author's attention that the Hon. Clive Mann-Formsby and Miss Harriet Snowe were married last month at the ancestral seat of Mr. Mann-Formsby's elder brother, the Earl of Renminster.

The newly wedded couple has returned to London to enjoy the winter festivities, as has Miss Susannah Ballister, who, as anyone who even stepped foot in London last Season will know, was courted rather assiduously by Mr. Mann-Formsby, right up until the moment he proposed to Miss Snowe.

This Author imagines that hostesses across town are now checking their guest lists. Surely it cannot do to invite the Mann-Formsbys and the Ballisters to the same events. It is frosty enough outside; an intersection of Clive and Harriet and Susannah will assuredly turn the air quite glacial.

LADY WHISTLEDOWN'S SOCIETY PAPERS,
21 January 1814

According to Lord Middlethorpe, who had just consulted his pocket watch, it was precisely six minutes after eleven in the evening, and Susannah Ballister knew quite well that the day was Thursday and the date was January the twenty-seventh, the year eighteen hundred and fourteen.

And at precisely that moment—at precisely 11:06 on Thursday, 27 January 1814, Susannah Ballister made three wishes, none of which came true.

The first wish was an impossibility. She wished that somehow, perhaps through some sort of mysterious and benevolent magic, she might disappear from the ballroom in which she was presently standing and find herself snuggled warmly in her bed in her family's terrace house on Portman Square, just north of Mayfair. No, even better, she'd be snuggled warmly in bed at her family's country home in Sussex, which was far, far from London and more importantly, far from all the inhabitants of London.

Susannah even went so far as to close her eyes while she pondered the lovely possibility that she might open them and find herself somewhere else, but not surprisingly, she remained right where she was, tucked away in a slightly darkened corner in Lady Worth's ballroom, holding a glass of tepid tea that she had absolutely no intention of drinking.

Once it became apparent that she wasn't going anywhere, either through supernatural or even quite ordinary means (Susannah couldn't leave the ball until her parents were prepared to do so, and from the looks of them, at least three hours would pass before they would be willing to retire for the evening), she then wished that Clive Mann-Formsby and his new wife, Harriet, who were holding court by a table of chocolate cakes, would disappear instead.

This seemed quite possible. The two of them were able-bodied; they could simply lift their feet and walk away. Which would greatly enrich the quality of Susannah's life, because then she would be able to attempt to enjoy her evening without having to stare at the face of the man who had so publicly humiliated her.

Plus, she could get herself a piece of chocolate cake.

But Clive and Harriet appeared to be having a wonderful time. As wonderful, in fact, as Susannah's parents, which meant that they would all be here for hours to come.

Agony. Pure agony.

But there were three wishes, weren't there? Didn't the heroines of fancy tales always receive three wishes? If Susannah was going to be stuck in a darkened corner, making foolish wishes because she had little else to do, she was going to use her full allotment.

"I wish," she said through gritted teeth, "that it wasn't so blasted cold."

"Amen," said the elderly Lord Middlethorpe, whom Susannah had quite forgotten was standing next to her. She offered him a smile, but he was busy drinking some sort of alcoholic drink that was forbidden to unmarried ladies, so they went back to the task of politely ignoring each other.

She looked down at her tea. Any moment now it would surely sprout an ice cube. Her hostess had substituted hot tea for the traditional lemonade and champagne, citing the frigid weather, but the tea hadn't remained hot for very long, and when one was skulking in the corner of a ballroom, as Susannah was, footmen never came to retrieve unwanted glasses or cups.

Susannah shivered. She couldn't remember a colder winter; no one could. It was, in a perverse sort of way, the reason for her early return to town. All the *ton* had flocked to London in the decidedly unfashionable month of January, eager to enjoy the skating and sledding and upcoming Frost Fair.

Susannah rather thought that bitter cold and icy winds and messy snow and ice was a deuced foolish reason for social congregation, but it wasn't up to her, and now she was stuck here, facing all the people who had so enjoyed witnessing her social defeat the summer before. She hadn't wanted to come to London, but her family had insisted, saying that she and her sister Letitia couldn't afford to miss the unexpected winter social season.

She'd thought she'd have at least until spring before having to return and face them all. She hadn't had nearly enough time to practice holding her chin up while she said, "Well, of course Mr. Mann-Formsby and I realized that we wouldn't suit."

Because she needed to be a very fine actress indeed to carry that off, when everyone knew that Clive had dropped her like a hot potato when Harriet Snowe's moneyed relatives had come sniffing about.

Not that Clive should have even needed the money. His older brother was the Earl of Renminster, for heaven's sake, and everyone knew he was as rich as Croesus.

But Clive had chosen Harriet, and Susannah had been publicly humiliated, and even now, nearly six months after the fact, people were still talking about it. Even Lady Whistledown had seen fit to mention it in her column.

Susannah sighed and sagged against the wall, hoping that no one noticed her poor posture. She supposed she couldn't really blame Lady Whistledown. The mysterious gossip columnist was merely repeating what everyone else was saying. Just this week, Susannah had received fourteen afternoon callers, and not a one of them had been polite enough to refrain from mentioning Clive and Harriet.

Did they really think she wanted to hear about Clive and Harriet's appearance at the recent Smythe-Smith musicale? As if she wanted to know what Harriet had worn, or that Clive had been whispering in her ear throughout the recital.

That meant nothing. Clive had always had abominable manners during musicales. Susannah couldn't remember even one in which he'd had the fortitude to keep his mouth shut throughout the performance.

But the gossips weren't even the worst of her afternoon callers. That title was reserved for the well-meaning souls who couldn't seem to look at her with any expression other than one of pity. These were usually the same women who had a widowed nephew from Shropshire or Somerset or some other faraway county who was looking for a wife, and would Susannah like to meet him, but not this week because he was busy escorting six of his eight sons to Eton.

Susannah fought an unexpected rush of tears. She was only twenty-one years old. And barely that, even. She wasn't desperate.

And she didn't want to be pitied.

Suddenly it became imperative that she leave the ballroom. She didn't want to be here, didn't want to watch Clive and Harriet like some pathetic voyeur. Her family wasn't ready to go home, but surely she could find some quiet room where she might retire for a few minutes. If she was going to hide, she might as well do it right. Standing in the corner was appalling. Already she'd seen three people point in her direction, then say something behind their hands.

She'd never thought herself a coward, but she'd also never thought herself a fool, and truly, only a fool would willingly subject herself to this sort of misery.

She set her teacup down on a windowsill and made her regrets to Lord Middlethorpe, not that they'd exchanged more than six words, despite having stood next to each other for nearly three-quarters of an hour. She skirted along the edge of the ballroom, looking for the French doors that led to the hall. She'd been here once before, back when she'd been the most popular young lady in town, thanks to her association with Clive, and she remembered that there was a retiring room for the ladies at the far end of the hall.

But just when she reached her destination, she stumbled, and she found herself face to face with—oh blast, what was her name? Brown hair, slightly pudgy . . . oh yes. Penelope. Penelope Somebody. A girl with whom she'd never shared more than a dozen words. They'd come out the same year, but they might have resided in different worlds, so infrequently had their paths crossed. Susannah had been the toast of the town, once Clive had singled her out, and Penelope had been . . . well, Susannah wasn't really certain what Penelope had been. A wallflower, she supposed.

"Don't go there," Penelope said softly, not quite looking her in the eye in the way that only the shyest of people do.

Susannah's lips parted in surprise, and she knew her eyes were filled with question.

"There are a dozen young ladies in the retiring room," Penelope said.

It was explanation enough. The only place Susannah wanted to be less than the ballroom was in a room full of twittering, gossiping ladies, all of whom would surely assume she had fled there to escape Clive and Harriet.

Which was true, but that didn't mean Susannah wanted anyone to know it.

"Thank you," Susannah whispered, stunned by Penelope's small kindness. She'd never spared so much as a thought for Penelope last summer, and the younger girl had repaid her by saving her from certain embarrassment and pain. Impulsively, she took Penelope's hand and squeezed it once. "Thank you."

And she suddenly wished she'd paid more attention to the girls like Penelope when she'd been considered a leader of the *ton*. She knew what it was like to stand on the edges of the ballroom now, and it wasn't fun.

But before she could say something more, Penelope murmured her shy farewells and slipped away, leaving Susannah to her own devices.

She was standing in the busiest section of the ballroom, which was not where she wanted to be, so she started walking. She wasn't really certain where she intended to go, but she kept moving, because she felt it made her look purposeful.

She subscribed to the notion that a person ought to look as if she knew what she was doing, even if she didn't. Clive had taught her that, actually. It was one of the few good things she'd gained from the courtship.

But in all her determined glory, she wasn't truly watching her surroundings, and that must have been why she was so taken by surprise when she heard *his* voice.

"Miss Ballister."

No, not Clive. Even worse. Clive's older brother, the Earl of Renminster. In all his dark-haired, green-eyed glory.

He had never liked her. Oh, he had always been polite, but then again, he was polite to everyone. But she had always felt his disdain, his obvious conviction that she was not good enough for his brother.

She supposed he was happy now. Clive was safely married off to Harriet, and Susannah Ballister would never taint the hallowed Mann-Formsby family tree.

"My lord," she said, trying to keep her voice as even and polite as his. She couldn't imagine what he could possibly want with her. There was no reason for him to have called out her name; he could easily have let her walk right by him without acknowledging her presence. It wouldn't even have seemed rude on his part. Susannah had been walking as briskly as was possible in the crowded ballroom, clearly on her way to somewhere else.

He smiled at her, if one could call it that—the sentiment never reached his eyes. "Miss Ballister," he said, "how have you been?"

For a moment she could do nothing but stare at him. He wasn't the sort to ask a question unless he truly wanted the answer, and there was no reason to believe he had any interest in her welfare.

"Miss Ballister?" he murmured, looking vaguely amused.

Finally, she managed to say, "Quite well, thank you," even though they both knew that was far from the truth.

For the longest while he merely gazed at her, almost as if he were studying her, looking for something she couldn't even begin to imagine.

"My lord?" she queried, because the moment seemed to need something to break the silence.

His head snapped to attention, as if her voice had brought him out of a slight daze. "I beg your pardon," he apologized smoothly. "Would you care to dance?"

Susannah found herself struck mute. "Dance?" she finally echoed, rather annoyed with her inability to come up with anything more articulate.

"Indeed," he murmured.

She accepted his proffered hand—there was little else she could do with so many people watching—and allowed him to lead her onto the dance floor. He was tall, even taller than Clive, who had stood a good head above her, and he possessed an oddly reserved air—almost too controlled, if such a thing were possible. Watching him as he moved through the crowds, she was struck by the odd thought that surely one day his famous control would snap.

And it would be only then that the true Earl of Renminster would be revealed.

David Mann-Formsby hadn't thought about Susannah Ballister for months, not since his brother had elected to marry Harriet Snowe instead of the dark beauty currently waltzing in his arms. A tiny shred of guilt over this started to niggle at him, however, because as soon as he'd seen her, moving through the ballroom as if she had somewhere to go, when anyone who took the time to look at her for more than a second would have seen the strained expression on her face, the pain lurking behind her eyes, he'd been reminded of Susannah's shabby treatment at the hands of the *ton* after Clive had decided to marry Harriet.

And truly, none of it had been her fault.

Susannah's family, while perfectly respectable, was not titled, nor were they particularly wealthy. And when Clive had dropped her in favor of Harriet, whose name was as old as her dowry was large, society had sniggered behind her back—and, he supposed, probably to her face as well. She had been called grasping, above herself, overly ambitious. More than one society matron—the sort who had daughters not nearly as arresting and attractive as Susannah Ballister—had commented that the little upstart had been put in her place, and how dare she even think that she might win a proposal of marriage from the brother of an earl?

David had found the entire episode rather distasteful, but what could he have done? Clive had made his choice, and in David's opinion, he had made the right one. Harriet would, in the end, make a much better wife for his brother.

Still, Susannah had been an innocent bystander in the scandal; she hadn't known that Clive was being courted by Harriet's father, or that Clive thought that petite, blue-eyed Harriet would make a very fine wife indeed. Clive should have said something to Susannah before putting the announcement in the paper, and even if he was too much of a coward to warn her in person, he certainly should have been smart enough not to make a grand announcement at the Mottram ball even before the notice appeared in the *Times*. When Clive had stood in front of the small orchestra, champagne glass in hand as he made his joyful speech, no one had looked at Harriet, who was standing by his side.

Susannah had been the main attraction, Susannah with her surprised mouth and stricken eyes. Susannah, who had tried so hard to hold herself strong and proud before she finally fled the scene.

Her anguished face had been an image that David had carried around in his mind for many weeks, months even, until slowly she slipped away, forgotten amid his daily activities and chores.

Until now.

Until he'd spied her standing in the corner, pretending she didn't care that Clive and Harriet were surrounded by a bevy of well-wishers. She was a proud woman, he could tell, but pride could carry a person only so far until one simply wanted to escape and be alone.

He wasn't surprised when she finally began to make her way to the door.

At first he'd thought to let her pass, perhaps even to step back so that she would not be forced to see him witnessing her departure. But then some strange, irresistible impulse had pushed his feet forward. It didn't bother him so much that she'd been turned into a wallflower; there would always be wallflowers among the *ton,* and there was little one man could do to rectify the situation.

But David was a Mann-Formsby to the very tips of his toes, and if there was one thing he could not abide, it was knowing that his family had wronged someone. And his brother had most certainly wronged this young woman. David would not go so far as to say her life had been ruined, but she had clearly been subject to a great deal of undeserved misery.

As the Earl of Renminster—no, as a Mann-Formsby—it was his duty to make amends.

And so he asked her to dance. A dance would be noticed. A dance would be remarked upon. And although it was not in David's nature to flatter himself, he knew that a simple invitation to dance on his part would do wonders to restore Susannah's popularity.

She'd appeared rather startled by his request, but she'd accepted; after all, what else could she do with so many people watching?

He led her to the center of the floor, his eyes never leaving her face. David had never had trouble understanding why Clive had been attracted to her. Susannah possessed a quiet, dark beauty that he found far more arresting than the current blond, blue-eyed ideal that was so popular among society. Her skin was pale porcelain, with perfectly winged brows and lips of a raspberry pink. He'd heard there were Welsh ancestors in her family, and he could easily see their influence.

"A waltz," she said dryly, once the string quintet began to play. "How fortuitous."

He chuckled at her sarcasm. She'd never been outgoing, but she had always been direct, and he admired the trait, especially when it was combined with intelligence. They began to dance, and then, just when he'd decided to make some inane comment about the weather—just so they would be observed conversing like reasonable adults—she beat him to the punch, and asked:

"Why did you invite me to dance?"

For a moment he was speechless. Direct, indeed. "Does a gentleman need a reason?" he countered.

Her lips tightened slightly at the corners. "You never struck me as the sort of gentleman who does anything without a reason."

He shrugged. "You seemed rather alone in the corner."

"I was with Lord Middlethorpe," she said haughtily.

He did nothing but raise his eyebrows, since they both knew that the aged Lord Middlethorpe was not generally considered a lady's first choice of escort.

"I don't need your pity," she muttered.

"Of course not," he agreed.

Her eyes flew to his. "Now you're condescending to me."

"I wouldn't dream of it," he said, quite honestly.

"Then what is this about?"

"This?" he echoed, giving his head a questioning tilt.

"Dancing with me."

He wanted to smile, but he didn't want her to think he was laughing at her, so he managed to keep his lips down to a twitch as he said, "You're rather suspicious for a lady in the midst of a waltz."

She replied, "Waltzes are precisely the time a lady ought to be most suspicious."

"Actually," he said, surprising himself with his words, "I wanted to apologize." He cleared his throat. "For what happened last summer."

"To what," she asked, her words carefully measured, "do you refer?"

He looked at her in what he hoped was a kindly manner. It wasn't an expression he was particularly accustomed to, so he wasn't quite certain he was doing it right. Still, he tried to look sympathetic as he said, "I think you know."

Her body grew rigid, even as they danced, and he would have sworn that he could see her spine turning to steel. "Perhaps," she said tightly, "but I fail to see how it is any of your concern."

"It may be that it is not," he allowed, "but nonetheless, I did not approve of the way you were treated by society after Clive's engagement."

"Do you mean the gossip," she asked, her face perfectly bland, "or the cuts direct? Or maybe the out-and-out lies?"

He swallowed, unaware that her situation had been quite so unpleasant. "All of it," he said quietly. "It was never my intention—"

"Never your intention?" she cut in, her eyes flashing with something approaching fury. "Never your intention? I was under the assumption that Clive had made his own decisions. Do you admit, then, that Harriet was your choice, not Clive's?"

"She was his choice," he said firmly.

"And yours?" she persisted.

There seemed little point—and little honor—in lying. "And mine."

She gritted her teeth, looking somewhat vindicated, but also a bit deflated, as if she'd been waiting for this moment for months, but now that it was here, it was not nearly as sweet as she'd anticipated.

"But if he had married you," David said quietly, "I would not have objected."

Her eyes flew to his face. "Please don't lie to me," she whispered.

"I'm not." He sighed. "You will make someone a very fine wife, Miss Ballister. Of that I have no doubt."

She said nothing, but her eyes seemed shiny, and for a moment he could have sworn that her lips were trembling.

Something began to tug at him. He wasn't sure what it was, and he did not want to think that he felt it anywhere near his heart, but he found he simply could not bear to see her so close to tears. But there was nothing he could do besides say, "Clive should have informed you of his plans before he announced them to society."

"Yes," she said, the word made brittle by a harsh little laugh. "He should have done."

David felt his hand tighten slightly at her waist. She wasn't making this easy on him, but then again, he had no reason to expect her to do so. In truth, he admired her pride, respected the way she carried herself straight and tall, as if she wouldn't allow society to tell her how she must judge herself.

She was, he realized with a shiver of surprise, a remarkable woman.

"He should have done," he said, unconsciously echoing her words, "but he did not, and for that I must apologize."

She cocked her head slightly, her eyes almost amused as she said, "One would imagine the apology would be better served coming from Clive, don't you think?"

David smiled humorlessly. "Indeed, but I can only deduce that he has not done so. Therefore, as a Mann-Formsby—"

She snorted under her breath, which did *not* amuse him.

"As a Mann-Formsby," he said again, raising his voice, then lowering it when several nearby dancers looked curiously in his direction. "As the head of the Mann-Formsby family," he corrected, "it is my duty to apologize when a member of my family acts in a dishonorable manner."

He'd expected a quick retort, and indeed, she opened her mouth immediately, her eyes flashing dark fire, but then, with an abruptness that took his breath away, she seemed to change her mind. And when she finally spoke, she said, "Thank you for that. I accept your apology on Clive's behalf."

There was a quiet dignity in her voice, something that made him want to pull her closer, to entwine their fingers rather than merely to hold hands.

But if he'd wanted to explore that feeling more closely—and he wasn't certain he did—his chance was lost when the orchestra brought the waltz to a close, leaving him standing in the middle of the ballroom floor, bending his body into an elegant bow as Susannah bobbed a curtsy.

She murmured a polite, "Thank you for the dance, my lord," and it was clear that their conversation was at an end.

But as he watched her leave the ballroom—presumably off to wherever it was she'd been going when he'd intercepted her—he couldn't quite shake the feeling—

He wanted more.

More of her words, more of her conversation.

More of *her.*

Later that night, two events occurred that were very odd, indeed.

The first took place in Susannah Ballister's bedroom.

She could not sleep.

This would not have seemed odd to many, but Susannah had always been the sort who fell asleep the instant her head hit the pillow. It had driven her sister batty back in the days when they had shared a room. Letitia had always wanted to stay up and whisper, and Susannah's conversational contributions never amounted to anything more than a light snore.

Even in the days following Clive's defection, she had slept like the dead. It had been her only escape from the constant pain and turmoil that was the life of a jilted debutante.

But this evening was different. Susannah lay on her back (which was odd in itself, as she much preferred to sleep on her side) and stared up at the ceiling, wondering when the crack in the plaster had come so much to resemble a rabbit.

Or rather, that was what she thought about each time she determinedly thrust the Earl of Renminster from her mind. Because the truth was that she could not sleep because she could not stop reliving their conversation, stopping to analyze each of his words, and then trying not to notice the shivery feeling she got when she recalled his faint, somewhat ironic smile.

She still could not believe how she'd stood up to him. Clive had always referred to him as "the old man," and called him, at various times, stuffy, haughty, supercilious, arrogant, and damned annoying. Susannah had been rather terrified by the earl; Clive certainly hadn't made him sound very approachable.

But she had stood her ground and kept her pride.

Now she couldn't sleep for thinking of him, but she didn't much mind—not with this giddy feeling.

It had been so long since she'd felt proud of herself. She'd forgotten what a nice sensation it was.

The second odd occurrence took place across town, in the district of Holborn, in front of the home of Anne Miniver, who lived quietly alongside all of the lawyers and barristers who worked at the nearby Inns of the Court, even though her occupation, if one could call it that, was mistress. Mistress to the Earl of Renminster, to be precise.

But Miss Miniver was unaware that anything strange was afoot. Indeed, the only person to make note of the occasion was the earl himself, who had instructed his driver to take him directly from the Worth ball to Anne's elegant terrace house. But when he ascended the steps to her front door and lifted his hand to the brass knocker, he found he no longer had any interest in seeing her. The urge was, quite simply, gone.

Which for the earl was quite strange indeed.

Chapter 2

Did you notice the Earl of Renminster dancing with Miss Susannah Ballister last night at the Worth ball? If not, for shame—you were the only one. The waltz was the talk of the evening.

It cannot be said that the conversation looked to be of the amiable variety. Indeed, This Author observed flashing eyes and even what appeared to be a heated word.

The earl departed soon after the dance, but Miss Ballister remained for several hours thereafter, and was witnessed dancing with ten other gentlemen before she left in the company of her parents and sister.

Ten gentlemen. Yes, This Author counted. It would have been impossible not to draw comparisons, when her sum total of partners prior to the earl's invitation was zero.

LADY WHISTLEDOWN'S SOCIETY PAPERS,
28 January 1814

The Ballisters had never had to worry about money, but neither could they have been called wealthy. Normally this did not bother Susannah; she had never wanted for anything, and she saw no reason for three sets of ear bobs when her one pair of pearls matched all of her clothes quite nicely. Not that she would have refused another pair, mind you; she just didn't see the need to spend her days pining for jewelry that would never be hers.

But there was one thing that made her wish her family was older, wealthier, possessed a title—anything that would have given them more influence.

And that was the theater.

Susannah adored the theater, adored losing herself in someone else's story, adored everything from the smell to the lights to the tingly feeling one got in the palms of one's hands while clapping. It was far more absorbing than a musicale, and certainly more fun than the balls and dances she found herself attending three nights out of seven.

The problem, however, was that her family did not possess a box at any of the theaters deemed appropriate for polite society, and she was not permitted to sit anywhere other than a box. Proper young ladies did not sit with the rabble, her mother insisted. Which meant that the only way Susannah ever got to see a play was when she was invited by someone who did possess a suitable box.

When a note had arrived for her from her Shelbourne cousins inviting her to accompany them that evening to see Edmund Kean perform Shylock in *The Merchant of Venice,* she had nearly wept with joy. Kean had made his debut in the role just four nights earlier, and already all the *ton* was abuzz about it. He had been called magnificent, daring, and unparalleled—all those wonderful words that left a theater lover like Susannah nearly shaking in her desire to see the production.

Except that she hardly expected anyone to invite her to share their box at the theater. She only received invitations to large parties because people were curious to see her reaction to Clive and Harriet's marriage. Invitations to small gatherings were not forthcoming.

Until the Worth ball on Thursday night.

She supposed she ought to thank the earl. He had danced with her, and now she was considered suitable again. She had received at least eight more invitations to dance after he had left. Oh very well, ten. She had counted. Ten men had invited her to dance, which was ten more than had in the entire three hours she'd spent at the ball before the earl had sought her out.

It was appalling, actually, how much influence one man could exert over society.

She was certain that Renminster was the reason her cousins had extended the invitation. She didn't think the Shelbournes had been consciously avoiding her—the truth was, they were distant cousins and she'd never known them very well. But when an opening had come up in their theater party and they needed another female to even the numbers, how easy it must have been for them to say, "Oh yes, what about Cousin Susannah?" when Susannah's name had been so prominently featured in Friday's *Whistledown* column.

Susannah didn't care why they had suddenly recalled her existence—she was going to see Kean in *The Merchant of Venice*!

"I shall be eternally jealous," her sister Letitia said as they waited in the drawing room for the Shelbournes to arrive. Their mother had insisted that Susannah be ready at the appropriate hour and not keep their influential relatives waiting. One was supposed to force prospective suitors to cool their heels, but not important relations who might extend coveted invitations.

"I'm sure you will find an opportunity to see the play soon," Susannah said, but she couldn't quite restrain her somewhat satisfied smile as she did so.

Letitia sighed. "Maybe they will want to go twice."

"Maybe they will lend the entire box to Mother and Father," Susannah said.

Letitia's face lit up. "An excellent notion! Be sure to suggest—"

"I shall do no such thing," Susannah cut in. "It would be beyond crass, and—"

"But if the subject comes up . . ."

Susannah rolled her eyes. "Very well," she said. "If Lady Shelbourne should happen to say, 'My dear Miss Ballister, do you think your family might possibly be interested in using our box?' I shall be sure to answer in the affirmative."

Letitia shot her a decidedly unamused look.

Just then their butler appeared in the doorway. "Miss Susannah," he said, "the Shelbourne carriage is parked outside."

Susannah jumped to her feet. "Thank you. I shall be on my way."

"I will be waiting for you," Letitia said, following her into the hall. "I shall expect you to tell me everything."

"And spoil the play?" Susannah teased.

"Pish. It's not as if I haven't read *The Merchant of Venice* ten times already. I *know* the ending. I just want to hear about Kean!"

"He's not as handsome as Kemble," Susannah said, pulling on her coat and muff.

"I've *seen* Kemble," Letitia said impatiently. "I haven't seen Kean."

Susannah leaned forward and placed an affectionate kiss on her sister's cheek. "I shall tell you every last detail about my evening. I promise you."

And then she braved the frigid cold and walked outside to the Shelbourne carriage.

Less than an hour later, Susannah was comfortably seated in the Shelbourne box at the Theatre Royal, Drury Lane, avidly gazing about the newly redesigned theater. She'd happily taken the seat on the farthest edge of the box. The Shelbournes and their guests were chattering away, ignoring, as was the entire audience, the farce that the acting company was performing as a prelude to the real performance. Susannah also paid no attention; she wanted nothing more than to inspect the new theater.

It was ironic, really—the best seats in the house seemed to be down in the pit with all the rabble, as her mother liked to put it. Here she was in one of the most expensive boxes in the theater, and a large pillar partially blocked their view. She was going to have to twist significantly in her seat, and in fact even lean on the ledge just to see the performance.

"Be careful you don't fall," murmured a low, male voice.

Susannah snapped to attention. "My lord!" she said in surprise, turning to come face-to-face with the Earl of Renminster, of all people. He was seated in the box directly next to that of the Shelbournes, close enough so that they could converse over the gap between the boxes.

"What a nice surprise," he said, with a pleasant and yet slightly mysterious smile. Susannah rather thought all his smiles a touch mysterious.

"I'm with my cousins," she said, motioning to the people next to her. "The Shelbournes," she added, even though that was quite obvious.

"Good evening, Lord Renminster," Lady Shelbourne said excitedly. "I didn't realize your box was next to ours."

He nodded his greeting. "I haven't had the opportunity to see very much theater recently, I'm afraid."

Lady Shelbourne's chin bobbed up and down in agreement. "It's so difficult to make time. We all have such busy schedules this year. Who would have thought so many people would find themselves back in London in January?"

"And all for a spot of snow," Susannah could not help commenting.

Lord Renminster chuckled at her quiet joke before leaning forward to address Lady Shelbourne. "I do think the play is beginning," he said. "It has been charming as always to see you."

"Indeed," Lady Shelbourne trilled. "I do hope you will be able to attend my Valentine's Day ball next month."

"I wouldn't miss it for the world," he assured her.

Lady Shelbourne sat back in her seat, looking both satisfied and relieved, then resumed her conversation with her best friend, Liza Pritchard, who Susannah was now absolutely convinced was in love with Lady Shelbourne's brother, Sir Royce Pemberley, who was also sitting in the box.

Susannah rather thought he returned the sentiment, but of course neither one of them seemed to realize it, and in fact, Miss Pritchard appeared to be setting her cap for the other unmarried gentleman in attendance, Lord Durham, who was, in Susannah's opinion, a bit of a bore. But it wasn't her place to inform them of their feelings, and besides they, along with Lady Shelbourne, seemed to be conducting a rather involved conversation without her.

Which left her with Lord Renminster, who was still watching her over the gap between their respective theater boxes. "Do you enjoy Shakespeare?" she asked him conversationally. Her joy at having been invited to see Kean's Shylock was such that she could even manage a sunny smile for *him*.

"I do," he replied, "although I prefer the histories."

She nodded, deciding that she was willing to carry on a polite conversation if he could manage the same. "I thought you might. They're rather more serious."

He smiled enigmatically. "I can't decide whether to be complimented or insulted."

"In situations such as these," Susannah said, surprised she felt so comfortable talking with him, "you should always decide to be complimented. One leads a much simpler and happier life that way."

He laughed aloud before asking, "And what about you? Which of the bard's plays do you prefer?"

She sighed happily. "I adore them all."

"Really?" he asked, and she was surprised to hear true interest in his voice. "I had no idea you loved the theater so."

Susannah eyed him curiously, cocking her head to the side. "I wouldn't have thought you'd have been aware of my interest one way or another."

"That is true," he acceded, "but Clive doesn't care much for theater."

She felt her spine stiffen slightly. "Clive and I never shared *all* of our interests."

"Obviously not," he said, and she thought she might have even heard a touch of approval in his voice.

And then—and she didn't know why she said this to him, Clive's *brother*, for heaven's sake—she said, "He *talks* incessantly."

The earl appeared to choke on his tongue.

"Are you unwell?" Susannah asked, leaning forward with a concerned expression.

"Fine," the earl gasped, actually patting himself on the chest. "You merely . . . ah . . . startled me."

"Oh. I apologize."

"Don't," he assured her. "I've always made it a point not to attend the theater with Clive."

"It's difficult for the players to get a word in edgewise," Susannah agreed, resisting the urge to roll her eyes.

He sighed. "To this day, I don't know what happened at the end of *Romeo and Juliet*."

She gasped. "You d—oh, you're bamming me."

"They lived happily ever after, didn't they?" he asked, his eyes all innocence.

"Oh, yes," she said, smiling wickedly. "It's quite an uplifting story."

"Excellent," he said, settling back in his seat as he focused his eyes on the stage. "It's good to finally get that cleared up."

Susannah couldn't help herself. She giggled. How strange that the Earl of Renminster actually had a sense of humor. Clive had always said that his brother was the most "bloody awful serious" man in all England. Susannah had never had any reason to doubt his assessment, especially when he'd actually used the word "bloody" in front of a lady. A gentleman generally didn't unless he was quite serious about his statement.

Just then the house lights began to dim, plunging the theatergoers into darkness. "Oh!" Susannah breathed, leaning forward. "Did you see that?" she asked excitedly, turning to the earl. "How brilliant! They're only leaving the lights on the stage."

"It's one of Wyatt's new innovations," he replied, referring to the architect who had recently renovated the fire-stricken theater. "It makes it easier to see the stage, don't you think?"

"It's brilliant," Susannah said, scooting toward the edge of her seat so that she could see past the pillar that was blocking her view. "It's—"

And then the play began, and she was rendered completely speechless.

From his position in the box next to her, David found himself watching Susannah more often than the play. He'd seen *The Merchant of Venice* on several occasions, and even though he was dimly aware that Edmund Kean's Shylock was a truly remarkable performance, it couldn't quite compare with the glow in Susannah Ballister's dark eyes as she watched the stage.

He would have to come back and view the play again the following week, he decided. Because tonight he was watching Susannah.

Why was it, he wondered, that he'd been so opposed to her marrying his brother? No, that wasn't entirely accurate. He hadn't been entirely opposed to it. He'd not lied to her when he'd said that he would not have objected to their marriage if Clive had settled on her rather than Harriet.

But he hadn't wanted it. He'd seen his brother with Susannah and somehow it had seemed wrong.

Susannah was fire and intelligence and beauty, and Clive was . . .

Well, Clive was Clive. David loved him, but Clive's heart was ruled by a devil-may-care urgency that David had never really understood. Clive was like a brightly burning candle. People were drawn to him, like the proverbial moths to flame, but inevitably, someone came away burned.

Someone like Susannah.

Susannah would have been all wrong for Clive. And perhaps even moreso, Clive would have been wrong for her. Susannah needed someone else. Someone more mature. Someone like . . .

David's thoughts were like a whisper across his soul. Susannah needed someone like *him*.

The beginnings of an idea began to form in his mind. David wasn't the sort to take rash action, but he made decisions quickly, based on both what he knew and what he felt.

And as he sat there in the Theatre Royal, Drury Lane, ignoring the actors on the stage in favor of the woman seated in the box across from his, he made a rather significant decision.

He was going to marry Susannah Ballister.

Susannah Ballister—no, Susannah Mann-Formsby, Countess of Renminster. The rightness of it seemed to sing through him.

She would make an excellent countess. She was beautiful, intelligent, principled, and proud. He didn't know why he hadn't realized all of this before—probably because he'd only ever met her in the company of Clive, and Clive tended to overshadow anyone in his presence.

David had spent the last several years keeping one eye open for a potential bride. He hadn't been in a hurry to marry, but he knew that he would have to take a wife eventually, and so every unmarried woman he'd met had been mentally inventoried and assessed.

And all had come up wanting.

They'd been too silly or too dull. Too quiet or too loud. Or if they weren't too something, they were not enough something.

Not right. Not someone he could imagine himself staring at over the breakfast table for years to come.

He was a picky man, but now, as he smiled to himself in the darkness, it seemed that the wait had most definitely been worthwhile.

David stole another glance at Susannah's profile. He doubted she even noticed that he was watching her, so engrossed was she by the production. Every now and then her lips would part with a soft, involuntary "Oh," and even though he knew it was beyond fanciful, he could swear that he felt her breath travel through the air, landing lightly on his skin.

David felt his body tighten. It had never occurred to him that he might actually be lucky enough to find himself a wife he found desirable. What a boon.

Susannah's tongue darted out to wet her lips.

Extremely desirable.

He sat back, unable to stop the satisfied smile that crept across his features. He had made a decision; now all he needed to do was formulate a plan.

When the house lights rose after the third act to mark the intermission, Susannah instantly looked to the box next to her, absurdly eager to ask the earl what he thought of the play thus far.

But he was gone.

"How odd," she murmured to herself. He must have crept out quietly; she had not noticed his departure in the least. She felt herself slouch slightly in her seat, oddly disappointed that he'd disappeared. She'd been looking forward to asking his opinion of Kean's performance, which was quite unlike any Shylock she'd seen before. She'd been certain that he would have something valuable to say, something that perhaps she herself had not noticed. Clive had never wanted to do anything during intermissions other than escape to the mezzanine where he might chat with his friends.

Still, it was probably for the best that the earl was gone. Despite his friendly behavior before the performance, it was still difficult to believe that he was amiably disposed toward her.

And besides, when he was near, she felt rather . . . odd. Strange, and breathless, somehow. It was exciting, but not quite comfortable, and it left her uneasy.

So when Lady Shelbourne asked if she wanted to accompany the rest of the party to the mezzanine to enjoy the intermission, Susannah thanked her but graciously declined. It was definitely in her best interest to stay put, remaining right there in the one place the Earl of Renminster most certainly was not.

The Shelbournes filed out, along with their guests, leaving Susannah to her own company, which she didn't mind in the least. The stagehands had accidentally left the curtain slightly open, and if Susannah squinted, she could see flashes of people scurrying around. It was strangely exciting and all rather interesting, and—

She heard a sound from behind her. Someone in the Shelbourne party must have forgotten something. Affixing a smile to her face, Susannah turned around, "Good eve—"

It was the earl.

"Good evening," he said, when it became apparent that she was not going to finish the greeting herself.

"My lord," she said, her surprise evident in her voice.

He nodded graciously. "Miss Ballister. May I sit?"

"Of course," she said, rather automatically. Good heavens, why was he here?

"I thought it might be easier to converse without having to yell between the boxes," he said.

Susannah just stared at him in disbelief. They hadn't had to yell at all. The boxes were terribly close. But, she realized somewhat frantically, not nearly as close as their chairs now were. The earl's thigh was nearly pressed up next to hers.

It shouldn't have been bothersome, since Lord Durham had occupied the same chair for well over an hour, and his thigh hadn't vexed her in the least.

But it was different with Lord Renminster. Everything was different with Lord Renminster, Susannah was coming to realize.

"Are you enjoying the play?" he asked her.

"Oh indeed," she said. "Kean's performance was nothing short of remarkable, wouldn't you agree?"

He nodded and murmured his agreement.

"I would never have expected Shylock to be portrayed in such a tragic manner," Susannah continued. "I've seen *The Merchant of Venice* several times before, of course, as I'm sure you have, too, and he has always been a more comic sort, wouldn't you agree?"

"It does make for an interesting interpretation."

Susannah nodded enthusiastically. "I thought the black wig was a stroke of genius. Every other Shylock I've seen was played with a red wig. And how could Kean expect us to view him as a tragic character with a red wig? No one takes red-haired men seriously."

The earl began to cough uncontrollably.

Susannah leaned forward, hoping she hadn't somehow insulted him. With his dark hair, she hadn't thought he could possibly take offense.

"I beg your pardon," he said, catching his breath.

"Is something amiss?"

"Nothing," he assured her. "Merely that your rather astute observation caught me off guard."

"I am not trying to say that red-haired men are less worthy than the rest of you," she said.

"Except us of the clearly superior dark-headed variety," he murmured, his lips creeping into a devilish smile.

She pursed her lips to stop herself from smiling back. It was so *odd* that he could draw her into a secret, shared moment—the sort that would develop into a private joke. "What I was trying to say," she said, attempting to get back to the matter at hand, "is that one never reads about men with red hair in novels, does one?"

"Not the novels I read," he assured her.

Susannah shot him a vaguely peeved expression. "Or if one does," she continued, "he is never the hero of the tale."

The earl leaned toward her, his green eyes sparkling with wicked promise. "And who is the hero of *your* tale, Miss Ballister?"

"I haven't a hero," she said primly. "I should think that was obvious."

He held silent for a moment, regarding her thoughtfully. "You should," he murmured.

Susannah felt her lips part, even felt her breath rushing across them as his words landed softly on her ears. "I'm sorry?" she finally asked, not entirely certain what he meant.

Or maybe she *was* certain, and she just couldn't believe it.

He smiled slightly. "A woman like you should have a hero," he said. "A champion, perhaps."

She looked at him with arched brows. "Are you saying I should be married?"

Again that smile. The knowing curve of his lips, as if he had a devilishly good secret. "What do you think?"

"I think," Susannah said, "that this conversation is veering into astonishingly personal waters."

He laughed at that, but it was a warm, amused sound, completely lacking in the malice that so often tinged the laughter of the *ton*. "I rescind my earlier statement," he said with a broad smile. "You don't need a champion. You are clearly able to take care of yourself quite well."

Susannah narrowed her eyes.

"Yes," he said, "it was a compliment."

"With you one always has to check," she remarked.

"Oh, come now, Miss Ballister," he said. "You wound me."

Now it was her turn to laugh. "Please," she said, grinning all the while. "Your armor is quite up to the task against any verbal blow I might strike."

"I'm not so sure about that," he said, so softly that she wasn't certain she'd heard him correctly.

And then she had to ask—"Why are you being so nice to me?"

"Am I?"

"Yes," she said, not even certain why the answer was so important, "you are. And considering how opposed you were to my marrying your brother, I can't help but be suspicious."

"I wasn't—"

"I know you said you weren't opposed to the match," Susannah said, her face almost expressionless as she interrupted him. "But we both know you did not favor it *and* that you encouraged him to marry Harriet."

David held still for a long moment, considering her statement. Not a word that she had said was false, and yet it was clear that she understood nothing of what had transpired the previous summer.

Most of all, she did not understand Clive. And if she thought she could have been the wife for him, perhaps she did not understand herself, either.

"I love my brother," David said softly, "but he has his flaws, and he required a wife who would need him and depend upon him. Someone who would force him to become the man I know he can be. If Clive had married you—"

He looked at her. She was staring at him with frank eyes, waiting patiently for him to formulate his thoughts. He could tell that his answer meant everything to her, and he knew that he had to get it right.

"If Clive had married you," he finally continued, "he would have had no need to be strong. *You* would have been strong for the both of you. Clive would never have had any reason to grow."

Her lips parted with surprise.

"Put simply, Miss Ballister," he said with startling softness, "my brother wasn't worthy of a woman like you."

And then, while she was trying to comprehend the meaning behind his words, while she was trying simply to remember how to breathe, he stood.

"It has been a pleasure, Miss Ballister," he murmured, taking her hand and gently laying a kiss on her glove. His eyes remained fixed on her face the entire while, glowing hot and green, and searing straight into her soul.

He straightened, curved his lips just far enough to make her skin tingle, and quietly said, "Good night, Miss Ballister."

Then he was gone, even before she could offer her own farewell. And he did not reappear in the box next to her.

But this feeling—this strange, breathless, swirling feeling that he managed to stir within her with only a smile—it wrapped itself around her and didn't leave.

And for the first time in her life, Susannah wasn't able to concentrate on a Shakespearean play.

Even with her eyes open, all she could see was the earl's face.

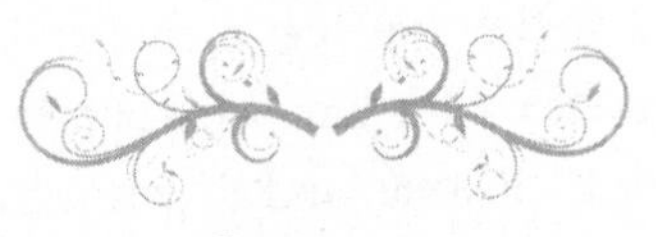

Chapter 3

Once again, Miss Susannah Ballister is the talk of the town. After achieving the dubious distinction of being both the most popular and the most unpopular young lady of the 1813 season (thanks, in whole, to the occasionally vacuous Clive Mann-Formsby), she was enjoying a bit of obscurity until another Mann-Formsby—this one David, the Earl of Renminster—graced her with his undivided attention at Saturday night's performance of The Merchant of Venice *at Drury Lane.*

One can only speculate as to the earl's intentions, as Miss Ballister very nearly became a Mann-Formsby last summer, although her prefix would have been Mrs. Clive, and she would have been sister to the earl.

This Author feels safe in writing that no one who saw the way the earl was looking at Miss Ballister throughout the performance would ever mistake his interest as fraternal.

As for Miss Ballister—if the earl's intentions are noble, then This Author also feels safe in writing that everyone would agree that she has landed herself the better Mann-Formsby.

LADY WHISTLEDOWN'S SOCIETY PAPERS,
31 January 1814

Once again, Susannah could not sleep.

And no wonder— *My brother wasn't worthy of a woman like you?* What could he have meant by that? Why would the earl say such a thing?

Could he be courting her? The earl?

She gave her head a shake, the sort meant to knock silly ideas right from her mind. Impossible. The Earl of Renminster had never shown signs of seriously courting anyone, and Susannah rather doubted that he was going to start with her.

And besides, she had every reason to feel the utmost irritation with the man. She had lost sleep over him. Susannah never lost sleep over anyone. Not even Clive.

As if that weren't bad enough, her restless night on Saturday was repeated on Sunday, and then Monday was even worse, due to her appearance in that morning's *Whistledown* column. So by the time Tuesday morning came along, Susannah was tired and grumpy when her butler found her and Letitia breaking their fast.

"Miss Susannah," he said, inclining his head ever so slightly in her direction. "A letter has arrived for you."

"For me?" Susannah queried, taking the envelope from his hand. It was the expensive sort, sealed with dark blue wax. The crest she recognized instantly. Renminster.

"Who is it from?" Letitia asked, once she'd finished chewing the muffin she'd popped into her mouth just as the butler had entered.

"I haven't opened it yet," Susannah said testily. And if she was clever, she'd figure out how not to open it until she was out of Letitia's company.

Her sister stared at her as if she were an imbecile. "That's easily remedied," Letitia pointed out.

Susannah set the envelope down on the table beside her plate. "I will deal with it later. Right now I'm hungry."

"Right now I'm dying of curiosity," Letitia retorted. "Either you open that envelope this instant or I will do it for you."

"I am going to finish my eggs, and then—Letitia!" The name came out rather like a shriek, as Susannah lunged across the table at her sister, who had just swiped the envelope in a rather neatly done maneuver that Susannah would have been able to intercept had her reflexes not been dulled by lack of sleep.

"Letitia," Susannah said in a deadly voice, "if you do not hand that envelope back to me unopened, I will never ever forgive you." And when that didn't seem to work, she added, "For the rest of my life."

Letitia appeared to consider her words.

"I will hunt you down," Susannah continued. "There will be no place you may remain safe."

"From you?" Letitia asked dubiously.

"Give me the envelope."

"Will you open it?"

"Yes. Give it to me."

"Will you open it *now*?" Letitia amended.

"Letitia, if you do not hand that envelope back to me this instant, you will wake up one morning with all of your hair cut off."

Letitia's mouth fell open. "You're not serious?"

Susannah glared at her through narrowed eyes. "Do I look as if I'm jesting?"

Letitia gulped and held the envelope out with a shaky hand. "I do believe you're serious."

Susannah snatched the missive from her sister's hand. "I would have taken several inches off at the very least," she muttered.

"Will you open it?" Letitia said, always one to remain intractably on subject.

"Very well," Susannah said with a sigh. It wasn't as if she was going to be able to keep it a secret, anyway. She'd merely been hoping to put it off. She hadn't yet used her butter knife, so she slid it under the flap and popped the seal open.

"Who is it from?" Letitia asked, even though Susannah hadn't even yet unfolded the letter.

"Renminster," Susannah said with a weary sigh.

"And you're upset?" Letitia asked, eyes bugged out.

"I'm not upset."

"You sound upset."

"Well, I'm not," Susannah said, sliding the single sheet of paper from the envelope.

But if she wasn't upset, what *was* she? Excited, maybe, a little at least, even if she was too tired to show it. The earl was exciting, enigmatic, and certainly more intelligent than Clive had been. But he was an earl, and he certainly wasn't going to marry her, which meant that eventually, she would be known as the girl who'd been dropped by two Mann-Formsbys.

It was more than she thought she could bear. She'd endured public humiliation once. She didn't particularly want to experience it again, and in greater measure.

Which was why, when she read his note, and its accompanying request, her answer was immediately no.

Miss Ballister—

I request the pleasure of your company on Thursday, at Lord and Lady Moreland's skating party, Swan Lane Pier, noon.

With your permission, I will call for you at your home thirty minutes prior.

Renminster

"What does he want?" Letitia asked breathlessly.

Susannah just handed her the note. It seemed easier than recounting its contents.

Letitia gasped, clapping a hand over her mouth.

"Oh, for goodness' sake," Susannah muttered, trying to refocus her attention on her breakfast.

"Susannah, he means to court you!"

"He does not."

"He does. Why else would he invite you to the skating party?" Letitia paused and frowned. "I hope *I* receive an invitation. Skating is one of the few athletic pursuits at which I do not appear a complete imbecile."

Susannah nodded, raising her brows at her sister's understatement. There was a pond near their home in Sussex that froze over every winter. Both Ballister girls had spent hours upon hours swishing across the ice.

They'd even taught themselves to spin. Susannah had spent more time on her bottom than on her skates during her fourteenth winter, but by God, she could spin.

Almost as well as Letitia. It did seem a shame that she hadn't yet been invited. "You could just come along with us," Susannah said.

"Oh no, I couldn't do that," Letitia said. "Not if he's courting you. There is nothing like a third wheel to ruin a perfectly good romance."

"There is no romance," Susannah insisted, "and I don't think I'm going to accept his invitation, anyway."

"You just said you would."

Susannah stabbed her fork into a piece of sausage, thoroughly irritated with herself. She hated people who changed their minds at whim, and apparently, for today at least, she was going to have to include herself in that group. "I misspoke," she muttered.

For a moment Letitia didn't reply. She even took a bite of eggs, chewed them thoroughly, swallowed, and took a sip of tea.

Susannah didn't really think her sister was through with the conversation; Letitia's silence could never be mistaken as anything but a momentary reprieve. And sure enough, just when Susannah had relaxed sufficiently to take a sip of her tea without actually gulping it down, Letitia said:

"You're mad, you know."

Susannah brought her napkin to her lips to keep from spitting out her tea. "I know no such thing, thank you very much."

"The Earl of Renminster?" Letitia said, her entire face colored by disbelief. "Renminster? Good heavens, sister, he's rich, he's handsome, and he's an *earl*. Why on earth would you refuse his invitation?"

"Letitia," Susannah said, "he's Clive's brother."

"I'm aware of that."

"He didn't like me when I was being courted by Clive, and I don't see how he has suddenly revised that opinion now."

"Then why is he courting you?" Letitia demanded.

"He's not courting me."

"He's trying to."

"He's not try—oh, devil take it," Susannah broke off, thoroughly annoyed with the conversation by this point. "Why would you think he wanted to court me?"

Letitia took a bite of her muffin and said rather matter-of-factly, "Lady Whistledown said so."

"Hang Lady Whistledown!" Susannah exploded.

Letitia drew back in horror, gasping as if Susannah had committed a mortal sin. "I can't believe you said that."

"What has Lady Whistledown ever done to earn my undying admiration and devotion?" Susannah wanted to know.

"I adore Lady Whistledown," Letitia said with a sniff, "and I will not tolerate slander against her in my presence."

Susannah could do nothing but stare at the deranged spirit she was certain had overtaken her normally sensible sister's body.

"Lady Whistledown," Letitia continued, her eyes flashing, "treated you rather nicely throughout that entire awful episode with Clive last summer. In fact, she might have been the only Londoner to do so. For that, if for nothing else, I will never disparage her."

Susannah's lips parted, her breath going still in her throat. "Thank you, Letitia," she finally said, her low voice catching on her sister's name.

Letitia just shrugged, clearly not wanting to get into a sentimental conversation. "It's nothing," she said, her breezy voice belied by her slight sniffle. "But I think you should accept the earl's offer all the same. If for no other reason than to restore your popularity. If one dance with him can make you acceptable again, think what an entire skating party will do. We'll be mobbed by gentleman callers."

Susannah sighed, truly torn. She *had* enjoyed her conversation with the earl at the theater. But she'd grown less trusting since Clive had jilted her last summer. And she didn't want to be the subject of unpleasant gossip again, which would certainly arise the minute the earl decided to pay attention to some other young lady.

"I can't," she said to Letitia, standing up so suddenly that her chair nearly toppled over. "I just can't."

Her regrets were sent to the earl not one hour later.

Precisely sixty minutes after Susannah watched her footman depart with her note for the earl, declining his invitation, the Ballisters' butler found her in her bedchamber and informed her that the earl himself had arrived and was waiting for her downstairs.

Susannah gasped, dropping the book she'd been trying to read all morning. It landed on her toe.

"Ow!" she blurted out.

"Are you hurt, Miss Ballister?" the butler asked politely.

Susannah shook her head even though her toe was throbbing. Stupid book. She hadn't been able to read more than three paragraphs in an hour. Every time she looked down at the pages, the words swam and blurred until all she could see was the earl's face.

And now he was there.

Was he *trying* to torture her?

Yes, Susannah thought, with no small measure of melodrama, he probably was.

"Shall I inform him that you will see him in a moment?" the butler inquired.

Susannah nodded. She was certainly in no position to refuse an audience with the Earl of Renminster, especially in her own home. A quick glance in her mirror told her that her hair wasn't too terribly mussed after sitting on her bed for an hour, and so with heart pounding, she made her way downstairs.

When she walked into the sitting room, the earl was standing by the window, his posture proud and perfect as always. "Miss Ballister," he said, turning to face her, "how lovely to see you."

"Er, thank you," she said.

"I received your note."

"Yes," she said, swallowing nervously as she lowered herself into a chair, "I surmised as much."

"I was disappointed."

Her eyes flew to his. His tone was quiet, serious, and there was something in it that hinted of even deeper emotions. "I'm sorry," she said, speaking slowly, trying to measure her words before she actually said them aloud. "I never meant to hurt your feelings."

He began to walk toward her, but his movements were slow, almost predatory. "Didn't you?" he murmured.

"No." She answered quickly, for it was the truth. "Of course not."

"Then why," he asked, settling into the chair nearest to hers, "did you refuse?"

She couldn't tell him the truth—that she didn't want to be the girl who was dropped by two Mann-Formsbys. If the earl began to accompany her to skating parties and the like, the only way it would appear as if he *hadn't* dropped her would be if he actually married her. And Susannah didn't want him to think she was dangling for an offer of marriage.

Good heavens, what could be more embarrassing than *that*?

"No good reason, then?" the earl said, one side of his mouth tipping up as his eyes never left her face.

"I'm not a good skater," Susannah blurted out, the lie the only thing she could think of on such short notice.

"Is that all?" he asked, dismissing her protest with nothing more than a quirk of his lips. "Have no fear, I shall support you."

Susannah gulped. Did that mean hands at the waist as they slid across the ice? If so, then her lie might just turn out to be the truth, because she was not at all certain that she could remain balanced and on her feet with the earl standing so close.

"I . . . ah . . ."

"Excellent," he declared, rising to his feet. "Then it is settled. We shall be a pair at the skating party. Stand now, if you will, and I shall give you your first lesson."

He didn't offer her much choice in the matter, taking her hand and tugging her upward. Susannah glanced toward the door, which she noticed was not nearly as far open as she'd left it when she entered.

Letitia.

The sneaky little matchmaker. She was going to have to have a stern talk with her sister once Renminster finally left. Letitia might wake up with her hair all chopped off yet.

And speaking of Renminster, what was *he* about? Expert skater that she was, Susannah knew very well that there was nothing to be taught about the sport unless one was actually *on* skates. She stood anyway, half out of curiosity, half because his relentless tug at her hand left her little choice.

"The secret to skating," he said (somewhat pompously, in her opinion), "is in the knees."

She batted her lashes. She'd always thought women who batted their lashes looked a bit dim, and since she was trying to appear as if she hadn't a clue about what she was doing, she thought it might be an effective touch. "The knees, you say?" she asked.

"Indeed," he replied. "The bending of them."

"The bending of the knees," she echoed. "Imagine that."

If he caught the sarcasm under her façade of innocence, he made no indication. "Indeed," he said again, making her wonder if perhaps it weren't his favorite word. "If you try to keep your knees straight, you will never keep your balance."

"Like this?" Susannah asked, bending her knees far too deeply.

"No, no, Miss Ballister," he said, demonstrating the maneuver himself. "Rather like this."

He looked uncommonly silly pretending to skate in the middle of the drawing room, but Susannah managed to keep her smile well hidden. Truly, moments like this were not to be wasted.

"I don't understand," she said.

David's brows came together in frustration. "Come over here," he said, moving to the side of the room where there was no furniture.

Susannah followed.

"Like this," he said, trying to move across the polished wood floors as if he were on skates.

"It doesn't seem terribly . . . smooth," she said, her face the perfect picture of innocence.

David eyed her suspiciously. She looked almost too angelic standing there watching him make a fool of himself. His shoes hadn't a scuff on them, of course, and they didn't slide at all on the floor.

"Why don't you try it again?" she asked, smiling rather like the Mona Lisa.

"Why don't you try it?" he countered.

"Oh, I couldn't," she said, blushing modestly. Except—he frowned—

she wasn't blushing. She was just tilting her head slightly to the side in a bashful manner that *should* have been accompanied by a blush.

"Learning by doing," he said, determined to get her skating if it killed him. "It's the only way." If he was going to make a fool of himself, heaven take it, so was she.

She cocked her head slightly, looking as if she were considering the notion, then she just smiled and said, "No, thank you."

He moved to her side. "I insist," he murmured, purposefully stepping just a little bit closer to her than was proper.

Her lips parted in surprise and awareness. Good. He wanted her to want him, even if she didn't understand what that meant.

Moving so that he was slightly behind her, he placed his hands at her waist. "Try it this way," he said softly, his lips scandalously close to her ear.

"My—my lord," she whispered. Her tone suggested that she'd tried to shriek the words, but that she lacked the energy, or perhaps the conviction.

It was, of course, completely improper, but as he planned to marry her, he didn't really see the problem.

Besides, he was rather enjoying seducing her. Even though—no, *especially because*—she didn't even realize it was happening.

"Like this," he said, his voice dropping nearly to a whisper. He exerted a bit of pressure on her waist, designed to force her to move forward as if they were skating as partners. But of course she stumbled, since her shoes didn't slide on the floor, either. And when she stumbled, he stumbled.

Much to his eternal dismay, however, they somehow managed to remain on their feet, and did not end up in a tangled pile on the floor. Which had been, of course, his intention.

Susannah expertly extricated herself from his grasp, leaving him to wonder if she'd had to practice the same maneuvers with Clive.

By the time he even realized that his jaw was clenched, he nearly had to pry it apart with his fingers.

"Is something wrong, my lord?" Susannah asked.

"Nothing at all," he ground out. "Why should you think so?"

"You look a little"—she blinked several times as she considered his face—"angry."

"Not at all," he said smoothly, forcing all thoughts of Clive and Susannah and Clive-and-Susannah from his mind. "But we should try the skating again." Perhaps this time he'd manage to orchestrate a tumble.

She stepped away, bright girl that she was. "I think it's time for tea," she said, her tone somehow sweet and resolute at the same time.

If that tone hadn't so obviously meant that he wasn't going to get what he wanted—namely, his body rather closely aligned against hers, preferably on the floor—he might have admired it. It was a talent, that—getting exactly what one wanted without ever having to remove a smile from one's face.

"Do you care for tea?" she asked.

"Of course," he lied. He detested tea, much as that had always vexed his mother, who felt it to be one's patriotic duty to drink the appalling beverage. But without tea, he'd have little excuse to linger.

But then her brows drew together, and she looked straight at him and said, "You hate tea."

"You remember," he commented, somewhat impressed.

"You lied," she pointed out.

"Perhaps I hoped to remain in your company," he said, gazing down at her rather as if she were a chocolate pastry.

He hated tea, but chocolate—now that was another story.

She stepped to the side. "Why?"

"Why, indeed," he murmured. "That's a good question."

She took another step to the side, but the sofa blocked her path.

He smiled.

Susannah smiled back, or at least she tried to. "I can have something else brought for you to drink."

He appeared to consider that for a moment, then he said, "No, I think it's time I departed."

Susannah nearly gasped at the knot of disappointment forming in her chest. When had her ire at his highhandedness turned into desire for his presence? And what was his game? First he made silly excuses to put his hands on her person, then he out-and-out lied to prolong his visit, and now, suddenly, he wanted to leave?

He was toying with her. And the worst part was—some little part of her was enjoying it.

He took a step toward the door. "I shall see you on Thursday, then?"

"Thursday?" she echoed.

"The skating party," he reminded her. "I believe I said I would come for you thirty minutes prior."

"But I never agreed to go," she blurted out.

"Didn't you?" He smiled blandly. "I could have sworn you did."

Susannah feared that she was wading into treacherous waters, but she just couldn't stop the stubborn devil that had clearly taken over her mind. "No," she said, "I didn't."

In under a second, he'd moved back to her side, and was standing close . . . very close. So close that the breath rushed from her body, replaced by something sweeter, something more dangerous.

Something utterly forbidden and divine.

"I think you will," he said softly, touching his fingers to her chin.

"My lord," she whispered, stunned by his nearness.

"David," he said.

"David," she repeated, too mesmerized by the green fire in his eyes to say anything else. But something about it felt right. She had never uttered his name, never even thought of him as anything but Clive's brother or Renminster, or even just *the earl*. But now, somehow, he was David, and when she looked into his eyes, so near to hers, she saw something new.

She saw the man. Not the title, not the fortune.

The man.

He took her hand, raised it to his lips. "Until Thursday, then," he murmured, his kiss brushing her skin with aching tenderness.

She nodded, because she could do nothing else.

Frozen in place, she watched mutely as he stepped away and walked toward the door.

But then, as he reached his hand toward the knob—but in that split second before he actually touched it—he stopped. He stopped, and he turned, and while she was standing there staring at him, he said, more to himself than to her, "No, no, that will never do."

He required only three long steps to reach her side. In a movement that was as startling as it was fluidly sensuous, he gathered her against him. His lips found hers, and he kissed her.

He kissed her until she thought she might faint from the desire.

He kissed her until she thought she might pass out from the lack of air.

He kissed her until she couldn't think of anything but him, could see nothing but his face in her mind, and wanted nothing but the taste of him on her lips . . . forever.

And then, with the same suddenness that had brought him to her side, he stepped away.

"Thursday?" he asked softly.

She nodded, one of her hands touching her lips.

He smiled. Slowly, with hunger. "I will look forward to it," he murmured.

"As will I," she whispered, although not until he was gone. "As will I."

Chapter 4

Good heavens, but This Author could not even begin to count the number of people sprawled most inelegantly upon the snow and ice during Lord and Lady Moreland's skating party yesterday afternoon.

It seems the ton *is not quite as proficient at the art and sport of ice skating as they would like to believe.*

LADY WHISTLEDOWN'S SOCIETY PAPERS,
4 February 1814

According to his pocket watch, which David knew to be perfectly accurate, it was precisely forty-six minutes past noon, and David knew quite well that the day was Thursday and the date was February the third, the year eighteen hundred and fourteen.

And at precisely that moment—at precisely 12:46 on Thursday, 3 February 1814, David Mann-Formsby, Earl of Renminster, realized three incontrovertible truths.

The first was, if one were going to be precise about it, probably closer to opinion than fact. And that was that the skating party was a disaster. Lord and Lady Moreland had instructed their poor, shivering servants to push carts about the ice with sandwiches and Madeira, which might have been a charming touch, except that none of the servants had the least bit of a clue as to how to maneuver on the ice, which, where it wasn't slippery, was treacherously bumpy due to the wind's constant sweep during the freezing process.

As a result, a flock of rather nasty-looking pigeons had congregated near the pier to gorge themselves on the sandwiches that had spilled from an overturned cart, and the poor hapless footman who'd been forced to push the cart was now sitting on the shore, pressing handkerchiefs up to his face where the pigeons had pecked him until he'd fled the scene.

The second truth that David realized was even less palatable. And that was that Lord and Lady Moreland had decided to host the party for the express purpose of finding a wife for their dimwit son Donald, and they'd decided that Susannah would do as well as any. To that end, they'd snatched her from his side and forced her into conversation with Donald for a full ten minutes before Susannah had managed an escape. (At which point they'd moved on to Lady Caroline Starling, but David decided that that simply couldn't be his problem, and Caroline would have to figure out how to extricate herself.)

The third truth made him grind his teeth, nearly into powder. And that was that Susannah Ballister, who had so sweetly claimed not to know how to skate, was a little liar.

He should have guessed it the minute she'd pulled her skates out of her bag. They didn't look anything like what everyone else had strapped to their feet. David's own skates were considered the height of new invention, and his consisted of long blades attached to wooden platforms, which he then tied onto his boots. Susannah's blades were a bit shorter than average, but more importantly, they had been attached to her actual boots, requiring her to change her footwear.

"I've never seen skates like that," he commented, watching her with interest as she laced up her boots.

"Er, it's what we use in Sussex," she said, and he couldn't be certain if the pink on her cheeks was a blush or merely from the blustery wind. "One doesn't have to worry about one's skates coming off one's boots if they're already attached."

"Yes," he said, "I can see where that would be an advantage, especially if one was not a proficient skater."

"Er, yes," she mumbled. Then she coughed. Then she looked up at him and smiled, although it did, in all honesty, look a bit like a grimace.

She switched to her other boot, her fingers moving nimbly as they worked the laces, despite being encased in gloves. David watched silently, and then he couldn't help commenting, "And the blades are shorter."

"Are they?" she murmured, not looking up at him.

"Yes," he said, moving so that his skate lined up next to hers. "Look at that. Mine are at least three inches longer."

"Well, you're a much taller person," she replied, smiling up at him from her position on the bench.

"An interesting theory," he said, "except that mine do seem to be a standard size." He waved his hand toward the river, where countless ladies and gentlemen were swishing across the ice . . . or falling on their bottoms. "Everyone's skates are rather like mine."

She shrugged as she allowed him to help her to her feet. "I don't know what to tell you," she said, "except that skates like these are quite common in Sussex."

David glanced over at the poor, hapless Donald Spence, who was presently being poked in the back by his mother, Lady Moreland. The Morelands, he was fairly certain, hailed from Sussex, and their skates didn't look a thing like Susannah's.

David and Susannah hobbled over to the edge of the ice—truly, *who* knew how to walk in skates on land?—and then he helped her onto the ice. "Mind your balance," he instructed, rather enjoying the way she was clutching his arm. "Remember, it's all in the knees."

"Thank you," she murmured. "I shall."

They moved farther out onto the ice, David steering them to a less populated area where he wouldn't have to worry so much about some buffoon crashing into them. Susannah seemed to be a natural, perfectly balanced and completely at one with the rhythm of skating.

David narrowed his eyes with suspicion. It was difficult to imagine anyone taking to skating quite so quickly, much less a wisp of a girl. "You *have* skated before," he said.

"A few times," she admitted.

Just to see what happened, he drew to a swift halt. She held her own admirably, without even a stumble. "More than a few times, perhaps?" he asked.

She caught her lower lip between her teeth.

"Maybe more than a dozen times?" he asked, crossing his arms.

"Er, maybe."

"Why did you tell me you couldn't skate?"

"Well," she said, crossing her arms in a perfect imitation of his, "it might be because I was looking for an excuse not to come."

He drew back, at first surprised by her show of honesty, but then rather impressed despite himself. There were many, many superb things about being an earl, and a rich and powerful one at that. But honesty among one's acquaintances was not one of them. David couldn't count the number of times he'd wished someone would just look him in the eye and say what they really meant. People tended to tell him what they thought he wanted to hear, which, unfortunately, was rarely the truth.

Susannah, on the other hand, was brave enough to tell him precisely what she was thinking. David was amazed at how refreshing it was, even when it meant that she was, in all truth, insulting him.

And so he just smiled. "And have you changed your mind?"

"About the skating party?"

"About me," he said softly.

Her lips parted with shock at his question. "I—" she began, and he could see that she did not know how to respond. He started to say something, to save her from an uncomfortable moment of his creation, but then she surprised him when she raised her eyes to his, and with that directness he found so enticing, said, quite simply, "I am still deciding."

He chuckled. "I suppose that means I will have to hone my powers of persuasion."

She blushed, and he knew she was thinking of their kiss.

This pleased him, as he'd been able to think of little else during the past few days. It made his torture a bit more bearable, knowing that she was enduring the same.

But this wasn't the time or place for seduction, and so he decided instead to uncover just how deeply she'd lied about her skating skills. "How well *do* you skate?" he asked, letting go of her arm and giving her a little push. "The truth, if you please."

She didn't falter for a moment, just swished a few feet away and then came to a stunningly swift halt. "I'm rather good, actually," she replied.

"How good?"

She smiled. Rather deviously. "Quite good."

He crossed his arms. "How good?"

She glanced about the ice, gauging the positions of the people around them, then took off—fast—straight in his direction.

And then, just when he was convinced she'd crash into him, toppling them both, she executed a neat little turn and circled around him, ending up right back where she'd started, in the twelve o'clock position.

"Impressive," he murmured.

She beamed.

"Especially for someone who doesn't skate."

She didn't stop beaming, but her eyes grew a little sheepish.

"Any other tricks?" he inquired.

She appeared undecided, so David added, "Go ahead. Be a show-off. I'm giving you permission."

She laughed. "Oh. Well, if *that's* the case . . ." She skated a few steps out, then stopped and shot him a glance that was pure mischief. "I would never dream of doing this without your permission."

"Of course not," he murmured, his lips twitching.

She looked around, obviously making sure she had room for her maneuverings.

"No one is even aimed in our direction," he said. "The ice is all yours."

With a look of intense concentration, she skated a few yards until she had built up a bit of speed, and then, to his complete surprise, she spun.

Spun. He had never seen anything like it.

Her feet never left the ice, but somehow she was twirling about, once, twice, thrice . . .

Good heavens, she made five complete rotations before she stopped, her entire being lit with joy. "I did it!" she called out, laughing on the words.

"That was amazing," he said, skating to her side. "How did you do it?"

"I don't know. I've never managed five rotations before. It's always been three, maybe four if I'm lucky, and half the time I fall." Susannah was talking quickly, caught up in her own exhilaration.

"Remind me not to believe you next time you say you can't do something."

For some reason, his words made her grin. From the smile on her face right down deep to her very heart and soul, Susannah grinned. She'd spent the last few months feeling like a failure, like a laughingstock, constantly having to remind herself of all the things she could not or should not do. Now here was this man—this wonderful, handsome, intelligent man—telling her that she could do anything.

And in the magic of the moment, she almost believed him.

Tonight she would force herself back to reality, back to remembering that David was also an earl and—even worse—a Mann-Formsby, and that she was probably going to regret her association with him. But for now, while the sun was glistening diamondlike off the snow and ice, while the cold wind felt like it was finally waking her up after a long, deep sleep, she was simply going to enjoy herself.

And she laughed. Laughed right there, right then, without a care for how she looked or sounded or even if everyone was watching her as if she were some deranged lunatic. She laughed.

"You must tell me," David said, skating over to her side. "What is so funny?"

"Nothing," she said, catching her breath. "I don't know. I'm just happy, that's all."

Something changed in his eyes then. He had gazed at her before with passion, even with lust, but now she saw something deeper. It was as if he'd suddenly found her and never wanted to tear his eyes away. And maybe it was a practiced look, and he'd used it on thousands of women before, but oh, *how* Susannah didn't want to think so.

It had been so long since she'd felt special.

"Take my arm," he said, and she did, and soon they were swishing silently across the ice, moving slowly but fluidly as they dodged the other skaters.

Then he asked her the one thing that she would never have expected. His voice was soft, and almost carefully casual, but his intensity was evident in the way his hand tightened on her arm. "What," he asked, "did you see in Clive?"

Somehow Susannah didn't stumble, and somehow she didn't slip, and somehow her voice sounded even and serene as she answered, "You almost make it sound as if you don't care for your brother."

"Nonsense," David replied. "I would give my life for Clive."

"Well, yes," Susannah said, since she'd never doubted *that* for a moment. "But do you *like* him?"

Several seconds passed, and their blades stroked the ice eight times before David finally said, "Yes. Everyone likes Clive."

Susannah looked at him sharply, intending to scold him for his evasive answer until she saw from his face that he intended to say more.

"I love my brother," David said, his words slow, as if he were making a final decision on each one mere seconds before he spoke it. "But I am not unaware of his shortcomings. I have every hope, however, that his marriage to Harriet will help him to grow into a more responsible and mature person."

A week ago Susannah would have taken his words as an insult, but now she recognized them as the simple statement of fact that they were. And it seemed only fair to answer him with the same honesty he'd given her.

"I liked Clive," she said, feeling herself slip into memory, "because—oh, I don't know, I suppose it was because he always seemed so happy and free. It was contagious." She shrugged helplessly, even as they rounded the corner of the pier, instinctively slowing down as they grew closer to the rest of the skating party. "I don't think I was the only one who felt that way," she continued. "Everyone liked to be near Clive. Somehow . . ." She smiled wistfully, and she smiled regretfully. Memories of Clive were bittersweet.

"Somehow," she finished softly, "everyone seemed to smile near him. Especially me." She shrugged, the motion almost an apology. "It was exciting to be on his arm."

She looked to David, who was regarding her with an intense expression. But there was no anger, no recrimination. Just a palpable sense of curiosity, of a need to understand.

Susannah let out a little breath—not quite a sigh, but something close to it. It was hard to put into words something that she'd never quite forced herself to analyze. "When you're with Clive," she eventually said, "everything seems . . ."

It took her several seconds to locate the right word, but David did not press.

"Brighter," she finally finished. "Does that make sense? It's almost as if he has a glow to him, and everything that comes into contact with it seems somehow better than it really is. Everyone seems more beautiful, the food tastes better, the flowers smell sweeter." She turned to David with an earnest expression. "Do you understand what I mean?"

David nodded.

"But at the same time," Susannah said, "I've come to realize that he shone so brightly—everything shone so brightly, actually—that I missed things." She felt the corners of her lips pinch into a thoughtful frown as she tried to find the words for what she was feeling. "I didn't notice things I should have done."

"What do you mean?" he asked, and when she looked into his eyes, she knew that he wasn't humoring her. He truly cared about her answer.

"At the Worth ball, for example," she said. "I was saved from what would surely have been a rather nasty episode by Penelope Featherington."

David's brow furrowed. "I'm not sure I know her."

"That's exactly my point. I never spared even so much as a thought for her last summer. Don't mistake my point," she assured him. "I was certainly never cruel to her. Just . . . unaware, I suppose. I didn't pay attention to anyone outside my little social circle. Clive's circle, in truth."

He nodded in understanding.

"And it turns out she's actually a very nice person." Susannah looked up at him earnestly. "Letitia and I paid a call upon her last week. She's very clever, too, but I never took the time to notice. I wish . . ." She paused, chewing on her lower lip. "I thought I was a better person than that, that's all."

"I think you are," he said softly.

She nodded, staring off into the distance as if she might find the answers she needed on the horizon. "Maybe I am. I suppose I shouldn't berate myself for my actions last summer. It was fun, and Clive was nice, and it was very exciting to be with him." She smiled wistfully. "It's difficult to refuse that—to be at the constant center of attention, to feel so loved and admired."

"By Clive?" David asked quietly.

"By everyone."

Their blades cut across the ice—once, twice—before he replied, "So it wasn't the man himself you loved, so much as the way he made you feel."

"Is there a difference?" Susannah asked.

David appeared to consider her question quite deeply before finally saying, "Yes. Yes, I think there is."

Susannah felt her lips part, almost in surprise, as his words forced her to think harder and longer about Clive than she had in some time. She thought, and then she turned, and she opened her mouth to speak, but then—

BAM!

Something slammed into her, knocking the very breath from her body, sending her skidding across the ice until she fell heavy and hard into a snowbank.

"Susannah!" David yelled, skating quickly to her side. "Are you all right?"

Susannah blinked and gasped, trying to blow the snow from her face . . . and her eyelashes, and her hair, and, well, everywhere. She'd landed on her back, almost in a reclining position, and she was very nearly buried.

She sputtered something that was probably a question—she wasn't sure whether she'd said who, what, or how, and then managed to wipe enough snow from her eyes to see a woman in a green velvet coat skating furiously away.

Susannah squinted. It was Anne Bishop, of all people, who Susannah knew quite well from the previous Season! She couldn't believe Anne would knock her down and then flee the scene.

"Why that little . . ."

"Are you hurt?" David asked, interrupting her quite effectively as he crouched beside her.

"No," Susannah grumbled, "although I cannot believe that she skated away without so much as a query to my welfare."

David glanced over his shoulder. "No sign of her now, I'm afraid."

"Well, she'd better have a good excuse," Susannah muttered. "Nothing less than impending death will be acceptable."

David appeared to be fighting a grin. "Well, you don't seem to be injured, and your mental capacities are quite clearly in working order, so would you like me to help you up?"

"Please," Susannah said, gratefully accepting his hand.

Except that *David's* mental capacities must not have been in working order, because he had remained in his crouch when he offered his hand, not realizing that he hadn't the proper leverage to yank her to her feet, and after a precarious moment, in which they both seemed to be suspended halfway between the ice and an upright position, Susannah's skates flew out from under her, and they both went tumbling down, back into the snowbank.

Susannah laughed. She couldn't help herself. There was something so wonderfully incongruous about the lofty Earl of Renminster buried in snow. He looked rather fetching, actually, with flakes on his eyelashes.

"Do you dare mock me?" he pretended to boom, once he'd spat the snow from his mouth.

"Oh, never," she replied, biting her lip to stave off a giggle. "I wouldn't dream of mocking you, My Lord Snowman."

His lips pursed into one of those expressions that tried to be annoyed but was really nothing more than amused. "Don't," he warned, "call me that."

"My Lord Snowman?" she echoed, surprised by his reaction.

He paused, assessing her face with an expression of mild surprise. "You haven't heard, then?"

She shook her head as best as one could in the snow. "Heard what?"

"Harriet's relatives were rather distressed at the loss of their surname. Harriet's the last of the Snowes, you realize."

"Which means . . ." Susannah's lips parted with delighted horror. "Oh don't tell me . . ."

"Indeed," David replied, looking very much as if he wanted to laugh but thought he shouldn't. "My brother must now be correctly referred to as Clive Snowe-Mann-Formsby."

"Oh, I'm evil," Susannah said, laughing so hard the snowbank shook. "I am truly an evil, unkind person. But I can't . . . I can't help it . . . I . . ."

"Go ahead and laugh," David told her. "I assure you, I did."

"Clive must have been furious!"

"That might be painting it a trifle too harsh," David said, "but certainly rather embarrassed."

"A doubly hyphenated name would have been bad enough," Susannah said. "I shouldn't like to have to introduce myself as Susannah Ballister-Bates—" She searched for an appropriately awful third surname. "Bismark!" she finished triumphantly.

"No," he murmured dryly, "I can see why you wouldn't."

"But *this*—" Susannah finished, stepping right on top of his soft words. "This is quite beyond the . . . oh dear. I don't know what it's quite beyond. My comprehension, I suppose."

"He wanted to change it to Snowe-Formsby," David said, "but I told him our Mann forebears would be quite upset."

"Forgive me for pointing it out," Susannah replied, "but your Mann forebears are quite deceased. I rather think they lack the capability to be upset one way or another."

"Not if they left behind legal documents barring monetary inheritance by anyone who drops the Mann name."

"They didn't!" Susannah gasped.

David merely smiled.

"They didn't!" she said again, but this time her tone was quite different. "They did no such thing. You only said that to torture poor Clive."

"Oh, it's *poor Clive* now," he teased.

"It's poor anyone who must answer to Snowe-Mann!"

"That's Snowe-Mann-Formsby, thank you very much." He shot her a cheeky grin. "My Formsby forebears would be quite put out."

"And I suppose they also blocked inheritance by anyone who drops their name?" Susannah asked sarcastically.

"As a matter of fact, they did," David said. "Where do you think I got the idea?"

"You're incorrigible," she said, but she couldn't quite manage an appropriately horrified tone. The truth was, she rather admired his sense of humor. The fact that the joke was on Clive was merely the icing on the cake.

"I suppose I shall have to call you My Lord Snow*flake*, then," she said.

"It's hardly dignified," he said.

"Or heroic," she agreed, "but as you'll see, I'm still trapped here in the snowbank."

"As am I."

"White suits you," Susannah said.

He gave her a look.

"You should wear it more often."

"You're quite cheeky for a woman in a snowbank."

She grinned. "My courage is derived from your position, also in a snowbank."

He grimaced, then nodded self-deprecatingly. "It's actually not too uncomfortable."

"Except for the dignity," Susannah agreed.

"And the cold."

"And the cold. I can't feel my . . . er . . ."

"Bottom?" he supplied helpfully.

She cleared her throat, as if somehow that would clear her blush. "Yes."

His green eyes twinkled at her embarrassment, then he turned serious—or at least more serious than he had been—and said, "Well, I suppose I ought to save you, then. I rather like your—don't worry, I won't say it," he interjected upon her gasp of horror. "But I wouldn't want to see it fall off."

"David," she ground out.

"Is that what it takes to get you to use my name?" he wondered. "A slightly inappropriate but I assure you most respectful comment?"

"Who are you?" she suddenly asked. "And what have you done with the earl?"

"Renminster, you mean?" he asked, leaning toward her until they were nearly nose to nose.

His question was so odd that she couldn't answer, save for a tiny nod.

"Perhaps you never knew him," he suggested. "Perhaps you only thought you did, but you never looked beyond the surface."

"Perhaps I didn't," she whispered.

He smiled, then took her hands in his. "Here is what we are going to do. I'm going to stand, and as I do so, I'll pull you up. Are you ready?"

"I'm not sure—"

"Here we are," he muttered, trying to heave himself up, which was no small task given that his feet were on skates, and his skates were on ice.

"David, you—"

But it was no use. He was behaving in a predictably manly fashion, which meant that he wasn't listening to reason (not when it interfered with an opportunity to make a show of his brute strength). Susannah could have told him—and in fact, she tried to—that the angle was all wrong, and his feet were going to slide out from under him, and they'd both go toppling down . . .

Which is exactly what they did.

But this time David didn't behave in a typically manly fashion, which would have been to get quite angry and make excuses. Instead, he just looked her straight in the eyes and burst out laughing.

Susannah laughed with him, her body shaking with sheer, unadulterated mirth. It had never been like this with Clive. With Clive, even when she'd laughed, she'd always felt as if she were on display, as if everyone were watching her laugh, wondering what the joke was, because one couldn't truly count oneself as part of the most fashionable set unless one knew all the inside jokes.

With Clive, she'd always known the inside jokes, but she hadn't always found them funny.

But she'd laughed all the same, hoping that no one noticed the incomprehension in her eyes.

This was different. This was special. This was . . .

No, she thought forcefully. This wasn't love. But maybe it was the beginnings of it. And maybe it would grow. And maybe—

"What have we here?"

Susannah looked up, but she already knew the voice.

Dread filled her belly.

Clive.

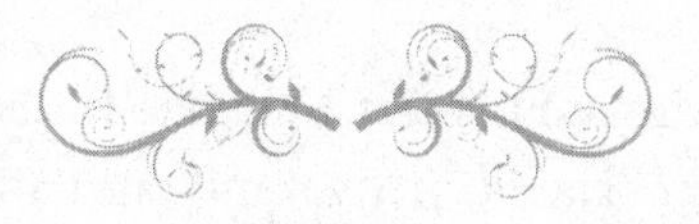

Chapter 5

Both Mann-Formsby brothers were in attendance at the Moreland skating party, although it can hardly be said that their interactions were amiable. Indeed, it was reported to This Author that the earl and his brother nearly came to blows.

Now, that, Gentle Reader, would have been a sight to see. Fisticuffs on skates! What could be next? Underwater fencing? Tennis on horseback?

Lady Whistledown's Society Papers,
4 February 1814

When Susannah placed her hand in Clive's it was as if she'd been transported back in time. It had been half a year since she'd stood so close to the man who'd broken her heart—or at the very least her pride—and much as she wanted to feel nothing . . .

She did.

Her heart missed a beat and her stomach flipped and her breath grew shaky, and oh, how she hated herself for it all.

He should mean nothing. Nothing. Less than nothing if she could manage it.

"Clive," she said, trying to keep her voice even as she tugged her hand away from his.

"Susannah," he said warmly, smiling down at her in that oh-so-confident way of his. "How have you been?"

"Fine," she answered, irritated now, since, really, how did he *think* she'd been?

Clive turned back around to offer a hand to his brother, but David had already found his feet. "David," Clive said cordially. "I didn't expect to see you here with Susannah."

"I didn't expect to see you here at all," David replied.

Clive shrugged. He wasn't wearing a hat, and a lock of his blond hair fell forward onto his forehead. "Decided only this morning to attend."

"Where is Harriet?" David asked.

"Off with her mother near the fire. She doesn't like the cold."

They stood there for a moment, an awkward triptych with nothing to say. It was strange, Susannah thought, her eyes drifting slowly from one Mann-Formsby brother to the next. In all the time she'd spent with Clive, she'd never known him to be without words or an easy smile. He was a chameleon, slipping and sliding into situations with perfect ease. But right now, he was just staring at his brother with an expression that wasn't *quite* hostile.

But it certainly wasn't friendly.

David didn't seem quite right, either. He tended to hold himself more stiffly than Clive, his posture always straight and correct. And in truth, it was a rare man who moved with the easy, fluid grace that Clive epitomized. But now David seemed almost too stiff, his jaw too tight. When they'd laughed so hard, just moments before in the snowbank, she'd seen the man and not the earl.

But now . . .

The earl was most definitely back.

"Would you like to take a turn about the ice?" Clive suddenly asked.

Susannah felt her head jerk with surprise when she realized that Clive was talking to her. Not that he would have been likely to want to take a turn about the ice with his brother, but still, it didn't seem quite appropriate that he do so with her. Especially with Harriet so close by.

Susannah frowned. Especially with Harriet's mother so close to Harriet. It was one thing to put one's wife in a potentially awkward position; it was quite another to do so with one's mother-in-law.

"I'm not sure that's a good idea," she hedged.

"We should clear the air," he said, his tone matter-of-fact. "Show everyone we've no hard feelings."

No hard feelings? Susannah's jaw stiffened. What the devil did he think he was talking about? *She* had hard feelings. Very hard. After last summer, her feelings for Clive were bloody well as hard as iron.

"For old times' sake," Clive cajoled, his boyish grin lighting up his face.

His face? Really, let's be honest, it lit up the entire pier. Clive's smiles always did that.

But this time, Susannah didn't feel her usual jolt of excitement. Instead she felt a little irritated. "I'm with Lord Renminster," she said stiffly. "It wouldn't be polite to abandon him."

Clive let out a little howl of laughter. "David? Don't worry about him." He turned to his brother. "You don't mind, do you, old man?"

David looked as if he minded very much, but of course he merely said, "Not at all."

Which left Susannah even more irritated with him than she was with Clive. If he minded, why didn't he *do* something about it? Did he think she *wanted* to skate with Clive?

"Fine," she announced. "Let us be off, then. If we're going to skate, we might as well do it before our toes freeze to black."

Her tone couldn't have been called anything but snippy, and both Mann-Formsby brothers looked at her with curious surprise.

"I shall be over by the vat of chocolate," David said, giving her a polite bow as Clive looped his arm through hers.

"And if it's not still warm, then you'll be over by the vat of brandy?" Clive joked.

David answered with a stiff smile to his brother and skated away.

"Susannah," Clive said, giving her a warm look. "Glad he's gone, eh? It's been an age."

"Has it?"

He chuckled. "You know it has."

"How is marriage treating you?" she asked pointedly.

He winced. "You don't waste any time, do you?"

"Neither did you, apparently," she muttered, relieved when he began to skate. The sooner they made their lap around the area, the sooner they would be done.

"Are you still angry, then?" he asked. "I'd hoped you'd managed to get past that."

"I managed to get past *you*," she said. "My anger is another thing altogether."

"Susannah," he said, although in truth, his voice sounded rather like a whine to her ears. He sighed, and she looked over at him. His eyes were full of concern, and his face had assumed a wounded air.

And maybe he really did feel wounded. Maybe he truly hadn't meant to hurt her and honestly thought that she would be able to shrug off the entire unpleasant episode as if nothing had happened.

But she couldn't. She just wasn't that nice a person. Susannah had decided that some people were truly good and nice inside and some people just tried to be. And she must have been in the latter group, because she simply couldn't summon enough Christian charity to forgive Clive. Not yet, anyway.

"I have not had a pleasant few months," she said, her voice stiff and clipped.

His hand tightened around her arm. "I'm sorry," he said. "But don't you see I had no choice?"

She looked at him in disbelief. "Clive, you have more choices and opportunities than anyone I know."

"That's not true," he insisted, looking at her intently. "I had to marry Harriet. I had no choice. I—"

"Don't," Susannah warned in a low voice. "Don't tread down that avenue. It isn't fair to me and it certainly isn't fair to Harriet."

"You're right," he said, somewhat shamefaced. "But—"

"And I don't care one way or another why you married Harriet. I don't care if you marched up to the altar with her father's pistol pressed against your back!"

"Susannah!"

"No matter why or how you married her," Susannah continued hotly, "you could have told me before you announced it at the Mottram ball in front of four hundred people."

"I'm sorry," he said. "That was shabby of me."

"I'll say," she muttered, feeling rather a bit better now that she'd had a chance to rail directly at Clive, as opposed to her usual arguments in absentia. But all the same, enough was enough, and she found she didn't particularly care to remain in his company any longer. "I think you should return me to David," she said.

His eyebrows rose. "It's David now, is it?"

"Clive," she said, her voice irritated.

"I can't believe you're calling my brother by his given name."

"He gave me leave to do so, and I don't see how it is any of your concern one way or another."

"Of course it is my concern. We courted for months."

"And you married someone else," she reminded him. Good Lord, was Clive *jealous*?

"It's just . . . *David*," he spat out, his voice unpleasant. "Of all people, Susannah."

"What is wrong with David?" she asked. "He's your brother, Clive."

"Exactly. I know him better than anyone." His hand tightened at her waist as they rounded the pier. "And he is not the right man for you."

"I hardly think you are in any position to advise me."

"Susannah . . ."

"I happen to like your brother, Clive. He's funny, and smart, and—"

Clive actually stumbled, which was a rare thing for a man of his grace. "Did you say funny?"

"I don't know, I suppose I did. I—"

"David? Funny?"

Susannah thought about their moments in the snowbank, about the sound of David's laughter and the magic of his smile. "Yes," she said with quiet reminiscence. "He makes me laugh."

"I don't know what is going on," Clive muttered, "but my brother has no sense of humor."

"That's simply not true."

"Susannah, I've known him for twenty-six years. I should think that counts for more than your acquaintance of, what—one week?"

Susannah felt her jaw set into an angry line. She had no desire to be condescended to, especially by Clive. "I would like to go back to the shore," she bit off. "Now."

"Susannah—"

"If you do not wish to accommodate me, I will skate off by myself," she warned.

"Just once more around, Susannah," he cajoled. "For old times' sake."

She looked over at him, which was a dreadful mistake. Because he was gazing at her with that same expression that had always turned her legs to butter. She didn't know how blue eyes could look so warm, but his were practically melting. He was looking at her as if she were the only woman in the world, or perhaps the last scrap of food in the face of famine, and . . .

She was made of sterner stuff now, and she knew she wasn't the only woman in his world, but he did sound sincere, and for all his childish ways, Clive was not at heart an unkind person. She felt her resolve slipping away, and she sighed. "Fine," she said, her voice resigned. "Once more around. But that is all. I came here with David, and it's not fair to leave him off by himself."

And as they pushed off to take one more turn around the makeshift course that Lord and Lady Moreland had set up for their guests, Susannah realized that she really did want to get back to David. Clive might be handsome, and Clive might be charming, but he no longer made her heart pound with a single look.

David did.

And nothing could have surprised her more.

The Moreland servants had lit a bonfire under the vat of chocolate, and so the beverage was blessedly warm, if not adequately sweetened. David had drunk three cups of the too-bitter brew before he realized that the heat he was finally beginning to feel in his fingers and toes had nothing to do with the fire to his left and everything to do with an anger that had been simmering since the moment Clive had skated up the snowbank and looked down on him and Susannah.

Damn and blast, that wasn't accurate. Clive had been looking at Susannah. He couldn't have cared less about David—his *brother*, for God's sake—and he'd gazed at Susannah in a way no man was supposed to look at a woman not his wife.

David's fingers tightened around his mug. Oh, very well, he was exaggerating. Clive hadn't been looking at Susannah in a lustful fashion (David ought to know, since he had caught himself looking at her in that exact manner), but his expression had definitely been possessive, and his eyes had fired with jealousy.

Jealousy? If Clive had wanted the right to feel jealous over Susannah, he should bloody well have married her, and not Harriet.

Jaw clamped like a vise, David watched his brother lead Susannah around the ice. Did Clive still want her? David wasn't worried; well, not really. Susannah would never disgrace herself by becoming too familiar with a married man.

But what if she still pined for him? Hell, what if she still loved him? She said she didn't, but did she really know her own heart? Men and women tended to delude themselves when it came to love.

And what if he married her—and he fully intended to marry her—and she still loved Clive? How could he bear it, knowing his wife preferred his brother?

It was an appalling prospect.

David set his mug down on a nearby table, ignoring the startled stares of his compatriots as it landed with a loud thunk, sloshing chocolate over the rim.

"Your glove, my lord," someone pointed out.

David looked down rather dispassionately at his leather glove, which was now turning dark brown where the chocolate was soaking in. It was almost certainly ruined, but David couldn't bring himself to care.

"My lord?" the nameless person queried again.

David must have turned to him with an expression approaching a snarl, because the young gentleman scurried away.

And anyone moving away from the fire on such a frigid day had to want to be somewhere else very badly indeed.

A few moments later, Clive and Susannah reappeared, still skating in perfectly matched steps. Clive was staring at her with that amazingly warm expression he had perfected at the age of four (Clive had never been punished for anything; one repentant look from those huge blue eyes tended to get him out of any scrape), and Susannah was staring back at him with an expression of . . .

Well, if truth be told, David wasn't exactly sure what sort of expression was on her face, but it wasn't what he'd wanted to see, which was full-fledged hatred.

Or fury would have been acceptable. Or maybe complete lack of interest. Yes, complete lack of interest would have been best.

But instead she was looking at him with something almost approaching weary affection, and David didn't know what to make of that one way or another.

"Here she is," Clive said, once they'd skated close. "Returned to your side. Safe and sound as promised."

David thought Clive was laying it on a bit too thick, but he had no wish to prolong the encounter, so instead all he said was, "Thank you."

"We had a lovely time, didn't we, Susannah?" Clive said.

"What? Oh yes, of course we did," she replied. "It was good to catch up."

"Don't you need to get back to Harriet?" David asked pointedly.

Clive just grinned back at him, his smile almost a dare. "Harriet is fine by herself for a few minutes. Besides, I told you she was with her mother."

"Nonetheless," David said, getting downright irritated now, "Susannah came with me."

"What has that to do with Harriet?" Clive challenged.

David's chin jutted out. "Nothing, except that you're married to her."

Clive planted his hands on his hips. "Unlike you, who is married to no one."

Susannah's eyes bobbed back and forth from brother to brother.

"What the devil is that supposed to mean?" David demanded.

"Nothing, except that you should get your own affairs in order before messing with mine."

"Yours!" David nearly exploded. "Since when has Susannah become your affair?"

Susannah's mouth dropped open.

"When has she been yours?" Clive volleyed back.

"I fail to see how that is any of your business."

"Well, it's more my business than—"

"Gentlemen!" Susannah finally interceded, quite unable to believe the scene unfolding in front of her. David and Clive were squabbling like a pair of six-year-olds unable to share a favorite toy.

And *she* appeared to be the toy in question, a metaphor she found she didn't much like.

But they didn't hear her, or if they did, they didn't care, because they continued to bicker until she physically placed herself between them and said, "David! Clive! That is enough."

"Step aside, Susannah," David said, nearly growling. "This isn't about you."

"It isn't?" she asked.

"No," David said, his voice hard, "it's not. It's about Clive. It's always about Clive."

"Now see here," Clive said angrily, poking David in the chest.

Susannah gasped. They were going to come to blows! She looked around, but thankfully, no one seemed to have noticed the impending violence, not even Harriet, who was sitting some distance away, chatting with her mother.

"You married someone else," David practically hissed. "You forfeited any rights to Susannah when—"

"I'm leaving," she announced.

"—you married Harriet. And you should have considered—"

"I said I'm leaving!" she repeated, wondering why she even cared whether they heard her. David had said quite plainly that this wasn't about her.

And it wasn't. That was becoming abundantly clear. She was simply some silly prize to be won. Clive wanted her because he thought David had her. David wanted her for much the same reason. Neither actually cared about her; all they cared about was beating each other in some silly lifelong competition.

Who was better? Who was stronger? Who had the most toys?

It was stupid, and Susannah was sick of it.

And it hurt. It hurt deep down in her heart. For one magical moment, she and David had laughed and joked, and she'd allowed herself to dream that something special was growing between them. He certainly didn't act like any of the men of her acquaintance. He actually listened to her, which was a novel experience. And when he laughed, the sound had been warm and rich and true. Susannah had always thought that you could tell a lot about a person from his laugh, but maybe that was just another lost dream.

"I'm leaving," she said for the third time, not even certain why she'd bothered. Maybe it was some kind of sick fascination with the situation at hand, a morbid curiosity to see what they would do when she actually started to walk away.

"No, you're not," David said, grabbing her wrist the moment she moved.

Susannah blinked in surprise. He *had* been listening.

"I will escort you," he said stiffly.

"You are obviously quite occupied here," she said, with a sarcastic glance toward Clive. "I'm sure I can find a friend to take me home."

"You came with me. You will leave with me."

"It's not—"

"It's necessary," he said, and Susannah suddenly understood why he was so feared among the *ton*. His tone could have frozen the Thames.

She glanced over at the iced-over river and almost laughed.

"You, I'll speak to later," David snapped at Clive.

"Pffft." Susannah clapped a hand over her mouth.

David and Clive both turned to stare at her with irritated expressions. Susannah fought another extremely ill-timed giggle. She'd never thought they resembled each other until now. They looked *exactly* the same when they were annoyed.

"What are you laughing at?" Clive demanded.

She gritted her teeth together to keep from smiling. "Nothing."

"It's obviously not nothing," David said.

"It's not about you," she replied, shaking with barely contained laughter. What fun it was to throw his words right back at him.

"You're laughing," he accused.

"I'm not laughing."

"She is," Clive said to David, and in that moment they ceased to be arguing with each other.

Of course they weren't arguing anymore; they were united against *her.*

Susannah looked at David, then she looked at Clive. Then she looked back at David, who was glowering so fiercely that she ought to have been frightened right out of her specially made ice skates, but instead she just burst out laughing.

"What?" David and Clive demanded in unison.

Susannah just shook her head, trying to say, "It's nothing," but not really succeeding in anything other than making herself look like a deranged lunatic.

"I'm taking her home," David said to Clive.

"Be my guest," Clive replied. "She clearly can't remain here." *Among civilized society,* was the implied end of his sentence.

David took her elbow. "Are you ready to leave?" he asked, even though she'd announced that very intention no fewer than three times.

She nodded, then made her farewells to Clive before she allowed David to lead her away.

"What was that all about?" he asked her, once they were settled in his carriage.

She shook her head helplessly. "You looked so much like Clive."

"Like Clive?" he echoed, his voice tinged with disbelief. "I don't look a thing like Clive."

"Well, maybe not in features," she said, plucking aimlessly at the fibers of the blanket tucked over her lap. "But your expressions were identical, and you were certainly acting like him."

David's expression turned to stone. "I never act like Clive," he bit off.

She shrugged in reply.

"Susannah!"

She looked at him with arched brows.

"I don't act like Clive," he repeated.

"Not normally, no."

"Not today," he ground out.

"Yes, today, I'm afraid. You did."

"I—" But he didn't finish his sentence. Instead, he clamped his mouth shut, opening it only to say, "You'll be home soon."

Which wasn't even true. It was a good forty minutes' ride back to Portman Square. Susannah felt every single one of those minutes in excruciating detail, as neither of them spoke again until they reached her home.

Silence, she realized, was quite deafening.

Chapter 6

Most amusing, Lady Eugenia Snowe was spied dragging her new son-in-law across the ice by his ear.

Perhaps she spied him taking a turn about the ice with the lovely Susannah Ballister?

And doesn't the younger Mann-Formsby wish now that he'd worn a hat?

LADY WHISTLEDOWN'S SOCIETY PAPERS,
4 February 1814

Just like Clive?!!!

David grabbed the newspaper he'd been attempting to peruse and viciously crumpled it between his hands. Then for good measure, he hurled it across the room. It was a wholly unsatisfactory display of petulance, however, since the newspaper was nearly weightless and ended up floating in a soft lob before settling gently on the carpet.

Hitting something would have been much more satisfying, especially if he'd managed to peen the family portrait that hung over the mantel, right in Clive's perpetually smiling face.

Clive? How could she possibly think he was just like Clive?

He'd spent his entire life hauling his brother out of scrapes and accidents and potential disasters. The most important word there being "potential," since David had always managed to intercede before Clive's "situations" turned calamitous.

David growled as he scooped the crumpled newspaper off the floor and tossed it into the raging fire. Perhaps he'd been too protective of Clive over the years. With his older brother around to solve all of his problems, why should Clive have learned responsibility and rectitude? Maybe the next time Clive found himself in hot water, David ought to just let him boil for a little while. But all the same . . .

How could Susannah say the two of them were alike?

Groaning her name, David slumped into the chair nearest to the fire. When he saw her in his mind—and he'd done so approximately three times per minute since he'd left her at her home six hours earlier—it was always with cheeks flushed from cold, with snowflakes bobbing precariously from her eyelashes, mouth wide and laughing with delight.

He pictured her in the snowbank, at that moment when he'd come to the most amazing, breathtaking realization. He had decided to pursue her because she'd make an excellent countess, that was true. But in that moment, as he'd gazed at her lovely face and had to use every ounce of his restraint not to kiss her right there in front of the entire *ton,* he'd realized that she'd be more than an excellent countess.

She would be a wonderful wife.

His heart had leaped with delight. And dread.

He still wasn't quite sure what he felt for her, but it was becoming increasingly apparent that those feelings resided rather stubbornly in and around his heart.

If she still loved Clive, if she still pined for his brother, then she was lost to him. It didn't matter if she said yes to his proposal of marriage. If she still wanted Clive, then he, David, would never truly have her.

Which meant the big question was—could he bear it? Which would be worse—to be her husband, knowing she loved someone else, or not to have her in his life at all?

He didn't know.

For the first time in his life, David Mann-Formsby, Earl of Renminster, didn't know his own mind. He simply didn't know what to do.

It was an awful, aching, unsettling sensation.

He eyed his glass of whiskey, sitting just out of arm's reach on the table by the fire. Damn, and he'd really wanted to get drunk. But now he was tired, and drained, and much as it disgusted him, he was feeling far too lazy even to get out of the chair.

Although the whiskey did look rather appealing.

He could almost smell it from there.

He wondered how much energy he'd have to expend to rise to his feet. How many steps to the whiskey? Two? Three? That wasn't so very many. But it *seemed* really far, and—

"Graves told me I'd find you in here."

David groaned without even looking to the door. Clive.

Not the person he wanted to see right now.

The last person, in fact.

He should have instructed his butler to tell his brother that he wasn't in. Never mind that David had never in his entire life been "not at home" for his brother. Family had always been David's first priority in life. Clive was his only sibling, but there were cousins and aunts and uncles, and David was responsible for the well-being of every last one of them.

Not that he'd had much choice in the matter. He had become the head of the Mann-Formsby family at the age of eighteen, and not a day had gone by since the moment of his father's death that he had had the luxury of thinking only of himself.

Not until Susannah.

He wanted her. *Her.* Just because of who she was, not because she'd make an excellent addition to the family.

He wanted her for himself. Not for them.

"Have you been drinking?" Clive asked.

David stared longingly at his glass. "Sadly, no."

Clive picked the glass off the table and handed it to him.

David thanked him with a nod and took a long sip. "Why are you here?" he asked, not caring if he sounded blunt and rude.

Clive didn't answer for several moments. "I don't know," he finally said.

For some reason, this didn't surprise David.

"I don't like the way you're treating Susannah," Clive blurted out.

David stared at him in disbelief. Clive was standing in front of him, his posture stiff and angry, his hands fisted at his sides. "*You* don't like the way I'm treating Susannah?" David asked. "*You* don't like it? What right, may I ask, do you have to offer an opinion? And when, pray tell, did I decide that I should care?"

"You shouldn't toy with her," Clive ground out.

"What, so that *you* can?"

"I'm not toying with anyone." Clive's expression turned angry and petulant. "I'm married."

David slammed his empty glass down on a table. "A fact you'd do well to remember."

"I care about Susannah."

"You should stop caring," David bit out.

"You have no right—"

David shot to his feet. "What is this really about, Clive? Because you know it's not about your looking out for Susannah's welfare."

Clive said nothing, just stood there glaring at his older brother as his skin grew mottled with fury.

"Oh dear God," David said, his voice dripping with disdain. "Are you jealous? Are you? Because let me tell you, you lost any right to feel jealousy over Susannah when you publicly humiliated her last summer."

Clive actually paled. "I never meant to embarrass her."

"Of course you didn't," David snapped. "You never *mean* to do anything."

Clive's jaw was set in a very tight line, and David could see by his shaking fists that he very much wanted to hit him. "I don't have to remain here and listen to this," Clive said, his voice low and furious.

"Leave, then. Be my guest. You're the one who came here unannounced and uninvited."

But Clive didn't move, just stood there shaking with anger.

And David had had enough. He didn't feel like being charitable, and he didn't feel like being the mature older brother. All he wanted was to be left alone. "Go!" he said harshly. "Didn't you say you were leaving?" He waved his arm toward the door. "Go!"

Clive's eyes narrowed with venom . . . and pain. "What kind of brother are you?" he whispered.

"What the—what do you mean?" David felt his lips part with shock. "How dare you question my devotion? I have spent my entire life cleaning up your messes, including, I might add, Susannah Ballister. You destroyed her reputation last summer—"

"I didn't destroy it," Clive quickly interjected.

"Very well, you didn't render her unmarriageable, you just made her a laughingstock. How do you think *that* felt?"

"I didn't—"

"No, you didn't think," David snapped. "You didn't think for a moment about anyone other than yourself."

"That wasn't what I was going to say!"

David turned away in disgust, walking over to the window and leaning heavily on the sill. "Why are you here, Clive?" he asked wearily. "I'm far too tired for a brotherly spat this evening."

There was a long pause, and then Clive asked, "Is that how you view Susannah?"

David knew he ought to turn around, but he just didn't feel like seeing his brother's face. He waited for further explanation from Clive, but when none came, he asked, "Is *what* how I view her?"

"As a mess to be cleaned up."

David didn't speak for a long moment. "No," he finally said, his voice low.

"Then how?" Clive persisted.

Sweat broke out on David's brow. "I—"

"How?"

"Clive . . ." David said in a warning voice.

But Clive was relentless. "How?" he demanded, his voice growing loud and uncharacteristically demanding.

"I love her!" David finally yelled, whirling around to face his brother with blazing eyes. "I love her. There. Are you satisfied? I love her, and I swear to God I will kill you if you ever make another false move against her."

"Oh my God," Clive breathed. His eyes widened with shock, and his lips parted into a small, surprised oval.

David grabbed his brother by the lapels and hauled him up against a wall. "If you ever, and I mean ever, approach her in a manner that might even hint at flirtation, I swear that I will tear you from limb to limb."

"Good God," Clive said. "I actually believe you."

David looked down, caught sight of his knuckles, turned white by the force of his grip, and was horrified by his reaction. He let go of Clive abruptly and walked away. "I'm sorry," he muttered.

"You really love her?" Clive asked.

David nodded grimly.

"I can't believe it."

"You just said you did," David said.

"No, I said I believed you would tear me from limb to limb," Clive said, "and *that* I still believe, I assure you. But *you* . . . in love . . ." He shrugged.

"Why the hell couldn't I be in love?"

Clive shook his head helplessly. "Because . . . You . . . It's *you,* David."

"Meaning?" David asked irritably.

Clive fought for words. "I didn't think you *could* love," he finally said.

David nearly reeled with shock. "You didn't think I could love?" he whispered. "My whole adult life, I've done nothing but—"

"Don't start about how you've devoted your life to your family," Clive interrupted. "Believe me, I know it's all true. You certainly throw it in my face often enough."

"I don—"

"You *do,*" Clive said forcefully.

David opened his mouth to protest once more, but then he silenced himself. Clive was right. He did remind him of his shortcomings too often. And maybe Clive was—whether any of them realized it or not—living *down* to David's expectations.

"It's all about duty to you," Clive continued. "Duty to family. Duty to the Mann-Formsby name."

"It's been about more than that," David whispered.

The corners of Clive's lips tightened. "That may be true, but if so, you haven't shown it very well."

"I'm sorry, then," David said. His shoulders slumped as he let out a long, tired exhale. How ironic to discover that he had failed at the one pursuit around which he'd built his entire life. Every decision he had made, everything he had done—it had always been about family, and now it appeared they didn't even realize it. His love for them had been perceived as a burden—a burden of expectation.

"Do you really love her?" Clive quietly asked.

David nodded. He wasn't sure how it had happened, or even exactly when during the brief time since they'd renewed their acquaintance, but he loved her. He loved Susannah Ballister, and somehow Clive's visit had jolted his feelings into startling clarity.

"I don't, you know," Clive said.

"You don't what?" David asked, his voice betraying his weary impatience.

"Love her."

David let out a harsh little laugh. "God, I hope not."

"Don't mock me," Clive warned. "I'm only telling you this because my behavior today might have led you to think that I . . . ah . . . Well, forget about all that. The point is, I care about you enough to tell you . . . well, you are my brother, you know."

David actually smiled. He hadn't thought himself capable of such an expression at that moment, but somehow he couldn't help it.

"I don't love her," Clive said again. "I only sought her out today because I was jealous."

"Of me?"

"I don't know," Clive admitted. "I suppose so. I never thought Susannah would set her cap for you."

"She didn't. I pursued her."

"Well, regardless, I suppose I assumed she'd be sitting at home pining for me." Clive winced. "That sounds terrible."

"Yes," David agreed.

"I didn't quite mean it that way," Clive explained, letting out a frustrated breath. "I didn't want her to spend her life pining away for me, but I suppose I thought she would anyway. And then when I saw her with *you* . . ." He sat down in the chair David had vacated a few minutes earlier and let his head rest in his hands. After a few moments of silence, he looked back up and said, "You shouldn't let her get away."

"I beg your pardon?"

"You shouldn't let Susannah get away."

"It had occurred to me," David said, "that that might be an advisable course of action."

Clive scowled at his brother's sarcasm. "She's a good woman, David. Not the right one for someone like me, but much as it wouldn't have occurred to me if you hadn't fallen in love with her, I think she might be exactly the right sort for you."

"How romantically put," David muttered.

"Pardon me for having trouble seeing you in the guise of a romantic hero," Clive said with a slight roll of his eyes. "I'm still finding it difficult to believe you've fallen in love at all."

"Heart of stone and all that," David quipped.

"Don't try to brush this off," Clive said. "This is serious."

"Oh, I'm aware of that."

"Earlier this afternoon," Clive said slowly, "when we were skating, Susannah said things . . ."

David jumped on his words. "What things?"

"Things," Clive said, giving his brother a stop-interrupting-me sort of glare. "Things that led me to believe she might not be unamenable to your suit."

"Will you speak English?" David snapped.

"I think she might love you back."

David sank down and found himself seated on an end table. "Are you sure?"

"Of course I'm not sure. I just said I *think* she might love you back."

"What a marvelous vote of confidence."

"I doubt she even knows her own mind yet," Clive said, ignoring David's words, "but she clearly cares for you."

"What do you mean?" David asked, desperately trying to find something definite to latch on to in Clive's words. Good God, the man could talk around an issue for hours without actually coming to the point of it.

Clive rolled his eyes. "All I'm saying is that I think that if you pursued her—really pursued her—she would say yes."

"You *think*."

"I think," Clive said impatiently. "Good God, when did I tell you I was a seer?"

David pursed his lips in thought. "What did you mean," he asked slowly, "when you said *really* pursue her?"

Clive blinked. "I meant you should really pursue her."

"Clive," David growled.

"A grand gesture," Clive said quickly. "Something huge and romantic and entirely out of character."

"Any type of grand gesture would be out of character," David grumbled.

"Exactly," Clive said, and when David looked up, he saw that his brother was grinning.

"What should I do?" David asked, hating that he was the one asking advice, but desperate enough to do it, anyway.

Clive stood and cleared his throat. "Now, what would be the fun in my telling you what to do?"

"I'd find great fun in it," David ground out.

"You'll think of something," Clive said, entirely unhelpfully. "A grand gesture. Every man can come up with at least one grand gesture in his lifetime."

"Clive," David said with a groan, "you know that grand gestures aren't in my style."

Clive chuckled. "Then I imagine you'll have to make them your style. At least for right now." His brow furrowed, and then he began to sputter with only slightly controlled laughter. "At least for Valentine's Day," he added, doing nothing now to contain his mirth, "which I believe is . . . ah . . . only eleven days away."

David's belly lurched. He had a feeling it was his heart dropping into his stomach. Valentine's Day. Dear God, *Valentine's Day*. The bane of any sane and reasonable man. If ever a grand gesture was expected, it was on Valentine's Day.

He staggered into his chair. "Valentine's Day," he groaned.

"You can't avoid it," Clive said brightly.

David threw him a killing glare.

"I can see that it's time I took my leave," Clive murmured.

David didn't even bother to acknowledge his brother as he left.

Valentine's Day. It should have struck him as perfect timing. Tailor-made for declaring one's love.

Ha. Tailor-made if one was the loquacious, romantic, poetic sort, which David most assuredly was not.

Valentine's Day.

What the devil was he going to do?

The following morning, Susannah woke up feeling not well-rested, not happy, hale, and hearty, and most definitely not refreshed.

She hadn't slept.

Well, of course she'd *slept,* if one wanted to be annoyingly precise about it. She hadn't lain awake the *entire* night. But she knew she'd seen her clock when it read half-one. And she had distinct recollections of half-two, half-four, a quarter past five, and six. Not to mention that she'd gone to bed at midnight.

So if she'd slept, it had only been in bits and snatches.

And she felt *awful.*

The worst part of it was—it wasn't just that she was tired. It wasn't even just that she was cranky.

Her heart ached.

Ached.

It ached like nothing she'd ever felt, the pain of it almost physical. Something had happened between her and David the day before. It had begun earlier, maybe at the theater, and it had been growing, but it had *happened* in the snowbank.

They had laughed, and she had looked into his eyes. And for the first time, she had really seen him.

And she loved him.

It was the worst possible thing she could ever have done. Nothing could have set her up for heartbreak with greater precision. At least she hadn't loved Clive. She'd thought she had, but in truth, she'd spent more of that summer wondering *whether* she loved him than declaring that she did. And in truth, when he had jilted her, it had been her pride that he'd battered, not her heart.

But with David it was different.

And she didn't know what to do.

As she'd lain awake the night before, she'd reckoned that she was caught in the midst of one of three scenarios. The first one was ideal: David loved her, and all she had to do was tell him she felt the same, and they would live happily ever after.

She frowned. Maybe she ought to wait for him to declare his love first. After all, if he *did* love her, he'd want to be romantic about it and make a formal declaration.

She closed her eyes in agony. The truth was, she didn't know how he felt one way or another, and in fact, the truth could be closer to the second scenario, which was that he had only been pursuing her to irritate Clive. If that was indeed the case, she had no idea what to do with herself. Avoid him like the plague, she supposed, and pray that broken hearts healed quickly.

The third scenario was, in her opinion, probably the most likely: David liked her well enough but didn't love her, and had only asked her to the skating party as a diversion. That seemed logical enough; men of the *ton* behaved that way all the time.

She flopped back on her bed, letting out a loud groan of frustration. It didn't really matter which scenario was the truth—none of the three had a clear-cut solution.

"Susannah?"

Susannah looked up to see her sister poking her head through the slim opening between the door and the doorframe.

"Your door was open," Letitia said.

"No, it wasn't."

"Very well, it wasn't," Letitia said, entering, "but I heard you making strange sounds and thought I should check as to your welfare."

"No," Susannah said, returning her gaze to the ceiling, "you heard me making strange sounds and wanted to know what I was doing."

"Well, that, too," Letitia admitted. Then, when Susannah made no reply, she added, "What were you doing?"

Susannah smirked at the ceiling. "Making strange sounds."

"Susannah!"

"Very well," Susannah said, since it was near impossible to keep a secret from Letitia, "I'm nursing a broken heart, and if you tell a single soul, I will—"

"Cut off my hair?"

"Cut off your *legs*."

Letitia smiled as she closed the door behind her. "My lips are sealed," she assured her, crossing the room to the bed and sitting down. "Is it the earl?"

Susannah nodded.

"Oh, good."

Curiosity sparked, Susannah sat up. "Why is it good?"

"Because I like the earl."

"You don't even know the earl."

Letitia shrugged. "It's easy to discern his character."

Susannah thought about that. She wasn't so certain that Letitia was correct. After all, she'd spent the better part of a year thinking that David was haughty, cold, and unfeeling. Of course, her opinion had been mostly based on what she'd been told by Clive.

No, maybe Letitia was right. Because once Susannah had spent time with David herself, without Clive . . . well, it hadn't taken long for her to fall in love with him.

"What should I do?" Susannah whispered.

Letitia was entirely unhelpful. "I don't know."

Susannah shook her head. "Nor do I."

"Does he know how you feel?"

"No. At least, I don't think he does."

"Do you know how *he* feels?"

"No."

Letitia made an impatient sound. "Do you think he *might* care for you?"

Susannah's lips stretched into an uncertain grimace. "I think he might."

"Then you should tell him how you feel."

"Letitia, I could make an utter fool of myself."

"Or you could end up blissfully happy."

"Or a fool," Susannah reminded her.

Letitia leaned forward. "This is going to sound dreadfully unkind, but really, Susannah, would it be so very terrible if you embarrassed yourself? After all, how could you possibly endure any greater mortification than you did last summer?"

"This would be worse," Susannah whispered.

"But no one would know."

"David would know."

"He's only one person, Susannah."

"He's the only person who matters."

"Oh," Letitia said, sounding a little bit surprised and quite a lot excited. "If that is how you feel, then you *must* tell him." When Susannah did nothing but groan, she added, "What is the worst that could happen?"

Susannah shot her a heavy look. "I don't even want to speculate."

"You *must* tell him how you feel."

"Why, so that you may vicariously live through my mortification?"

"Through your happiness," Letitia said pointedly. "He will love you in return, I'm sure of it. He probably already does."

"Letitia, you haven't the least bit of facts upon which to base such a supposition."

But Letitia wasn't paying attention. "You must go tonight," she said quite suddenly.

"Tonight?" Susannah echoed. "Where? I don't even think we've any invitations. Mama was planning for us to remain at home."

"Exactly. Tonight is the only night this week that you will be able to sneak out and visit him at home."

"At home?" Susannah very nearly shrieked.

"What you need to tell him must be said in private. And you will never find a moment's privacy at a London ball."

"I can't go to his home," Susannah protested. "I'd be ruined."

Letitia shrugged. "Not if no one found out."

Susannah grew thoughtful. David would never tell anyone, of that she was certain. Even if he rejected her, he wouldn't do anything that would place her reputation at risk. He would simply bundle her up, find a carriage without his crest on it, and send her discreetly home.

In a way, she had nothing to lose except her pride.

And, of course, her heart.

"Susannah?" Letitia whispered. "Are you going to do it?"

Susannah lifted her chin, looked her sister straight in the eye, and nodded.

Her heart, after all, was already lost.

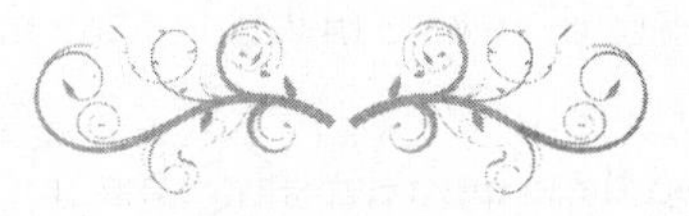

Chapter 7

And amid all this cold and snow and ice and frigid wind and . . . well, amid this abominable weather, if one is going to state it quite honestly, may This Author remind you, Gentle Reader, that Valentine's Day is fast approaching?

Time to get thee out to the stationers' shop for valentine notes and perhaps, for good measure, the confectioner and the florist.

Gentlemen of the ton, *now is the time to atone for all of your sins and transgressions. Or at least to try.*

LADY WHISTLEDOWN'S SOCIETY PAPERS,
4 February 1814

David's study was ordinarily spotless, with every book in its proper place on the shelf; papers and documents organized into neat piles, or better yet, tucked away in appropriate files and drawers; and nothing, absolutely nothing, on the floor save for the carpet and the furniture.

Tonight, however, the room was littered with paper. Crumpled-up paper. Crumpled-up valentines, to be precise.

David wasn't much of a romantic, or at least he didn't think he was, but even he knew that one was supposed to buy one's valentines at H. Dobbs & Co. And so, that morning, he'd driven out to New Bridge Street, clear across town by St. Paul's Cathedral, and bought himself a box of their best.

All of his attempts at flowery script and romantic poetry were disasters, however, and so at noon he found himself once again in the quiet confines of H. Dobbs & Co., purchasing another box of their best valentines, this time a package of twelve instead of the half dozen he'd bought earlier that day.

The entire affair had been embarrassing, but not nearly as embarrassing as when he dashed into the store that evening, precisely five minutes before they were due to close, after having raced his curricle across town at speeds that could only have been termed reckless (although *stupid* and *insane* had also come to mind). The proprietor was clearly a professional through and through, because he didn't even crack a smile as he handed David their largest box of valentines (eighteen in all), and then suggested that he also purchase a slim book called *Valentine Writers,* which purported to offer instructions on how to write a valentine for any type of recipient.

David was appalled that he, who had taken a first in literature at Oxford, was reduced to using a guidebook just to write a bloody valentine, but he'd accepted it without a word, and in fact, without a reaction save for the burning sensation on his face.

Good God, a blush. When was the last time he'd blushed? Clearly, the day could not possibly descend any further into hell.

And so at ten in the evening, there he was, sitting in his study with a single valentine on his desk, thirty-five others strewn about the room, in various states of crumpled disaster.

One valentine. One last chance to get this bloody endeavor right. He suspected that H. Dobbs might not be open on Saturday, and he knew they weren't open on Sunday, so if he didn't do a good job on this one, he was probably stuck until Monday with this awful task hanging over his head.

He let his head fall back and groaned. It was just a valentine. A valentine. It shouldn't be so difficult. It couldn't even qualify as a grand gesture.

But what did one say to a woman one wanted to love for the rest of one's life? The stupid little *Valentine Writers* book had offered no advice on that quarter, at least none that would apply when one feared that one might have angered the lady in question the day before with one's stupid behavior, quarreling with one's brother.

He stared down at the blank card. And stared. And stared.

His eyes started to water. He forced himself to blink.

"My lord?"

David looked up. Never had an interruption from his butler been so welcome.

"My lord, there is a lady here to see you."

David let out a tired sigh. He couldn't imagine who it was; maybe Anne Miniver, who probably thought she was still his mistress since he hadn't quite gotten around to telling her that he was through with mistresses.

"Show her in," he said to his butler. He supposed he might as well be thankful that Anne had saved him the trouble of going all the way out to Holborn.

He let out an irritated little snort. He could have easily stopped by her home in Holborn any one of the six times he'd nearly passed right by it today on his way to and from the stationers' shop.

Life was just full of delightful little ironies, wasn't it?

David stood, because it really wouldn't be polite to be sitting when Anne arrived. She might have been born on the wrong side of the blanket, and she certainly lived her life on the wrong side of propriety, but she was still, in her own way, a lady, and she deserved no less than his best behavior under the circumstances. He walked over to the window as he awaited her arrival, pulling the heavy drapes back to stare out into the inky night.

"My lord," he heard his butler say, followed by, "David?"

He whirled around. It wasn't Anne's voice.

"Susannah!" he said in disbelief, nodding curtly to dismiss his butler. "What are you doing here?"

She answered him with a nervous smile as she glanced around his study.

David groaned inwardly. The crumpled valentines were everywhere. He prayed she'd be too polite to mention it. "Susannah?" he asked again, growing worried. He couldn't imagine a circumstance that would compel her to visit him, an unmarried gentleman, in his home. In the dead of night, no less.

"I—I'm sorry to bother you," she said, looking over her shoulder even though the butler had closed the door when he'd left.

"It's no trouble at all," he replied, restraining the urge to rush to her side. Something must be amiss; there could be no other reason she would be here. And yet he didn't trust himself to stand next to her, didn't know how he could do so without taking her into his arms.

"No one saw me," she assured him, catching her lower lip between her teeth. "I—I made sure of it, and—"

"Susannah, what is the problem?" he said intently, giving up on his vow to remain at least three paces away from her. He moved quickly to her side, and when she did not answer, took her hand in his. "What is wrong? Why are you here?"

But it was as if she hadn't heard him. She stared over his shoulder, clenching and unclenching her jaw before finally saying, "You won't be trapped into marriage with me, if that's your worry."

His grip on her hand slackened. It hadn't been his worry. It had been his greatest desire.

"I just—" She swallowed nervously and finally brought her eyes to his. The force of it nearly buckled his knees. Her eyes, so dark and luminous, were glistening, not with unshed tears, but with something else. Emotion, perhaps. And her lips—dear God, did she have to *lick* them? He was going to be sainted for not kissing her that very minute.

"I had to tell you something," she said, her voice dropping to a near-whisper.

"Tonight?"

She nodded. "Tonight."

He waited, but she didn't say anything, just looked away and swallowed again, as if trying to work up her nerve.

"Susannah," he whispered, touching her cheek, "you can tell me anything."

Without quite looking at him, she said, "I have been thinking about you . . . and I . . . I . . ." She looked up. "This is very difficult."

He smiled gently. "I promise . . . Whatever you say, it will remain between the two of us."

She let out a little laugh at that, but it was a desperate sound. "Oh,

David," she said, "it's not that sort of secret. It's just . . ." She closed her eyes, slowly shaking her head. "It's not that I've been thinking about you," she said, reopening her eyes but glancing to her side to avoid looking at him directly. "It's more that I can't *stop* thinking about you, and I—I—"

His heart leaped. What was she trying to say?

"I was just wondering," she said, her words tumbling out in a rush of breath and speech. "I need to know . . ." She swallowed, closed her eyes yet again, but this time she almost seemed to be in pain. "Do you think you might care for me? Even a little?"

For a moment he didn't know how to respond. And then, without speaking, without even thinking, he cupped her face in his hands and kissed her.

He kissed her with every pent-up emotion that had coursed through his body for the past few days. He kissed her until he had no choice but to pull back, if only to take a breath.

"I care," he said, and kissed her again.

Susannah melted in his arms, overcome by the intensity of his passion. His lips traveled from her mouth to her ear, trailing a white-hot path of need along her skin. "I care," he whispered, before unbuttoning her coat and allowing it to fall to the floor. "I care."

His hands moved down the length of her back until they cupped her bottom. Susannah gasped at the intimacy of his touch. She could feel the hard, hot length of him through their clothes, could sense his passion in every beat of his heart, every rough catch of his breath.

And then he said the words she'd been dreaming of. He pulled himself away, just far enough so that she could gaze deeply into his eyes, and said, "I love you, Susannah. I love your strength, and I love your beauty. I love your kind heart, and I love your wicked wit. I love your courage, and—" His voice broke, and Susannah gasped when she realized there were tears in his eyes. "I love you," he whispered. "That is all there really is to say."

"Oh, David," she said, gulping back her emotions, "I love you, too. I don't think I even understood what it meant to love until I met you."

He touched her face, tenderly, reverently, and she thought she might say more about how much she loved him, but then she saw the oddest thing . . .

"David," she asked, "why is there paper all over your study?"

He pulled back, then actually began to scurry around the room, attempting to gather up every piece. "It's nothing," he muttered, snatching up the dustbin and shoving the paper inside.

"It's not nothing," she said, grinning at the sight of him. She'd never thought a man of his size and bearing could scurry.

"I was just . . . I was . . . ah . . ." He leaned down and scooped up another crumpled-up piece of paper. "It's nothing."

Susannah spied one that he'd missed, slightly underneath his desk, and she bent down and grabbed it.

"I'll take that," David said swiftly, reaching out to grab it from her.

"No," she said, smiling as she twisted away so that he couldn't reach it. "I'm curious."

"It's nothing interesting," he mumbled, making one last attempt to retrieve it.

But Susannah had already smoothed it out. *There are so many things I'd like to say,* it read. *Like how your eyes . . .*

And that was all.

"What is this?" she asked.

"A valentine," he muttered.

"For me?" she asked, trying to keep the note of hopefulness out of her voice.

He nodded.

"Why didn't you finish it?"

"Why didn't I finish any of them?" he countered, waving his arm toward the room, where dozens of other unfinished valentines had been strewn about. "Because I couldn't figure out what I wanted to say. Or perhaps I knew that, just not how I wanted to say it."

"What did you want to say?" she whispered.

He stepped forward, took both her hands in his. "Will you marry me?" he asked.

For a moment she was struck dumb. The emotion in his eyes held her mesmerized, filled her own with tears. And then finally, choking on the words, she replied, "Yes. Oh, David, yes."

He lifted her hand to his lips. "I should take you home," he murmured, but he didn't sound like he meant it.

She didn't say anything, because she didn't want to go. Not yet, at least. This was a moment to be savored.

"It would be the right thing to do," he said, but his other hand was stealing around her waist, drawing her closer.

"I don't want to go," she whispered.

His eyes flared. "If you stay," he said, his voice soft, "you won't leave here an innocent. I can't—" He stopped and swallowed, as if trying to keep himself under control. "I'm not strong enough, Susannah. I'm only a man."

She took his hand and pressed it to her heart. "I can't go," she said. "Now that I'm here, now that I'm finally with you, I can't go. Not yet."

Wordlessly, his hands found the buttons at the back of her dress, nimbly slipping each one free. Susannah gasped as she felt the cool rush of air hit her skin, followed by the startling warmth of David's hands. His fingers slid up and down her back, feather-light in their caress.

"Are you certain?" he whispered harshly in her ear.

Susannah closed her eyes, touched by his final show of concern. She nodded, then made herself say the words. "I want to be with you," she whispered. It had to be said—for him, for her.

For them.

He groaned, then picked her up and carried across the room, kicking open a door leading to . . .

Susannah looked around. It was his bedroom. It had to be. Lush and dark and intensely masculine, with rich burgundy drapes and bedcoverings. When he laid her down on the massive bed, she felt feminine and deliciously sinful, womanly and beloved. She felt naked and exposed, even with her dress still loosely hanging from her shoulders. He seemed to understand her fears, and he moved to remove his clothing before returning to hers. He stepped back, his eyes never leaving her face as he undid the buttons at his cuffs.

"I have never seen anything so beautiful," he whispered.

Nor had she. As she watched him undress in the candlelight, she was struck by the pure masculine beauty of him. She had never seen a bare male chest before, but she couldn't imagine that there was another to compare with David's as he let his shirt fall to the floor.

He slid onto the bed beside her, his body matching the length of hers, his lips finding hers in a hungry kiss. He touched her reverently, gently tugging her dress down until it was nothing but a memory. Susannah caught her breath at the sensation of his skin against her breasts, but somehow there wasn't time or space to feel embarrassment as he rolled her onto her back, pressing his body against hers, moaning hoarsely as he settled his still-clad hips between her legs.

"I have dreamed of this," he whispered, lifting himself up just far enough to look at her face. His eyes were hot, and even though the dim light didn't allow her to see the color, somehow she felt them, burning a fierce, bright green as they swept across her.

"I've been dreaming of you," she said shyly.

His lips curved into a dangerously masculine smile. "Tell me," he gently ordered.

She blushed, feeling the heat of it sweep across her entire body, but still she whispered, "I dreamed you were kissing me."

"Like this?" he murmured, kissing her on the nose.

Smiling, she shook her head.

"Like this?" he asked, brushing his lips against hers.

"A bit like that," she admitted.

"Or maybe," he mused, his eyes taking on a devilish gleam, "like this." His lips trailed down the length of her throat, moving over the swell of her breast until they closed over her nipple.

Susannah let out a little shriek of surprise . . . which quickly melted into a low moan of pleasure. She'd never dreamed that such things were possible, or that such sensations existed. He had a wicked mouth and a naughty tongue, and he was making her feel like a fallen, depraved woman.

And she loved every moment of it.

"Was that it?" he asked, his torture unceasing, even as he murmured the words.

"No," she said, with shaky voice, "I could never have dreamed that."

He lifted his head to gaze hungrily at her face. "There's so much more, my love."

He rolled off her and quickly stripped off his breeches, leaving him amazingly, startlingly naked. Susannah actually gasped at the sight of him, causing him to chuckle.

"Not what you expected?" he asked as he resumed his place at her side.

"I don't know what I expected," she admitted.

His eyes grew serious as he stroked her hair. "There is nothing to fear, I promise you."

She looked up at his face, barely able to contain her love for this man. He was so good, so honest, so true. And he cared for her—not as a possession or a convenience, but for *her,* the person inside. She'd been out in society long enough to have heard whispers of what transpired on wedding nights, and she knew that not all men behaved with such consideration.

"I love you," he whispered. "Never forget that."

"Never," she promised.

And then words ceased. His hands and lips brought her to a fever pitch of excitement, to the edge of something daring and unknown. He kissed her and caressed her and loved her until she was straining and quivering with need. Then, just when she was certain she couldn't possibly bear it a moment longer, his face was once again opposite hers, and his manhood was pressing against her, urging her legs further open.

"You're ready for me," he told her, the muscles in his face pinched with restraint.

She nodded. She didn't know what else to do. She had no idea if she was ready for him, wasn't even sure what it was she was supposed to be ready for. But she wanted something more, of that she was certain.

He moved forward, just a touch, but enough so that she gasped with the shock of his entry.

"David!" she gasped, clutching at his shoulders.

His teeth were gritted together, and he looked almost as if he were in pain.

"David?"

He pushed forward again, slowly, allowing her time to accommodate him.

Her breath caught again, but then she had to ask, "Are you all right?"

He let out a rough chuckle. "Fine," he said, touching her face. "Just a little . . . I love you so much, it's hard to hold back."

"Don't," she said softly.

He closed his eyes for a moment, then kissed her once, gently, on the lips. "You don't understand," he whispered.

"Make me understand."

He pushed forward.

Susannah let out a little "oh" of surprise.

"If I go too quickly, I will hurt you," he explained, "and I couldn't bear that." He inched forward, groaning as he did so. "But if I go slowly . . ."

Susannah didn't think he was particularly enjoying going slowly, and truth be told, she wasn't so much, either. There was nothing *wrong* with it, and the fullness of the feeling was rather intriguing, but she'd lost the sense of urgency she'd felt just moments earlier.

"It may hurt," he said, pressing further within her, "but only for a moment, I promise."

She looked up at him, cradling his face in her hands. "I'm not worried," she said quietly.

And she wasn't. That was the most amazing thing. She trusted this man completely. With her body, with her mind, with her heart. She was ready to join with him in every way, to connect her life with his for eternity.

The thought of it gave her so much joy she feared she might explode.

And then suddenly he was fully within her, and there wasn't any pain, just the slightest twinge of discomfort. He held still for a moment, his breath coming in short, harsh rushes, and then, after whispering her name, he began to move.

At first Susannah didn't even realize what was happening. He moved slowly, with a steady rhythm that mesmerized her. And that excitement she'd been feeling, that desperate need for fulfillment, began to grow again. It started small, like a tiny seed of desire, and then grew until it wrapped itself around every inch of her body.

Then he lost his rhythm, and his movements grew frenzied. She met him with every thrust, unable to contain her need to move, to writhe beneath him, to touch him wherever her hands could reach. And just when she didn't think she could possibly bear it any longer, that she would surely die if she continued on this course, her world exploded.

David's entire body changed at that moment, as if he suddenly let go of the last thread of his control, and he let out a triumphant shout before he collapsed atop her, unable to do anything but breathe.

The weight of him was stunning, but there was something so . . . comforting about having him there. Susannah never wanted him to leave.

"I love you," he said, once he was able to speak. "I love you so much."

She kissed him. "I love you, too."

"Will you marry me?"

"I already said I would."

He grinned wickedly. "I know, but will you marry me tomorrow?"

"Tomorrow?" she gasped, squirming out from under him.

"Very well," he grumbled, "next week. It'll probably take me at least a few days for a special license."

"Are you certain?" she asked. Much as she wanted to shout in delight at his hurry to make her his own, she knew that his position in society was important to him. Mann-Formsbys did not marry in hastily arranged ceremonies. "There will be talk," she added.

He shrugged boyishly. "I don't care. Do you?"

She shook her head, her smile spreading across her face.

"Good," he growled, pulling her back into his arms. "But perhaps we need to seal the deal more firmly."

"More firmly?" she squeaked. He seemed to be holding her quite firmly indeed.

"Oh yes," he murmured, taking her earlobe between his teeth and nibbling until she shivered with delight. "Just in case you weren't quite convinced that you belong to me."

"Oh, I'm"—she gasped when his hand closed around her breast—"quite convinced, I assure you."

He smiled devilishly. "I need more assurance."

"More?"

"More," he said, quite definitely. "Much more."

Much, *much* more . . .

Epilogue

Happy Valentine's Day, Gentle Readers, and did you hear the news? The Earl of Renminster has married Miss Susannah Ballister!

If you are grumbling because you did not receive an invitation, you may take solace in the fact that no one received invitations, save, perhaps for her family and his, including Mr. and Mrs. Snowe-Mann-Formsby.

(Ah, how This Author loves to write that name. Brings a smile to the face, does it not?)

By all accounts, the couple is blissfully happy, and Lady Shelbourne has reported, quite delightedly, and quite to everyone who will listen, that they have agreed to attend her ball this evening.

Lady Whistledown's Society Papers,
14 February 1814

"We're here," murmured the Earl of Renminster to his new wife.

Susannah just sighed. "Do we have to go?"

He raised his brows. "I thought you wanted to attend."

"I thought *you* wanted to attend."

"Are you jesting? I'd rather be home, stripping you naked."

Susannah blushed.

"Aha. I see you agree with me."

"We *are* expected," she said, but without conviction.

He shrugged. "I don't care. Do you?"

"Not if you don't care."

He kissed her, softly, slowly, nibbling at her lips. "May I begin the process of stripping you naked now?"

She lurched back. "Of course not!" But he looked so crestfallen she had to add, "We're in a carriage!"

His glum face didn't perk up.

"And it's cold outside."

He burst out laughing, then rapped on the carriage wall and directed the driver to return home. "Oh," he said, "before I forget. I have a valentine for you."

"You do?" She smiled delightedly. "I thought you'd given up on those."

"Well, I have. And it's a good thing you're already well and truly married to me for eternity, because you shouldn't expect flowery words and fancy valentines in the future. This attempt nearly killed me."

Curiously, she took the paper from his hands. It was tri-folded, and sealed with a festive red bit of sealing wax. Susannah knew that he usually sealed his correspondence with a serious dark blue, and she was touched that he'd gone to the extra effort with the red.

With careful fingers, she eased the missive open and smoothed it out on her lap.

There were only three words.

"It was really all I meant to say," he said.

"Oh, David," she whispered, her eyes filling with tears. "I love you, too."

Julia Quinn

#1 *New York Times* bestselling author JULIA QUINN began writing one month after graduating from college and, aside from a brief stint in medical school, she has been tapping away at her keyboard ever since. Her novels have been translated into forty-three languages and are beloved the world over. A graduate of Harvard and Radcliffe Colleges, she lives with her family in the Pacific Northwest.